I0657772

Betrayed

Love and Murder
in the Adirondacks

J.E. Irvin

**The New
Atlantian Library**

Habent Sua Fata Libelli

The New
Atlantian Library

Manhanset House
Shelter Island Hts., New York 11965-0342

bricktower@aol.com • tech@absolutelyamazingebooks.com
• absolutelyamazingebooks.com

All rights reserved under the International and Pan-American Copyright
Conventions. No part of this publication may be reproduced, stored in a retrieval
system, or transmitted in any form or by any means, electronic, or otherwise, without
the prior written permission of the copyright holder.
The New Atlantian Library colophon is a trademark of
J. T. Colby & Company, Inc.

Library of Congress Cataloging-in-Publication Data
Irvin, j.e.
Betrayed—Love and Murder in the Adirondacks
p. cm.

1. FICTION / Thrillers / Psychological. 2. FICTION / Romance / Suspense.
3. FICTION / Mystery & Detective / International Mystery & Crime
Fiction, I. Title.
ISBN: 978-1-955036-61-0, Trade Paper

Copyright © 2023 by J.E. Irvin
Electronic compilation/ paperback edition
copyright © 2023 by Absolutely Amazing eBooks

December 2023

Betrayed

Love and Murder
in the Adirondacks

The Second Book in the
Love and Murder in the Adirondacks *Series*

J.E. Irvin

Dedicated to the inhabitants of the real Wanakena
who have welcomed me into their hamlet and their hearts...
this one's for you.

Other books by J.E. Irvin

The Dark End of the Rainbow
Hopewell 1

The Rules of the Game
Hopewell 2

The Strange Disappearance of Rose Stone
Hopewell 3

A Principle of Light

Broken
Love and Murder in the Adirondacks 1

Carrion
A Byrd & Crowe Mystery

…a rush to judgment…

Strings of Christmas lights shimmied in the distance, interspersed with the warning beacons on the orange cones lining the construction zone. I dodged a swirl of debris in the middle lane, then shot east out of Akron just after one in the morning. My eyes blurred as I checked the rearview mirror. No one was following me, right? I rubbed my forehead and peered into the night, unable to trust my tired brain to identify a threat before it struck. A car crowded my back bumper, then roared into the passing lane and sped away. Another followed, slowed, headlamps wavering through the snow that fell in lazy swirls. The driver took the next off-ramp and disappeared. Uncertainty added to the panic gnawing at my guts. I was Emma Pearson, no, Emma Evans now. *Get it right, Em.* "All right," I said aloud. "Emma Evans, elementary teacher on the run." Nervous laughter escaped, along with the realization that I was way out of my element and scared shitless.

To be safe, I took the exit toward Kent, then pulled into a storage lot, cut the lights, and stared down each vehicle, very few this time of night, that passed along the road. After scanning for traffic, I checked the rearview mirror again. The twins slept in their car seats, chocolate-smudged cheeks resting against slumped shoulders, oblivious to the fear nestled inside me and the fury that wound like a strangler vine around my shattered heart. I was so tired I could cry but had to press on. I

1

planned to make it as far as Erie by morning, then stop to feed Evan and Mollie, entertain them until naptime, and snag a few hours of sleep before the wintry day melted into night, providing the cloak I needed to conceal our escape. Until I could reach the Adirondacks and disappear into six million acres of wilderness to save me and the children from the fate sniffing at our heels.

A semi lumbered south along the access road, the extended trailer blocking the sign for the ramp back onto I-76. I rested my head against the wheel. *Just for a minute.* The words whispered out. My eyes closed, and I drifted into recall, reviewing every action since we left Poplar Street and the only life my kids had ever known. In the back seat, Mollie whimpered. I jerked upright, drool trickling down my chin, and checked the dash clock. We'd been idling in the lot for more than half an hour. Time to get back on the road. I stiffened, stretched, looked to the side. A shadow prowled on the other side of the chain link fence encircling the storage lockers. Condensation from our breathing fogged the windows. I scrubbed at the glass. What was out there? The dark figure crept closer, head lowered, a deep growl echoing around the deserted space. I pressed my face to the window, recognized the muzzle of a giant Doberman. Swallowing down a yell, I turned on the headlights and exited the lot, pursued by two sharp warning barks and a lunge that rattled the fence.

The past, and my gullibility, sneered at me as I eased back onto the Interstate, guided by the disembodied voice of the navigation app, and headed east, the unknown ahead preferable to the wreckage behind me. Wind buffeted the late-model Land Rover I'd purchased from a seller on Hopewell's Internet Marketplace for all cash and no questions. My mom and dad, bless them, had helped load our belongings and refrained from asking the question uppermost in their minds. *When will we see you again?* I didn't offer any explanations. Keeping them in the dark was the only way to ensure their safety. I shrugged off the reminders to call when I got there, wherever there was, buckled the kids into their seats, and pretended we were making a fast-food run, in case anyone was within listening range. That included passersby and the agents who'd been watching the house since the murders in Kansas City. My father waited to open the garage door until the street had emptied, until the neighbors were tucked in for the night and the surveillance team distracted by the fake call for assistance Dad had placed from his new burner phone.

I had taken every precaution. No one knew our destination, not my co-workers at Hopewell Elementary, not the pediatrician whose office handed over the twins' records without comment, not even the federal agent assigned to handle our case. No, not ours. Gary's. The husband I thought I knew with a secret no one could have guessed. When I closed my eyes, the photographs of the murder scene flashed across my mind like the trailer of a horror movie. Full color and black and white. Gary lying face up in the doorway of a modest bilevel. A woman slumped over a highchair, an infant visible behind her, blood pooling on the tray.

I stifled the sob demanding release. Again, my eyes threatened to close. I yawned, pinched my cheeks, rolled my neck. The cell phone chirped with incoming news blasts, the screen lighting up like a firefly. Not even Mom and Dad had the new number. I had deactivated my Facebook and Instagram accounts, stripped the location tracker from every device I owned, erased Emma Pearson to reconstruct Emma Evans, the woman I'd been before I met Gary at The Ohio State University, before I fell in love and said yes to his proposal, before I had his babies. I expunged Emma 'dumbass' Pearson, the woman I'd been before the visit from law enforcement detailing my husband's death and revealing the double life he'd lived. I wanted to blot October fifteenth from my mind, but purging Gary Pearson seemed impossible. His children slept behind me. My finger still bore the indent from my wedding rings. His betrayal tainted every memory of the past six years. There was no coming back from that.

...a matter of logistics...

Chuck Mouse tucked the brown delivery shirt into the brown trousers, checked the boxes piled in the back of the truck, and punched in the coordinates for 110 Poplar Lane, Hopewell. Dispatch would be calling to check on his progress as a new hire. They also had an app to read his location, which would delay his approach to the Pearson home until one of the neighbors ordered another box of cleaning supplies or a year's worth of toilet paper. Mouse sniffed his disgust at the petty consumptions of humans even as he found it helpful in his work. Surveillance came easy when the average Jane or Joe had no idea who cruised their streets, or why. Even his sister Cheryl, two states away in Ames, Iowa, never questioned how he earned the money that paid her mortgage, nor did she ever ask how he could afford the trips to Disneyland he gifted his nieces every spring.

Mouse wasted no time in moral puzzling. He was good at what he did, discrete, efficient, untraceable, despite the residue of guilt after the last job. It was nothing personal, just unfortunate collateral damage. That loss would have been avoided if the woman hadn't risen to shield the infant. Mouse sloughed off the brief stab of remorse. He had a job to finish. Gary Pearson and the woman snitch had been taken care of, but the real threat to his boss remained. Turning toward the subdivision that housed the Pearsons, he rehearsed the plan. Find Emma and the twins. Locate the information her husband had stolen. Eliminate all the loose ends the undercover cop had left behind. Avenge Pearson's insult to the boss. A simple matter of logistics.

He cruised down Poplar, pretending to check his phone for the address. The RV, property of the woman's parents, that had occupied the curb was gone. The Feds were parked two doors away, the satellite dish on top announcing a cable company working in the neighborhood. Mouse snorted. As if they could hide their presence from him. For the past three days, he had cruised the area in a van, the magnetized A-One Plumbing signs on the side panels guaranteeing no one even blinked at his presence. He'd noted Emma Pearson's parents coming and going with armfuls of grocery bags. Maybe they were preparing for a siege. The thought amused him. He was the battering ram to bring down the castle. If the mother and father were there when he took it down, so be it. The agent behind the wheel of the fake cable company truck looked up as Mouse passed, waved, and returned to his phone. Mouse saluted with a forefinger, pulled in front of the Pearson driveway, and retrieved a package. He tightened his grip on the box, patting the weapon in the underarm holster. He didn't intend to use it tonight, but who knew? Maybe he'd get lucky and finish this job in time to join his family for a New Year's Eve funfest.

Standard procedure for the delivery company meant depositing the package on the porch or front step, knocking, or texting, then returning to the truck. Instead, Mouse rang the bell, tapping his foot as he waited and peered around. If anyone were to notice him, they'd see an anxious man, a driver hurrying to do his job. No one answered the first buzz. He pressed the ring button again, aware of the camera poised to capture his face. He hoisted the box higher, turned in a circle, and noticed one of the agents had exited the car. If the Pearsons were home, they were ignoring his summons. He shook his head, pretended to check the address, and hopped off the porch, shoulders slumped. He crunched across the half-frozen grass to the neighboring house, rang the bell, then tucked the package against the front door.

Tiny ice pellets bounced off his shoulders and the brim of his cap. The officer had retreated into his vehicle. Mouse twisted his lips into an expression of dismay as he jogged toward his van. If Emma Pearson and her children weren't in their home, where were they? Time for more aggressive action. Much as he'd like to be in Ames for the last holiday of the year, the job came first. Money was money, especially with the offer of a bonus for a speedy resolution. The boss had been quite clear in his instructions. Find the missing data. Kill Gary Pearson's family, all of them. No one fucks the boss over and survives.

…into uncharted territory…

Erie, Pennsylvania, was cold and windy, but the hotel had an indoor pool, which helped relax the twins and send them into early naptime. I'd barely closed my eyes when my cell phone blared a warning. Resetting the alarm, I dragged the cooler from the car, prepared a light supper, then entertained the children with a Lego movie until Evan nodded off. Mollie stayed awake until I returned from checking us out, my explanation of a family emergency not enough to get my money back. I carried Evan out to the car and helped Mollie buckle in as she, too, fell asleep. Feeling light-headed, I stopped for coffee and a Danish at an all-night drive-thru, then continued the push toward Syracuse, the glove of night enclosing me in a soft grip of anxiety and relief. No suspicious headlights followed behind us, although the intermittent blasts of light from the phone whenever a news story broke provided eerie backup to the noise in my head. Shrugging off the why's and what if's that threatened to choke me, I plotted my next stop. One more day to hide and sleep, then a final push north into the wilderness where Emma and the Pearson twins could vanish and stay alive.

As I turned north, a brisk wind stirred the snowflakes drifting from the leaden sky. The roads had been plowed from the previous storm, the mountainous drifts piled along the roadway witness to the area's reputation for record snowfall amounts. Evan and Mollie awoke cranky, their questions about where we were going and when Daddy would be coming to meet us pounding at me until I wanted to scream, but I kept my voice low and calm. No need for the children to sense how scared I was. Their world had been upended enough.

We made it to Syracuse before nightfall. I was scouting the roadway for a budget motel when I realized Mollie's EpiPen was missing from the toiletry kit. Panic rose like the tide. Gripping the wheel with my left hand, I scrabbled in my purse for the handful of prescriptions. Once I located the one I needed, I scanned the strip shopping malls for pharmacies. Evan kicked the back of my seat and whined.

"Mommy, my tummy hurts."

I recognized the advent of car sickness, a malady my son had been prone to since infancy. "Mollie? Can you hand your brother one of his tummy pops?"

"They're all gone," Mollie said. In the rearview mirror, I glimpsed my daughter leaning toward Evan. "Don't throw up, bro-bro."

"Listen to your sister, Ev. We're almost ready to stop for the night." I continued to search for drugstores along the way. Finally, I spotted a CVS sign sandwiched between a print shop and a computer repair business. A median separated the lanes. Unable to turn, I drove a mile farther, looped around, and took an access road to the store. Overhead, an airplane roared. We must be close to the city's main airport. Finding a place to stay wouldn't be difficult, but it might be expensive. I mentally counted the bills in my wallet and sighed. The cash wouldn't last forever. Once we reached the parking lot, I hurried to unbelt the twins and shepherd them inside. I located the Prescription drop-off counter and, ordering the children to stay close, spoke with the pharmacist.

"This is from an out-of-state doctor." The woman narrowed her eyes.

I pulled out the tab on my key fob that identified me as a customer. "If you scan this, I'm sure you'll see there's no problem."

Once the pharmacist verified the information, she informed me the wait would be at least fifteen minutes. To distract the kids, I took them down the toy aisle, the shelves loaded with Christmas items already marked down. Valentine's Day cards sat in boxes waiting to be displayed. I coaxed them to behave by buying Santa candy dispensers, then returned to the pharmacy counter when I heard my name over the loudspeaker. Relieved and ready to settle in for the night, I clutched the bag with the EpiPen and the anti-nausea suckers and herded the twins back to the car. I re-set their tablets for another Disney movie, filled Evan's cup holder with pops, and returned to the interstate. Ten minutes later, I pulled into the lot of a no-tell motel and rehearsed my spiel for the clerk at the counter.

In the morning, after my first full night's sleep in weeks, I checked the nav app, treated us all to a big breakfast, and started north. At an exit labeled Parish, I stopped to top off the fuel tank. Running out of gas was not a pleasant thought deep in upstate New York at any time, but especially during the winter. I determined to leave nothing to chance. The farther north we traveled, the wilder the scenery, the fewer signs of habitation. When the GPS instructed me to turn, I did, ignoring the unease that curled low in my belly. I was in unknown territory, at the mercy of the weather and strangers. To keep my mind from darker thoughts, I tried memorizing landmarks. I knew we were getting close when I saw the signs for Fort Drum, a training base for special forces soldiers, I recalled. Soon we were winding our way along two-lane rural roads. Of course, nothing looked familiar, and the closer I got to Wanakena, the more apprehensive I became. What if we couldn't find a place to live? What if I didn't find work? The question uppermost in my mind, however, the one that kept me gripping the wheel until my fingers went numb, was this: would the men who killed Gary find us?

...chameleon schemes...

Forty-eight hours of drive-bys, deliveries, and night-vision surveilling, with nothing to show for it. Mouse gathered the empty fast-food wrappers and stuffed them into the garbage bag in the back seat. He detested a dirty car and planned to have this, his personal vehicle, detailed as soon as this job ended. Which began to look like never. Neither the Pearson woman and her children nor her parents had shown up at the Poplar Street residence for two days. The FBI watch had tapered off as well, which caused Mouse to wonder why. The last glimpse he'd had of the family was Monday when they'd all gone out at dinner time. The kids had chattered about happy meals and a trip to the bouncy place, the grandparents all touchy-feely as they helped load the children into the Land Rover, then rumbled away in the RV, shouting about seeing everyone later. Mouse wiped his chin with a napkin, then scanned the street again. He removed the camera from the dash and stowed it away, yawned, and stretched. Fuck this waiting game. Time for more proactive measures. Tonight, he was getting into the house.

The outdoor lights at the Pearson house flicked on. So did the ones in the kitchen area. Were they operating on timers, or was someone hiding inside? If so, how had they slipped by him? Mouse checked his face in the rearview mirror, his reflection muted by the approaching dusk. His was a nondescript visage, not unpleasant but perfectly unremarkable, on a man of average height, average build, the muscles he cultivated concealed beneath clothing a size larger than necessary. No outstanding features. No scars or tattoos to attract or frighten. His was the face of a chameleon, capable of blending into any crowd, calling no attention to himself. Not attractive or unattractive. Not memorable. Not a killer. He smiled. The man in the mirror smiled back. Pleasant, affable, unthreatening. The phone alarm buzzed, reminding him it was time to call his sister, speak to his nieces before bed, to pretend to a normal life before he let the beast out to play.

The home improvement store by the local mall hummed with after-Christmas shoppers looking for discounted decorations. Mouse ambled down the lighting aisle, checking prices, then headed toward the section devoted to construction gear and safety vests. He filled a basket with tools, grabbed a roll of duct tape and several of blue painter's tape, and headed to checkout.

"Gearing up for work?" the clerk commented as she scanned the prices and bagged each item.

Mouse favored her with a wry smile. "Some asshole stole my stuff out of my truck over the weekend. Makes me fair crazy."

"I hear you. Here it is Christmas, and there are some still doing the Devil's work. Well, that'll be ninety-seven eighteen."

He handed over a hundred dollars, grinning as she fingered the bill. "Santa must've been good to you."

"I'm blessed," Mouse said. "Got a bonus."

"Well, praise the Lord," she intoned as she punched in the sale. The register dinged open. Mouse waved off the change.

"Put it in the Children's Hospital jar." He pointed at a donation poster taped to a canister on the counter." Eying the line behind him, he grabbed his bags and strolled away, confident the woman wouldn't spend more than a minute remembering one encounter among the many still to come.

Back at the cheap motel along the highway, Mouse spread his purchases on the bed, then rummaged through his stash of uniforms until he located the Duke Energy overalls he'd acquired in the flea market in nearby Monroe. Outdated gear, but most consumers paid little attention to what workers wore. As long as he sported an ID card on a lanyard, he'd be fine. Once he facilitated a power outage, he could slip into the Pearson home without anyone raising suspicions. Even if the FBI grunts showed up, they'd welcome his arrival. No one liked sitting in the dark. He thought about taking a shower, but it could wait until after. If he found the family, there'd be blood to wash off. One more glance at the clock assured him he had enough time to chat with his sister. Digging out the phone he used for legitimate calls, he settled onto the bed, legs stretched in front of him, and became the man Cheryl thought he was.

…getting off wrong-footed…

The early morning overcast had turned to an afternoon snow sky. An occasional flake drifted down, pasted itself to the windshield, then left a wet fingerprint as it slid down the glass. I checked the map on the phone and followed the winding road while my irrational mind screamed, *Lost! You're lost!* The temptation to turn back clutched at my throat. Then I spotted the sign — **Gateway to the Wilderness** — guarding a fork in the two-lane road. Exhausted and strung out by worry, I veered left, then right, then right again, pulling to a stop in front of a red clapboard building with a sandwich board out front announcing Otto's Abode. Mollie kicked the back of the seat. "I'm hungry, Mommy."

"I know, baby." I hustled to free the twins from the car seats. "We're going to take a break here, have some lunch, and then find out how to get to Aunt Riley's house."

"Auntie Riley?" Evan hopped down, snow puffing up around his feet as he landed. His little face beamed up at me, so full of hope it tugged my heart. "We're going to see Auntie Riley?"

Before I could answer, boots pounded along the porch behind me. A voice, rich, deep, and surly, boomed at us. "Snowstorm's coming. Foolish to be on the road when it hits, especially with small children. You should hurry back where you came from."

I shuddered at the rebuke in the man's words. How dare some stranger speak to me like that? Herding Evan and Mollie up the stairs, I glimpsed a pair of dark brown, hooded eyes and the scowling face of the man who had spoken and now stood at the top of the stairs, guarding the entrance like a backwoods gargoyle. A very handsome gargoyle. Riley's most recent account of the hamlet's local inhabitants came to mind, my friend's description of the brooding negative energy that had arrived with the return of this man to Wanakena on full display.

"You're Anton Storms, aren't you?" I paused to take in the broad shoulders, the brow shadowed with grief, the mouth that might, if relaxed, convey warmth and invitation. A kissable mouth, if I were interested in that anymore. A masculine, sensual man and a grumpy one whose demeanor radiated confrontation. Determined not to allow him to orchestrate the moment, I met his stare with one of my own. "Riley and Josh—"

"You're Emma?" He growled my name, his gaze shifting over me before landing on the children clutching my legs. "Those the twins?"

I cupped a gloved hand around each small head, pulled them close, and nodded. "Riley mentioned you'd come back to Wanakena. Thanks for the warm greeting."

Storms ignored my sarcasm as he brushed past me, his thick coat rubbing mine at the elbow, the contact sending a charge up my arm. He paused at the bottom of the steps and looked up, his eyes filled with fury and regret. "Go back where you came from, Emma Pearson. We don't need any more outsiders here."

Evan twisted to watch the man stomp over to an older model camper truck. "Is he a friend of Auntie Riley?"

I followed Evan's pointing finger as Anton Storms settled a stocking cap more securely over his head. I started to reply when my son grabbed my hand and squeezed, his next words an additional blow to my already damaged heart. "Don't be angry, Mommy. He's just sad, like you."

"Mommy!" Mollie tugged at my sleeve, yanking me back from sorrow's ledge. "I have to go potty."

Shrugging off the encounter with Wanakena's resident grump, I ushered the twins inside Otto's and stopped dead. Riley's description of the place from her first summer working at the general store didn't match the configuration in front of me. The register had relocated to the center of the room. To the left, another counter flanked a seating area with a loveseat and two chairs, while an antique telephone booth occupied space next to the entry door. On the right, several rows of shelving jutted out from the wall. Beyond the shelves, I noted a freezer with ice cream treats and, deeper into the store, displays of dry goods and produce. Wall coolers took up the back wall of a second, smaller alcove. Mollie continued to tug at my hand.

"Hello?" I shuffled the children toward the register. A door to the left of the sales counter banged open, and a man in a flannel shirt, work pants, and hiking boots hurried in. His beard reached the middle of his chest, the white contrasting with the ruddiness of his cheeks, lending him the appearance of an old-fashioned Santa.

"Sorry about that." He gestured over his shoulder with his thumb. "Carl's got me doing inventory, and I didn't hear you come in."

I smiled at his apology. "Not a problem, but we've been traveling for a while, and my children really need to use the restroom. Is there one available?"

He motioned for us to follow him through the door he'd just exited, then pointed out a second door down the hall and stood back, arms folded.

"Come out front when you're done. I'll be waiting for you."

Still puzzled by Storms' surly greeting, I helped the twins use the toilet, washed everyone's hands, and led them back into the store. "Who's Otto?"

"Of Otto's Abode? That would be Ms. Beamish's nephew, Otto Beamish. He generally runs the store now, but he's off making a delivery today."

I looked around. "The place is so different from what I expected."

"Don't know who set your expectations, although I have my suspicions, but I agree that Otto's made a few changes, including dragging that phone booth all the way from a state building over in Watertown. Quite the conversation starter, don't you agree?"

"I do, and you, if my instinct and Riley's description are correct, must be Jesse Livetree." I waited for him to take my outstretched hand.

Livetree grinned, eyes twinkling, and shook. "One and the same. The bigger question is, who are you? And you and you?" He poked a finger at Mollie's nose, then did the same to Evan.

"I think you know, Mr. Livetree. I'm Emma, who was once Pearson. It's, um, Evans now. And these are the twins, Mollie and Evan. We're friends of Riley and Josh Waylon, which I think you already figured out. I was hoping you could give me directions to their place."

"Well, Mollie and Evan, it's a pleasure to finally meet you, as your mother's friend Riley has shared quite a few pictures of your growing-up days. From when your name was Pearson."

I blushed. "Long story, and not the time or place for it. We always planned to visit Wanakena, but life didn't work out quite the way I thought it would."

Jesse's knowing look made me want to cry. How much did he or the other inhabitants of the hamlet know about my situation? Of course, the murders had been in the papers and on the nightly news, but only until other, more catastrophic world events unfolded. And not even Riley knew the worst of it. Shame and humiliation surfaced, threatening to overpower the anger keeping me upright. *Get over yourself, Em.* I acknowledged the interior pep talk and stiffened my spine. No one from Hopewell or the FBI knew where I was. So what? I was well and truly on my own, but I had no time for self-pity. The children needed me. I had to stay strong. I looked around Otto's before turning back and mustering a smile. "We could use some lunch. Is there a restaurant near that's open?"

"Not this time of year, Emma, but I'm guessing I can round up some alphabet soup and crackers and a cookie or two."

"Cookies!" Evan shouted. Mollie rubbed her tummy. Livetree folded his arms, waited for the children to settle down, and then hooked his chin at me.

"I'll feed you, but if you're looking for Riley, you're out of luck. Josh took her away for some surprise pampering, just the two of them. Left Timmy and Michael with Josh's parents."

The mayor's announcement shot down my plan for a place to spend the night. I leaned on the counter to steady myself. "When will they be back?"

"Not until the day after tomorrow."

Despair crept over me like a shadow. I tapped my nails on the soup bowl. I was too strung out to drive any farther today. I also couldn't expect the twins to remain quiet and cooped up for another two hours without some playtime. What was my next move? Jesse reached beneath the counter to pull out napkins and spoons. He handed them over and cocked his head. "You settle in. Help yourself to milk from the cooler while I heat up that soup. And don't stress yourself, Emma. We'll find you a place to stay."

I brushed a hand through my hair, longer now than I'd ever worn it, long enough to hide my face when I didn't want to be seen, when the tears came despite my best efforts to keep them at bay. I wiped my nose with my sleeve and lifted my shoulders. *One step at a time, Em,* I whispered. *One at a time.*

"Mommy?" Mollie patted my hip. "Don't be sad. I love you." My daughter's declaration brought the tears I'd been fighting. How could someone so young be so empathetic?

"I love you, too, Mollie Moo, and Evan Bevan." Whenever I used their pet names, they giggled, the sound of their laughter the best antidote to my sorrow. I hustled them over to the counter stools and ordered them to sit still, then fiddled with my phone, anxious to avoid the calculating look in Jesse Livetree's eyes when he returned. The man knew more than he was letting on. The realization settled like an unscratchable itch beneath my skin.

Four packages of crackers and a shared glass of milk later, Livetree returned, the bowls of hot chicken soup steaming on the tray he carried. A plate bearing chocolate chip cookies nestled among them. "No treats until you eats," he said, winking at the twins.

Mollie winked back. Evan tucked his napkin beneath his chin and blew on the soup. I sank onto a stool, the weight of the past three months an anvil on my back. Livetree waited until the children were fully engaged in eating before he slipped a paper into my palm. "While the soup was heating, I called around. Ordinarily, Ms. Beamish would have you stay in the cabin that was Riley's when she first came to Wanakena. But the insufferable woman's off-site, too, visiting friends in Saranac Lake for a few days. However, Ron and Amy Dugas happen to have a vacancy at the Lodge. The Moose Room has a queen bed and a single, perfect for you and the young ones. Funny how things work out, isn't it?"

I wondered at the rancor evident in his reference to Carl Beamish, especially since Riley had mentioned they had a thing for each other, but I shrugged it off. Local relationships were not my concern. "You didn't have to do that, Mr. Livetree."

"No problem, Emma, Riley's friend. That's how we do for each other in this town."

He meant it. I searched for the right words and came up empty. "I'm so grateful."

The mayor nodded and, while we ate, busied himself rearranging the items next to the register, then returned to collect our empty bowls. The twins curled up on the couch, their heads buried in a *Where's Waldo* book. He wiped crumbs from the counter, then wrapped the cloth around one gnarled fist. "Trouble following you, Emma?"

"I hope not," I whispered, moving to the door. I squinted into the snowflakes falling more steadily now. Already the tracks of Storms' tires and those of the Land Rover had disappeared beneath a layer of white. "But I can't promise that. I can't promise anything anymore."

Jesse cleared his throat, sidled closer. "Some days, Miss Emma, the only way out of trouble is to pass through it."

Returning to the counter, I secured the lid on the milk, wrapped the remainder of the cookies in a napkin, and laid a twenty by the register. Jesse disappeared into the back of the store while I wandered around, inspecting the produce bins, the juice and dairy products in the coolers, and planned menus for future meals. I paused before a sign taped to the side of the ice cream freezer.

Volunteer
Drivers Needed
to Transport Veterans In
Clifton/Fine Area

The poster included a phone number. I snapped a photo, then studied the directions Jesse Livetree had given me. With a safe place to stay, I could look for a job, begin to build a new life, hold off the dark thoughts pressing on me. Meanwhile, I would confide in no one, not even the best friend I'd ever had. Riley Waylon didn't need to know all the details of my husband's betrayal, just the one that sent me and my children here.

...on the hunt...

A quick pass down Poplar Street assured Mouse that nothing had changed at the Pearson home. Inside the house, the lights timed off as midnight approached. The RV had not returned. He cruised past the spot where the federal agents usually parked. Their vehicle was gone, too. Maybe they knew something he didn't. He'd have to reach out to his contact, see what was stirring on his end. He waited an extra half hour to be sure the house was empty. When no one appeared inside or outside the home, Mouse eased the utility truck to the curb, the extension ladder on top swaying in the wind. Climbing out, he adjusted the tool belt at his waist and checked for traffic. Then he made his way to the third house to the left of the Pearson property. He switched on the headlamp mounted on his hard hat and pretended to mark off items on a clipboard. He used a handheld meter to check for gas leaks, then tripped a circuit breaker, plunging the west side of Poplar into darkness, and moved on. Nobody came outside to investigate the disruption. At the Pearson's, he knocked, waited, knocked again, then, glancing around, picked the locks and let himself in. He announced his presence and referenced the company as though someone inside had answered, an extra precaution and a useless one. No one was home.

Drawing his weapon, he searched the premises, room by room. The place screamed empty, the air stale, every room neat, tidy, and devoid of recent activity. Tucking the gun away, Mouse slipped out to restore the power. Back inside, he checked the time and began the search for information. If neither the woman nor the kids were here, he had to figure out where they went. The pressure was on him to locate the missing data and end the Gary Pearson saga before the stolen information exposed his boss and all the other players in the game. If he didn't deliver soon, the next family on the chopping block would be his.

Despite a thorough search, Mouse uncovered nothing of interest or value. The house had been stripped of any useful data. Even the refrigerator magnets were gone. He exited through the back door, skirted the abandoned swing set and sandbox, and checked the street. Down the block, the federal agents had returned to the stakeout. He made a show of stowing the clipboard in his pack to squat by the utility boxes in the side yard, pretending to examine the connections. Irritated and angry, he yanked the cover off the electric panel. Searching the home had yielded nothing. If he didn't know better, he'd suspect the feds themselves had sanitized the place. Did their sporadic presence indicate they had no more info than he did, or was something else going on? It was as if the family had never lived here. Distracted, he fiddled with the wires, then lifted the cover panel and kicked it into place. Above, a single star glimmered in the darkened sky. The streetlights flickered. Mouse cursed softly and headed toward the utility vehicle. He had to return it before morning.

Looking back toward the house, he pretended to consult his clipboard again and stepped onto the driveway. He'd scoured every drawer and desk, pawed through empty closets and folded linens but found no calendar, daybook, photo albums, or baby books, not even old bills, or holiday cards. When he reached the curb, he paused. The mailbox. He feigned forgetting to leave a card in case one of the neighbors had awakened to observe his movements, although now that power was restored, he doubted anyone cared what he was doing. Retracing his steps, he hunched over the mailbox, then flipped it open. He directed the headlamp at the interior. Empty. He stuck a hand inside and touched an envelope at the back of the box. He tugged it free, stuffed it in his pocket, and returned to the truck he'd commandeered for the evening. Headlights flashed down the block, indicating renewed interest in his presence. Mouse stowed his gear, chugged past the surveillance team, and waved. Once he left the development, he increased his speed. At the storage lot, he parked the truck, tucked the keys and an envelope of cash beneath the floor mat, and returned to his car. He was ready for a shower, a drink, and some serious thinking about his next move.

The fleabag motel where he'd registered under a fake name slumbered under the dark gray sky, occasional outbursts of sleety rain pinging against the metal roof. Mouse pulled into a spot that fronted the room he'd rented, his old-model Chevy blending with all the other second-hand vehicles. He dumped his late-night Waffle House breakfast and coffee on the scratched top of the bistro table snugged under the window, flung his coat onto the bed, and extracted the card he'd found in the mailbox. Something was better than nothing, and this was the only lead he had.

Moisture and mishandling had erased the return address and smudged the postmark, although Emma Pearson's name was still legible. The stamp, a generic Forever flag of the United States, revealed nothing. Mouse teased open the flap with a penknife and eased out the card. **Thank you** was scrawled across the front in an elaborate font. The sender had included a big exclamation mark and a crowd of smiley faces. The interior was covered in writing. He skipped to the signature, R, then returned to the beginning.

Ems,

Thank you so much, bestie, for the gifts. Love, love, love the overalls and jeans for Michael, the tee shirt for Josh, and the gift certificate to Amazon, and Timmy adores the game you sent him for his new console. He and J spend way too much time street racing each other in the virtual. With all you have on your plate, dear heart, that you found time to think of us touches me deeply. I hope our package arrived in time for the holiday and that you are coping with the constant presence of bodyguards and surveillance. Please, please, please, consider coming to stay with us, if only for a few days. I have a huge surprise for you, which I've been saving for

MONTHS now, and which I will only reveal in your presence or, if necessary, on FaceTime, but please say you'll fly up soon. Michael will enjoy having the twins to play with, and I will make you tea and scones and hold you when you cry. Waiting to hear from you and sending you so much love. R

PS Actually, I have two surprises, one for you and one for the twins. All I'm going to say is puppies! Come see us...I miss you!

Mouse scarfed down the hotcakes, finished the coffee, and re-read the note. What had he learned? R lived far enough away that the Pearsons would have to fly to reach her. R was probably a female. No man he knew would draw smiley faces on a card. What else? Ah, the woman's man was named Josh, and they had two boys. Not much. But a start. Time to put deliveryman Mouse and utility worker Mouse to bed and resurrect Charles Mouse, decorated agent of the Federal Bureau of Investigation. He couldn't wait to hear what Emma Pearson's colleagues would say about her best friend R.

...without reservation...

Snow continued to fall in lazy swirls as I drove west on Hamele Street. I made the left turn onto the steel bridge, then a right onto Reed Road, remembering Riley's garbled description of the night she arrived in Wanakena. *I think she mixed things up just a little.* A giggle slipped free as I recalled my friend's adventure four years ago, the one that led her to the love of her life, Josh Waylon. A lump I couldn't swallow formed in my throat. I no longer believed in love like that.

The Rover bounced along the rutted roadway. I passed several homes, including the cabin where the Dugas family lived. Turning in at the Backpackers Lodge sign, I squeezed in between an Outback Subaru and a truck that looked exactly like the one grumpy Anton Storms had driven off in. My stomach clenched. The lump remained. All I needed was another nasty encounter with the dark-eyed man, and I'd throw myself in the river rushing over the stony channel behind the Lodge.

The front door bore a welcome sign and a request to show proof of Covid vaccination upon registration. I sighed. The twins were too young to be vaxed. I hoped that wouldn't be a problem. I cracked the door open and yelled a greeting. No response. Mollie clung to one leg, and Evan wrapped around the other as I stalked into the great room, where a fire flickered behind a glass screen.

"Both of you sit here while I bring in our suitcases. Don't move, and don't touch anything. Please?" I grabbed their little screens from my bag and dropped them in their laps. Evan flopped back, yawning as his red curls splayed over the cushions. I brushed a hand over his sweet face and bent down to kiss both children. By the time I returned, they had fallen asleep, entwined in each other the same way they'd lain in my womb. I bit my lip to stop the quivering. In slumber, they resembled their father, the bastard. I gritted my teeth, exchanging sorrow for rage, and set the suitcases on the floor, then began searching for a door with a moose cutout on the outside panel. I located the designated room on the second floor at the end of the hall, the mustiness of unused quarters assailing me as I shoved my way in, dragging backpacks with me. No matter. The room was clean and warm and charming in its simplicity. There were no chests for the children's clothing, only a few pegs along the entry wall. Riley's place would be a better arrangement, but it also had drawbacks. Adding three more bodies to the Waylon's small ranch would test everyone's comfort level. What I needed was a place to call our own. I prayed Jesse's mention of the cabin at Carl Beamish's house would pan out and offer a more permanent solution. For better or worse, I had come to Wanakena to start anew where no one knew me or the full extent of the horrors I'd left behind.

Giggling from the first floor interrupted my unpacking. Sliding my oversize backpack underneath the bed, I scurried down the hall, leaned over the railing, and watched Anton Storms pull coins out of Evan's and Mollie's ears. The twins clapped and begged him to do it again. Magic tricks? The grumpy fisherman did sleight-of-hand for little kids? Hadn't he warned her an hour ago to go back where she came from? She narrowed her gaze on the man.

The grump had removed his heavy coat, revealing shoulders and a broad chest that strained at his flannel shirt. Rolled up sleeves exposed muscled forearms, each bearing tattoos that entirely covered his ropey-looking skin. Blue jeans and sturdy hiking boots completed his attire, but my eyes were drawn upward. His dark hair, short on the sides, longer on top, barely covered the scar a bullet had carved into his head. The skin along the right side of his neck revealed evidence of grafting after the burns from the explosion at the trailers. OMG, I thought. Riley's description of his injuries hadn't conveyed the full extent of the damage. I must have made a sound because Storms chose that moment to raise his head and glare at me while the children clamored for another trick.

"Didn't take my advice." He shook his head as he shuffled the cards he held before placing them on an end table and turning away. He didn't have to say more. I read the dismissal in his eyes. I sighed and headed down for more belongings, expecting to hear him leave. Instead, when I reached the bottom of the stairs, he was waiting, coat on, stocking cap once again hiding the wound on his head. "Hope you know what you're doing, Pearson, for their sakes."

He slammed the door behind him, setting off a reverberation of violence under my skin. I abandoned our gear to herd the children into the dining area. Retrieving the items I'd bought at Otto's, I placed the food in the refrigerator beside the beverage counter. Then I opened the game of Chutes and Ladders. While the kids set up the board, I stared out the wall of windows at the falling snow, recalling Storms' chilling remark. *I hope I do, too, Mr. Grump. If I don't, we'll all be dead.* That outcome I refused to accept.

Content for the time being, Evan and Mollie groaned each time one of their tokens slid down a ladder. I sat beside them, checking the phone for news, then retrieved the photo of the sign at Otto's asking for volunteers and copied the number into my contacts. It probably wasn't a paid position, but it would provide a way to learn the area and make connections. Networking was the key. I took a deep breath, rehearsed what I wanted to say, then brought up the number and hit *Call.* A recorded voice welcomed me to the Veteran's Assistance Center for the Clifton/Fine area, stated that Sergeant Phil Gordon was out of the office until January 2, and asked me to please leave a message after the beep. I waited for the signal, then recited my name and phone number. "I'm looking to settle here in Wanakena," I said, my voice only a little shaky, which I blamed on the cold weather. "I would be more than happy to meet with you and assist in any way. My father served twenty years in the Air Force, and my cousin is a Marine currently stationed somewhere in the Middle East. I have a vested interest in helping vets." I repeated my name and number and ended the call. With the twins happily engrossed in their game, I wandered through the downstairs rooms of the Lodge, noted the tees and fleeces available for purchase, and pondered my next move. The snow had picked up. A storm of this magnitude would keep most people indoors, especially the killers who might come after me.

...more than a paper trail...

Hopewell Elementary appeared deserted during the holiday break, but a skeletal cleaning staff had to be on-site most days to check for heating or water issues. Small towns like Hopewell were overzealous in their care for their children and the buildings where they studied. If Mouse got lucky, he'd encounter a conscientious teacher prepping for next week's back-to-school classes. He straightened his tie and double-checked the badge and ID identifying him as an agent of the Federal Bureau of Investigation, all the more ironic because it was true, or had been. The incident that forced him out of the Bureau hadn't been his fault, but the higher-ups didn't give a rat's ass. He'd pulled the trigger, so he was the goat they scaped. Water under the bridge, anyways. He hitched his pants, settled the crease down the front of each leg, and pressed the buzzer mounted on the outside wall. These days no one was admitted without a thorough inspection. While he waited, he did a slow pivot, taking in the empty lot, the icy low spots, the bare limbs of honey locust trees slumbering through winter. He leaned on the buzzer five more times before a woman pushing a mop and a bucket approached the door. She bent over the squawk box and shouted, "Ain't no one here, mister. Come back next week."

He shoved his badge against the window and smiled. "Sorry to disturb you, ma'am. I'm with the Federal Bureau of Investigation, and we're doing some routine interviews in connection with the Gary Pearson murder. I expect you've heard about that."

The woman's face drooped. "Oh, Emma and those poor babies of hers. It's a terrible tragedy, it is."

"Yes, ma'am, that it is." Mouse pressed his face to the intercom and let a note of melancholy infuse his next words. "I'd really like to finish up before the holiday, spend some time with my family. Would you mind answering just a few questions? It won't take long, I promise."

The custodian shrugged, looked over her shoulder, and unlocked the door. "Suppose you want to sit down somewhere," she said.

"I'd like to see Mrs. Pearson's classroom if you don't mind."

"Won't do you much good. The sub packed up all Emma's things. They're in the storage closet in the teacher's lounge."

"Mrs. Pearson isn't teaching anymore?"

The woman gave him a squinty look. "Thought you Feds would know that much. Poor woman's taken a leave of absence for the remainder of the school year. Can't blame her none. Well, since you're here, I'll give you the tour."

Mouse followed her down the hall and into Emma's former classroom. Books lined low shelves. Tables and chairs clearly meant for small bodies were stacked in the corners, along with enough bean bags to create a fort. He wandered over to the desk, sifted a hand through the papers stacked there, then returned to the custodian. "Have you worked here long, Mrs.—?"

"Miss. Della. Over thirteen years. Seen a lot of children fill these seats. Lots of teachers come and go, too. Emma was one of the good ones."

"Oh, I believe you. Tell me, who were her closest friends? You know, who might know Emma Pearson best?" He hurried to dispel the suspicion lowering her eyebrows. "It's important we speak to all her family and acquaintances to ensure we have all our facts. We want to find her husband's killer and keep her and her children safe."

"Uh-huh." Della fiddled with the keys on her belt. "Once Riley left, Emma didn't have a bestie, you know, on account of they were so close."

"Riley?"

Again, a sideways look of distrust. "You sure don't seem to know much about her yet."

Mouse blushed. "I'm new on the case, not up to speed, but I'm trying. That's why I'm here bothering you today. You were saying about Riley?"

"Miss Riley was a sweet young woman. Taught third grade until her parents went to Florida, and she went someplace north for the summer and never came back."

"What did you say her last name was?"

"I didn't."

"Sorry. Do you know where she went up north?" He folded his hands and waited.

"Maine. Vermont. Somewheres up there. Emma was right sorry to see her leave, but then Riley found herself a real looker, a forest ranger. Saw his picture once. Better than that turd Warren Carstairs, excuse my language. Now, if that's all?"

Mouse had more questions, but he saw her antenna going up. Della didn't trust him, feared she'd already said too much. But he had two more names to contact and a direction. Maybe Emma and the children had taken their friend up on her invitation to visit. All he had to do was find out where.

...an invitation she couldn't refuse...

The phone call from the hamlet's reigning empress ordered me to report for dinner and a confab at five o'clock sharp. Who said confab these days? Still, I needed what Carl Beamish had to offer. I shrugged off the fact that, contrary to what Jesse Livetree had stated, the woman was, in fact, in the hamlet after all. I loaded the kids into the Rover and prepared to meet the most formidable personality in Wanakena.

Mounds of snow lined both sides of Reed Road all the way to the Beamish home. A narrow path led to the newly enhanced entrance to the cabin, which included a deck and screened-in porch that, according to Riley, Josh and Anton had built under duress and constant supervision from Ms. Beamish. Diffused light speared out from the windows of the home that belonged to Carl Partlowe Beamish, matriarch of Wanakena and the woman who had rescued Riley from herself. Maybe she could work her magic for me, too. I helped the twins from the car, and we shuffled down the trail. We had almost reached the steps when the door swung open and Carl waved us in.

"Well, I'm flubbered," she announced, "absolutely flubbered, for sure. Is it really you, Emma Pearson, and those two adorable children who promised to visit more times than I can count and never did?"

I accepted her pat on the back, then instructed the children to stomp the snow off their boots and slip them off before venturing farther into the home. In the great room, the fireplace beckoned, and the dining table, set for a feast, sparkled. From my spot in the hall, I noted the moose paraphernalia decorating every surface. Feeling awkward and a little intrusive, I toed off my boots and stumbled toward the warmth.

"Ms. Beamish, if this is a bad time, we can talk tomorrow."

"Nonsense. You can't back out now, my girl. Besides, I invited you. Enough said."

"Yes, but," I gestured at the fancy table, "it looks like you're expecting company."

"Well, I am. And now that my company is here, we can eat. Of course, I'd have invited the Waylons, but," Carl lifted her chin and winked, "that Josh has turned into a right romantic soul, and Mayor Livetree minds his own schedule, no matter what I say or don't say. Plus, he's person non grateful these days, on my sh—, my list, if you know what I mean. Two rotten peas in a pod, me and the mayor." Carl frowned, then wrapped me in a huge hug. "You are welcome, Emma, dear. Riley will be tickled pinkie to see you."

"Well, I thank you for your kindness, Ms. Beamish. Truly."

"Again, nonsense, Emma. Any friend of Riley's is welcome in my home. I just can't help but wonder why she isn't here to greet you herself?"

I licked my lips, avoiding her gaze. "Riley doesn't know we're here."

Carl raised her eyebrows. "Oh, gracious, it's a long way to come for a surprise visit."

Mollie climbed into Carl's recliner and immediately began to rock. Evan, my storyteller, snatched a stuffed moose from the hearth and dropped to the rug to craft a scenario involving the fireplace bellows, two throw pillows, and the animal itself. Glad for the distraction, I admonished the children to respect Ms. Beamish's home while Carl folded her arms and tapped her foot, waiting for an excuse or an explanation.

I fiddled with the buttons on my cardigan. How much should I tell Carl, that fiery force of nature whose nose for news fed the gossip pipeline in the hamlet? Whatever she knew would soon be common knowledge. I ticked through my options. Tell exactly what happened? Reveal partial truths, enough to keep the woman from prying further? Or concoct a story to keep my secrets, to hide the horror I'd run from? I decided to share only a little of the truth of the past four months, at least until after I spoke with

Riley, but even then, I had to keep the worst of it from all of them. I couldn't risk their lives.

I nodded at the children, then took Carl by the elbow and herded her toward the kitchen, speaking in a hushed voice. "My husband died, Carl. He was murdered in Kansas City while working on an undercover job."

"Oh, mercy, Emma, no. You poor thing, and those sweet babies. Well, you need a strong drink, and so do I." She scampered into the dining room, returning with two tumblers, a bottle of Crown Royal, and a determined air. She poured us both a generous amount and shoved one of the glasses into my trembling hand. "No, don't talk. Drink."

"But—" Carl shoved my glass toward my mouth, then drank hers in one gulp.

"Bottoms up, dear," she said with a wink as she poured herself a second shot.

"Should you be drinking with your, um, heart thing?" I circled a finger around my chest.

"Doctor fixed me right up. The spot on my lung was nothing but an old, calcified something or other, and I've been right as raindrops for almost four years now. Don't you go worrying about me, my dear." Carl looked back at the children, now snuggled under a fleece blanket in front of the fire. "You put your efforts into keeping those precious children safe. Now, dinner's almost ready."

While Carl fussed in the kitchen, I wandered in and out of the room, all the restless thoughts from the past three days piling up like sawdust. Finally, I leaned against the refrigerator and sighed. "Isn't there anything I can do to help?"

Carl shoved a stool my way. "Stop fidger-faddling and distracting. Sit, and tell me what's really going on."

A wail from the great room interrupted our conversation. I hurried from the kitchen to intervene in the latest sibling squabble. The twins were huddled beneath the blanket, eyes wide and wet with tears. I picked them up and sat them on the couch. Mollie's lip quivered. Evan crossed his arms in imitation and scrunched his face into a scowl that reminded me so strongly of Gary that my eyes filled with tears. I brushed them away, crouched in front of the children, and took their hands in mine. "What's going on, Mols? Did Evan hit you? Did you hit him?"

My daughter threw herself down, sobs shaking her shoulders. Evan uncrossed his arms, covered his sister's body with his own, and gazed up at me.

"We miss Daddy," he said. "When can we go home?"

The enormity of their loss settled over me like the snowstorm currently burying Wanakena. I moved between them and curled them into my lap. The ache of loss and guilt threatened to consume me. How did I miss the signs of Gary's deception? And how could I ever make this right?

The gentle weight of Carl's hand brought me back to the present situation. "Dinner's ready, Em. Come along now, little cubs. I can't eat all these blueberry muffins by myself."

The mention of blueberries distracted the twins just enough to get everyone moving toward the table where a chicken casserole, a basket of fresh-baked muffins, and child-size bowls of homemade applesauce begged to be eaten. Soon they were asking Carl about the moose head mounted over the fireplace and when they could play in the snow. Mutzi, Carl's cat, emerged from beneath the sideboard and meowed her way around the table, begging for a scrap or two of dinner. After a dessert of Rice Krispy bars, Carl stowed the leftovers, while I settled the children into Riley's old room, once more snuggled under a blanket as they watched another episode of "Captain Underpants" on Evan's tablet. I returned to help Carl finish the dishes, although I found it difficult to focus. Several times I caught myself staring at the wall, replaying the flight from Hopewell, picking apart every move to see if I had left some clue behind or missed some piece of information that might lead to Wanakena. As I placed one last dish in the cupboard, a noise from the bedroom reminded me of Evan's question. When can we go home? He deserved an answer, but what could I tell him or Mollie about the crime that had upended their lives? Three-and-a-half was too young to confront such scary truths. How could I possibly explain a life on the run or the need to hide from a shadowy presence dedicated, if the federal agents were correct, to hunting us down?

"Emma?" Carl tugged on my sleeve. "Come sit and tell me the rest of it, all of it."

"I can't, Carl. The less you know, the safer you'll be."

"I didn't make it to my age by playing it safe. You're as pale as a gull-darned snowflake, so thin a mountain breeze would blow you right over. You're a right tall woman, my dear, and you've lost too much weight to be healthy. So," she patted the table, "I promise this one time to keep whatever you tell me to myself, and that's not something I say lightly. Lord knows I love good gossip."

I joined her at the now-cleared dining table. She smoothed out the moose placemat in front of her and inhaled sharply. "I don't know where this story begins. Why don't you start there?"

"I don't even know when my life began to unravel. It's such a jumbled mess."

Carl folded her hands. "Start where you think it does. We can prognosticate the details later."

"All right." I stopped before the sob could choke me, before Carl's delicious dinner could come back up, before my gullibility could wrack me again. I paused long enough to regain my bearings. "Four years ago, my husband Gary attended a conference in Kansas City to give a presentation at a policing convention. At least, that's what he told me. He even asked to borrow a small recording device I had to tape his speech. While he was there, or so I've been informed, he was hired to conduct undercover work, which entailed multiple return trips to the state. He had a partner there, a woman he worked with and then married, even though he was already married. To me. He fathered a child with her around the time the twins turned two."

Despite the pain, it felt good to finally let the story out, to tell someone every ugly detail. Ms. Beamish waited, no hint of pity or judgment in her, until I recovered enough to continue. My voice cracked on the following sentence, but I spit it out before it could strangle me. "Whatever he did pissed off the wrong people, who sent someone to murder him and his other family before coming after me and mine."

Carl sucked on her bottom lip, then nodded in my direction. "You think you'll be safe here."

"I hope so, but I'm scared we won't, and now that you know, I'm afraid you're in danger. Whoever is after me and my children will hurt you, too."

Carl reached across the table. "You have enough to worry about without adding me and Wanakena to the list. We're smarter and stronger than you know, Emma Pearson."

"I'm not Pearson anymore. I took back my maiden name. Evans."

"Emma Evans. Good to know. And you need a home, don't you?" At my nod, she scraped a thumb over her chin. "Which I have. No one's living in Riley's old cabin, so it's yours so long as you need it. We'll negotiate a fair rent. But not tonight. You're too tired and upset to think this through right now."

I escaped to the great room before I broke. The lodging was just what I needed, but her acceptance and offer to help overwhelmed me. Carl followed me, patted my shoulder, held out a tissue.

"Don't even think about getting all grateful on me, Evans. Be better to have that small cabin in use than sitting vacant. Taxes are coming up. Got utilities to pay, and someone's got to check on the place at least once a month. Which Storms was doing for me, but he'll be right pleased to let that burden go. Long as you keep the place clean and pay on time, it's yours."

I thought about Riley's tales of bears and the mystery prowler who had tried to kill her, but it was a different season now. Bears hibernated in the winter, and my human predators didn't know where I was. A sliver of hope pierced my frazzled defenses. What was it my grandfather used to say? God willing, and the creek don't rise? Wishing for a thing and making it so didn't always happen at the same time, but I had few options. Even if the creek did rise, I was committed to making a stand here in Wanakena, at least until spring.

...beauty and the beastly storms...

I rehearsed saying my name for the twentieth time. Emma Evans, Emma Evans. It should have been easy, but I kept stumbling over the vowels. Before I lost my nerve, I checked on the twins, nestled under a blanket fort, and dialed the Veteran's helpline for the tenth time, expecting the answering machine. Instead, a gruff voice bellowed out a greeting, the echo indicating they were on speaker phone.

"Gordon here. Help you?" When I didn't respond immediately, Gordon tried again. "Phil Gordon for the Veteran's Center. You there, sport?"

"Hello. My name is Emma Evans. I'm interested in the volunteer position driving veterans to appointments."

"Oh? Oh, you're the woman left that message, right? Wow, that's great." Gordon's gracious tone made me smile. He yelled at someone in the background. "Hey, Tony, we got a live one about the driving gig. Want me to schedule a meet and greet, boss?"

A faint response followed by the slam of a door indicated that Tony had just arrived. The oddly familiar voice grew louder as the new arrival approached Gordon. "Have him come in this afternoon at four."

"Copy that," Gordon said. "You hear, Evans? Director says to come around four o'clock. Bring your vax cards and references. Oh, and if you're a vet, bring your discharge papers."

"I'm not a vet, although my hus—" I choked up, swallowed hard, and kept going. "My husband was."

"Look, I've got another call coming in. See you later, Evans." Gordon hung up before I could correct the misunderstanding. Maybe that was for the best. What the man didn't know couldn't hurt me yet. At least I had an interview. I brushed a hand down the over-sized pullover I wore to disguise my chest. Motherhood had altered my once-slender body into a curvy pain-in-the-ass hourglass. Despite the weight loss of the past few months, there was no way to hide my boobs. Dislodging a few more crumbs from the breakfast muffins Carl had sent over, I entered the address for the Veteran's Center where I was supposed to show up in exactly, I checked my phone, six hours. The twins had grown quiet under the tent canopy. I lifted one flap to find them curled in each other's arms, traces of tears down their soft cheeks. I closed my eyes against the rush of emotion. Damn Gary! Damn him for all eternity. I knelt to kiss each forehead, then set about making beds, vowing never, ever again to let any man find a foothold in my heart.

The twins eventually woke up, rubbing their eyes and demanding lunch. Around one, Carl Beamish called to suggest I take a copy of my resumé to the Clifton-Fine School District's Central Office. "It's a small school, Emma dear, but you have unique qualifications, what with your reading and special ed credentials. So, don't do any prevaricating."

"I won't, Ms. Beamish."

"Carl."

"Carl." I blushed at the rebuke in the older woman's voice. Calling her by her first name would take time. "By the way, I have an interview at the Veteran's Center about that volunteer driving position. I thought it would help me learn the area and get to know more of the residents."

The momentary pause stretched into a lengthy one. Finally, Carl spoke. "The hell you say. Who did you talk to?"

"Um, a man who said his name was Phil Gordon, and then someone named Tony came in. I guess he's the one making the decision."

Another pause, shorter, followed by a snort and a chuckle. "Well, Emma Evans, Wanakena's going to be a lively place with you here. I suspect you're going to be as much trouble as your friend Riley, and I mean that in a good way."

I frowned at the phone. "Why do you say that?"

"Never you mind, missy. Just wear your big-girl pants, and don't let Tony," she barked the name, "do any intimidating, okay? Stand your ground. Oh, and the person you want to see at the school district is Elaine Narbow. Come back for breakfast tomorrow, you and the twins."

"Speaking of the twins, can you watch them while I'm at the interview? I'll be glad to pay you."

"Hush your mouth, woman. No need to pay me for looking after those cubs of yours. Does my heart good to hear them laughing and carrying on."

"Thank you, Carl, but why are you being so good to me? I'm a stranger with nothing but trouble trailing behind like a shadow."

Carl laughed. "Nonsense. You're a new chapter in Wanakena's winter tale. I look forward to hearing more about your adventures, so plan to stay for dinner after you talk to those men."

She hung up before I could decline the invitation. Riley always said Carl Beamish was formidable. Guess she was right. Thinking of Riley reminded me that the Waylons were due home from their vacation later today. Tomorrow I'd take the twins to visit. Tonight, I needed some time after the children went to bed to consider how best to explain my sudden, unexpected appearance in Wanakena and how to talk Riley and Josh out of contacting the authorities. Setting aside that uncomfortable conversation, I cleaned up the lunch mess and crawled into the makeshift tent to play bear hunt, one of the twins' favorite games. I decided to save the story of Auntie Riley's encounter with a real mama bear and cubs for when the children were older and not prone to nightmares. The past few months had introduced enough trauma into their lives. No need to invite more.

The alarm on my phone blared at exactly 3:15. Not certain how long it would take to reach the Center for the interview, I decided to allow plenty of time to get there. Since Carl had agreed to look after the twins, promising a rousing game of hide and seek before putting them to work making sugar cookies, I could relax a bit during the drive.

The roads were snow-covered and slick on the way out of Wanakena, but the stretch into the Fine Town Hall had been plowed and salted. I relied on the navigation app for directions, and it didn't disappoint. Half an hour of driving delivered me right to the door. Kicking snow off my boots, I stomped over the threshold and into a deserted hallway with doors lining both sides. I tried each handle until I found one that opened into a medium-sized space. A receptionist's desk occupied the area to the left of the entrance. Above the desk, a big-screen TV tuned to Fox News had been muted, rendering the commentators and their opinions unintelligible. A chest-high counter lined with brochures divided the remaining space. When I peeked around the divider, I noticed two well-used sofa chairs and an electric fireplace tucked behind it. Another door, currently closed, indicated more space, perhaps a conference room for group meetings or a separate office. Photos on the lounge wall paid tribute to local veterans who had died in wartime. A gym bag slumped next to one of the chairs. I heard no voices or sounds that would indicate anyone was around. I took a deep breath and steeled myself for what was to come.

"Hello?" I approached the desk, looking for a bell to ring or another way to attract attention. "Excuse me? Is anyone here?"

Boots thumped down the outer corridor, skidded to a halt. The door banged open, revealing a man wearing Army fatigues. His hair was buzzed short, and his eyes, dark gray and creased with fine lines at the corners, looked me over. "Evans? You're ten minutes early."

"Mr. Gordon?" I extended a hand. "I wasn't sure how long it would take to get here from Wanakena. Is that a problem?"

Phil Gordon rubbed his hands down his thighs before shaking, then slipped past me to stand behind his desk. "I thought you'd be older."

I blushed and shoved my hands in my pockets. What could I possibly say to that? I'm sorry I'm not older, too? "Nope, still thirty-two last time I checked my driver's license, which is just a standard-issue Ohio one. Do I need a special permit to do this volunteer driving?"

"Tony will have to answer that if he decides to take you on. He'll be here in," Gordon pursed his lips and tapped his watch, "five, four, three, two, one second."

The door I'd spied in the lounge area opened, and a man backed into the room, his flannel shirt rolled to the elbows. His muscled forearms strained under the weight of a bottle meant for a water cooler, which I hadn't seen in the office. Gordon and I stepped toward him simultaneously, arms outstretched to help with the heavy load. Gordon reached him first and helped wrestle the bottle to the counter. "Evans here yet?" The man turned as he spoke, stroking his lower lip with a thumb.

"Storms?" I took a step back. Gordon looked back and forth between us and frowned.

"What are you doing here?" he growled.

"Tony," Gordon waved in my direction, "this is the volunteer I told you about."

Tony, AKA Anton "Grumpy" Storms, narrowed his gaze. "You didn't say Evans was a woman."

I bristled. "What difference does my gender make? You need a driver, and I'm willing to drive. Get over yourself, Storms."

Gordon scooted around us and exited into the corridor, mumbling about a microwave. Tony Storms glared at me. I glared back.

"You can't be serious about driving vets to appointments. You don't know the area."

I held up my phone. "There's this modern convenience called a navigation app, which I can use quite well, thank you."

"You'll be a," he ran a hand through the hair that covered the scar along his temple, "distraction."

"Why is that? Because I'm a woman? Or is it because I'm an outsider? Oh, wait, maybe you think I'm looking for a hookup? Puh-lease. I care deeply about the men and women who have served our country, and for your information, Mr. Storms, I have no intention of being with a man ever again." I clapped a hand over my mouth before any more stupid revelations could spew free. Storms cocked his head, his mouth working over my words.

"You'll be a distraction, Evans, because you're god-damned beautiful and have those sad, puppy-dog eyes men love. The older vets will want to adopt you. The young ones—" He shook his head. "Go back home, woman. Save us all a shit ton of grief."

"Mr. Storms. Tony." I swallowed hard to dislodge the word beautiful from my mind. Was the man blind? I'd barely showered in a week. My shoulder-length hair, longer than I'd ever worn it, had escaped the tie to tumble around my face in a riot of curls, and my once-tight body had acquired a little more flesh than I thought attractive in the belly area. "I'm a responsible, sensible, educated woman who needs to do something good to counteract all the ugliness in my life. You bloody well need someone. I'm here. So, stick your stereotypes up your ass and give me a chance. You might be pleasantly surprised."

Tony didn't take his eyes off me during the entire tirade. Now, he licked his bottom lip, a move I found vaguely disturbing, and shrugged. "What happens when you get a job? I'm guessing you're looking for work. We'll be left in the lurch again."

"Lurch?"

Despite the tension between us, Tony's lips twitched. "A Jesse Livetree word. Been spending way too much time with that old man. If, and that's a big if, I give you a shot, I don't want to hear about you speeding or stopping off for a beer here and there."

"What? Why would I ever do that?" I paused, then raised a finger. "Oh, the guys lobby for unauthorized stops on their way home."

Tony picked up a folder from the desk and handed it over. "Male or female, vets are people like the rest of us. They can try your patience. Most are elderly and need special care. There are also a few with serious mental health issues."

I hugged the folder. "Does this mean I'm hired?"

"On a trial basis, Evans. One bad report and you're history. And fill that out before you leave."

"You're a real confidence builder, Storms." I leaned on the counter, took out the paperwork, and started to read the application, jumping when he leaned over my shoulder. His body heat swept over me.

"You'll need to be fingerprinted."

I planted my pen in his chest and pushed him away. "I've already been. Teachers in Ohio do this routinely, and I have my records."

"References?"

My hand trembled. I couldn't allow anyone to contact Hopewell. Luckily, my teaching credentials were all in my maiden name. "Riley, Josh, and Ms. Beamish will speak for me."

"Got it all figured out, have you?"

Not really, I thought, easing away from him and his intimidating presence. I finished filling out the form and handed it back, along with a copy of my fingerprint check. "When can I start?"

...flight plans...

Despite repeated visits to Poplar Street, the stakeout at the Pearson property had ended with a whimper. No additional mail delivery. No FBI surveillance vehicles, and no further evidence of human habitation. The whole damn family had vanished like the sun on a cloudy day. Mouse dedicated two days to hacking airport databases hoping to find reservations under the Pearson name. When that search came up empty, he phoned hotels in and around Orlando, claiming a family emergency and the need to contact Gail and Fred Evans immediately. He learned nothing of value until he expanded the search to include retirement communities close to popular family destinations. The third venue – Orlando Springs West – had a Mr. and Mrs. Fred Evans registered in Bungalow 33. When the operator offered to connect him to the residence, Mouse ended the call. The hunt was on. But first, he had to report in.

He keyed the number of an auto parts store in Emporia. A woman answered, waited for Mouse to ask to speak to a mechanic, then placed him on hold. After a brief pause, a synthesized voice rasped his name. "Mouse?"

"Mechanic?" A guttural affirmative verified he had reached his employer. "The search for parts is taking longer than expected. I have a few more stores to check off my list. Then I'm on my way to Florida to interview a dealer."

"Will you be able to finalize the sale?"

"Uncertain if the parts match the specs. I may need to do further searching."

The Mechanic cleared his throat. "Whatever it takes. Standard rates apply. Try not to do further damage to the vehicles when extracting the needed items."

"Understood." Ten minutes later, Mouse checked his online bank app. An additional five thousand dollars had landed in his account. Satisfied and ready to continue the hunt, he opened the weapons bag, laid out a cloth, and began to clean his guns.

...renewing old acquaintances...

The wind whistled a mournful tune through the tall pines along the riverbank. The lights in the Lodge flickered but did not go out, a reminder to keep a flashlight and candles handy once the kids and I had our own place. I shuffled through the schedule of doctor's appointments and shopping trips that Storms had given me for my first volunteer run three days from today. I entered the dates and times into my phone and stuffed the paperwork in my bag. Before I started the driving gig, I needed to arrange daycare for the twins and set up a bank account locally. For that, I needed Riley. Overwhelmed, I dropped my head in my hands. So much to do. How long before the pain went away? I poured a packet of hot chocolate mix into a mug, added hot water, and moved to stare at the Oswegatchie rumbling by at the back of the property. The twins, sleeping now, had spent their time at Carl's drawing pictures of Wanakena to send to their father. I was tired of lying to them, but I honestly had no idea how to tell them the truth. I swallowed a scream along with a host of tiny marshmallows and rubbed away the headache behind my eyes.

Tomorrow, I would move us into Carl's small cabin. Then we'd go surprise Riley and Josh, and float my idea for hiding the few assets I'd brought with me. Right now, the promise of seeing my friend again was the only thing keeping me from a complete and total meltdown. Setting the mug aside, I picked up my phone, the urge to contact my parents overpowering. I found their number, rubbed a thumb over the contact, hesitated. I didn't dare call, afraid to even hint at my location. What if the FBI or Gary's killer went to Florida, found Mom and Dad, threatened them into talking? "Like it or not, Emma P, er, Evans," I told the map of Wanakena decorating the wall beside me, "you're on your own."

After checking to see if I had everything I needed, the Lodge owners, Ron and Amy, returned to their home up the road. I double-checked that the doors were locked, climbed to the second floor, and undressed in the dark. The single bed was narrow, the mattress lumpy, but the blankets were clean and warm. I snuggled deeper, missing the comfort of a warm body next to me, but what I thought was a loving presence had been a lie. Despite my vow not to cry, the tears came. Betrayed as I had been, how could I ever love again? The specter of living the rest of my life alone chilled me. It was a long time before I slept.

In the morning, Carl served us breakfast, a gigantic stack of blueberry pancakes, along with bacon, peaches the woman had canned herself, and a litany of snowstorm stories. Someone had cleared the path between the large cabin and the one we would occupy, but the kids and I still tracked in a fair amount of snow along with the boxes and suitcases. Mollie and Evan towed their roller bags into the kitchen, then spent the next two hours climbing snowbanks. By lunchtime, everyone was exhausted, the kitchen floor covered in melted snow, and the furnace working overtime to heat the cabin. Carl plopped into a chair, fanning herself and breathing hard. I remembered the woman had had heart surgery only a little over three years ago.

"That's enough, Ms. Beamish. You rest while I fix lunch, and then you can go back to your place. I'll clean up the mess we made."

Carl didn't argue, but she did insist I return to the large cabin and bring down the tuna salad she'd prepared earlier. Exhausted and hungry, the twins gobbled their sandwiches, then settled onto the sofa to read books. It wasn't long before they fell asleep.

"I guess all that fresh air worked some magic," Carl said, slipping into her plaid anorak. "I'll leave you to it, then. You around tonight for dinner?"

I rinsed a dish, dried my hands, and hugged her. "I'm going to see Riley as soon as the kids wake, so don't wait on us. But thank you so much." I swiped at my eyes. "I don't know what I'd have done without you."

"Pshaw, woman, you're tough like Riley. Here." Carl fished a paper from her pocket. "Found someone to watch the kids. Asa Cleary. She's raised eight kiddos, all grown and productive citizens now. She knows how to keep children out of mischief. Call her, and don't forget to take some time for yourself, Emma girl. God and all his angels know you need it."

I stood at the back door, watching my benefactor trudge along the now-rutted walkway, gather up Mutzi, and go inside. I checked the time. With luck, the twins would sleep for two hours, long enough for me to unpack and discard the nostalgia I'd foolishly included in our hurried departure. Gary's briefcase. The letters we'd written each other before our marriage, missives I'd believed proved our love. I shoved the case under my bed and stashed the letters under the sink, where all trash deserved to go. Then I attacked the suitcases. By the time the children woke, the cabin had warmed, the rooms no longer resembled the aftermath of a hurricane, and I felt a little more settled. Time for a heart-to-heart with my best friend.

The directions Carl supplied matched the map on my GPS, but the roads had grown slick again, and I was carrying the most precious items I possessed. I took my time, content to rumble along and let more eager drivers pass me by. Mollie tapped the back of my head with a mittened hand. "Mommy? Are we there yet?"

"Almost, baby." I checked the app. One point three miles to go.

"I can't wait to see Auntie Riley," Evan chirped. "And Timmy and Mikey. And Uncle Josh."

I shared my son's excitement, although a fair amount of anxiety coursed through me. I had decided to reveal the truth about our flight from Hopewell. Would my friends help? Or would Josh, that upright, good, solid man, insist I inform the local authorities and let the FBI agents know where we were? I prayed he wouldn't. The only way to keep the children safe was to disappear, if not here in Wanakena, then somewhere else in the vastness of the Adirondacks. When the tidy ranch appeared up ahead, I noticed a new addition to the right of the original structure. So like Riley's man, to add space for their growing family. I couldn't deny the envy that replaced a bit of my joy. As soon as the kids spotted the house, they began to yell. I pulled in next to the Forest Service truck Josh drove and killed the engine.

"Remember, kids, there are inside voices and outside voices, and mind your manners." I helped them down from their car seats and ushered them onto the front porch. The doorbell rang loudly, and someone called, "I'll get it." When the door opened, Timmy Waylon shifted his crutches to one hand, braced his legs, and smiled. "Aunt Emma."

"Tim." I stepped around the twins to wrap him in my arms. The boy had grown taller, his head at my shoulders now, and his speech was much improved. A small hand waved from around the corner of what must be the living room, followed by a dark-haired toddler nine months younger than Mollie and Evan. I squatted to face the boy and held out my arms. "You must be Michael. I'm your Aunt Emma, and I've wanted to meet you for a long time."

The smell of spaghetti sauce drifted toward the open door. "Tim, who is it?" Riley came into the hall, wiping her hands on a dishtowel, gasped, and waddled toward me. "Emma? Oh, my God, Em. Mollie! Evan! What are you doing here?"

I rose, ready for a hug, then stopped, hands on hips. "OMG, Riley, you're pregnant again!" I folded her into my arms, bending around the bulge of her stomach, and hung on, unable to stop the tears.

"Hey, Riley? Tim? What's going on?" Josh stepped into view, hair wet from a recent shower, shook his head, and laughed. "I should have guessed. Only my wife's best friend could elicit such squealing. Well, come in, Pearsons, and tell us why you're here."

Tim closed the door. "Want to watch me play Planteaters?" Giggling, the twins dumped boots, hats, mittens, and winter coats on the floor and followed him into the room where Michael had been. The toddler looked at his father, eyes wide, then scampered to join the children. Riley led me into the kitchen, where we hugged again before she pushed me into a chair, then eased herself down with a sigh. Josh moved behind to massage his wife's shoulders. I blinked the tears away. Riley deserved this happiness. I smiled and squeezed her hand. Outside, a dog barked, then pawed at the back door. A second bark sounded, this one from beside the refrigerator, accompanied by mewling noises. Mollie and Evan ran in from the TV room to peek around my chair. "Puppies!"

"Kids!" I grabbed for them but missed, then stood to corral them as they crawled toward a white-coated retriever nursing pups.

"Momma." Mollie's voice came out hushed and reverent. "Auntie Riley has puppies. Eight puppies! Can we have one? Please."

"Please, Mom." Evan tugged my sleeve. "Can we?"

Riley extricated me from Evan, shooed the twins over to Timmy, and led me back to the table. "That's the deal, Em. You take a puppy, or we're not friends anymore."

I snorted. "What possessed you to get another dog?"

Josh gave his wife a pat on the butt and chuckled. "Seems like we're real good at breeding things, right, Ri?"

Riley shared a look with her husband, then plopped down again. "Josh found Iris abandoned in the Five Ponds area six months ago. When he brought her home, she and Ike bonded." My friend shrugged. "The pups are mostly spoken for, but we have two who need homes. A male and a female. You can have one or both."

"OMG, Ri, I can barely take care of the twins on my own. How am I going to raise puppies?" I worried the zipper of my fleece. "But we'll discuss the pups later. More important stuff first. Why didn't you tell me you were pregnant? How far along are you?"

"Eight months, two weeks, and three days, but who's counting?" She looked at Josh and smiled, then patted her stomach. "Our little miss is sort of a surprise, but that's what you get when you camp out under the stars during a meteor shower."

I looked away, the devotion between my friends palpable. Once I thought I had that, too. The loss felt unbearable. "The kids can't hear us, right?"

Riley patted my hand. "They can't. Spill, Emma. What's going on?"

Josh moved to the counter. "I think this calls for a drink. Want a glass, Em?"

I looked at the bottle of wine in his hand and nodded. One drink couldn't hurt, and I could use some liquid courage to get through another recital of Gary's betrayal. "You know Gary was killed in Kansas City. What you don't know are the circumstances of his murder. I-I couldn't tell you before because it's too awful."

Riley took my hands. "But you can tell us now, Em."

I sipped from my drink, straightened my shoulders, and went on. "The truth is he had another wife and a child in KC. They were murdered, too. Apparently, he was involved in an undercover investigation that got out of hand."

Riley didn't flinch. Josh stirred the pasta sauce. "Why would he do that?"

"I don't know." Tears again. I scrubbed them away. I was so tired of crying. "The thing is the FBI believes, claims they have proof even, that my husband's killers are coming after me. Don't ask what proof. I don't know. What I do know is I don't want to live in witness protection. I don't want my kids caught up in that kind of lie, either. So, I ran away. I came here."

Josh adjusted the flame under the sauce and crossed his arms. "And no one knows you're here."

"Right."

"What about your parents?" Riley said.

"They helped me leave, but they don't know where I am." I choked out the next words. "I'll never see them again. It's too dangerous."

"You think the people chasing you will go after your parents?"

"I think they'll go after anyone who can lead them to me. I probably shouldn't even be here. I could be putting you and your family in danger." I fisted my hands. "I'm sorry, Riley. Josh. I didn't know where else to go."

Filling a pot with water, Josh set it on a burner. "Emma, relax. You and the kids will stay for supper, and we'll figure things out."

"Josh is right. You're staying." Riley levered herself up to rummage for silverware. "So, Em, how are you planning to pull this off? Your name? The kids' records for doctors and school?"

"I brought all the paperwork with me. Wanakena isn't exactly a thriving metropolis. No one would think I'd come here. And I was careful not to leave any clues behind." I accepted plates from her and set them out on the table. "I've taken back my maiden name."

Riley stared at me, then burst into laughter. "You're seriously going to saddle your son with Evan Evans?"

I stared back, then laughed myself. "I never thought of that. Guess my long-range planning isn't as good as I thought. I do need a job, though, so I'm handing in my resumé at the school office next week. Ms. Beamish has offered me the cabin you used. I moved in today. And I'm hoping you'll agree to help me open a bank account that uses your name but gives me access to the funds."

"That's a big ask."

"I know. I just can't be traceable. My funds are limited, but if I find a job to supplement what I brought with me, I'll have enough to get us through till spring."

Josh and Riley exchanged a look. "The school might not have anything full-time, but you could probably sub. You'll need references."

"Yeah, that's what they said at the Veteran's office."

Riley added spaghetti to the boiling water. "Why were you there?"

"They need a volunteer to drive vets to appointments. I need to learn my way around and make some contacts. It wasn't easy, but I convinced them to let me try."

More eye rolls from Riley. "Geez, Em, you sure know how to poke the bear."

"Why do you say that?"

Josh kissed the top of Riley's head and grinned. "The bear is one Anton Storms. Among other things, he runs the vet programs for the region, and he's not easy to get along with."

"Oh, I found that out real quick. Tony Storms ordered me to leave Wanakena and go back where I came from."

"Not surprising." Josh drew his wife closer and laid a hand on her belly. "Sit, babe. I'll get the kids to wash their hands."

Riley watched him go, her hand where his had been. When she turned back to me, she sighed. "You going to let Storms intimidate you?"

"Not a chance in hell, girlfriend. I'm done being manipulated by men."

...interview with a jerk...

Mouse spent two days holed up in the motel, phoning contacts, and searching the Internet for pictures of Riley Finn, a name he discovered in copies of old grade-school yearbooks at the local library. He eventually found photographs tagged in other people's feeds, but every picture was at least three years old. Wherever the Finn woman went, she had not left a cyber trail, which was weird. Most women in her age group were addicted to posting selfies and reporting every wrinkle in their ordinary lives. She had managed to erase herself from social media. That took skill and determination. Perhaps he had underestimated both her and Emma Pearson. He wouldn't make that mistake going forward.

New Year's Eve came and went without a break in the chilly drizzle that marked the end of the old year and the beginning of the new. Mouse phoned his sister, complained of problems in his job that kept him away from home. He ate fast-food from cardboard containers, watched porn and grade-B action movies, and contemplated his next move. The custodian at Hopewell Elementary had provided a substantial lead, but he needed more. As soon as school was in session again, he would track down the ex-boyfriend of the Riley woman. If that interview turned into a dead-end, he'd locate Emma Pearson's parents, at their Florida place. He did a few more drive-bys past the Pearson house, convinced that the FBI had abandoned their surveillance. That had to mean something, although

Mouse wasn't sure what, exactly. But no mail had been delivered since December 26. No one had removed the lights decorating the pine tree in the front yard, and the timer-based electric candles in the windows still lit up at night. Despite the attempt to fool casual observers, the place gave every indication of being deserted.

Mouse rooted through his retinue of disguises, then decided to create a new persona, that of a stereotypical engineer, complete with pocket pens and a thin mustache. Satisfied with the look, he put in a call to Hopewell High, requesting a conference with the principal about enrolling his daughters there. The secretary scheduled him for the first appointment on January 3rd.

A short, fit man, Principal Warren Carstairs, stood in the foyer, welcoming students back with a stern expression and a firm handshake. Some kids accepted the gesture. Most giggled and slipped past him. Observing the varied reactions, Mouse waited for the crowd to taper off before approaching the woman at the front desk. He showed his driver's license, had his picture taken, and pasted a name tag to his oxford button-down. Then, adjusting his tie, he took a seat in the waiting area. Ten minutes later a secretary escorted him into the principal's office.

"Mr. Champion?" The principal rose to greet him. "Warren Carstairs. I understand you're new to the area."

"I am." Mouse set his briefcase down and shifted from one foot to the other. "My wife is joining me in a few weeks, and our children's schooling is of the highest priority. We're looking for a good district with a strong academic reputation, which Hopewell appears to have. And I understand you run a tight ship. No discipline problems, I take it?"

Carstairs settled behind the desk. He picked up a folder and handed it over. "Our reputation is outstanding, Mr. Champion. I've gathered some materials for you and your wife which speak to our curriculum and certification. One of the brochures contains our most recent evaluation by the state. We rank highly in all academic areas, especially here in Warren County. I've also included a copy of the school handbook. Our policies are well-defined. What grades are your daughters in?"

"Mariah is a freshman, so she would be a student here. Nevaeh's in third grade. I understand you have a great staff at the elementary school, too, but have recently lost a few of your best teachers?" Mouse opened his case to pull out a newspaper clipping and slid the article across the desk.

"This woman, Emma Pearson, wasn't she involved in some sort of scandal a few months ago?"

The principal folded his hands. "Her husband was murdered in Kansas City. However, Mrs. Pearson was not implicated in any way in that affair."

"Well, that's both tragic and reassuring. The article mentions an award she received a few years ago, she and a fellow teacher. I'm sorry, I don't remember her colleague's name."

"Pearson worked on a team, so, yes, the group was honored with an outstanding teaching award by the county. Well-deserved, too."

Mouse tapped his fingers on top of the folder Carstairs had given him. "Who were those other teachers? Are they still teaching here? Wasn't one of them a Riley something?"

At the mention of Riley's name, Carstairs frowned and checked his watch. "I'm afraid I have a meeting in a few minutes, Mr. Champion. If there's anything else you need, our guidance counselor, Ms. Wilson, will be more than happy to speak with you."

Mouse recognized dismissal when he heard it. He also noted that Warren Carstairs did not want to discuss the Riley woman. Thanking the man for his help, Mouse carried the information folder with him until he rounded the corner of the office. Then he dumped the paperwork into a trash can along with the briefcase. He was planning his next move before he reached the parking lot.

...a little knowledge is a dangerous thing...

The line at the rental car desk was long, and the clerk slow. Mouse chafed at the delay, but it was time to hide his tracks again. He handed over the keys, paid the bill in cash, and took an Uber to the Dayton Airport, where he used his fake federal ID and a spiel of equal parts flattery and intimidation to talk his way onto a full flight to Orlando. The passenger bumped from the flight complained loudly until the airline agent offered a sizeable compensation and a promise to book him a first-class seat on the next flight out.

Given that most schools were now back in session, Mouse was surprised at the number of families heading south for vacation. The plane hummed with the excited chatter of children wearing Disney gear and waving Harry Potter wands. Bored, he slipped in earbuds, selected one of his favorite heavy metal albums, and zoned out for the three-hour flight.

The gated community of Orlando Springs West was a sprawling maze of ranch homes centered around a spacious building that housed registration and sales, with an outdoor swimming pool, tennis, pickleball, and shuffleboard courts. The roads bustled with golf carts. Pedestrians strolled along trails that meandered past several ponds skirting the golf course. Mouse noted the alligators sunning themselves along the banks, but none of the residents paid any attention to the reptiles. The hitman showed his badge to the guard and eased the Jeep he'd rented down the main thoroughfare, following the GPS instructions to the rental property occupied by Emma Pearson's parents. Locating the condo was easy. Finding a parking space proved more difficult. He cruised two streets over before finding an open curb space. He walked back to the Evans residence, sweat stains blooming on his shirt under the jacket he wore. His weapon sat heavily against his ribs. When he reached the duplex, he paused to scan the street. Then, assuming his trusted-law-enforcement face, Mouse rang the bell.

A perky redhead, an older, more petite version of Emma Pearson, cracked open the door and scrunched her nose at him. "No soliciting in the village, sir." She started to shut him out. Mouse lodged his foot against the frame, lifted his badge, and held it up. The woman didn't smile, but she did relax into the hand that gripped her shoulder. A tall, powerfully-built, older man, bald and wearing metal-rimmed glasses, stepped up beside her. "Now is not a good time," Fred Evans said. "Give me your card, and I'll contact your supervisor."

Gail Evans patted her husband's hand, then swung the door wider, revealing a cluster of people in the great room. Each head swiveled toward Mouse.

Evans held out his hand. "Card?"

Mouse bowed his head. "I believe I'm at the wrong house." He pulled a small notebook from his jacket and consulted it. "This is the Finester residence, correct?"

"No." The woman began to close the door again. "You must be in the wrong place entirely. We know all our neighbors. None of them are named Finester."

For the first time, Charles Mouse didn't know what to do. Establishing surveillance in a development that touted a neighborhood watch program would be impossible, especially since Emma's parents and all their friends had seen him. Damn. This misstep could cost him days. He needed to re-think the game plan here, and he was thirsty. He rewound his way to the entrance and drove along the main highway until he spotted a sports bar advertising Jimmy Buffet margaritas and parrot jokes.

When he stepped into the dimly lit interior, Mouse knew he'd struck paydirt. A display of one-armed slot machines lined the side wall. Glenn Miller and Elvis Presley competed for jukebox plays, and a woman in her late sixties wearing a crop top and shorts more suitable on a teenager sipped from an over-size margarita glass while swaying on her stool. A lanyard bearing the flamingo crest of Orlando Springs West dangled from her neck.

Mouse hitched up his pants, smoothed back a few stray hairs on the gray wig he wore, and sidled up to the bar.

"Give us one of what the lady's having," he said, cocking a thumb in her direction. The woman raised her eyebrows, looked him over, and grinned.

"Fresh meat for the grinder," she sputtered, then slurped more of her drink. "You look like a man in search of a friend."

"You got that right, ma'am. My company sent me down here to this charming community to find an insurance beneficiary, and all I've run into is stonewalling and misdirection." Mouse laid on the southern accent, thanked the bartender for his drink, and laid two twenty-dollar bills on the bar. The woman stretched her fingers toward the money, licking her lips. He helped himself to a handful of bar nuts and waited for her to make the first move. She tapped her fake fingernails against the rim of her drink and stuck out her hand.

"Trudi Funtain, pariah of Springs West due to my," she giggled, "preference for strong drinks and stronger males. Tell me, Mr. Fake Hair, how much of that money are you willing to spend to find your missing heir?"

"Who says she's missing?"

"Your face and that gun under your jacket." Trudi Funtain sipped the last of her margarita and rapped on the bar for another. "I may be old, but I'm not stupid. Used to work for the sheriff's department in Ocala."

Mouse ignored the hiccup that followed that disclosure. He nodded at the bartender to take her drink from his stash, then pulled out another twenty and placed it beside the others. "Who do you know in Orlando Springs West?"

Funtain laid a hand on his arm and squeezed. "Everyone, sugar. Used to volunteer at registration until management decided they wanted a younger face at the old folks' home."

Mouse waited while she cackled, coughed, and took another swallow from her fresh drink. She stared into the mirror behind the bar and patted her hair. When she turned back to him, he covered her restless hand with his own. "Tell me about Fred and Gail Evans."

Trudi did, offering move-in dates and dietary restrictions, favorite restaurants, and recreational choices. Two more margaritas and she was spouting off next-of-kin information, her words slightly slurred but the information crisp as kindling. "Saw pictures of them twins, their grandkids, you know, and their son and daughter. Derrick lives in Colorado, runs some ski resort out there. That Emma, met her once before all that crap with her faithless husband. You know about that?"

Mouse nodded. "I didn't know she'd come to stay with her parents."

"Because she didn't." More hiccupping. Funtain signaled the bartender, who shook his head. "He's cutting me off 'cause I have to get back before my daughter starts looking for me. She met Emma and the twins once, too, before they went away. Liked them. Doesn't like me."

Mouse leaned in, stroked the back of her hand. "I'll take you home, Ms. Funtain, soon as you tell me where Emma is."

One eye opened wider than the other. "You got me drunk so's you could pump me for information?"

"Maybe." Mouse slid the bills toward her. "Take the rest of this and have a few on me tomorrow."

When she grabbed for the money, he tightened his grip on her wrist. "Where's Emma, Trudi?"

The bartender caught Trudi's grimace and started toward them. Funtain tugged at the bills, then sighed. "Gail didn't tell me, but I overheard her ask Fred about the weather in the Adirondacks this time of year, so if I had to guess, I'd say she's somewhere in New York, hiding in the mountains."

Mouse released his hold. The money disappeared into a pocket before he could blink. The Adirondacks, six million miles of wilderness, but at least he had a direction now. It might take a while, but he'd find Pearson and the data she carried, and when he did, he'd end the threat to the boss and finally work off his debt. Only three more murders, and he'd be free.

...doing the snowshoe shuffle...

New Year's Eve had been fun. The hours spent with the Waylons helped salve the wounds on my soul. Despite misgivings, Riley agreed to accompany me to the Chase Bank in Star Lake at the end of the week to set up a custodial account under her name. It wasn't an ideal solution, but if I could hide my location from prying eyes until I could establish the new identity, I'd buy us time and protect the twins. Given the insular nature of the region, the arrangement seemed unlikely to raise eyebrows or trigger questions. Riley and I had a long history of friendship, and my intention to establish roots in the community worked in my favor. In return, I promised to go with her to the next scheduled Lamaze class. Josh would be away checking the backcountry for potential avalanche conditions and answering calls for Ranger assistance from people who failed to prepare for winter conditions in the wilderness and need rescuing. I'd learned about the incidents in the online Adirondack Almanac and swore I'd never get myself in similar situations. Riley also convinced me to be her emergency contact should the baby decide to make an appearance before the scheduled due date.

I spent the next two days establishing a routine for Mollie and Evan, washing clothes, and arranging our belongings. The cabin had acquired a lived-in look, cluttered but homey, although the twins continued to ask about their father. I hated lying to them. Like it or not, I'd have to tell them the truth soon. My chest ached just thinking about it.

My phone call to the woman Carl had recommended for daycare ended with an invitation to bring those little ones over "toot sweet." When I pulled in front of the single-story home, I immediately noticed the fenced-in play equipment crowding the backyard. Most of the structures were buried in snow, but someone, maybe one of the children Carl had mentioned, had packed the sliding board to form a chute. I shook my head, wondering which of the twins would be the first to break an arm attempting to slide down headfirst. However, when I rang the bell, Asa Cleary's welcoming face eased my fears.

"You come right on in, Miss Emma, Miss Mollie. And you must be Evan. My, aren't youse the spitting image of your mama." The aroma of cabbage wafted from the woman's apron like a cloud. "Sorry, so sorry, but I be about my sauerkrauting today. Won't always smell like this. And I saw you frowning at the backyard ski run. Not to worry about that, either."

Mollie slipped off her boots, dropped her coat, hat, and mittens, and scurried into the front room, overflowing with games, puzzles, building blocks of every size, and a flat-screen TV. Game controllers draped themselves over the console. Suddenly shy, she looked back at me, her tiny eyebrows raised in question, which the Cleary woman immediately answered with a wave of the towel in her hand.

"Go right ahead and play, young missy." Asa nudged Evan with her elbow. "Bet you like to play that car racing game, don't you?"

Suddenly shy, Evan waited for me to remove his coat and boots before tiptoeing toward the game console, eyes wide, mouth a round O of wonder. As soon as they settled in, I followed Asa to the kitchen. "They'll be fine, Miss Emma, and not to worry about broken bones. Scrapes are just a part of growing up, but I was a nurse in my first life before the children claimed me." She laughed and stirred the soup pot with a long-handled wooden spoon. "I can send you copies of my degrees and certifications if it'll ease your mind."

"Thank you, Mrs. Cleary. To be honest, I'm a little overwhelmed. Carl made it seem like you were, well, a volunteer."

The woman laughed. "Beamish tends to understate and overstate most things. I have eight children, twenty grandchildren, with more in the pipeline, and I be happy to take care of them all. But the childrens, six of them live far away, so we only gather here at Christmas and in the summer. Then this big house fills with noise. Wish my Edward were still here to see it. But that's life. You're a widow, too, I understand. We womens must help each other, no? I take good care of your precious babies, and you go do good things in the world, ok?"

I sat in the chair she set out for me. "We should discuss your fee."

Cleary brushed her cheek with the back of her hand, then grabbed a slip of paper from her apron pocket and set it in front of me. "This be good, or no?"

The figure was half what I was expecting. "This is more than generous, Mrs. Cleary."

"Call me Asa, dear heart, and bring their favorite snacks and drinks. Children settle in better with food in their bellies. I make lunch for them, all right?" She turned to me and winked. "Not sauerkraut! Promise!"

With the children safe at the Cleary residence and the cabin clutter settled more or less into order, I tackled the next item on my agenda – a job. So far, no one in Wanakena except Riley, Josh, and Carl knew the truth about my relocation, and I intended to keep it that way. I had sworn Ms. Beamish to secrecy, going so far as to make her take an oath not to tell Jesse Livetree anything about Gary's death and the threat of retaliation hanging over my family. Anxious to complete my tasks, I left the Cleary home and headed toward Clifton. The tires skidded on Route 61 going out of town, reminding me that all it takes is one miscalculation and everything, including my life and my children's, could be lost. *Damn you, Gary Pearson!* Anger returned to stand next to fear, an unsettling combination. I concentrated on going forward. It was too late to turn back.

This time the navigation app deposited me at 11 Hall Avenue, where the school district offices and the two school buildings were also located. It was a small district, only a little over three hundred students, which probably meant not much opportunity to land a full-time position, but maybe they needed substitute teachers or volunteers. Any role was a way to get my foot in the door. Both Carl and Riley had agreed to be my references. Gathering my purse and my courage, I tromped through the entrance to explain my mission to the secretary behind the plastic screen. The woman accepted my application and supporting materials, handed me a business card, and announced that someone from the office would contact me. It wasn't precisely a brush-off, but it didn't leave me hopeful.

Good thing I had a backup plan in place. I'd mailed the same materials to Harrisville, Hermon, and Gouverneur schools. Although each was farther from Wanakena and meant more time away from the children, I couldn't afford to be picky.

Satisfied I'd accomplished my plan for the day, I stopped at the pharmacy for toothpaste and Band-Aids, then followed the highway east until I spied an observation post above a boggy area and a sign indicating a snowmobile trail. Checking for vehicles and hikers, I pulled over, opened the rear door of the SUV, and lifted the cover hiding the spare tire. I looked around one more time to be sure I was alone, then took out the package I had concealed there. I unwrapped the towel around the box, keyed the lock, and ran a finger over the weapon within, the one I'd discovered hidden in Gary's toolbox in the basement workshop. Although I hadn't found the opportunity to fire it, I had practiced loading and aiming the weapon until I felt comfortable with its lethal firepower. Terrified at the thought of Mollie or Evan finding it, I had buried it beneath the tire, but I refused to get rid of it. No matter the cost in moral terms, I would protect my children. Lie, steal, kill, I'd do it. Replacing the box, I slipped the gun into my purse and headed for Riley's, in need of some friend time.

...what we hide in the light, we share in the dark...

"Am I glad to see you." Riley wrapped her arms around me and squeezed as tight as her expanded belly would allow. The baby kicked, a jolt I felt through the thick down coat.

"Baby's acting up today, big time." Riley rested a hand over the press of a tiny foot and pushed it down. She took my coat and hung it on a hook in the hall. "Leave your boots on the rug, Ri, and join me in my baking frenzy."

I shuffled after her into the warmth of a kitchen, smack into the midst of a chocolate explosion. "Have you taken over Carl's baking chores at the grocery?"

Riley laughed until she cried, then waved a spoon at the mess. "The sugar cookies are for the boys. The snickerdoodles are for Josh and his guys. The double chocolate fudge brownies are all mine. But I'll share one with you."

"Very generous of you, girlfriend." I perched on a bar stool and sighed. "It's great to see you so happy, Riley."

She slid a tray of cookies into the oven and hurried over to me. "I can't believe what that rat-ass did to you, Em. Hope he rots in hell. But I know you held something back last night. Care to expound now that Josh is at work, Timmy's at school, and the wee monster's engrossed in sorting his Legos?"

"I want to say more, Riley, but the last thing I want is to endanger you or your family. I probably should have gone straight to Canada, but I just couldn't take such a final step."

"You really believe the person who killed Gary and his other family is after you?"

"Well, they're after something. Look at this." I rummaged in my purse for the zip-lock baggie I'd discovered in the case with the gun. I set the bag on the counter and stared at the contents. Riley poked the bag, frowned, leaned closer.

"Thumb drives?"

"Yeah, five, all loaded with MP3 files of country music, one for each decade from the 50s through the 90s. I didn't think Gary even liked country. He was more of a rock and roll guy." The memory of frequent squabbles over which radio station to play during car trips intruded. I shoved down the urge to retch.

"But, Emma, why would your...why would he have these?"

"I don't know."

"And you think the people after you are trying to find these?"

I rolled my eyes. "Riley, I don't know. If they were diamonds, I'd say yes in a minute. But music?"

"Say they are searching for these." Riley poked at the thumb drives again. "What could be on them worth slaughtering a family?"

"Great question." I stared at the drives, mesmerized by the idea that these small items may have cost three people their lives and ruined mine. "They must know I have them."

"Why do you think that?"

I took out my phone to scroll to the video recorded by the camera I'd installed before I left Hopewell. The shadowy footage revealed a man in a utility worker's overalls shining a flashlight around the kitchen and into the living room. The video recorded nothing but darkness for seven minutes before the intruder returned, shoulders hunched. He punched a fist into a wall, then sifted through the drawer in the hall table, holding up pieces of paper, inspecting them, then tossing them aside.

"Why are the lights off?"

"I don't know. Maybe there was a power outage?"

"But your camera's working."

I nodded. "Yeah. Battery-powered. I'm not sure how long until it runs out."

"Why not go to the police? Tell the FBI?"

"My husband," I ignored the hitch in my chest when I said the words, "was in law enforcement. Didn't keep him alive, did it? No, Riley, I'm doing this my way." I shoved the drives back in my purse, set it on the couch, and gave the gun inside a mental pat. Definitely doing it my way this time, even if it meant I had to kill someone.

...doing the due diligence...

The aviator glasses cut the glare from the tarmac as Mouse waited for the call to board. He'd booked a flight to Syracuse and a suite at the Best Western Airport Inn and ordered cold weather gear and several electronic devices delivered there from Amazon, paying extra for rush shipping. With luck, he could set up his computer and search for signs of the Pearson woman in the area as soon as he arrived at the hotel. He rubbed his newly shaved head. Change the look, change the attitude. If Emma Pearson had holed up in the mountains, he'd have to proceed with caution. He loved the chase, loved the idea of a new identity, of becoming someone who'd blend in, someone capable of gaining the woman's trust.

The challenge was to figure out how to get what he needed without rousing her suspicions. Emma Pearson was cagey, clever, an opponent worthy of his talents. Of course, she didn't know he was coming. Advantage, Mouse. And after what happened in Kansas City, Mouse intended to be extra careful. He pushed aside the image of the infant bleeding out in the highchair. Dammit it to hell, he hadn't counted on that kind of collateral damage, and he wasn't keen on doing kids again. But was it his fault? No. He wandered back to the bathroom. No use wasting time on regrets. It was what it was. If he finished this job, the reward would be worth all the aggravation. He tended to his needs, glanced in the mirror, and returned to his seat. Minutes later, conscience untroubled, he settled into first-class pampering, the new plan in place as he dozed off. *I'm on my way, Emma Pearson, and you'll never see me coming.*

Rush-hour traffic crowded the highway as Mouse rode the shuttle bus to the hotel and the room with a view of the airport conning tower. The place offered easy access to the I-81 highway and the Northwoods. The items Mouse had ordered online were already waiting in his room. He set up the monitoring system in record time. Satisfied and eager to start this phase of the hunt, he called room service and ordered dinner, his mind already working out ways to locate Emma Pearson and her children. When the food arrived, he asked the waiter to leave the tray outside. When he was sure no one remained in the corridor, he collected the turkey sandwich, chips, and chocolate cake, hung a *Do Not Disturb* sign on the doorknob, and returned to his research.

Pearson's profile over the last six years had been scrubbed clean, but a search through the Hopewell Schools directory yielded a list of fellow teachers. Somewhere among their Facebook posts, he'd find a reference to Emma and her friends, especially the mysterious Riley Finn, who had also vanished into the wilderness. If he were a gambling man, he'd bet on them being together. Hours of trolling through family photos and group shots had him yawning. He printed out several class pictures that featured Emma and other teachers standing behind rows of elementary students. He also found a slew of holiday party snaps, women smiling or laughing, drinks prominently featured. Midnight came and went. Mouse dozed off and on and helped himself to a soda from the room refrigerator. At 3 a.m., he called it a night. Despite the time constraints, he had perseverance and motivation on his side.

...riding the storm...

I kicked the crusty snow off my boots, welcoming the rush of warm air against my cold cheeks. The man who had greeted me on my initial visit sat hunched over paperwork on the desk.

"Mr. Gordon?" I called, whispering in case he had fallen asleep.

"Gordo." He grunted the name and looked up, a smirk on his chiseled features.

"I'm sorry to interrupt you. Emma Evans, remember, Mr. Gordon? I'm here to drive veterans to their appointments."

"Gordo. No one calls me Mister Gordon."

"All right. Gordo. How are you?"

A crash sounded behind the door beyond the lounge area, followed by faint mutterings, a louder thud, and silence. Gordo raised one eyebrow and sniffed. "Good luck to you, Red."

"Emma. My name's –" Gordo raised a hand before I could finish.

"You work here, you earn a nickname. Given that mane of yours, I reckon Red will suffice, unless you prefer something else?"

I bit my tongue to keep from saying something snarky. I'd deal with Mr. Gordo later. "I have the list, and I've loaded all the coordinates on my navigation app. Does Mr. Storms have any further instructions for me?"

Gordo chuckled. "You better tighten your belt, Red. The boss is in a rare gloom today. Take these, but don't admit I gave them to you."

I closed my hand around an electronic key fob with three keys and slipped it into my pocket. The door to the inner office creaked open. Storms staggered through the lounge, a white, button-down shirt clinging to his muscular chest. His jeans rode low on his hips, his cheeks and chin bore a hint of a beard, and he cursed again. All signs pointed to a morning meltdown. "Gordo, I can't find the December sign-in sheets."

"In the filing cabinet in your office, Tony. Bottom drawer. Folders for each calendar month complete with invoices and receipts."

"About that." Storms abandoned buttoning his shirt to scratch his chin. "I accidentally pulled out the drawer, and everything spilled out."

"I'll take care of it, Boss."

"Good, Gor—" Storms looked up and stopped walking. "What are you doing here?"

I backed away from the desk as Gordon stepped toward him. "Red's ready to drive that schedule for the vets' appointments today."

"You told me to be here today at," I interrupted Gordo to tap my phone, "noon. I'm twenty minutes early."

"Well, at least you're on time." He ran a hand over the scar on his temple, then turned to the desk. "Where are the keys? Gordo?"

I smirked and held up the key fob. "Got them right here, Storms."

Scowling, he confronted Gordon, who grabbed his empty coffee cup and scampered out of reach. "Red can take it from here, Tony. Maybe you should put your files back in order while she gets to know the guys. You know, after the all-nighter you pulled."

"Don't start with me, Sarge."

Gordo laid a hand on Storms' shoulder. "You talked him down, Tony. Got Weems to agree to counseling. There's no need to feel guilty about what he did before you reached him."

I watched them carry on a silent conversation, how they leaned toward each other as they confronted the previous night's events. I didn't know the details, but their grief was palpable.

Storms shook off Gordon's hand, retrieved his coat from behind the partition, and gestured toward the door. "You're right, as usual. Let's go, Evans."

"Red," Gordo shouted from the coffee station. I scampered into the hall.

"Red?" Storms followed, his long legs a match for mine.

"Guess that's me now, To-ny." I looked back and drawled his name. "Gordo says everyone here has a nickname."

"You're not part of here."

"Not yet." I pushed through the outer door and scanned the lot. "What am I driving?"

Storms waved toward a green van with a handicapped lift and the VA logo on the side panel. "You're only a volunteer, lady. You're not one of us."

His words were cruel, arrogant, and cut like the wind that whipped my hair into my face. I gathered the thick strands in a knot, shoved the whole mess under my stocking cap, and climbed in. "Only a matter of time, Storms."

"Like hell." He muttered something I couldn't make out, swung up in one swift, agile move, and settled into the passenger seat. Then he leaned over to check the gas gauge. We bumped heads when he reached for the ignition button. He backed off, handed me a paper, and snarled. "Here's the list for today, Evans."

"I already have the list, remember? You gave it to me when I applied for the job."

"Well, there have been a few updates. Hit your turn signal when you pull out of the lot."

"Back off, Storms. I'm driving. Today you're just my wingman."

"What? Are you in the Air Force now?"

"I watch movies, read books, follow the news."

"Armchair female warrior. Great."

"And you're a backwoods badass." I punched in the address of the first stop, waited for the app to calibrate, and drove onto the road. "What can you tell me about our first guy, Vic Gmoser?"

"I'm not as backwoods as you think, Red." A hint of sarcasm in a voice meant for seduction. Damn this prickly man! I repeated the question, emphasizing each word like I would for the twins. Storms brushed a hand over the dash. "Sixty-five. Dialysis twice a week. Served twenty years in the Coast Guard. Wife died last year. She was a redhead, too, so you might deal with some repressed emotion."

I kept quiet. When Tony offered nothing more, I decided to use my people skills, which he was testing to the max. "Thank you. Details matter. The more I know, the better service I can provide. Maybe you can call me Emma around him?"

Storms leaned against the headrest and closed his eyes. "His four daughters all live on the coast, visit for holidays and in summer, but most of the time, he's on his own. Unless you take your hat off, he won't even know you're a ginger."

"I won't always be wearing a hat."

"You won't be around long enough for the weather to change." He crossed his arms, slumped deeper into the seat, and snored lightly. I scrunched my face and blew him a silent raspberry, wondering at the desperate sadness that enveloped him. The mysterious events of last night were part of it, but I felt sure there was more to his story than a veteran needing to be talked down from suicide. Maybe the man had suffered a betrayal as deep as my own, but I refused to feel sorry for him when he was being such an ass. *Won't be around long? That's what you think, Tony Storms. I've exhausted my one free runaway card. This time, I'm staying.*

...night terrors...

Physical exhaustion replaced the adrenaline rush from the first day of volunteering. My brain hummed with all the new information I'd acquired during the afternoon drives. I put away the dinner leftovers, gave the kids a quick bath, and settled in for story time. Our bedtime routine was a sacred rite, one I refused to abandon no matter how exhausted I was, but the minute I turned off the light and closed the door, doubts about my course of action began to circle. A glass of wine. That's what I needed to calm my nervous stomach and the nagging fear that whoever killed Gary was coming for us. I also needed the weapon I'd stashed back under the spare tire. I checked on the twins, made sure all the doors and windows were secure, then crunched my way down the path past Carl's cabin. The sky had cleared, although the local weatherman promised more snow. Above, stars sparkled among the scudding clouds, crowning the night with light that had traveled more miles than my brain could comprehend. The stars might be long dead, but their gift remained.

I pressed the button, and the rear hatch slid up. I grabbed the bottle of Sauvignon Blanc, set it down, and lifted the wheel cover. I hated to bring a weapon into the house, but I'd feel safer with it by my side. I shifted the tire and paused, then reached for the wrapped gun. A shadow fell over me. I screamed and, slipping on the icy ground, stumbled backward.

"Quiet, woman," a deep voice muttered as a man pulled me against his chest. "You'll wake Carl."

I hugged the gun, stifled a curse, and pounded the man through his jacket. "What the hell, Storms! You scared the shit out of me."

Big sigh, but he didn't lessen his hold on my waist. "You left these in the van." He waved a pair of gloves in my face.

"And you thought showing up in the dark at half past nine was an acceptable way to return them?" He shrugged. His grip relaxed, and I sprang away, pointing the Glock in its terrycloth wrap at him. "I could have shot you."

"Could have, but you didn't." Our stare-down lasted long enough for me to wonder why the hell I came out here without my coat. It was freezing. Suddenly, being in Storms' arms didn't seem like such a bad idea. He pressed the button to close the hatch. "I was going to leave them on your porch. Didn't expect you'd be dumb enough to come outside without proper clothing."

"Well," I said, "I didn't expect to be out here very long. And now I'm going inside. Wait, why couldn't you just give them to me tomorrow?"

He considered my question for a minute. "Seemed important you have them, especially after Vic Gmoser's story about losing a toe to frostbite. It upset you."

"Well, I'm not. Upset. I mean, I was a little, thinking about what if that happened to my kids, but I'm fine now." I snatched the gloves, tucked the weapon under my arm, and leaned down for the bottle.

"Why exactly are you out here in the dark?" Storms poked the towel-wrapped gun. "And why do you have a gun, Red?"

"That's none of your business." I turned to go back to my cabin when Carl's porchlight snapped on. Ms. Beamish stepped out, a rifle balanced in the crook of her arm.

"Who's messing around my yard this time of night?" She stepped onto the packed snow, her untied boots flapping around her ankles. "Anton Storms and Emma Evans. Mind explaining this suspicioutous meeting?"

"I needed something from my car, Carl. Storms just showed up. Brought me my gloves."

Carl chewed her lip, then chuckled. "Well, this sounds like a funny coincidence. Come on in and get warm. Fire's going good. You can tell me all about it over a glass of that wine you're toting."

I backed away. "I can't leave the children alone. I only meant to be out here a minute."

"Fine." Carl herded me and Storms ahead of her toward the smaller cabin. "We can talk at your place just as well as mine, though it'll be a mite cramped. Seeing as Storms here's a big man and takes up a lot of space."

Tony held up his hands. "I'm leaving," he said.

"No, Mr. Storms, you are not." Carl prodded him with the rifle barrel. "It's impolite to cause a ruckus and then disappear. Which you have always been real good at doing. Nuh-uh. No equivocatin'. Go along, then."

Arms full and mind racing, I led the way back to my cabin. Inside, boots off, gloves tossed on the top of the refrigerator, I decided a drink was more essential than ever. I located the corkscrew from the jumble of kitchen utensils, but Tony took it from me, set the bottle on the counter, and opened the wine. Carl stashed her weapon on the porch, then searched for glasses.

"Um, this is my place, isn't it?" I said. She smirked and proceeded to open every cabinet and drawer. I didn't know what to do with my gun and ended up cradling it in my lap. I felt trapped by her solicitude and Storms' irritating arrogance.

Eyes twinkling, Carl waited for Tony to pour the wine, then lifted her glass in a toast. "To another interesting year in Wanakena. Drink up, kids."

Storms ignored her. "I have to go."

Carl waggled her eyebrows. "A man's gotta do what he's gotta do, but firstly, tell us why you really came here tonight."

"I already did. The woman left her gloves in the vets' van."

"I see, and you, Anton Storms, have never exactly been a knight in shining armor, leastways not so anyone could see. Does our Ms. Evans pique your interest?"

I swear he growled at her. "I didn't plan to come over, Ms. Beamish, but Vic found her gloves and insisted I bring them to her. If it were up to me, she'd be back on the road to Ohio tomorrow."

"Why do you want me to leave so badly?" I set the gun under the chair and rose to confront him. "What's it to you?"

Instead of answering, he pulled on his ski cap, buttoned his coat, and yanked the door open. I locked it behind him, then plopped down in front of the fireplace, where the last of the evening's embers glowed. Carl joined me. We drank in silence for several minutes until the older woman patted my arm. "Man's got a lot of past to unpack, Em. A woman like you is a threat to his oath."

"What oath is that?" I hiccupped.

"After Amanda Waylon humiliated him and Riley almost died under his watch, and the fire and the bullet scarred him, he decided never to trust his feelings again."

"What feelings? The man hates me. But I understand where he's coming from. I'm never letting a man into my heart again. Never. Ever. End of story."

Carl finished her wine, ambled into the kitchen, and set her glass in the sink. "Humans," she said, "have a way of painting themselves into corners, but sometimes, they find a way out through the window. And never is a very long time to deny your nature."

"Carl, don't even go there."

"You're a woman, Emma Evans, with a huge hole in your life. One day you'll want to fill it with a good man." Carl struggled into her boots. "Best hide that gun where the twins can't find it."

I watched the woman stride down the path, angry that everyone and his brother thought they knew more about my heart than I did.

...if it weren't for bad luck...

Mouse blamed the recycled air in the plane for the sore throat and runny nose that morphed into full-blown flu symptoms by the afternoon of his second day at the Best Western. Between chills, fever, and bathroom runs, he found it impossible to concentrate on the computer screens for longer than fifteen minutes at a time. After requesting refills of tissues from housekeeping, he abandoned the attempt to locate the Pearson woman. He took another hot shower, climbed into bed, and slept ten hours before waking to a coughing fit that left him drained. The hotel was concerned enough to send a doctor to the suite. Mouse accepted the medication the man offered but turned down a check-up. He didn't want anyone to see the network of computers and scanning devices he'd installed around the room. When his phone chimed on the third day, he struggled to sit up. Worry lines creased his forehead. Only two people had this number: the boss and his sister. He checked the number, then answered the call with a spate of coughing.

"Chuck?" Cheryl's voice squeaked down the line. "You there?"

"I told you not to call," a new round of coughs doubled him over, "unless you had an emergency. Something wrong with the girls?"

"The girls are fine. Are you okay?"

"Just a really nasty cold. What's up?"

"A man came around last night, looking for you. Said he had a message." Cheryl stuttered through the next words. "Remember the contract."

"Geezus H.—" Mouse choked off the response. "What did he look like?"

"Medium height. Slender. Spoke with a twang. Oh, and he wore a cowboy hat."

Mouse scratched at the stubble on his chin. Sounded like one of the boss's personal bodyguards sent to intimidate and frighten. His sister whispered his name. "Chuck? You still there? I'm concerned, Chuck."

Stifling a groan, he shifted from the bed to the window. Beyond the highway, a plane circled the airport. "Listen, sis, take the girls and go to that place we discussed last time I was home. No, don't say the name on the phone."

"Now you're scaring me, big brother. Is this why you didn't come home for New Year's? Because I didn't know your job was dangerous."

"It's not, Cher. We just have a disgruntled employee determined to cause trouble. It would be best if you went away until the man's taken care of. Do you understand? Don't worry about the cost. I'll deposit funds in your account."

"You're a good brother, Chuck. We'll," she swallowed hard enough for the sound to carry through the phone, "leave tomorrow. You take care, okay? And, Chuck, when will you be back?"

"Not sure. You and the girls get settled in. I may be out of touch for a while, but you can always leave a message."

The connection ended. Mouse stared at the phone, throat raw, eyes weeping, stomach in knots. Sick or not, he'd have to go out the next day. His employer was worried. Getting nervous, even. Not a good sign. Was it possible the Feds found out about the missing data files? But the boss threatening his family? Not acceptable. He'd find the Pearson woman and take care of her. Then he'd go after the man himself. Head and body aching, Mouse crawled back into bed.

Around the middle of the day, the fever abated. Although every part of his body ached, he spent another two hours renewing his online search. The desperation in his sister's voice forced him to suck it up and get on with the plan, as flimsy as it was. When he uncovered no additional information, he showered, shaved his beard and head, and ventured into the strip mall down the highway. At the Print & Pay, he handed a one-page flyer bearing Emma Pearson's picture to a faux-hawk-wearing teenager, who ran off fifty copies, collected his money, and stuffed the papers into a bag without ever removing his earbuds. Mouse fought the urge to slap the kid, then doubled over with a coughing fit. Spotting the sign for a CVS Pharmacy, he hurried into the store. The pharmacist was closing for an afternoon break as Mouse approached the window.

"Excuse me," he placed the packet of flyers on the counter. The woman reached up to pull down the accordion door and paused. He exaggerated his cough, although not much. She stepped back. "I need something for this cough. What do you recommend?"

The pharmacist frowned. "You should see a doctor, sir."

Mouse cocked his head, covered his mouth until the hacking slowed, and nodded. "Have an appointment tomorrow, but I can't spend another night like the last one. Please?"

When she leaned forward to point out a display of cold remedies across the aisle from the pharmacy counter, she knocked the packet to the floor. The flyers fanned out, Emma Pearson's pretty face smiling up at them. "Oh, my God, I'm so sorry." She hurried out to help Mouse gather the fallen papers. Holding one up, she frowned. "This woman is missing?"

"It's my sister." Mouse bowed his head. "She drove here to visit a friend, but no one's heard from her for days. My family and I, we just want to know she's all right. Would you post one of these flyers in your store?"

Standing, the woman shoved the flyers she'd recovered into his hands. "No need. I saw her and those twins of hers when she stopped to fill a prescription."

Mouse dug his nails into the meaty part of his hand and coughed to hide a grin. Now came the delicate part. "Do you know, um, did she say where she was going?"

"North, I think. The little boy mentioned a gateway." She shook her head, pulled a bottle of cough syrup from the shelf, and handed it to him. "Get some cough drops, too. They'll help with the sore throat. Bet you didn't get your flu shot, did you?"

Mouse offered a weak smile, ignoring the condescension in her voice. He paid for his purchases, folded a flyer and stuffed it in his pocket, and dropped the rest of the missing person announcements in a recycle bin on his way out. North and gateway, two clues more than he had when he arrived in Syracuse. Emma Pearson was as good as found. As good as dead. And Charles Mouse was on his way to freedom.

...pigtails and puppy dog trails...

Life, as it often does, settled into a routine, each day a step forward into an uncertain future. Grieving, nursing an anger hangover that threatened to stay forever, I had no choice but to lower my head and plow into the winds of change. Asa Cleary was happy to accept the children on an as-needed basis, which meant texting Gordo at seven each morning, setting up the schedule of appointments, and contacting the woman before feeding the twins. I received a letter from the school board informing me of their intention to hire me as a substitute teacher. The communication included instructions on how to check with the schools on the days I was available. I also reached out to Carl's nephew, Otto, who suggested I clerk at the store, again on an as-needed basis. The Abode only opened two days a week during the winter season, so unless Otto was doing a supply run or his kids were sick, I'd rarely be needed, but it was an opportunity to get to know more people. I gladly accepted his offer. Now, unexpectedly, I had three jobs, each providing a distinct opportunity to become a part of the community. My anxiety shifted into low gear. I could do this, as long as I didn't add one more thing to the mix.

The children refused to drop the dog issue. First thing every morning, Evan asked when we were getting a puppy. Mollie repeated the request each night after prayers. Riley also brought it up again when I stopped by on my way home from filling out paperwork for the substitute teaching job.

"The pups won't be ready for new homes until March, Em. You have plenty of time to get ready. And Josh will ensure they're potty trained before you get them."

"Them? I can't handle all the irons I've got in the fire now, Riley. Puppies? I don't know."

She laughed. "You don't give yourself enough credit, my friend. Look at all you've accomplished after barely two weeks in Wanakena."

"All right. Stop with the lobbying. I promise to think about it."

On the drive back to the hamlet, I considered what Riley had said. Settling-in had gone quicker than I imagined. The speed with which I had acquired contacts was matched only by the animosity of my main boss and principal pain in the ass, Anton Tony Storms. The man was unrelenting in his effort to ignore me outright at the office or persuade me to return to Hopewell whenever we rode together to pick up veterans. A couple of shared ridealongs to acclimate me to the schedule had morphed into a two-person tag team. To his credit, he did let me drive, although he was a ruthless critic. *Not so fast. Take this curve slower. Make sure you have enough gas to make it back to the Center.* If he wasn't giving me grief about the driving, he was slumped and sulky and pretend-napping in the passenger seat. Today, I decided to change the dynamic.

When I entered the office, Gordo sat at the computer screen, his eyes racing back and forth over whatever app he'd pulled up.

"Hey," I called, slipping off my winter coat and plopping into the chair across from his desk. "I understand we have a full schedule today."

Startled, he shook his head. "What time is it?"

Noting his distracted look, I got up to lean over his shoulder. "Gordo, what is all that?"

He closed the screen, folded his arms, and frowned. "Eldercare issues. My favorite uncle passed away last year, and his wife's having mobility issues."

"Does she live near here?"

"That would be a negative, Red. Like it or not, I need to go to South Carolina to see about getting her into an assisted living facility. Which means," he swiveled his chair, stood, and grabbed me by the arms, "I need a huge favor."

I didn't remember seeing such naked worry on the stoic soldier's face.

...a little luck and some retribution...

Mouse propped his feet on the coffee table and savored the steam rising from the chamomile tea. The cough syrup had tamed the convulsive hacking, but his nose ran like a faucet, and he couldn't get warm enough. When was the last time he'd been this sick? He didn't remember, but it didn't matter. Maybe he had Covid. Too bad. Healthy or ill, he had a job to do. He glanced at the setting on the thermostat, noted the fan laboring to force hot air into the room, and eyed the results of Googling the words 'north of Syracuse' and 'gateway.' He fingered the few pages of information he'd uncovered on Riley Finn, who also seemed to have disappeared into the Adirondacks. Three years ago, the woman had an active social media presence. Strangely, after the summer of 2018, she had virtually disappeared from the Internet. Her accounts had been deleted or set to private and, therefore, were inaccessible to him. Unless she had changed her name and migrated the old posts to new ones. But like the Pearson woman's photos and posts, they had also been scrubbed.

He swallowed a few more aspirin, helped himself to a swig of cough syrup, and finished the chicken noodle soup from room service. His head throbbed. After a long, steamy shower, he plopped onto the bed and pondered the lucky coincidence that had landed him in the same pharmacy where the woman had stopped almost two weeks ago. Some mobster god had to be looking out for him, not the God he'd grown up with, the stern, unyielding Old Testament deity who condemned murder as one of the worst sins. Mouse's hands were too stained to ever wash clean. Shoving aside the thought of languishing in his parents' version of hell for all eternity, he turned off the light and burrowed under the covers. Perhaps he'd think clearer in the morning.

Light, watery and diffuse, trickled through the heavy curtains at the window. Mouse woke feeling better than he had for days. His head had stopped throbbing, he could swallow without choking, and not every part of his body ached. He decided to help himself to the breakfast buffet in the lobby, then spend one more day working over the clues. Back in the room, he spread a map of New York over the coffee table and traced I-81 on its northward journey. It seemed unlikely that Pearson would go to the St. Lawrence and cross into Canada. Mouse wondered if she had assumed a different name. As far as he knew, the children didn't have passports. Even if they did, she had no sponsor and no good reason to emigrate without revealing her real identity to Canadian authorities. No, Pearson would stay in the States. Eventually, she had to turn northeast, head into the mountains, and choose a small town to lie low. The obvious choice was Watertown, but that seemed unlikely for a number of reasons, the first being its size and location along the highway. His prey was looking to hide. Six million acres of remote land offered a lot to choose from, but he had to start somewhere. Mouse wrote down the names of the towns and hamlets located along Route 3: Natural Bridge, Harrisville, Pitcairn, Fine, Star Lake, Wanakena, Cranberry Lake. He stopped at Childwold. He'd check those eight first. If nothing showed up, he'd keep going north toward Saranac Lake. Sitting with the laptop in front of the window, watching snowflakes drift and dance as airplanes crisscrossed the sky, Mouse scanned the list, entering each name and looking up the history of each settlement. It didn't take long to find the "Gateway to the Wilderness." Wanakena. Pearson had to be there. His gut and the Internet said so. Now to cement his cover.

Long experience and his connections to the black-market underworld led Mouse to a local purveyor of fraudulent documents. By eight o'clock the following morning, he was ready for phase two. The twenty-something with a scruffy beard and no scruples had suggested using the military as cover. After all, the kid insisted, Fort Drum was just outside Watertown. Perfect cover for anyone engaged in black ops. Yeah, he actually said black ops. Mouse forked over the money and returned three hours later to collect the credentials now spread across the bed. A somber face peered up from the new driver's license. The DD214 looked worn and official, perfect for a man discharged ten years ago. He spent two hours syncing his real history with the false backstory and practicing a slight Kentucky accent to match that of ex-Army sharpshooter Harlan Clouse turned itinerant photographer. Cover story in place, he'd begin the search at the Veteran's Center in Clifton-Fine. Establish his identity, attend a few group meetings, build a network. Ex-military guys knew the areas where they lived, and the old-timers lived to gossip. All he had to do was find a place to stay. Might as well contact the Center before he got on the road. Mouse called three times, hanging up when someone answered. Finally, he got a recording. He left a brief message and ended the recording. The lure was cast. Now all he had to do was wait for someone to return his call. Then the real hunt would begin.

...on the edge of the whirlwind ...

The twins adapted to the routine much faster than me, sleeping like the babies they still were, occasionally asking when Daddy was coming to see them. I woke to the slightest noise, pacing the small kitchen with the gun in my hand, alert for a danger I couldn't see and didn't understand. I worried about my parents in their Florida condo. With so many friends around them, they'd be safe, wouldn't they? I got called to sub twice, both times for the third-grade teacher who was pregnant with her fifth child. The staff at the elementary school were friendly but a little distant. I didn't blame them. No one knew how long I'd be around. The next few weeks at the Veteran's Affairs office were going to be interesting, especially after Gordo asked me to assume his duties, and I accepted. How, I wondered, would grumpy Anton Storms react when he realized I'd be working full-time with him?

The Wednesday before the weekend Gordo planned to leave for North Carolina, Storms took off for Lake Placid. The sergeant excused himself to tidy up loose ends, he said. I closed the Center early, picked up the kids, and dedicated the rest of the afternoon to cleaning the cabin's tiny kitchen. The twins were settled at the table, making snowmen with construction paper, twigs, and googly eyes, when someone rattled the screen door, then clomped onto the porch and rapped on the window. I opened the door to a Gordo in formal dress uniform clutching a crate full of paperwork and a bottle of wine.

"Gord? What are you doing here?" I took the wine and ushered him in, rubbing my arms at the cold air that rushed in with him.

The man set the crate on the counter and straightened to his full height. "Apologies, Red. Kids."

Mollie waved but continued drawing. Evan bounced from his chair to tug on the sergeant's jacket. "We're getting a dog, Mr. Soldierman."

"Is that so?" Gordo squatted to look Evan in the eye, then placed a hand on my son's shoulder. "That's a big responsibility, young man. Are you ready, willing, and able to care for a dog?"

Evan matched the man's solemn stare and saluted, his tiny hand trembling above his eyebrow. "Yes, sir." I blinked back tears as I watched my boy's small palm disappear into the larger one, and the two shook over the promise. I had put off my decision to the pup question. Now, like it or not, it was a done deal.

Phil Gordon rose to confront me. "Sorry to spring this on you today, Red, but the situation with my aunt has escalated. She needs me now. So, you start tomorrow at the Center. You can have all calls sent to voice mail when you're out on the road, then take care of the requests when you return to the office. Here are the keys. I've labeled each one, so you shouldn't have any problems finding things. Oh, and if any new vets show up, you have them fill out the intake form, label a folder with their name on it, and pass the info along to Storms. He'll do the rest."

The speed with which the man accomplished the handover left me speechless. I accepted the keyring, glanced at the box of files, and sputtered, "What about those?"

"Thought you might like to know more about our clients." Gordo actually smiled. He rubbed a thumb over one eyebrow, patted Evan's shoulder, and winked at Mollie, who had sidled up beside her brother. I recognized the yearning in the twins' faces. They missed their father, missed having a man to tease and play with them. It was impossible to prevent the ache in my chest or the rush of tears that had me turning away to fuss with a dish towel. Gordo touched my elbow. I faced him again. "I'll do my best, Gordo."

"You'll do fine, Red. Don't let Storms scare you off. The man's had his share of grief." Gordo looked away, his eyes clouded with his own particular sorrow. "Stand your ground, and he'll back off. Now, kids, I expect to be invited back to meet that new puppy when it comes home."

Evan repeated the salute. Mollie poked a tentative finger at the stripe running down his pants. "Semper fi, Mr. Soldier?"

"Semper Fi, young miss." He headed for the door. "I'll check in periodically, Red. My number's in my file. Call if you need anything."

"I don't know what to say except thank you, Gordo."

He offered his hand. When I took it, Gordon pulled me closer. "I filled out the employment forms for you. Driving is volunteer work, but doing my job pays well. It'll help with whatever you've got going in your life. A piece of advice? Don't be late. Be early. Drives Tony crazy to be beaten at anything."

I stood on the porch, shivering in the cold as the sergeant drove away. Tomorrow, I started a new job at the VA Center, one that involved a group of feisty old men and a boss who hated my guts. *Yeah, me!* I whispered a prayer for all lost things and tossed it into the wind.

...a second chance for snow...

A dark sky loomed over the hamlet, adding to my unease. I hadn't yet accustomed myself to winter in the mountains. But Mrs. Cleary's home was brightly lit, the Christmas decorations still on display, and the children's playroom a welcome space. The twins shrugged out of their coats and raced for the bouncy balls stashed in the corner. Asa offered coffee and fresh-baked Danish, but I was determined to heed Gordon's advice to arrive early at the Center. I took a cinnamon roll to go and headed out, fiddling with the radio until I located a local station predicting snow before nightfall and groaned. Why couldn't the universe give me one problem at a time to deal with? Stuck behind a slow-moving truck dumping sand on the roadway, I thumbed on the phone and called Riley.

"Hey, girl! Oof!" Riley's yelp sent me on high alert.

"Ri? It's me. Are you in labor?"

"Emma? No, this little-big child in my womb is determined to destroy my bladder before she ever sees the light of day. Or dark, as it were. A January birth...who would have suspected?"

"That's what happens when you have unprotected sex after celebrating Earth Day from the bed of a Ranger's truck." We giggled together. "Seriously, are you okay?"

"Fine, but it's getting closer to show time. What's up with you?"

"Two things. First, I'm taking over for Phil Gordon at the Vet Center while he takes care of some family business in Greensboro."

"As in North Carolina?"

"Yep. More importantly, we, Mollie, Evan, and I, will take a pup...or two. When they're ready."

"Oh, Em, I'm so glad. It won't be a bad thing, you'll see. As for the new job, um, Storms?"

"Yeah, that. I'm apprehensive, but Gordo assured me the man's bark is worse than his bite. Ugh. I hate clichés."

"Listen, if anyone's a cliché, it's Tony Storms." Riley groaned again as the baby continued her morning workout. "But I'm pretty sure he has a big heart somewhere inside that muscled body of his. He's had a pretty tough three years, Em. Do what you can to cut him some slack."

"If you say so. Listen, the snowplow truck finally pulled off, and I don't want to be late. Gotta go." With a promise to call again that night, I floored the accelerator, kept an eye out for wandering moose, and reached the Center with half an hour to spare.

Gordon had placed a vase with a yellow rose and a smiley-face note on the desk, which warmed my heart, but the room was freezing. How do men stand it so cold? I located the thermostat, set at sixty-eight degrees. I glanced over my shoulder and, hearing no noise from Storms' office or the hall, hiked the temp to seventy-three. Once the room began to warm, I returned to the car for the files Gordo had left me and settled in at the desk. I sniffed the rose, smiled, and spotted an envelope addressed to me peeking from beneath the calendar. When I opened it, an index card slipped free and floated to the floor.

"Damn it!" Tugging off my gloves, I crouched down and crawled after the errant card. My head was buried beneath the desktop, my butt wiggling like the hind end of Josh's dog Ike when someone coughed. Retrieving the card, I backed out of the cubbyhole, rose to my knees, and found Storms, arms crossed over that formidable chest, scowling down at me.

"What," he barked, "in the Sam Hell are you doing here?"

I held up the card and read the names of two new clients. "Rescuing our newest patrons from oblivion. Why?"

"You're early. Where's Gordo?" Tony scratched his head.

"Gone to Carolina." I failed to prevent a snort from erupting at the use of that old James Taylor line. "And not in his mind."

My boss frowned. "Wait. He left?"

I nodded, placed a hand on the chair, and hauled myself up. "He had important family matters to take care of, so he left me in charge."

"Oh, no. No, no, no. You, Red, are not going to be a thorn in my side every damn day."

I blinked. He called me Red. Anton Storms was not a man for nicknames. Was Phil Gordon rubbing off on the grump? I sat to write the names and contact numbers of the new clients in the logbook for the day. A hand clamped over mine, sending an immediate charge up my arm.

"Your job is to drive people to appointments, not serve as receptionist."

I looked from his hand to his face and back again. "Remove your hand, Mr. Storms. Sergeant Gordon hired me as his replacement, so, technically, you are not the boss of me. You only get to lord it over me when we're in the van, which you shouldn't have to be any longer. I can handle that part of the job by myself from now on."

Storms was staring at his palm. When he looked up, consternation had replaced the frown. He stamped his booted foot, spun around, and marched to the coffee machine, which remained unplugged and empty on the shelf by the snack basket. "Make yourself useful and get this machine pumping out caffeine."

"A please would be nice," I said. Storms shot me another glare and bulled his way through the lounge and into his office. He braced a hand against the doorframe, pointed at me, and muttered something I couldn't catch before raising his voice to thunder, "Better not screw up, Red."

"Better not screw up, Red," I mimicked as I reviewed the schedule for the day. I had fifty minutes before I had to leave, enough time to contact the new guys. Well, I couldn't be sure they were guys. *Don't be sexist*, I reminded myself. *Women serve our country, too.*

David Yang's voice mail recording clicked in on the first ring, his voice a pleasant tenor, the message accompanied by Lee Greenwood's anthem to America playing in the background. I introduced myself and read through the list of procedures Gordon had outlined for me, then requested Yang return the call with times he was available to come into the office for an intake interview.

The second call rang ten times before a pre-recorded greeting by a soft-spoken ex-Air Force captain named Harlan Clouse asked me to leave

my name, number, and a brief message, and he'd get back to me soon. I
didn't give my name, but I did mention our scheduled meeting times,
requested he contact us again, and hung up. Next, I recorded my own
message for any callers that rang in while I was out of the office, checked
that the coffee was ready, and refilled the snack shelf with more granola
bars and fewer jawbreakers. Satisfied that the office looked as good as when
Gordon was here, I collected my coat and the keys to the van. I had almost
reached the outer door of the building when a clomping behind me
announced the rushed arrival of Tony Storms.

"Where do you think you're going?" He crowded me back against
the wall.

"I don't need your help anymore, Storms, and we don't work well
together."

"That's an understatement, but there's a weather advisory out for the
county, so like it or not, I'm coming with you."

"I don't want you to come with me. And stop yelling."

"I'm not yelling."

"Yes." I flicked his nose with one gloved finger. "You are."

He grabbed my hand in a vise-like grip. "Give it up, Red. You're stuck
with me so you don't get stuck in the storm."

"Hah." I tried to free my hand, but he didn't let go. "Looks like I get
the storm no matter what. Which is unfair. Why don't you trust me?"

He backed off, cut his eyes away, and pulled his ski cap lower. "Trust
is not the issue. I'm coming with you."

"Are not."

"Am too." He had edged closer again. Our chests collided, the heavy
coats preventing close contact, but the proximity was enough. I put my
hand on his chest to push him away, once again jolted by a charge that
settled this time in a much lower part of my anatomy. Which was
ridiculous because I hated men, and I especially despised this surly,
uncooperative bully whose dark eyes now seemed fixated on my mouth.

"Red?" My name came out part growl and part something else I
didn't have time to parse. One of Tony's eyebrows shot up. He covered my
hand with his own and squeezed. "You can drive. I promise not to talk,
but you're not going out on these backroads alone. Anything could happen,
and those kids of yours, they already lost a father. They deserve a mother
who's around to see them grow up."

Wow! I hadn't seen that coming. The passion with which Anton Storms deflated my argument and made me feel guilty for even debating the issue. I blinked away the sudden onslaught of tears, stepped around him, and pushed into the cold. "Fine, Stormy. Way to play the guilt card. No, don't say one more word. Just shut up and get in."

Storms ducked his head, but not before I saw a grin lift the corners of his mouth. I handed him the list and pulled up the directions to the first stop for the day. Tony played with his phone, checked the weather channel on the radio, and hummed to himself, but he didn't talk. Which was good. I didn't want a replay of our previous confrontation, and I certainly didn't want to expose the rawness of my grief and anger to this giant hunk of angry man who, upon close examination, was too hot to be single and too cranky to make a good mate. Not that I ever wanted another man in my life. Never ever again. Once betrayed, forever on guard.

It was almost two before we found time to consider lunch. I had packed a tuna sandwich but felt awkward eating in front of Storms, not to mention smelling like fish for the rest of the drive. Despite our earlier argument, we had reached a détente of sorts, and the day turned out to be a pleasant one. Tony greeted the clients, sharing anecdotes with them, but he didn't speak directly to me until we dropped off the last morning patient at the dentist's office in Star Lake.

Snowflakes drifted in lazy whorls onto the hood and windshield as we idled outside the walk-in clinic. Storms pointed down the road at a single-story diner bearing a slanted sign above weathered siding. A plume of smoke rose from the chimney atop the shingled roof. "Kelson's serves great barbecue."

"I'm good," I said.

"Right. I can hear your stomach growling from here." He put a hand on the wheel, forcing me to face him. "Let's get something to eat, Red. You need your strength in case this snow turns into more than flurries."

Unable to mount a valid argument while my stomach growled like a grizzly bear, I caved to his suggestion. Inside the restaurant, several locals greeted Storms with upraised fists and high fives. One guy whistled when he spotted me. "This be the new woman? Tony, Tony, Tony. You holding out on us?"

"Calm your hormones, Fry. Ms. Emma Evans is the new driver for the Veteran's Center. Show some respect."

Fry stood and saluted. "Aye, aye, captain."

I jiggled Tony's sleeve. "Did he serve in the Navy?"

Tony pulled out a chair and motioned for me to sit. "Nope. Fry motored off to Canada during the Viet Nam era, but he's in the early stages of dementia and forgets that fact. I'll order for both of us."

He slipped away before I could object. When he returned with two large sodas, napkins, and silverware, I rolled my eyes.

"What?" He plopped everything down, including himself. Seated across from the man, I was struck again by his presence. Hulking, yes, and domineering, but beneath all the bluster, I detected something kinder, gentler. Like the way he joked with the old vets and asked about their pets and their wives. A conundrum. One I wasn't interested in solving.

A man wearing a greasy apron and a dirty towel over his shoulder approached, set two plates of barbecue and fries on the table, and patted Tony on the back. "On the house, Storms."

I bit into the sandwich and moaned with delight. But my thoughts returned to the man across from me and how the other men we encountered deferred to him. Anton "Tony" Storms was a well-liked and respected man here. What was I missing?

...an invitation he can't refuse...

The final trip of the afternoon involved ferrying an overweight diabetic, Nick Ayers, for a routine checkup at the clinic in Star Lake. I was beyond grateful that Storms was with me on that run. It took both of us working together to maneuver Mr. Ayers from the van into the clinic and then back inside his house afterward. Once we returned to the office, Storms escaped to his lair, leaving me alone to sort the mail, unplug and rinse the coffeepot, straighten the cushions on the couch, and reposition the chairs in the lounge. An ashtray filled with butts indicated someone had taken advantage of the open house policy. I found a sticky note with a thank you below an inked crooked heart taped to the counter, accompanied by an illegible signature. When I turned on the answering machine, it burped out several requests for rides the following Tuesday, the eighteenth, and a follow-up from one of the new enrollees, David Yang. The other man, Harlan Clouse, had not yet responded to my call. I shrugged off the chill that raced down my back and entered the doctor visits on the master schedule, then glanced at the clock. I had an hour and a half to go. Might as well re-file all the folders Gordo had dropped off for me to study. I juggled my phone, the urge to check on the children strong enough to make my fingers itch, but hearing their voices would only make me miss them more. I was stuffing the cell in my pocket when a loud bang brought me to my feet. Was there a shooter in the building? I debated whether to lock the entry door when a string of muffled cursing, accompanied by a second explosion and the rasp of metal against wood, alerted me to the source of the noise. A fire alarm blared. I scampered through the lounge, put my hand on the doorknob to Storms' office, then knocked twice.

"Storms? Tony? I'm coming in."

"Do. Not. Come. In."

"Too late." I swung the door wide and stepped into the man's private chamber. Tony stood, bare-chested and breathing hard, over the charred remains of what vaguely resembled a frozen dinner. A long-sleeved flannel he'd used to smother the flames dangled from one hand. The door to the microwave hung open, wisps of smoke curling from the interior. The smell of burned meat and cloth competed with the blare of the alarm for my attention. I approached Storms, grabbed his wrists, and turned his scarred palms toward me. "Are you hurt?"

He stiffened in my grasp and tried to pull away, but I didn't relax my grip. "Red." My name, low and frantic on his lips, sent fresh shivers down my back. "Let go."

I released one wrist, ran my fingers over the front and back of his other hand. "No blistering, but you could use some aloe for the sting. What happened?"

He tried to free himself again, mumbling something about dinner. Aware of how close we were, I released his hand, picked up a folder from his desk, and fanned the ceiling-mounted smoke detector until it stopped shrieking. Then I surveyed the damage.

"First aid kit?" Tony pointed toward a cabinet above the sink. I rummaged inside until I found it. Extracting the burn cream, I squeezed a glob into my palm and waited for him to give me his hand again. "Don't be a baby."

Storms dropped his head, but not before I registered the panic in his eyes. Then I put it together, the scars on his arms, the one from the bullet along his head. Anton Storms had been shot and seriously wounded in an explosion and fire three and a half years ago. His reaction was more than macho bluster. The man suffered from PTSD. Instead of applying the burn cream myself, I handed the tube to him and wiped the amount in my palm on a towel. *Change the subject, woman.* I glanced around, noticed a cot tucked into a corner, blankets piled on top. "Um, you're not sleeping here, are you?"

Storms shrugged as he spread the ointment over the reddened skin. He nudged the ruined meal with his bare foot, drawing my attention to his decidedly masculine body. I didn't want a man, had sworn off men forever, but I wasn't dead, and I definitely wasn't immune to the appeal of a robust, virile guy. Tony Storms checked all those boxes. I ordered my female parts to behave and called upon my motherly instincts for reinforcement. Protect and comfort. Before I could think it through, I grabbed a handful of paper towels and knelt to scoop up the soggy mess.

"Listen. I've got pot roast in the crock pot, more than the twins and I can manage to eat in three days, so get dressed, GI, and follow me home." Tony crossed his arms, causing his biceps to bulge. I avoided looking directly at him. "No excuses, boss. If I have to, I'll enlist the big guns. Beamish and Livetree will have you drawn and quartered, and me along with you, if I leave you here by yourself tonight."

"I'm not going to your cabin."

I held the charred and ashy carnage at arm's length as I brushed past him. "Yes, you are, Storms, or I'm telling the locals how you placed a metal container in a microwave and almost burned down the Clifton-Fine Vet Center."

"You're blackmailing me?"

"If the shoe fits...come on, Tony, everyone loves my pot roast." I turned away, but not before I saw him scratch his chest, then his chin, and shake his head like a wounded deer.

Snow covered the trash bin outside the building. I brushed off the hinged lid and tossed the ruined shirt and the smelly residue of a chicken enchilada dinner inside. At least the cold would prevent any chance of the fire restarting in the trash. Back in the office, I washed up in the restroom and tidied up the desk. I checked the machine one more time to see if Yang or Clouse had phoned me back. Nothing. Well, I could follow up with both men tomorrow. I called out to Storms as I shrugged into my coat. The January night had already closed in when we left, Tony a reluctant captive of my threat to expose his accident. "I have to pick up the twins. I'll meet you at the cabin." I watched him trudge to his truck, not certain he'd show up, not sure why I cared.

...setting things in motion...

Everything was in place. Mouse checked out of the hotel, then engaged a cab to ferry him to a used car lot. He needed an older model, one so nondescript it wouldn't raise a second thought in anyone's mind. He also required enough photography gear to fit his cover story. He completed the auto purchase, then followed the dealer's directions to Johnson Camera. While the clerk searched trade-ins for the items Mouse requested, he used his cell to do a quick dive into available rentals in and around Wanakena. He didn't intend to stay in the hamlet, but he did need to be close enough to the Vet Center in Fine. Maybe a bolder move would pay off. Who, he wondered, was the go-to person in the tiny hamlet?

The clerk returned with an armload of gear, a spiel about getting a great deal, and twenty questions about where he was going up north. Mouse ignored the push for information. He paid cash, thanked the man for his help, then located a sports bar where he could continue his research while nursing a beer. He spent two hours reading through various websites that featured stories associated with the Gateway area, including articles about the Ranger School in Wanakena. Next, he searched back issues of the *Adirondack Almanac*, tagging postings related to seasonal activities and events. He skipped over announcements about summer concerts and canoeing competitions. He would be long gone by that time.

When a waiter approached his table, he paused to order a pizza, then did a virtual happy dance when he stumbled across the *Wanakena Gazette* and articles by a journalist named Mariah Kimby, who billed herself as the "voice of the mountains." It was only curiosity that had him Googling a piece with the headline, "The Wilderness Strangler," and pure luck that he discovered a three-year-old photo of a smiling Riley Finn and her new husband, Ranger Josh Waylon, flanked by a woman named Carl Beamish and a man identified as Jesse Livetree, mayor of Wanakena. Drinks in hand, the group was posed in front of a gazebo. Mouse bookmarked the page and made a note to check out Beamish and Livetree. When the food arrived, he ate and scrolled simultaneously, intrigued by the story of the murders and the role the petite Finn had played in apprehending not one but two killers. The irony made him laugh. If Emma Pearson had fled to be with her friend, her choice of hiding places offered a rare opportunity to pull off his own coup and thumb his nose at people who thought they were smarter than him. *But, no more children,* his conscience clamored. He cut off the thought before it could gain traction, and emailed the Kimby woman, admiring her work and requesting her assistance. Wounded vet photographer seeking employment and accommodations around Cranberry Lake. He included several photos pilfered from online sites to demonstrate his ability, then settled in to read about the Wanakenan bigwigs. They were the ones to cultivate in his search for the missing Pearson woman and the information she carried. Satisfied, he sent a quick text to the boss in Kansas City.

Found the missing link…details to follow

He was surprised at the speed of the response. **Good news M…assistant on route to help with retrieval**

Mouse gritted his teeth. He didn't need help, didn't want it, and the threat was clear. The boss didn't trust Mouse to finish the job himself. Angry, he responded by touting his success rate and insisting he worked best alone, but that fuckup, his fuckup, in Kansas City had brought unwelcome attention. Careful not to sound ungrateful, Mouse said he was close to bringing the search to a swift conclusion, that extra personnel would only complicate things. The boss did not reply, nor did he identify the assistant. Time was not on Mouse's side. He had a day, maybe two, to solve the problem, and the stakes had risen. He now had a target on his back. He had to find and dispose of the Pearson woman before the second assassin arrived.

...the best-laid plans and other surprises...

The stars in the sky above the forest canopy twinkled like fairy lights among the clouds streaming eastward. The snow had stopped, but the wind continued to howl, polishing the road in long stretches of black ice. I was relieved when we reached the cabin. I hurried the twins down the path, the cold tickling my nose hairs and reminding me that little fingers and toes were at risk of frostbite. Once inside, I ushered Mollie and Evan into the bathroom to wash their hands while I set the table. The place smelled wonderfully warm and inviting, the rich aroma of beef, carrots, and potatoes scenting the air. I glanced at the clock, aware of the minutes ticking away and no Tony, but I set an extra plate anyway. Evan noticed first.

"Is Daddy coming home tonight?" he said, climbing into his booster seat and spreading the napkin over his lap. I smiled at how well my etiquette lessons had taken root, even as my heart lurched at the question. Mollie chimed in, too, clapping her hands as she settled in. I served up spoonfuls of pot roast, considering how best to respond, when footsteps on the porch caused all three of us to turn toward the entrance.

"Daddy!" Mollie cried and began to climb down. I stopped her. The screen door banged open, the main door creaked, and Tony Storms, arms wrapped around two moose toys and a paper bag dangling from one hand, stomped in. He kicked the door closed with one foot, then toed off his wet boots and frowned.

"Did someone here call for a moose patrol?" He lowered his eyebrows at me when I stepped forward to take the wine from him. Shifting the stuffed animals to one arm, he slipped off his jacket and winked at Evan, who blinked back a tear. Mollie, caught between disappointment and joy, resettled into her chair.

"Not Daddy," she whispered. I set the wine aside, brushed my daughter's hair back from her face, and handed her a fork.

"No, sweetheart, not Daddy, but Mr. Storms had an accident with his dinner, so I invited him to share ours. Is that all right with you?" I included Evan in the question. The twins exchanged a glance, stared at the gifts Storms held, and nodded. "Good. Tony, please help yourself while I open the wine." Instead of sitting, he followed me and, leaning over my shoulder, took the bottle and opener away.

"This doesn't mean we're friends, Evans," he whispered.

I snatched the corkscrew back and scowled. "Got it, Storms. Sit. I'll take care of this."

"Well, hurry up then. I'm starving." Positioning the stuffed moose on the couch, he joined the twins at the table. I poured the wine and set a glass by his plate, then sat, alternating between sadness and a tiny ping of joy at the intimacy of a meal shared, conversation not freighted with tension. Tonight, the children and I were not alone.

After dinner, Tony offered to clean up, but I waved him off. So, he sat on the floor with the twins, trying out names for their new stuffies and reading every book Mollie dragged in from her room. The pleasant drone of their voices washed over me. When Mollie giggled at something Storms said, I felt the tightness in my chest relax. I dried the dishes, then my hands, and prepared for the usual bedtime argument when my cell chimed. Riley. Tony looked up.

"What?" he said.

I stared at the screen a moment, then picked up. "Hey, Ri, everything all right?"

Nothing, only the void when a call dropped. Shit. I was about to hang up and call her back when Riley breathed heavily. "Em, can you come now? Carl's coming, too, to watch our boys. You can bring the twins, and she'll watch them all here. Josh is gone, I'm bleeding, and I need you with me at the hospital." More heavy breathing accompanied by a few pants.

"I'll be there in fifteen, tops. Try not to panic. Stay on the line." I clutched the phone to my chest and took a deep breath.

"Red?" Tony sat Mollie and Evan on the couch and came over. "What is it?"

"Riley's in labor. I need to help her. I'll have to take the twins with me."

"Is Josh gone?" I nodded. He leaned closer. "Call the squad, Emma. Then go be with her. I'll stay with the kids."

"I can't ask—" He stopped me with a nod toward Mollie and Evan, who were staring at us, panic on their upturned faces. "It's all right, kids, nothing's wrong, okay? But Auntie Riley's baby wants to be born now, and Uncle Josh is doing his Ranger job, and I need to go help her. Mr. Storms is going to stay here until I get back. Okay?"

The twins scrambled over to Storms. Mollie slipped her hand in his. He winced but didn't pull away. "Go," he said.

With a reminder to brush their teeth and a flurry of hugs, I grabbed water, snacks, and a book to read and checked my pockets for the gloves Tony had returned to me. "Thank you," I mouthed to Storms before heading out, perplexed by the man who warned me to stay away even as he pulled me deeper into his debt.

...a light in the darkness...

Patches of ice. The shimmer of snow flocking the pines along the road. My pulse beat at my wrists and neck as I skidded and slipped my way from the cabin to Riley and Josh's home. I arrived just as the EMTs were evaluating my friend, who lay swollen and tearful on the couch. Josh's son Timmy leaned against the wall, his face shrouded with concern. Carl paced beside him. The older woman's face lit up when I rushed in.

"Great goodness sakes, Emma, I'm glad you're here. Our Riley's about to pop, and our Ranger Josh is unreachable. Where are those two precious little bears of yours?" Carl stomped around the emergency responders to grab my shoulders. Riley reached out a hand, which I took and held.

"I'm here, Ri, and I'll follow you to the hospital." I raised my eyebrows at the female tech, who mouthed eight centimeters, then conferred with her companion. They lifted Riley onto a gurney, tucked a sheet and a warm blanket around her and her taut belly, and wheeled her out the door. I maintained my grip on her hand as I looked back. "Twins are fine, Carl. Tony's with them."

The amazement on Beamish's face matched Riley's. The door slammed open behind them, and the cold slapped my face. I let go so they could lift Riley into the ambulance. Once she was loaded, I edged my way back to the Rover and climbed in. I texted a carefully worded message to Josh, informing him that we were leaving for the hospital and assuring him that everything was under control. But it wasn't. My best friend in the world was in labor, a man who hated me was watching my children, and the secret burner phone I'd bought specifically to keep in touch with my parents was pinging inside the glove box. I stretched across the seat to retrieve it, corrected the slide of the wheels as I spun out of the lane and onto the highway, and punched in the code only I knew. A text popped up, tinted blue from the dashboard glow. Ice formed in my gut as I scanned the message from my mother.

Em...surprise fake FBI visitor here scared us dad snapped picture r u all right?

Embedded in the text was a video from their doorbell camera. I strained to inspect the grainy image of a gray-haired man in a plaid shirt, navy sport coat, and khaki trousers knocking on the door. He looked around, then glanced straight into the lens. There was nothing special about his features, until I looked in his eyes. His stare caused a visceral reaction. I held the phone closer to study his gaze. Dark. Cold. Menacing. This man was a predator. Had he threatened my parents? Had he learned anything from his visit to Florida? Was he coming after me?

I wanted to ask Mom for more details, but I hesitated. My parents understood what was at stake. They would send additional information if they judged the danger imminent. At least I had a face to commit to memory. Right now, there were other, more immediate concerns. I pressed the gas pedal, afraid to fall too far behind the ambulance. I wasn't sure I knew where we were going, and I hadn't had time to plug in the navigation app. Heat gushed from the dashboard vents as I hurried as safely as possible along the backroads, wondering if every decision I'd made had been wrong. Perhaps I should have stayed in Hopewell and let the FBI deal with threats to me and the children. Maybe I should have agreed to enter witness protection, even though that would cut the children off from all the friends and family they had ever known. Well, regret was a cold dish. I had made the call for all of us. Nothing to do now but see it through. Meanwhile, Riley's baby was about to be born, and I didn't want to miss her arrival.

The emergency vehicle halted beneath the covered entry into Clifton-Fine Hospital in Star Lake. I parked, gathered my bag, and trudged through the slush-covered ground to meet the crew unloading Riley. Despite the contraction currently demanding her attention, my friend looked up at me. When our eyes locked, she nodded, then returned to breathing through the pain. Alerted by the ambulance driver, a nurse waited just inside the door, her face a mirror of calm competence that soothed Riley and me the moment the doors whooshed closed behind us.

"Emma?" Riley lay back, panting.

"I'm here, Ri. I'll take care of the paperwork. You concentrate on bringing that little bit of love into the world."

"Josh?" Another contraction spiked. Riley's gaze turned inward, all her focus now on the final act of the birthing process. The emergency tech shared Riley's vitals with the nurse. Given the advanced stage of labor, the nurse directed them toward the critical care ward immediately. I stepped to the counter and handed over the documents Riley had given me when I had agreed to be Josh's stand-in. The woman at the desk hummed "You are my sunshine" as she typed in the information and pulled up Riley's file.

"Where's Ranger Lieutenant Waylon now?" she inquired.

I held up my hand, realized I still had the clandestine burner phone, and stuffed it into a pocket before retrieving my other cell. "I've been texting, and the network has been alerted. I'm sure he's doing his best to get here, but in the meantime, I'm Mrs. Waylon's support team."

"Well, Miss Emma, you better get a move on. From what I saw, that baby's arrival is imminent." She handed me a visitor pass and pointed toward the elevator. Murmuring thanks, I hurried through the open door, pushed the button for the upper floor, and shrugged out of my coat. I checked for a response from Josh, then sent a message to Storms. How are the twins? His reply was instant, as though he had been waiting for my text.

Tucked in and sleeping soundly... Seconds ticked off. Then **Don't worry, Red. I've got your 6**

It took me a second to connect the dots from his reference to the military equivalent of looking out for a buddy to the weird love-hate relationship growing between us. For some reason, the image of him in his office, shirtless, barefoot, distraught, and sexy as hell, intruded. At that moment, I had wanted to wrap him in my arms, soothe his pain, and erase the look of devastation and despair that loomed in his eyes.

The elevator dinged, the door whisked open, and I headed toward the voices in the delivery room. Riley was already on the table, her feet in stirrups. An anesthesiologist waited for directions as the nurse finished checking the baby's progress and signaled the tech to page the doctor on call. When Riley looked over, I set down all my gear and looked around for scrubs. The nurse opened a cabinet, withdrew a packet, and tossed it to me.

"Won't be long now, dear." The woman patted Riley's leg. "Your baby's eager to join us. Now, don't push yet, Mrs. Waylon. That handsome ranger of yours is probably busting his tail to reach you, but if he isn't here soon, we'll welcome the little one ourselves."

"I can't wait." Riley squeezed my hand hard enough to crunch the bones together. "I need to push now."

"Hey, Ri, look at me." I moved to block her sightline to the door. "You've got this. He'll be here as soon as he can." My regular phone vibrated. I read the text and held it up so Riley could read it, too.

Tell Riley hang tough love her on my way

Riley's eyes filled with tears. She bit her lip, inhaled, and breathed through the pain as the next contraction swept over her. The doctor, a young woman dressed in camo scrubs, strolled in, checked the chart, and placed a hand on Riley's belly. "Yep, you're ready to go. I'm just going to check the dilation. Gentlemen and ladies?" She raised her eyes to the EMTs and me and nodded toward the door. The emergency personnel left. Riley gasped my name and an emphatic no. The doctor raised an eyebrow.

"I'm her designated partner until her husband gets here."

"Fair enough." The woman turned back to Riley, slipped a gloved hand up the birth canal, and smiled. "Crowning. It's showtime, honey. Ready?"

I stood beside the birthing table, arm under Riley's shoulders, reliving my labor with the twins. Like Josh, Gary had been absent, too. Unlike the ranger, my husband hadn't sent a message like the one that Josh had written. I was happy my friend had found such a good man, but I couldn't deny the sadness welling up in me, the loss threatening to push out the tears of anger and sorrow I had held in for so long. Riley must have sensed my dismay. She exhaled at the end of the push, stroked a hand down my arm, and smiled before gritting her teeth as the doctor encouraged her to bear down again. The baby's head appeared. The door burst open, and Josh rushed in, hair wild, cold air streaming from his winter coat. Relieved, I stepped back. Josh kissed her forehead, placed his arm around her, and whispered, "She's almost here, babe."

Riley groaned into one more push. The doctor murmured a final instruction, sat on a stool, and eased the child free of Riley's body. We all waited, holding our breath for one, two, three seconds before a lusty yell made us all grin. Baby Cara continued to wail as the nurse took her to be cleaned and weighed.

"You have a beautiful baby girl," the doctor said. "Good work, Mom." She returned to tend to Riley, catching the afterbirth as it slipped free, sharing pleasantries with the nurse as they recorded the time of birth, the weight, all the details essential to a new beginning.

Josh waited, arms open, to hold his daughter. "Hello, little bit of heaven," he said, placing a soft kiss on the baby's forehead. "Welcome to the family."

The warmth and joy on his face was the final tug that released my tears. I tiptoed out of the room, placed a hand on the wall to steady myself, and set off to wander the corridor. I was so happy for my friends and utterly, impossibly, irrevocably sad for the fate that had betrayed me and smashed forever my belief in a one, true, everlasting love.

The drive back to Wanakena under a sky brimming with cold fire failed to calm my restlessness. I stood outside the cabin, hunched into my down coat, and stared at the river, the water half-frozen now but still moving beneath the ice. When I finally gathered my courage to go inside, I noticed a nightlight by the sink, a thoughtful touch and unexpected. I tiptoed into the twins' room, kissed their cheeks, and resettled the blankets over their sleeping forms. I returned to the living room, another blanket in my arms, to gaze at the sleeping form of Anton Storms, in slumber more relaxed than he ever looked awake. The scar along his temple reflected a pale white. The stubble on his cheeks gave him a subtly mysterious air and an alluring one. I spread the blanket over him, smoothed back the hair that had fallen over his cheek, and began to move away when his eyes popped open. We stared at one another for a long moment.

"Everything good?" Storms said.

"Yes." Part of me wanted to lie down beside him, to feel protected and safe again. Part of me wanted to order him out of the house. I resisted both urges. Toeing off my boots, I bent to retrieve them and backed toward my bedroom. "Thank you."

"You're welcome, Red." He shifted to his back, crossed his arms behind his head. "Always."

I thought I would have trouble falling asleep, but my physical exhaustion, accompanied by the emotional turmoil of the past four hours, had drained my reservoir. Instead of rehashing the evening, I sighed and glided into slumber, inexplicably content that the grumpy Tony Storms guarded the cabin from his sofa bed. For a moment, I listened to the wind soughing a melody in the pines around the house. An owl hooted as it glided along the riverbank, seeking dinner. I fell into dreams, reminded that somewhere out there, a gray-haired predator with fake FBI credentials plotted to find me and my children and end the game my husband set in motion.

...opportunity knocks...

Satisfied with his purchase, Mouse patted the hood of the 2010 Corolla with a noisy muffler and a few rust spots on the front rocker panel. He loaded the trunk with the used cameras and tripod he had picked up at the shop on Kinne Road, then checked into a cheaper hotel for one more night. His throat still rasped. Every cough made his chest ache, but the worst of what he could only think of as the god-damned flu was over. He was perusing listings for rentals close to Clifton when he stumbled across an ad in the *Adirondack Almanac* placed by Denver Lorang, a disabled veteran who had served in the Korean War. Lorang was looking for a fellow vet to live in and help care for his personal needs. Mouse used Google Earth to scope out the location. The one-story homestead occupied ten acres west of Fine and was secluded enough to provide the cover he needed while he worked up the next part of his plan. He rehearsed his story, then called the number listed in the ad. By the time he and Denver hung up, Mouse had convinced the man that he was his new best friend and the perfect choice for an in-home assistant. Then his work cell rang, reminding him of the potential for unpleasant repercussions if he didn't find the Pearson woman.

"Cheryl?" He rested the tips of his fingers on the barrel of his Glock. "Everything all right?"

His sister hemmed and hawed her way through a recital of the inconvenience of moving from Ames, Iowa to the bungalow in Omaha, then thanked him for the money he had wired to her account. "When," she asked, her words carefully measured so as not to provoke him, "will we be able to go home, Chas?"

He observed the second hand on his watch make one complete revolution before he answered. "I understand it's rough, Sis, but you can't go back until I close the file on this crazy employee."

"So, you're being careful, too?"

Mouse caught a glimpse of his face, pale and gaunt, in the mirror above the suitcase rack. He was glad he hadn't engaged Facetime. He cared for his sister, the only remaining member of the Mouse family besides him, but she was a ditz. Right now, he didn't need her asking more questions. Clearing his throat, he forced a laugh. "Careful as a fox in a henhouse. Now, let me say a quick hello to my nieces and end this before anyone taps the line."

His sister squeaked. "Can they do that?"

"Don't worry. Long as we make this short, it'll be all right. Now, I won't be in touch for a while, going to be super busy working with management and the lawyers, but I'll be fine."

"Whatever you say, big brother. Here's Nancy."

Mouse talked a minute with each girl, spinning tales that made them giggle and promising to send postcards for their collection. Exhausted by the interaction and doubled over with a coughing fit, he collapsed into a chair to finish cleaning the guns he'd acquired from a pawnshop in the grittier part of the city. He hadn't heard back from the voicemail he'd left the Beamish woman, but Livetree had left a message inviting Mouse to stop by the local grocery, Otto's Abode, in Wanakena as soon as he was settled in. He chuckled at the confluence of events moving him ever closer to his goal. Maybe when he'd cleared his debt with the boss, he'd take Cheryl and the girls to Disneyworld.

...shaken, stirred, and dismayed...

When the phone alarm sounded, I lay still, listening for sounds from the living room. In the bedroom next door, Evan banged a leg against the wall, rattling the moose photographs hanging above my bed, but nothing disturbed the whoosh of the propane heating system as it fed hot air through the ducts. I hurried to dress, ran a brush through my hair, and prepared a short thank-you speech, which died undelivered when I found the blanket neatly folded and no sign of Tony Storms. Unable to decide if I was upset or relieved, I opened the cereal cabinet to a sketch of a bull moose with THANK YOU printed between the antlers and two smiley faces labeled Mollie and Evan. The note stirred something in my gut. Maybe Mr. Grumpy wasn't so bad. Still, last night had been awkward, and now I had to work the entire day knowing that he'd spent the night not twenty feet away from me. *And nothing happened.* Before I could extract more meaning from that thought, two four-year-olds barreled into my legs, knocking me off balance. I recovered enough to snatch them up and whirl us around before collapsing onto the couch where Tony had slept.

"Did Auntie Riley have her baby?" Mollie inquired.

"Where's Tony?" Evan said. "He promised we could play with my army soldiers today."

"Auntie Riley had a beautiful baby girl whose name is Cara." I brushed Mollie's hair from her face and kissed the top of her head. "Mr.

Storms had to go to work, but he left a note thanking you for keeping him company last night."

Evan yawned, climbed from my lap to settle into a chair, and banged a spoon on the table. "He wasn't sad last night, Mommy," he said. "Because he wasn't alone."

I felt the words like a punch to the heart. Kids knew things instinctively. We adults had to figure everything out the hard way. I placed juice, cereal, and a vitamin in front of each twin, poured milk, and waited for the tea kettle to boil. "Did he tell you that, Evan?"

Mollie tried to talk through a mouthful of Cheerios. Tiny O's sprayed across the placemat. "He didn't have to, Mommy. We could tell cause he smiled when we kissed him good-night."

While my bagel toasted, I dipped a tea bag up and down in my mug, wondering how my children had developed such insight. I used to think I had that gift, too. Now, I just felt lost. Of course, they didn't know the truth about their father. Someday, I would have to tell them all of it. What would happen to their innocence then?

I dropped the children at Asa's house and checked the gas gauge, then worried all the way into Clifton that I'd run out of fuel. I coasted into a station right before the warning light flashed. Standing at the pump, nozzle in hand, I recalled Riley and Josh cuddling little Cara. The baby was precious. Her arrival provoked a daydream of having another baby one day. I shook off the thought. That would entail trusting another man enough to let him into my heart, and that, I assured my imaginary self, would never happen. However, I couldn't shake the sight of Tony Storms sprawled half-naked and asleep on my couch. Forever was a long time. I was a woman, after all, and I couldn't let Gary Pearson rob me of everything good in life. There might come a time when I'd want a man in my bed. Not Storms, though. God, no. He did, however, have a hot body. I stamped my foot to stifle that image and replaced the gas cap on the combustible thoughts.

As usual, the office thermostat rested in the sixties, so the first thing I did was turn up the heat. Next, I checked the calendar. No appointments today, although 7:30, followed by a question mark, had been scribbled under today's date. Since regular group therapy sessions took place on Tuesdays, I tucked the added piece of information away to ask about later. The answering machine blinked, reminding me of the need to confirm meet and greets with the new veterans who had moved into the area, David

Yang and Harlan Clouse. I settled into Gordon's chair, placed my insulated cup of tea on a coaster, and cued up the messages. Clouse had requested an afternoon appointment for Monday. The man named Yang hemmed and hawed a bit before asking essentially the same thing. I attempted to contact both men, hoping to confirm specific times, and once more found myself routed to voice mail.

Shrugging off the phone tag blues, I decided to check out the folders in the top two drawers of the filing cabinet. Big mistake. The haphazard system Gordon blamed on his predecessor screamed chaos. Apparently, neither man understood the concept of alphabetization. The number of folders labeled with a giant question mark on a sticky note required serious reorganization. I started, logically, at the top, carrying a handful of files to the desk, re-sorting them, and setting aside the ones marked *Deceased*, intending to ask Tony about them later. Thinking of the man reminded me I hadn't seen or heard from him. Remembering how I'd found him yesterday, I blushed. Whatever else the man was, he was undeniably in good shape. I had half-decided to risk encountering him in a similar situation by trying his office door when said door banged open, and the grump himself stomped into the room. I grinned.

"You don't look like you slept on a couch."

Storms ran his hands through his hair, still damp from a shower. I made a note to check out the bathroom he used, do inventory, and order the necessary grooming supplies. He shoved his hands in the pockets of his jeans and narrowed his eyes.

"About that."

Before he could say something mean, I ticked off three quick facts on my fingers. "One, the kids loved your note. Two, I love that you took such good care of them, and three, Evan says you promised to play army with his toy soldiers."

He smiled. My heart did one of those flippy things, which I blamed on heartburn. "What did they name the baby?"

"Cara, and nice try changing the subject, but uh-uh. A promise made to a four-year-old is an obligation to be honored. Tonight is spaghetti and meatballs at the Pears-, um, Evans house, and you're invited."

"I can't."

"Yes, you can." I rose from the chair, fisted my hands on my hips, and advanced toward him.

"No, Red, I really can't tonight. I have a meeting."

I shook my head, confused, before I remembered the time penciled onto the desk calendar. "Group isn't usually scheduled on a Friday."

Tony scrubbed his mouth with the back of his hand. "This is something extra. We have an emergency with one of the guys, and I need to be here."

Embarrassed, I dropped my objection. Of course, he had to be here tonight for his guys. Whatever he saw on my face had him moving closer. He rested his hands on my shoulders and bent to look in my eyes. "Hey, what's wrong?"

Caught in the backdraft of memory, I struggled against the emotion threatening to spill out. Gary, late for dinner. Gary, with one excuse after another for not being home, for traveling again over a weekend. One betrayal after another. Hearing similar words from Tony Storms reopened the wound. But this man wasn't my husband. He wasn't even a friend. So, suck it up, pretend everything was fine, and shift pasta night to Saturday so my son could have a man to play army with him.

"Nothing an organized file cabinet won't cure. You can come tomorrow or sometime next week." I slipped from his grip and returned to the folders on the desk. With my back turned, I didn't have to watch the look of relief, disgust, or whatever Storms felt about me and my children flicker over his face. When his shadow fell over me again, I flinched. "What?"

He crouched, one hand on the back of my chair, the other settling with a thump on top of the paperwork. "Why don't you come back tonight? Meet the guys? Help them settle in. Finish your busy work."

I tried to ignore the smirk in his words, then huffed. "Busy work? Sergeant Gordon gave me specific instructions about what needs doing around here," I waved my arm, "and I'm doing it."

"Does that mean you'll come back? You can bring the kids." He waited for me to meet his gaze, then cocked his head toward the corner of the lounge where a large bin of toys and games rested.

I wanted to say no. Instead, I closed my eyes to avoid looking at him and groaned. "Do I get paid for overtime?"

"No," Storms said, rising. "But if you come tonight, I'll treat you and the twins to donuts at Otto's in the morning. And I'll come for dinner tomorrow night and play Army guys with Evan. Deal?"

Reluctantly charmed by the offer, I nodded my head. "How could anyone refuse such a reasonable suggestion? Deal."

"Bring the moosies."

"Moosies?"

"Yeah." He headed back to his office. "Mollie and Evan named them both Moosie."

I returned to the folders, surprised by the excitement rising like dough in the pit of my stomach. When I reached the S's, I shuffled through the stack until I found the one labeled Anton Storms, then stuffed it in my purse. Tonight, after the kids were asleep, I intended to do a deep dive into my boss's background.

...a little stop along the road...

The sandwich boards on the front porch listed the specials available at Otto's Abode the two days a week it was open during the winter season. Mouse knocked the slush from his boots, then angled past the bistro table and chair beside the front entrance. The bell above the door jingled a greeting as he stepped into the coffee-rich air of Wanakena's central meeting place. A woman stood perusing the coolers in the back while a bearded man wearing a hunter's cap and a corduroy vest over a plaid shirt and jeans busied himself rearranging items by the register. The man raised a hand and hollered a greeting.

"Make yourself at home. Let me know if you need any help."

Mouse had taken two steps toward the bearded guy when a deep, cultured voice arrested his progress. "Welcome, stranger. Jesse Livetree, mayor of Wanakena. What brings you to our hamlet this snowy day?"

Turning to his left, Mouse looked straight into the narrowed eyes and tilted chin of an older man whose shoulders and arms indicated attention to fitness despite his age. Adjusting the camera slung over his shoulder, Mouse proffered a smile. "I believe you invited me via email. I'm considering relocating here and wanted to check out what the area offers."

"Ah, that was you who left that cryptic phone message?" Livetree waited for me to offer my name. Instead, I deflected.

"No, I didn't make any calls. But an acquaintance of mine said this was a nice place to live, mentioned that his daughter lives around here.

Riley Waylon? Said a friend of hers recently moved here as well. Emma Pearson?"

Livetree folded his arms. "How do you know Riley?"

Mouse raised his hands, palms out. "I don't know her personally, just what my friend told me that she told him. That Wanakena and the other towns around here were friendly to veterans." He looked around until he spotted a poster asking for volunteers to assist local vets with driving and home chores and gestured toward the placard.

Livetree tilted his head. "You're a veteran, then?"

"Yes, sir." Mouse drew himself up and saluted. "First Cav from '95 to 2015 when I took a few rounds that shattered my kneecap."

"You walk pretty good." Livetree glanced at Mouse's legs.

"Docs fixed me up pretty good, but they mustered me out on a disability. On account of I can't run anymore."

Otto finished his register cleanup and joined them. "Otto Beamish. My aunt and I own this place. So, you're thinking of moving here? Got a place to stay yet?"

Mouse bobbed his head. "I'm bunking with Denver Lorang. Man needs some help, I understand, and I can use a base of operations. I'm an amateur photographer looking to turn it into a profession."

"Lots of great places to take pictures around here," Otto said. "Can I get you anything?"

"A cup of that coffee to go." Mouse pulled a five from his pocket and slapped it on the counter. Otto finished the pour, capped the cup, and handed it and the change to Mouse. "Thanks. Nice to meet you both. I'd better get moving if I'm going to be at Lorang's by noon."

Livetree and Otto followed Mouse out, watching as he slung the camera onto the passenger seat and got in. The stranger pulled away just as Trooper Sandra Kellerman swung her patrol car into the plowed area in front of the store. As she exited the vehicle, Otto greeted her with a wave and an offer of coffee and a pecan roll, Carl's morning treat for the day. Jesse pursed his lips. "Man never did give his name, did he?"

Otto nodded. "Seem strange to you, him asking about Riley and Emma?"

"Yeah. If you see Emma, don't say anything to her, but fill in Trooper Kellerman. I'll call Josh, let him know someone's asking around about our girls."

...constructing a trap to snare a fox...

Snow flurries flirted with the windshield as Mouse brought the Corolla to a stop before a deteriorating ramp leading to a front door desperate for a fresh coat of paint. The cedar siding had warped in spots. Green moss decorated the cinder block foundation. The low-slung ranch belched smoke into the wintry sky. He checked the address, then heaved himself out of the car and into the frigid air. As he scuffed up the icy ramp, the door eased open, and a burly man with a sallow complexion and a scattering of moles over his bald head spit a wad of tobacco juice into a can in his lap. The wheelchair scraped against the doorjamb.

"Denver Lorang?" Mouse approached with an outstretched hand and his friendliest smile. "We spoke on the phone. About me helping you out in exchange for lodging?"

Another spurt of tobacco juice, and the man rolled the chair backward. "Clouse, is it?"

Mouse removed his stocking cap and followed the man through a narrow mid-century living room into the kitchen. Beyond the window over the dining table, he could see a shed, a detached garage, and a large expanse of dense woodland skirted by scrub trees. A split-rail fence bordered the back of the property. "Nice view you got here, Mr. Lorang."

"Denver'll do. Got your discharge papers?"

"Right here." Mouse patted his breast pocket, then took out the pages and slapped them onto the table.

"Had lunch yet?" Lorang took out his phone and snapped pictures of the paperwork before adding to his collection of juices. Mouse looked around. No evidence of a female presence but plenty of stuffed deer, bear, and fish trophies. Also, a display of family photographs of boys fishing and girls canoeing.

"Nice family." Mouse jerked a thumb at the pictures. "Live close, I gather."

"Not very," was all the response Lorang gave.

"You're a hunter and fisherman, I gather."

"Back in the day." The old vet's eyes glazed over at the mention of the past, then returned to the present to size up his new assistant. "First, we'll eat, then I'll show you where to stash your belongings and where the bathroom is. I know the house ain't up to your standards, but I haven't been able to do much since the diabetes. Anyway, don't feel sorry for me 'cause I don't feel sorry for myself. No whining and carry on's my motto."

"Good way of thinking," Mouse replied, liking the man despite the circumstances. If things went sour, he might have to kill him. He draped his coat over the back of a chair, inspected the plate of sandwiches Lorang had set out, and gestured toward the refrigerator. "Mind if I help myself to a drink?"

Lorang wheeled closer to the table. "Help yourself," he said. "And hand me a water."

They sat munching on chips and making small talk until Lorang flicked the remote, and the TV roared to life. He apologized with a grin. "Time for my soap opera fix. Sometimes a man's got to have a little drama in his life." Mouse choked off a reply. That's the last thing he wanted, more drama, especially when he checked his phone, which he did as soon as Lorang turned to watch the screen. There was only one message, repeated three times so he'd be sure to get it: additional asset in place send details now

...knights of the round table...

"Cold enough to freeze your nose hairs." Carl Beamish stomped her booted feet on the welcome mat and raised a gloved hand to push back the hood of her coat. I swallowed the come-on-in I had prepared, seeing as the woman was already inside the cabin.

"Carl? What are you doing here this time of day?" I dried my hands and rescued the grocery tote from the woman's twitching fingers. The twins ran out from their bedroom, snowsuits over their pajama-clad legs and moose lovies tucked under their arms.

"Momma says we're going to see soldiers tonight." Evan's shouted proclamation filled the small space. Carl covered her ears and hooted.

"Inside voice, young bear, or I'm going to tell your momma to leave you behind."

"No-o-o." Mollie clapped a hand over her brother's mouth and whispered, "Be quiet, Evan, or we'll miss our adventure."

Carl raised her brows. I shrugged. "They're just a wee bit excited. But seriously, what is all this?"

Ms. Beamish tugged the camera strap slung around her neck and grinned. "Mariah Kimby's covering some environmental conference in Watertown and asked me to find out about the benefit event Tony and the Center's planning for Denver Lorang. Been a while since I've had an official assignment. You mayn't have met the man yet, but the poor thing lost both

116

legs to a land mine in Viet Nam, and now he needs a new ramp to get in and out of his house. Anyway, Mariah called, then Tony called, and here I am, rambling on. Get a move on, Red, and let's get this party started."

"Party? Momma," Mollie tugged my pantleg, "are we going to a party? Will there be cake?"

Carl scooped the girl up and pulled Mollie's hat down to cover the child's ears. "Your ears are bigger than a rabbit's aren't they, little Red?"

"Little Red?" Mollie giggled.

"Yes, little Red. Your momma's big Red because of her hair, because, you see, it's flambulous."

Mollie giggled again. I scowled at Carl. "Who gave you permission to call me Red?"

The older woman flashed a coy smile as she exited the cabin, hefting the child in her arms, and tromped down the path past her cabin. "Don't forget the cookies. Phil Gordon made a few calls before he took off for those southern mountains. You've made quite an impression, Red, a good one, it seems."

"My name's not Red," I grumbled as I clutched Evan's hand and followed my landlord to the car. "Have you spoken to Riley or Josh today? I haven't had a minute to check with them."

"No need to fret yourself." Carl deposited Mollie into her car seat and thumped over to the passenger side of the vehicle. "Julia's watching the boys, Josh has taken two weeks' vacation, and mother and baby are shining like rock stars at the clinic. Half the hamlet is over the moon at the chance to hold a newborn."

I pulled into the night, grateful for the news about Riley. Above, clouds scudded through a broken field of stars. The moon, if there was one tonight, remained hidden. The drive to the Center was uneventful. The children chattered to their moosies while Carl regaled me with more local gossip, much of it about inhabitants I had yet to meet.

The outdoor light above the Center's entry door cast an eerie glow along the shoveled walkway from the parking lot. The icicles hanging from the eaves loomed like giant teeth. The sky had temporarily cleared, offering a view of the constellation Orion. I pointed it out to the twins before shepherding them along, then shivered. Was there another hunter out there looking for me?

Inside, I settled the kids by the toys in the lounge and paused to watch Tony talking with five men, three of whom I recognized from van runs. They had gathered around an octagonal table that hadn't been there when I left earlier. The table took up most of the space in the reception area, but no one seemed to mind being crowded together. Storms acknowledged me with a nod, then returned to stare at the tablet in his hand. The vets raised their heads and chorused, "Red!" I groaned but waved back. When they turned to watch Carl set up her camera gear and called her name, the older woman smirked.

"Don't try none of that soldier bull-slinging on me, gentlemen. I'm here in a strictly observatory position as the celebrated journalist Mariah Kimby couldn't make it to our patch of the wilderness tonight. And watch your language. We've got youngins among us this evening." She cocked her head toward the twins, who were engrossed in a game of Chutes & Ladders.

Eager to help, I unwrapped the boxes of chocolate chip and peanut butter cookies and arranged them on the tray Carl had remembered to pack, then reached around Storms to set the snacks within easy reach of the men. My chest brushed his shoulder. My nipples tightened, leaving me startled and unable to stop the sharp intake of breath that escaped. The muscles in Storms' back tensed, the only sign that he, too, had felt the electricity between us. I stepped back and hurried toward the coffee station, willing my pulse to stop racing. Whatever was simmering between me and the boss, I had to squelch it now. I jumped when he called my name.

"Ms. Evans? Will you please keep notes for us tonight?" The courteous tone surprised me. When I swung around, Tony held the tablet out. I glanced at the children, who had abandoned the game and were now setting up a confrontation between scores of plastic dinosaurs. Carl was engaged in muted discussion with a vet whose name, I recalled, was Thomas Cross. I accepted the proffered tablet, scrolled to the notetaking feature, and dragged a folding chair closer to the group. Tony began the meeting by thanking the men for coming out in the cold.

"So, Denver. He's been an active member of our center for ten years, but in addition to his leg injuries, he's developed diabetes. His wheelchair has reached the end of its useful life, and the ramp outside his house needs replacing."

Tom spoke up. "The inside needs a facelift, too, Tony."

"Good point, Tom. All right, what's a reasonable amount of money we can raise to help him out?" Tony leaned back, fiddling with a pencil, while the men discussed and discarded ideas, so many that I struggled to record them all. The depth of caring they displayed was touching. When the group finally agreed on an amount, an event, and a date, the cookies were mostly gone, Carl had finished snapping photos and offering her opinion, and the twins had fallen asleep on the couch, their moosies tucked between their entwined limbs. As the meeting wrapped up, one of the men cornered Tony.

"Good meeting tonight, Storms, and Lorang will be grateful. By the way, he told me this morning he's got a fellow vet moving into the area and into his house to help him with daily care."

"That's great news, Phil. Thanks for letting me know."

"Guess we'll have a new member to add to the group."

"Maybe three. Red scheduled two other new guys for an intake interview Monday."

"Only one's confirmed," I said. I returned the tablet, along with a printed copy of the minutes. My fingers grazed Tony's, igniting the same spark I'd felt earlier. "Carl? You ready?"

"As I'll ever be. Which twin do you want me to carry?"

"Neither one, Ms. Beamish." Storms headed for the couch. "I've got this." He leaned down to whisper to them, and the children instinctively reached out. Scooping each child into his arms, he stood up, then nodded to me and Carl to get their coats. Once they were dressed against the cold, he settled them close to his chest and strode out behind the men who waited to hold the door for him. I tidied up the cups and crumbs, rinsed the coffee pot, and checked to ensure all lights were off except the one in the reception area. Then I followed Carl into the night, uneasy over the sense of belonging growing in my chest and the warmth lower in my belly every time I looked at Storms.

...a little night reading...

Carl helped me carry the twins into the cabin, then waited until I had them tucked in for the night. When I returned to the kitchen, the older woman had opened a bottle of wine and set out the leftover cookies on a paper towel. She wrapped an arm around me and guided me to a chair.

"You didn't eat a thing while those men chowed down, so sit, drink a little vino, and relax." Carl pushed a second chair closer to the table, then lifted each of my feet to remove my boots.

"Why are you being so solicitous, Carl?"

Hands on hips, Carl fixed me with a quizzical look. "My, aren't you just as over-educated as our Ms. Riley and just as clueless. When a woman reaches my age, Red, she's entitled to do a little mothering, especially when she missed the opportunity a long time ago."

Noting the wistful look on Carl's face as she turned toward the darkened window and the forest beyond, I accepted the glass of wine and cocked my head. "Are you sorry you didn't have children?"

"Yes, and no. I've lived life on my terms, but there are days when I'd like to have a son or a daughter to ease my way into retirement."

"Aren't you already retired?" I sipped the Riesling and sighed, the sweet taste lingering on my tongue.

Carl speared me with a patented Beamish scowl. "Retired means dead, and I'm not there yet. Short answer's no, and don't you forget it."

"Well, how old are you?"

"Sixty-nine my next birthday."

"When's that?"

"Whenever I say it is." Carl rapped her knuckles on the table, then wrestled into her coat. "Take care of them precocious little bears of yours, Red, and try not to be too hard on our Tony."

"I will, and I'm not upset with Storms, although he has made it clear how he feels about me."

Carl shook her head. "You and your best friend may have a world of book learning, but when it comes to men, you both need some schooling. Tony Storms is absolutely undone by your arrival. That man has no idea what to do about you."

"Come on, Carl. He disapproves of me intensely and scowls my way every chance he gets."

Carl smirked. "Yeah, he's looking. A lot. And he's been hurt ten ways to Sunday, so don't you be breaking him any more than he's already been broken. Well, look at the time. I'm in need of my beauty sleep. I'll get my camera stuff out of your car tomorrow, or at least by the time you go to work Monday."

"Oh, there's no rush. I'm not going into the center until the afternoon on Monday. The twins have routine checkups with the new pediatrician in the morning, and then we're off to Riley's to see her and baby Cara. Sunday's possible, but tomorrow, we have other plans." She cocked her head, waiting for me to share, but I didn't. Those plans included Tony Storms, a fact I didn't feel like sharing right then. "What about you? Have any plans of your own for the weekend? I thought you and Jesse—"

She cut me off. "Not going there, Red. Not gonna open that can of wormy past."

"I'm sorry." I looked at her. She turned away. "Riley told me you two were good friends, so I assumed." I stopped babbling when she shook her head.

"In the past, my girl. Not your concern."

I apologized again for prying. She shrugged. "It's fine. I'll see you Sunday, then."

"Sure. Come for dinner, Carl."

"Okay, I'll leave you to your reading."

"What?"

"Think I didn't spot Storms' file peeking out of that gigantic purse of yours? Lock up when I leave." Carl didn't wait for a response. She whisked through the door like a sprite. The screen banged, and I listened to the crunch of boots on frozen snow until I didn't hear them anymore. Then I shook my head, poured more wine, and lifted Tony's file from my bag. I carried it to the couch and settled in.

The fire had spread into a blanket of embers that winked and glowed like the holiday lights we had passed on our drive north. I snuggled deeper into the cushions, flannel pajamas and knee-high socks not enough to dispel the chill from earlier in the evening. I grabbed a second fleece throw and tucked it around my feet, smiling at the moose images on the border. I was eager to learn Tony's story and also wary. What if it was worse than what I already knew? I poured more wine, took a healthy gulp, and set the glass on the side table, unable to recall the last time I'd enjoyed a drink without feeling guilty. Carl and the other inhabitants of the gateway to the wilderness made me comfortable in a way I hadn't experienced since long before Gary's death and the revelation of his betrayal. I would always be grateful for their welcome. Now, to find out more about the inscrutable Anton Storms. I laid the folder bearing his name on my lap and took a deep breath. This was an invasion of privacy. I was crossing a line. Should I? Probably not. Could I do it? Of course. The file, along with the truth of his past, was in my possession. My fingers itched to open and read it. Still, I hesitated. If only Riley were here to give advice or encouragement. Riley Finn was many things. Indecisive wasn't one of them. All right, I'd consider my next move as if she were sitting beside me. Mind made up, I grabbed the glass, chugged the rest of the wine, and started to read.

Anton Clever Storms, born February 14, 1988. Four siblings – two sisters and two brothers. Father deceased. Mother remarried. Nothing further about his birth family. *Graduated summa cum laude with a degree in Poly Sci from Boston College.* BC? Holy crap, the man was smart. *Served in Army from 2010-2014. Worked for DEA as an undercover operator Injured in 2018 while investigating drug ring.*

I stopped reading. I knew this part, about the trailer blowing up, about Ranger Gus shooting Tony, the explosion that scarred his hands and arms, the ones the tattoos covered. I'd seen them when he rolled up his sleeves. Was the ink a tribute to his father? I wanted to know but doubted a man as moody and close-mouthed as Storms would explain their origins to me. Riley had hinted at the man's complicated past with Josh's murdered ex-wife, but my friend also insisted that Tony could be charming and funny, a side I glimpsed when he engaged with the twins. I'd like to see more of that from him.

By the time I finished reading, the fireplace had grown cold. I checked the time. Half past eleven. Too late for a mother with small children who roused early and with enough energy to power a generator. As a precaution, I smothered the remnants of the fire, rechecked the locks, and peeked in on the twins. Reluctant to leave Tony's folder where anyone could see it, I tucked it in my bag, then carried my burner phone with me to my room. My heart stuttered when it vibrated. Caller ID flashed my mother's name. I plopped down on the bed to read the incoming text. PLEASE CALL ME! Moving back to the kitchen, I punched in the number. My mother answered before it could ring a second time.

"Emma? Thank God, honey. Are you all right? Are the kids?"

"Mom? I told you only to call in an emergency. Is something wrong with Dad?"

"Your father's fine. I'm fine. I know we shouldn't talk long, but I needed to tell you about that man in the photograph, the one I sent you?"

"I got it, Mom. Thank you. It helps to have a face to look out for."

"Well, that man in the picture talked to Trudi Funtain, and she told him about Riley and you and where you might be."

"Who's Trudi Fountain?"

"Not Fountain, Funtain, and her name's as screwy as she is. Always knew that woman was a bitch, but, honey, listen. You need to call the FBI, or go home, or come here, because if that man had anything to do with what happened to Gary, you're not safe."

"Calm down, Mom. Is Dad there?"

"Right here, Em. You're on speakerphone. Listen to your mother, okay?"

"I understand, and I'll be careful. But I can't uproot the kids again so soon. Let me think about this for a day or two."

"Emma," my mother swallowed a sob. "We love you, and we're worried."

"It'll be all right. I have friends here, and I'm being careful, honest. You stay safe, too. We should get off now."

"Emma girl." My father's gruff tone let me know how upset he was. "If anything happened to you or those precious grandchildren—"

"I know, Dad. I'll check in soon. Bye." I hung up before I started crying. First, the fear, like a weight on my chest. Then the guilt. Finally, the anger. Not me. Not my children. I retrieved the gun from the locked case in the closet, checked the clip and the safety, and jammed it under the spare pillow. The only way to my children was through me, and I vowed that would never happen.

...a midnight conversation...

Something ticked in the wall. Once, twice, followed by a scrabbling Mouse thought had to be mice. He snorted, Mouse hearing mice, and rolled over to lay with his hands behind his head, staring at the water stain on the ceiling and wondering how his life had narrowed to a musty mattress in a decrepit house in the middle of six million miles of wilderness. His mind rationalized the job, balancing the risks against the money and the promise his boss had sworn to uphold – to release him from his employ after this one last assignment. So, he held on to the promise in the man's words, even though his gut was telling him otherwise. He couldn't trust the boss because the man no longer had faith in Mouse. It was past time to get out.

The window screen rattled. Mouse got up to check that the casement lock still held and returned to bed. Looking after Lorang's physical needs had sobered him. The man's present circumstance could be Mouse's future. True, he hadn't lost his legs, but he was alone, and he carried the ghosts of his victims, the burden increasingly heavy. Every one of those dead souls had friends and family who may not know his identity but were looking for revenge just the same. One whisper from his employer and retribution would find him. Mouse closed his eyes. The image of the infant in Kansas City, the red-silk pool of blood spreading across the highchair tray, swam behind his lids. Abandoning the attempt at sleep, he swung his legs over the edge of the lumpy mattress and wished he had a cigarette.

The bedroom his host had assigned him overlooked the eastern portion of the man's property. The trickster wind had sculpted dunes in the now-frozen snow, giving the land the appearance of an alien beach. The rustling in the wall continued, unfazed by his pacing. Tomorrow he'd suggest setting traps around the place. He switched on the lamp beside the bed, watched it sway on its uneven base, and rummaged through the bag he'd brought inside. His photographic gear and most of the weapons he'd purchased remained in the trunk. Safer to have them there than risk questions from Lorang, who seemed far more curious by dinnertime than he had when Mouse first arrived. Setting out the new documents, he checked the passport and the driver's license, reciting the specifics of his new identity until they came readily to mind. He needed to be pitch-perfect when he went into the Vet Center Monday. Satisfied that his answers did not sound rehearsed, he retrieved the cell phone he used only for contact with his employer and fed in the code. When the message screen popped open, he entered his location, his schedule for the next few days, and a brief account of his stop at Otto's Abode in Wanakena. He was stuffing the cell back into the bag's lining when a vibration indicated a response. A muscle in his jaw twitched. The boss never responded to messages this quickly. Outside the door, Lorang's wheelchair squeaked down the hall. Mouse reached for the handgun he'd shoved under his pillow and held his breath. The noise subsided. After a minute, it began again. Soon he heard water running and the low drone of voices from the TV. The old vet couldn't sleep either.

Mouse waited for Lorang to check on him, but the man remained in the living room. Only when he was confident he wouldn't be interrupted did he read the message.

Looking forward to working with you Clouse watch your back I am

A laughing emoji accompanied the text. Despite his desire to smash the phone, Mouse erased the conversation before zipping the phone into the lining of the bag. Then, rubbing a hand over his mouth, he went out to join his benefactor.

...when everything turns upside down...

The reminder flashed on the phone...*meet Tony ten a.m.* The time was the last thing he'd whispered before he left us last night. I thought about the information in his personnel file, balanced his past against the care and concern he displayed with each of the veterans, the way he had of making the children smile, and I set my reservations aside. I'd pretend today was a routine outing and avoid contact beyond that required of an employee with her boss. However, Mollie and Evan had no such reservations about our trek to Otto's. They tugged up their snow pants, zipped up coats, and stood waiting by the door, eager to begin our Saturday adventure.

Our boots squeaked over the snow-covered street and thumped against the metal railings of the bridge over the Oswegatchie as we slipped and slid our way toward Otto's. The moosies rode in backpacks, antlers flopping up and down with each step. I snapped several photos, dragging my feet the closer we got to the Abode. Tony's truck was already parked by the stairs, along with half the cars in Wanakena, but there was no sign of the man himself. We kicked the snow off our boots on the bottom step, clambered onto the porch, and stepped inside an Otto's teeming with people. Everyone turned at the tinkling of the bell over the entrance, raised a drink, and shouted, "Surprise, Red!"

Alarmed and embarrassed, I grabbed the twins and began to haul them back through the door when Jesse Livetree stopped me. "Don't go, Emma. This is your informal, formal welcome to our hamlet. Besides, today's my birthday. We have cupcakes, punch for the young ones," he bent down to wink at Mollie and Evan, "and stronger libations for the adults." Another wink, and he pulled me into the crowd, introducing people as we shouldered our way to the register. Two small heads bulled toward us, the Dugas boys, if I remembered Riley's descriptions correctly. Between them, a blonde-haired cutie, Annie, squealed when she saw Mollie and held out her arms. Excited to see someone roughly their own age, my children hurled their coats at me and wormed their way back to the sofa and the mini art camp set up there.

A tug on my sleeve had me turning to confront a smirking Anton Storms. "Did you orchestrate this, Mr. Storms?"

Tony tugged his ear, offered a half-smile, and cocked his head toward the back of the store where Carl Beamish stood, arms crossed, a look of triumph on her face. "Hey, Red, welcome to Wanakena's Wacky Winter Weekend. You're the flavor of the week. Stop frowning and help yourself to the punch." Carl gestured toward a silver soup tureen balanced precariously on the ice cream freezer.

I leaned over, pressed my lips to Tony's ear, and hissed. "You should have warned me."

"What," he stiffened but didn't pull away, "would be the fun in that?"

"This is funny to you?"

"Sort of." His dark eyes examined me head to toe. I shivered. "You're not gonna run away, are you?"

"You'd like that, wouldn't you?" I poked his solid, muscled, spectacular chest, withdrew my finger before he could capture it, and smiled. "Not a chance, Storms. Not now, not ever."

"Careful what you promise, Red." He brushed a strand of my hair off my shoulder, let it slip through his fingers. We stared at each other until Carl stepped between us.

"Enough of this bullmoosing, you two. Come with me, Emma. There's a few people I want you to meet."

The crowd remained until Otto began to ease them out the door, claiming he needed to make room for paying customers. Laughter, jokes, invitations to visit or arrange play dates with other children. For two hours, I forgot the reason I had brought the children here, why I needed to be cautious and alert. The reality of the situation returned full force when a tall state policewoman sauntered into the store. Otto greeted her and escorted her over. Trooper Sandra Kellerman shook hands, welcomed me to the community, and offered her card, eyeing me the whole time like I was a new specimen she planned to add to her collection. I shrugged off that feeling, thanked Otto and Carl, and suited up the twins for the walk home. Tony left with us. He stood by his truck, watching as we headed down Hamele Street, then called, "What time's dinner?"

I had forgotten I had invited him to pasta night. I raised my ungloved hands over my head and held up six fingers, unwilling to face him. Before, I'd noted disdain, then confusion, but the way Storms was looking at me in Otto's looked a lot like desire.

In the few short weeks we'd been in Wanakena, my children had outgrown naps. I did, however, insist on quiet time while I prepared dinner. I enjoyed cooking, something else Riley and I had in common, and took pleasure in creating meals that my children would eat. While the meatballs baked in the oven, mini-sized ones for the children, standard size for Tony and me, I iced the brownies, then slathered melted butter on the ciabatta, added herbs, and set the bread aside. Wine wasn't a prerequisite on my grocery list these days, but I did have a few bottles of beer in case Tony wanted to drink something other than water. I intended to change out of my tomato-sauced top before our guest arrived when the bang of the screen door announced his arrival. I wiped my hands and went to let him in. Evan raced past me, Mollie on his heels. They attacked Tony before he could step into the kitchen, Evan yelling about playing Army soldiers and Mollie yanking on his jeans to ask what he brought them. Tony raised the bags he carried above their heads, laughed, and looked my way for help. I peeled the children off, ordered them behind me, and reached for the bags. He shook his head.

"You look like you could use a few minutes of me time. I'll handle this." When he refused my offer a second time, I decided to take advantage of his presence and slipped down the hall to my room. I released my hair from the clip, changed into tights and a tunic top, and slapped on some rouge and lipstick. Then I stared at my reflection, noted the light in my eyes, and leaned on the sink. Was that all it took? Someone showing a little kindness for me to find the Emma I used to be? An excited squeal from Mollie brought me out of my funk.

The children were seated on the sofa. A fire blazed on the hearth, and Tony Storms crouched before them, reprising the same trick he'd played the day we arrived in Wanakena. He pulled silver dollars from their ears, then turned and looked my way. A spark jumped between us. I inhaled past the guilt and went to tend the pot of boiling water. On the counter, I spotted a bottle of red wine beside a bouquet of winter roses. I couldn't breathe past the thoughtfulness. My boss had brought me flowers. I brushed the tears away and stirred the spaghetti.

Dinner was a riot of children's laughter, compliments to the chef, and more magic tricks. After the brownies, Tony stretched out on the floor to help set up Evan's collection of toy soldiers. It took half an hour to construct the battle and all of three minutes to destroy everything. Mollie sat on the couch, talking to her moosie, the silver dollar Tony said belonged to her forever clutched in her hand. I cleaned and dried the dishes, divided the leftover sauce and meatballs into two containers, and was about to join them when Tony came to me. He reached for his coat hanging on one of the hooks by the door and stepped closer.

"Time for me to go, Red."

"You don't have to leave yet." I harbored a secret wish to sit by the fire with him, to believe, for one night, I lived a normal life.

He rubbed his chin, his eyes on my mouth. "I think I do."

I thrust the container of leftovers at him. "This plastic is microwave safe."

"Good to know." He stepped closer, his hesitancy palpable, bent to my ear. "Thank you, Emma. See you Monday." And he was gone.

I didn't move, aware of my body's reaction to his when he brushed against me, when his lips grazed my cheek. Did he kiss me? Or had I imagined that moment when never became maybe.

...a man with a plan has second thoughts...

Mouse picked an eight of hearts from the pile, considered his options, and discarded a spade three. Lorang spat into his coffee can and picked up the three. When he laid his hand down and declared gin with a yellow-toothed grin, he slapped Mouse's shoulder. Mouse forced a smile. "You want a refill?"

Lorang tipped his mug to inspect the contents and shook his head. "You seem kinda restless, Clouse. You got somewhere to be?"

"Nah." Mouse rinsed his mug and set it in the dish drainer. "Kind of anxious about my interview at the Vet Center tomorrow. I don't like to talk about my service."

"You got somethin' to hide?" Lorang muted the sound on the TV and wheeled to face his new housemate.

Mouse thought about his actual experiences, contrasted them with the cover story he had created, then decided a small truth among a heap of lies couldn't make much difference. "I've seen a lot of war, Denver. Shot my share of," he paused at the irony, "corpses. It ain't pretty."

"With your camera, you mean?" Lorang twisted to read the weather crawler spooling along the top of the HD screen. Mouse remained silent, aware of the moment when the man's attention shifted from him to the details of more storm activity heading their way. He busied himself wiping down the counters while his mind scrolled through the pantheon of his victims, unable to move past the unfortunate collateral damage in K.C. Maybe that's why the boss had sent backup. Well, for the moment, he had to go along with it, but he didn't have to like it.

Denver muted the TV, but he did not turn it off. He wheeled over to the laptop on the table and entered his password, unaware that Mouse was studying his keystrokes. When the voice of a preacher boomed from the speakers, Mouse edged toward the bedroom. Lorang grabbed the tail of his untucked shirt. "Not a religious man, Harlan?"

"I see no need to worship some dude who promises redemption that never arrives. At least not for men like me." He tugged free of Lorang's grip and grabbed a book from the shelf in the hall.

"That's curious, then."

Mouse turned around. "What is?"

Lorang pointed at the book in the hitman's hand. "You reading *The Brothers Karamazov*. It's all about faith and doubt. Seems you have a fair amount of the latter."

"I'll be in my room if you need me." Mouse didn't like the way Lorang looked at him, the way he seemed to see things Mouse preferred to keep hidden.

In the room, he retrieved his hidden phone and reread the messages from the boss. No name for his new partner. No day or time for them to meet. He rolled his shoulders, sensing the target on his back. He looked out at the sculpted field and felt the urge to abandon the plan, to escape to some foreign destination where no one knew him or what he'd done. Was it possible for a man to erase the past? To atone for it? He slipped into the bathroom for a piss, returned to the bedroom, and opened the book to a random page where he read a paragraph underlined in a wavering hand.

"Above all, don't lie to yourself. The man who lies to himself and listens to his own lie comes to a point that he cannot distinguish the truth within him, or around him, and so loses all respect for himself and for others. And having no respect he ceases to love."

"That's not me," Mouse whispered. "I love. My sister. Her kids." And the words whispered back, "Do you?"

Later that evening, Lorang suggested they play chess. With the pieces arranged on the board, whiskey glass at his elbow, Mouse gazed with intent at the white and black squares, determined to beat Lorang at this game while the message of Fyodor Karamazov echoed in his brain.

...baby toes and big girl woes...

In the three weeks we'd been gone from Hopewell, I had forgotten what a hassle it was to ferry children from one place to another in wintertime. Pulling on and removing snowsuits, boots, hats, gloves. Buckling and unbuckling car seats. Stocking up on snacks and drinks and, in Evan's case, enough tummy pops to prevent car sickness. The new pediatrician was efficient and personable, which helped when he had to administer vaccines. Luckily, the twins didn't need many, and the promise of a surprise from the doctor's "treasure chest" sweetened the deal. After a morning of running around, we were all ready to relax at home. Mollie and Evan settled in with their moosies and little screens, allowing me to to process the revelations about my taciturn boss as well as the late-night phone call from my parents. I needed an hour of quiet time to evaluate what I'd learned. But first, I wanted to check in with Riley and make sure it was all right for us to stop over with dinner. A knock at the door interrupted my dialing.

"Carl?" Surprised to see the woman, I undid the deadbolt and motioned her in. She toed off her boots and swept toward the children glued to their little screens while the fireplace crackled, spreading warmth throughout the room.

"Hey, little bears, how are you today? Ready for a new adventure?"

Mollie abandoned her drawing to crawl into the older woman's lap. She took Carl's face between her hands and stared into her eyes. "Are you a fairy godmother, Ms. Beamish?"

Evan grunted. "She's too big to be a fairy, Mollsie. She's a mama moose."

"Are you a moose mother?" Mollie giggled when Carl tickled her, then enveloped her in a hug.

"Go finish what you were doing while I talk to your mama."

I raised my eyebrows, then gestured at the coffee pot. "Don't mind if I do," Ms. Beamish said, groaning as she padded in her stockinged feet over to the counter.

"What's up?" I placed a mug in front of Carl and slid the sugar bowl toward her.

"Thought you might like to visit Riley without the little ones. My nephew's giving snowshoe lessons to all the preschoolers in town this afternoon. Might be a good thing for Mollie and Evan to learn how." She glanced at my slippered feet. "You, too, I might add, but Tony can take care of teaching you that skill. Among other things."

The woman wriggled her eyebrows. I groaned. "Carl, don't go there."

"Riley must have told you I'm a hopeless busybody, Red, and Wanakena's a small town with lots of characters. Somebody's got to keep the conversation flowing. Besides, it's winter. We need a juicy scandal to warm us up."

"Well, I'm not going to be your drama queen." I toyed with the tea bag in my mug before looking up. "I did read Anton's history last week. He's a hero who acts like an antihero. Why is that, Carl?"

"Despite that rugged and very fine exterior, the man's a sensitive and caring soul, a fact he does not want out as general knowledge. He went into the Army and afterward to the DEA because he hoped to make our country a better place. Then his dad passed, so he came here, already hurting, and ran into the steamroller that was Amanda Waylon. She messed him up emotionally when he was at his most vulnerable. Then the explosion ripped him up physically, and it took a long while for those outer injuries to heal. I believe the interior pain runs so deep that he still hasn't recovered, and he's closed himself off."

"Wow, you've really thought about this, Carl."

"Man's important to me, Red. Guess my mother bear instincts exist after all. Wanakena takes care of its own."

"Doesn't mean he has to be so surly, especially to me." I thought about last night, when he hadn't seemed surly at all, and shivered.

Carl patted my shoulder. "Don't tell me you don't know why he's acting all hot and cold?"

"I have no idea."

"Yes, Red, you do. You are the farthest thing from stupid I've ever met, so don't go pulling that with me, honey. You threaten the walls he's built around his heart. I mean, look at yourself, a gorgeous woman with two young cubs out on her own insinuating herself into his world, challenging the status quo with the men he serves. To Tony Storms, you're a temptation he can't resist and an enigma he can't resolve." Carl sipped from her mug. "Does he know your story?"

I shook my head, then glanced over to ensure the twins remained engaged in their learning games. Neither paid me any attention, their moosies tucked between their legs, their attention centered on YouTube videos about Minecraft monsters. "No, and I don't intend to tell him. You'd better not, either. Only you, Riley, and Josh know what really happened."

Lips pursed, head down, Carl drew circles on the countertop before she spoke again. "I promised not to say anything, and I won't. But it would be best if you told him, Red, and soon. He finds out from someone else, and he'll see it as another betrayal. I don't want him hurt like that again. Now, about those lessons."

"Of course, you can take them. I'll zip over to Riley's and be back in," I checked my watch, "two hours. Is that too long?"

"Perfect. I'll fix hot chocolate and share moose stories at my place until you're back."

"Thank you, Carl, for being so good to us. It means the world to me."

The woman took my hand. "I don't know you well, Red, but I know hearts, and yours isn't meant to go through life solo."

Phone in hand, I watched the children skip down the path beside the older woman, their laughter drifting back until they rounded the corner and disappeared. I tapped Riley's name in my contacts and pressed CALL. "Hey, new momma. Got time for a quick visit? I've got a chicken casserole with Waylon on it that I need to drop off."

"Yes, please," Riley squealed. "I'm exhausted, I smell like milk and spit up, and I'd love to see you, but the twins will have to be very quiet. Cara is sleeping. I'm praying she stays that way until at least four o'clock."

"No worries, then, since Mollie and Evan are at snowshoe lessons with Ms. Beamish."

"Even better. How soon can you get here?"

"Packing up the food now." I settled the casserole into a carry bag and slipped into my boots. Then, feeling guilty for not heading to the Center as intended, I texted Tony an explanation, then added a question. Did our new vets check in yet? I didn't expect an immediate reply, but one came anyway. **Yes thanks see you tomorrow**. No emoji, but the fact that he responded so quickly had me smiling all the way to the Waylon's.

Riley answered the door in fuzzy bunny slippers, a wrinkled NYU sweatsuit, and a receiving blanket over one shoulder. Her dark hair, caught up in a high ponytail, brushed my cheek as she wrapped me in a fierce hug and tugged me, along with the food bags and a rush of icy breeze, into the warm shelter of her home. Ike and Iris raced up, nails clicking on the wood floor, tails wagging. I crouched to nuzzle both and cooed my happiness at seeing them again.

"They really are great dogs, Ri. Are the puppies still in the kitchen?"

"No, we moved them to the basement. They are way too mobile to have up here now." Shooing the dogs away, she deposited the bags on the counter and returned to pull me into another hug. "So glad you're here, and don't take this the wrong way, but without my two beautiful godchildren. I need me some Emma time."

I draped my coat over the back of a chair and collapsed into it. "I feel the same, Riley, and don't take this the wrong way, but you look exhausted and supremely happy. How are you feeling?"

"I'm tired, my bottom hurts, and my boobs resemble Mt. McKinley, but I'm beyond content." Riley folded the blanket and placed it on the table next to a pile of freshly laundered baby clothes. She rested a hand on her still-swollen stomach and looked around. "I never expected to have any of this. It's so much more than I deserve, and I will not complain about one single bit of it."

I snagged a tissue from the box on the counter and held it out. "God, I remember the weepies. Seems like every happy thought brought them on. Can I see Cara?" Riley led me to the room where her daughter lay sleeping. We stood in silent contemplation of the wonder that was a newborn. I ran a gentle finger down the baby's down-soft cheek. "She's perfect. You're so lucky."

"Do you think," Riley slipped an arm around my waist, "you'd ever want another baby?"

"To do that, I'd have to love another man, and I don't ever plan to take that chance again." I sniffed and tiptoed out of the room. "Where's Josh?"

"Neat way to change the subject, bestie." Riley blew her nose and grinned. "He's taken Michael out to look for tracks in the snow."

"Ri! He's so little!"

"Ranger Josh says kids start training early up here. And with Timmy's disabilities, some things were not possible when he was Mikey's age. Besides, they'll build a snow fort, after which my pistol of a son will take a nice long nap. Now, how about some hot chocolate while you detail your encounters with the grumpy Anton Storms? Oh. OH! Something's going on there!"

My face warmed. I shrugged her off. "Nothing's going on. He hates me. But he's super good with the twins, and he stayed over the night before last. No, not for that reason. He just, I don't know, sends mixed signals. I don't want a relationship, although it was nice to have a man pay attention to my children, to hear them laugh again. They've been so sad."

It was Riley's turn to offer a hug and a hanky. "Em, this, too, shall pass, right? Does Tony know about your husband?"

"No. I don't want anyone at the Center to know the truth. And after talking to my parents last night, I wish I hadn't come here."

"What happened with your parents?"

I picked up the baby clothes. "I'll put these away for you."

"Nice try sidestepping, Red, but we will talk about that later. Meanwhile, you should tell Tony the truth." Josh's sudden appearance jolted me, and his words carried the impact of a command. "The man's had enough surprises in his life. Don't you be one of them."

I turned to confront him, then noticed the boy asleep on his shoulder. Riley half-rose to take their son. Josh waved her off. "I'll put him down, love. Then we'll talk."

I met his stare and nodded. Riley and I traded gossip and kid stories until the tall ranger returned. He ran a hand across his wife's shoulders, dropped a kiss on top of her head, then helped himself to an apple from a bowl on the counter.

"How much paternity leave do you get, Josh?" I asked.

"Enough. Good to see you, Em. Riley missed you."

Grateful for his kind words, I swallowed hard. "Thank you. That means a lot. But I do have to share something with you, and I'm very sorry I brought this to your doorstep."

He sat, rested his elbows on his knees, and steepled his fingers under his chin.

"You have proof your husband's trouble followed you here?"

I gulped back a second apology and opened my phone. "I don't know. I hope not. Here. My parents sent me a photo of a man who showed up at their Florida condo unannounced. They sent him away, but it made them suspicious. Then, last night, they called to tell me he'd found out about you from a gossipy acquaintance of theirs who mentioned Riley's name and this area. That's the man."

Josh studied the images from the ring camera. "Mind if I copy this?" When I agreed, he forwarded the message and attachments to his phone.

"I'm afraid I've put your family in danger, and I don't know what to do. Maybe I should move on."

"No." Josh gripped my wrist, his firm yet gentle touch steadying me. "You need to tell Anton what happened to Gary and why you came here. This community protects its own, Emma. Like it or not, you're one of us now."

"How can that be?"

"The veterans are already talking about the redhead with the kind eyes and her firebrand kids." He smiled, and I saw what had captivated my friend four years ago. Josh Waylon didn't just work in the wilderness. Like so many of the people I'd met in Wanakena, he was a force of nature unto himself. Corny, maybe, but the thought felt right. But tell Tony Storms about the ugliness of my husband's life and death? Show how inadequate a wife I'd been, how unlovable, that my husband had to find another woman to satisfy him? Sharing that truth would validate his opinion of me as a weak woman, a bad mother. No, I didn't want to see that condemnation in Tony's eyes.

* * *

Josh gathered Riley close as they watched Emma slog through the drifting snow to the SUV and then drive down the lane. Sensing her husband's concern, Riley moved to confront him. "What aren't you telling me, Ranger Waylon?"

"You mean besides how you're so beautiful it makes my chest ache?"

"Stop." She placed a hand over said heart and rested her head against him. "I can tell when you're keeping something back."

Silence, then a deep sigh. "Would you object to taking the kids to my parents for a few days?"

She leaned back to stare into those blazing blue eyes. "Is Emma right? Are we in danger?"

Her husband shook his head. "I don't know. Jesse called me Friday while I was out on patrol. Sent me a photo."

When he hesitated, Riley poked his stomach. "And?"

"Men have been asking about Riley and Emma at Otto's."

"Men, as in plural?" Something skittered in her gut." "Was one of them the man in the photo Em showed us?"

"He was."

"And the other one?"

"Don't know, but that extra sense we rangers develop out in the woods is sparking like mad. Jesse got the same feeling, and he only spoke with the one who visited Emma's parents in Florida. Otto met the other one. Neither stranger gave his name."

"This is bad, isn't it?"

"Could be, which is why I'd feel better, babe, if you and the children were out of here for a while."

"What about Tim's school?"

"You can help him with the assignments for a few days." He gathered her close and kissed her. When they broke apart, he bent his forehead to hers and sighed. "It'll be a long three months until you're healed, babe."

Riley allowed her hand to drift lower, to cup her husband through his jeans. "There are other ways to take care of you, love."

Josh groaned. "Don't start something you can't finish."

"Who says I can't?" She batted her eyes, then hugged him again. "What about Emma? Should she come with me to your mom and dad's?"

Josh led the way back to the kitchen and the coffee, now cold in the mugs. He placed them in the microwave and pressed the timer. "Maybe. Let me talk to Jesse again. If she doesn't tell Storms what's going on by this time tomorrow, I will. He deserves to know."

Riley accepted the heated mug and settled onto the pillow in her chair. "I think so, too, but Emma insists on keeping those who know to a minimum. I know she told Carl. Is that how Jesse found out?"

Josh joined her at the table. "Despite their ongoing quarrel, Carl can't keep anything from him."

"Are they," Riley giggled, "a thing?"

Her husband cocked an eye over the top of his mug. "Right now, they're more of a nothing. Far as I know, they only had that one night after you and I got together."

"Did we ever." Riley's gaze turned inward, revisiting the memory of their first coupling. When she felt his hand cover hers, she sighed. "Okay, focus on the moment, Riley," she said. "That picture Em's parents took... the man seemed innocuous. I wouldn't give him a second look if I saw him walking down the street."

"Exactly." Josh frowned.

"So, what makes you think he's dangerous?"

"The moment he looked into the camera, I saw it." He fisted one hand in the other. "The man has a killer's eyes."

...ignition...

All through dinner, Mollie and Evan vied for who could tell the most fantastic story about their snow adventure with Auntie Carl. I reminded them about using their indoor voices but remained captivated by their eager descriptions of falling into snowbanks and making snow angels and building a fort. Exhausted from their outdoor adventures, they didn't protest a warm bath and fell asleep in front of the fire. Carrying them one at a time to bed, I reflected on the day's activities, Josh's advice pinballing through my thoughts every few minutes. To tell or not to tell. With the twins settled, I fished Anton's file from my purse and paged through the documents again. Would my story add to his trauma, cement his disapproval, or force him to fire me to protect the Center and its clients? Maybe I should call a psychic hotline for advice. Groaning at my blatant self-pity, I rechecked my phone. No new messages from anyone. Feeling peevish and lonely, I huddled in front of the dying fire and worried myself into a restless night of wild dreams and endless speculation.

Tuesday morning Mrs. Cleary was delighted to welcome the children back to the playhouse, as she referred to the toy room, and I was relieved that they had someone else to regale with their snowshoe stories. Weak sunlight filtered through the pines lining the road, casting a misty glow over the drainage ditches and the snow-covered open fields. When I arrived at the Center, Tony's truck was nowhere in sight. Grateful for more

142

time to consider how best to reveal my tawdry past, I returned his file to the cabinet, cranked up the thermostat, and booted up the computer, surprised by an email from Josh and Riley that included a video of the puppies and a banner advising me to CLAIM YOUR PUPS NOW BEFORE THEY'RE GONE! Despite the work, worry, and financial drain they would bring, I had to admit the puppies were adorable. If I agreed, Mollie, Evan and I could be pet owners in roughly six weeks. But how would the children ever decide who got which dog? Engrossed in the antics of the squirming pups, I didn't hear Tony arrive. When a hand clamped down on my shoulder, I squealed and jumped from the chair. Storms chuckled and backed away.

"Put the weapon down, Red." His mouth twitched when he spotted the letter opener in my hand. I tossed it on the desk and crossed my arms.

"Where did you come from?" Goosebumps skittered down my back. How would I protect my family from a stalker if I didn't even know when my boss came into work?

He bobbed his head toward his office, then narrowed his eyes. "You're freezing."

"I tried boosting the thermostat. Maybe it hasn't kicked in yet."

Scowling, Storms turned and disappeared into his room, emerging with a cream-colored fisherman's sweater. He tossed it at me. "Put that on, Red. I'll check the furnace."

I watched him stride down the hall toward the utility closet, clutching the sweater to my chest, aware of a familiar scent drifting from the garment, snow and forest and shaving cream. It had been months since I'd experienced *eau de man*. I held the sweater to my nose, caught in the memory of a time when those smells signified warmth, security, and love. *Stop, Emma.* I worked my arms into the sleeves, which hung past my wrists, ducked my head, and tugged the garment down, but the sweater refused to slip on. Mumbling to myself, I extricated one arm and wormed it up to my neck. A loose thread had tangled itself on the back of the diamond stud I'd purchased for myself when Gary forgot our third anniversary. I picked at the knot, but it remained stubbornly attached to my ear. I tried removing the sweater. No luck. I stamped my foot and did a circle dance, swearing as I attempted to loosen the back of the earring and free myself, when an arm snaked around my waist. A warm breath tickled my cheek.

"What's going on, Red?"

At that moment, I wished I could click my heels and transport myself home like Dorothy in *The Wizard of Oz*. "I'm stuck."

Tony leaned his head against mine. "Say again?"

"Your sweater's stuck on my earring, and I can't get it loose." I didn't imagine the snort that erupted. He was laughing at me. "Go away!"

"No. You look like a female version of the headless horseman." More laughter. "Hold still." I stopped shuffling. He leaned closer and shifted the sweater onto my head until he could see where it had caught. "I'm going to touch you now, Red, okay?"

I mumbled okay, mortification making my eyes water. I ordered my clumsy self not to cry over such a silly thing, but my emotions were not under control. Storms' calloused fingers untangled the skein enough to release the earring back and pull the stud free. Once the tension disappeared, I began to remove the sweater. Tony's hand slipped around my neck, gentle and soothing.

"Put it back on, Emma. Please." I followed his command, grateful for the warmth it brought as it fell to mid-thigh. Once I had the sleeves rolled up, he moved closer again. "Hold still while I put this back in."

His breath warmed my cheek once more as he inserted the post and snapped the back in place. When he finished, he caught my eye, a grin erasing his usual scowl. I smiled back. "Thanks for rescuing me from certain suffocation, Sir Knight."

"You're welcome, my lady." His hand still rested on my neck. I had the urge to step into his embrace, to let go of the burden I carried. It would feel so good just to be held. *But,* I reminded myself, *he doesn't really like me. And I don't trust men. Not anymore.* Still, the longing remained. To break the spell, I cleared my throat, an action that caused his gaze to shift from my eyes to my lips and linger there. Then he released his hold, shuttered his look, and motioned toward the desktop. "I left the intake forms for you to enter in the computer and then file away."

I busied myself with re-rolling the sleeves of the sweater until my pulse returned to normal. "Both men showed up yesterday?"

"They did." He rubbed his chin with a thumb. "I invited them to the meeting tonight. Be good if they can connect with a few guys while settling in."

"You sound concerned." I picked up the registration papers, then located the member spreadsheet in Gordo's directory.

"Maybe. It's unusual to have two new vets move to this area in January."

"I moved here in January."

He focused on me again. A shiver tickled my spine. "Yes, you did, Red. Can't say whether that's a good or a bad thing yet, but it sure is interesting. I'll be in the hole if you need me."

"You call your office a hole?" I didn't have to keep asking questions, but I wanted him to keep talking. No way to parse that strange notion. I glanced up to catch him staring at me. He tucked his hands in his pockets.

"My foxhole. When I'm in there, nobody bothers me."

"That right?" I couldn't keep from smirking. "Nobody?"

"You heard me, Red. Stay in your space, and I'll stay in mine. Now, get back to work."

Despite the dismissive words, I experienced a feeling of belonging. Gordo had told me about Tony's penchant for "holing up" in the office. Now that I realized he slept there, too, and after reading his file, I understood the desire to be in a safe space. I wished I had one. Maybe this pull I felt toward him meant that someday I wouldn't mind sharing my life with a man I could depend on. Of course, where would I find such a sterling example of mandom? No, not in the cards for me. Squaring my shoulders, I concentrated on entering the data of David Yang and Harlan Clouse, who appeared, on paper, like carbon copies of each other. Maybe that's what had Tony's spidey sense twitching. I felt a little of that unease myself.

Tony didn't come out of his hole at lunchtime. I heated leftovers from last night's meal and tidied up the notes from the Friday fundraising committee. At one, I left to pick up the appointments for the day. When I arrived at the final stop, the man was too ill to venture out and begged off, which meant I was back in the office in time to complete next week's schedule. At three, I taped a note on Tony's door saying I'd return for the regular group meeting at seven, then hurried to pick up the kids. Carl had insisted on babysitting tonight, claiming she and the children hadn't finished inventing their moosie stories. I was surprised that Mollie and Evan didn't mind her gruff ways and occasional strange wordings. The woman had a way of insinuating herself into people's lives, then making them glad she did.

At dinner, I shared the puppy video with the kids, who immediately claimed their pups. They even announced names, Clue and Blue. I had no idea where they got the idea for the monikers, but it seemed adopting the puppies was a done deal. I delivered them to Carl, promising to pick them up as soon as the meeting ended. As I tucked my scarf into the collar of my coat, I recalled the weight of Tony's hand on my skin and how good it felt to be touched again.

The parking lot at the Center was almost full by the time I arrived. Inside, two women and three men arranged chairs in a circle while a guy with a cane and another using a walker chatted by the coffee bar. When I entered, everyone turned and shouted, "Hi, Red!"

I waved my hand to quiet them and divested myself of hat, gloves, and coat. The room had warmed to a more tolerable seventy-two degrees. I mouthed a thank you to the furnace gods and scanned the room. Tony held a clipboard as he circled the group, recording names and votes on an issue from a previous discussion. I made my way over to rescue the tray of cookies balanced precariously in the crook of his elbow.

"What can I do?"

He nodded at a man standing on the fringes, a paper cup of cider balanced in one hand, phone in the other. The stranger wore a ball cap with the Kansas City Chiefs logo, extremely out of place among the sea of Buffalo Bills paraphernalia on display around the room. Fear became a fist in my throat. "Can you introduce the new guy to the others, get him settled?" Tony said. "He's recovering from head trauma from an IED and may come across as a little spacey."

"Of course. Which one of the newbies is he?"

"Yang. Marine. Reports he served three tours in the Middle East doing some type of intelligence work."

"I remember that from his information sheet. Sounds very secretive. You don't think he was telling the truth?"

"Not sure." Storms caught his lower lip between his teeth. "I put out a few feelers, just in case, so don't get too chatty, Red. Okay?"

I righted the tray before the cookies tumbled off. "Don't intend to, boss. What else?"

"Can you turn on the TV and set up the Zoom? You have the password, right?"

I assured him I did, set the tray next to the drink cups, and worked my way over to Yang. "Hi, I'm Emma Evans, Jill of all trades here at the Center," I said. "You're David Yang, right?"

Yang ran his eyes over me and looked away. "You're not a vet."

"No, I'm staff. I drive guys to appointments, answer the phone, file paperwork. Typical volunteer stuff. I'd like to introduce you to some of the other vets."

"I'm good," Yang said. He sipped his drink, his eyes distant. In the face of his dismissal, I nodded and turned away. He grabbed my arm. When I tried to tug free, he refused to release me.

"You know the area, right?" He stuffed the phone he'd been trolling into his pocket and reached inside his jacket. I wondered if he had a weapon. "It's safe? No terrorists hiding in the woods?"

"Far as I know, bears and wolves are the only things to be afraid of out here." I freed my sleeve from his grip and corralled two men walking by. "David, meet Tom Sinclair and Eddie Marner. Guys, can you make our new vet feel at home?"

The men shook hands while I backed away and took a deep breath. David Yang had the glassy stare of a drug addict and the posture of a wounded man. I made a mental note to contact the psychiatrist on call about my observations, then restocked the napkin dispenser and counted the attendees. Fifteen. A good turnout despite the weather. I was about to sit when the thump of the entry door hitting the wall caught my attention. A man dressed in combat fatigues stepped in and scanned the room, pausing when he spotted me, then raised a hand to Tony, who rose to greet him. I adjusted my stocking cap against the blast of cold air that accompanied him and hurried to close the door before more heat could escape. The group turned to stare at the newcomer. He straightened and saluted Storms. Tony shook his hand.

"You're the sergeant from Fort Drum who called this morning?"

"Klaman, Eric, yes, sir. I've been assigned as liaison to the group."

Tony rubbed a thumb over his lower lip. "Strange timing. We've never had one before, although I've asked. Well, glad you could join us. We welcome any support the Fort can provide."

"Thank you, sir." Klaman turned his gaze toward me. I looked down, uneasy at the intensity of the man's stare. That made twice I'd felt uncomfortable tonight. Funny how I never felt that way with the regulars when I drove them around the area. Tony noticed my reaction. He frowned but led the sergeant to a chair beside the other newcomer, Yang, and continued to chat with those at the drink station. I snatched the iPad from the desk and opened the online session, blushing when each member joining the meeting shouted, "Hi, Red!" I was never going to live down that nickname.

By five minutes to seven, all scheduled participants had signed in and were using the chat box to greet each other. Tony asked those lingering by the snacks to take a seat. He opened with the pledge of allegiance and recited the serenity prayer, his voice filling the space as the others murmured along with him. After reviewing the agenda, he paused to thank them for the work on the Denver Lorang fundraiser and gestured toward the TV. "Denver's joining us this evening, thanks to his new housemate, who has figured out how to connect D's computer to our program."

A scattering of applause. Denver offered his thanks. Behind him, a man's jean-clad legs moved through the room. Denver motioned the man over. "This here's my new helper. Harlan, say hello to the vets at the center." The man jerked away. Lorang grabbed his shirt and tugged him closer to the camera. As the stranger's face swam into focus, my stomach churned. I dropped the iPad onto Tom Sinclair's lap and edged out of camera range. Unable to reach the exit and stay offscreen, I stumbled through the chairs and into the lounge. I banged a shoulder against Tony's office door, shoving it against the wall, and disappeared inside. I didn't care about invading his space. I didn't care that the whole room would think me crazy. I reached the toilet in Tony's small bathroom before my dinner came barreling up, smearing the seat and dripping down the outside of the bowl. When nothing was left but dry heaves, I rocked back on my knees and rummaged in the cabinet below the sink. I found a roll of paper towels and cleaned up the mess I'd made. I removed my hat, scrubbed it and the strands of hair splattered with vomit, then cowered inside the shower stall, shaking with cold and fear and anger. I didn't know how much time elapsed before the office door snicked open and Tony's shadow fell over the darkened room.

"Can I turn the light on, Red?" I mumbled okay. He flipped the switch, throwing the room into glaring light. I shrank back against the wall. Tony crouched down to face me. "Everyone's worried, Em, but they're gone now. I told them you were sick." He touched my cheek, ran a hand over my wet hair, and tugged my chin to make me look up. "Want to tell me what's going on?"

"I need to go home now." I struggled to stand, sidestepped him, and made it as far as the door before he curled a hand around my bicep.

"Red?"

"Let go, Tony. I can't breathe. I can't think. I can't talk about this now." When he released me, I hurried into the outer office and grabbed my coat. I opened the door, then slammed it shut and pressed against the wall. Tony had matched my steps and now stood a mere foot away.

"Emma, tell me what's going on."

I worried the fringe on my scarf while a thousand scenarios presented themselves in my rattled mind. Had the man in Lorang's house seen me? What if he wasn't alone? I clutched the sleeve of Tony's flannel. "Check the parking lot for me. Please. Tell me if anyone's out there."

Tony frowned but did as I asked. He stomped back in, dusting snowflakes from his hair and shoulders. "It's clear. We're the only ones left."

"What about," I clenched my fists, my words slipping out in whispers, "down the road? Any cars parked there that shouldn't be?"

He shook his head. "If anyone is waiting out there, they're well hidden. What kind of trouble are you in, Red?"

"The kind I don't want you involved in. I can't put anyone else in danger."

"Well, darling, that train's left the station. I'm your boss, and I'm responsible for your safety. You have to tell me what this is all about."

I toyed with the buttons on my coat before looking him in the eye. "Josh told me I should tell you, but I don't want you to know because it's awful and dangerous and humiliating. And I really, really need to get home to make sure the twins are all right."

"The kids are in trouble, too?"

Tears I didn't want and couldn't afford sprang free and rolled down my cheeks. "I have to get to them before he does."

Tony nodded as though the internal debate he was waging had concluded. "Take the back road toward the Jones house, then head over to Wanakena. I'll be right behind you."

I waited while he set the alarm and turned off the lights, then ran to the Rover, locking the doors as soon as I slid into the driver's seat. The roads, covered in a fresh dusting of wet snow, were slick but empty of vehicles. I checked the rearview mirror obsessively, reassured by the constancy of Storms' headlights behind me. When no other cars appeared, the band around my chest eased. I drew out my phone to call Carl, to make sure nothing had happened, that my children were safe. The face of the man at Denver Lorang's house leered at me as it had in the video from my parent's Florida condo. Thank God I hadn't been at the Center yesterday when he came by. But who was he, this man claiming to be a veteran named Harlan Clouse, and why was he so intent on finding me? I passed the Jones property and neared the turnoff for Wanakena. Tony flashed his lights, a reassuring brightness that had me sobbing with relief until he turned left while I continued right, heading straight over the bridge and onto Reed to Carl's place. Tony had left me. I didn't want to know why that made my chest ache.

The Dugas's lodge was dark. Without a moon or streetlights, the road seemed to narrow into nothingness. My eyes burned from staring hard into the woods that lined the way, searching for predators of the animal and human variety. I pulled to a stop in front of Carl's cabin, jumped from the car, and raced down the snowy path to my place. The only illumination came from the fanlight over the stove. If Carl and the twins were asleep, I didn't want to frighten them, but I had to see my children's faces. I had to know they were warm and safe and alive. I stopped in the living room. No one was on the couch. I paused in the hall that led to the bedrooms. Had Ms. Beamish fallen asleep with the kids? While I considered what to do, a board creaked on the porch. Someone was here. I opened the door to the children's bedroom. The nightlight illuminated enough of the room to make me gasp. The twins were gone.

The noise outside sounded again. I needed a weapon. Frantic, I turned in circles, almost forgetting Gary's gun, locked in a case and hidden under the bed. Except at night, when I slipped it under the pillow beside me. I crept into my room, dropped to my knees by the bed. Listening for footsteps, I slid the case toward me and fumbled with the digital lock. When the tumbler whirred free, I closed my hand around the grip and lifted it to my chest. I didn't remember loading it and didn't have time to do so now. The kitchen floor squeaked, then a soft footstep in the hall. I raised the gun and released the safety. Crouched on one knee, I prepared to shoot to kill.

...a step too far...

The smell of corn beef and cabbage permeated Denver Lorang's clothing, causing Mouse to avoid close contact until the computer screen popped open and the Vet Center gathering zoomed into view. He didn't care who else had joined online. All his focus was centered on those attending the night's meeting in person. He concentrated on the screen as it panned the room, following Anton Storms, who, clipboard in hand, greeted those in attendance. Storms spoke to everyone, although his eyes, narrowed and intent, appeared to follow someone off-screen, someone Mouse couldn't see. He turned his attention to those he could, noting a younger man among the aging vets. Hovering over Lorang's shoulder, he committed names to memory, searching for the asset he knew was already in place. The idea of being under surveillance himself stung. He'd never worked with a partner and didn't appreciate it now. He blamed the Pearson woman. When he found her, he'd make sure she knew exactly how much trouble she'd caused him. Maybe, he mused, it ran in the family. Her husband had crossed both his federal contacts and the KC mob and paid the price for his disloyalty. Now, even Pearson's parents had outplayed him. The woman would not be so lucky.

After the pledge of allegiance and the salute to all the fallen soldiers, Storms began the agenda for the evening. When he brought up the fundraiser for Lorang, he invited the man to introduce his new helper and speak about what the coming event meant to him. Mouse did not want to be seen, but Lorang grabbed his shirt and tilted the computer until both men were in full view of the assembled vets. Mouse lurched forward and tilted the screen down. Mumbling about the lack of privacy online, he walked out of the kitchen, then returned in time to see Storms introduce Sergeant Eric Klaman. A younger man whom Mouse had noticed earlier, glanced at the new arrival, tipped his chair back, and shook his head. He set the chair back down, clenching and unclenching his hands as he muttered to himself. Caught up in Yang's reaction to the guy in uniform, Mouse jumped at a loud crash off-camera. Everyone turned toward the noise. Storms started forward, shrugged, and offered an excuse Mouse didn't catch. The group returned their attention to the front of the room.

"Nothing to worry about, guys. Red's feeling a little under the weather. Now," Storms glanced at the wall clock, "let's call it a night and let you all go home."

Lorang scrubbed at his beard. "Wonder where Gordo is?"

Alert to the change in topic, Mouse settled at the table out of camera range. "Who's Gordo?"

"Phil Gordon, retired Marine who runs the office for Tony. Don't know for sure who Red is. Maybe it's that new volunteer driving vets around to appointments."

"The new person have a name?"

"Red's all I know." Lorang huffed. "Gordo gives everyone a nickname. Mine's Colorado."

"Why Colorado?"

Lorang shrugged, eyes focused on the screen as the men dispersed. "He was stationed there once, liked it, says I remind him of a friend he used to know who lived there, too."

Mouse toyed with a napkin he'd neglected to dispose of after they ate dinner. Emma Pearson had red hair. Could this mystery volunteer be her? That would be a stroke of luck. He looked up to see Lorang eyeing him. "What?"

Lorang held up two passports, one for Harlan Clouse and the other bearing the name and image of Charles Mouse.

"You went through my stuff?"

Lorang shrugged. "Man's in my home, I got a right to know who he is and what he's doing out here in the wilderness, pretending to be something he's not."

"You have no idea who I am." Mouse had underestimated the old man's curiosity. He wandered over to the couch, picked up a throw pillow. Stiff and heavy in his hands, it was too bulky for what he had in mind. He watched the man reach into his lap for the Glock hidden there. Mouse raised an eyebrow. "And when I'm in another man's home, I make sure he can't harm me."

Lorang squeezed the trigger. Nothing happened. Lorang threw the gun. Mouse sidestepped the weapon and swept around from behind to apply a chokehold. Lorang struggled, but Mouse squeezed harder and counted, leaning his full weight into the struggle. Eight seconds, and Lorang slumped back, unconscious.

...if the truth will out, what else will follow?...

A dark figure stepped in through the open door, halted, then skipped back out of sight.

"Do. NOT. Come. Closer," I punctuated each word with a sob. The figure returned, hands in the air.

"Red? Don't shoot. It's me, Tony."

"You said you would follow me home." I didn't intend it as an accusation, but it came out that way.

Tony took a step forward but didn't lower his hands. "I know. I wanted to talk to Jesse. Are you going to shoot me?"

I lowered the weapon and slumped back against the bed, the cold from the floor seeping through my corduroys. I dropped my head on my knees and exhaled long and slow. "I thought you were him."

"Can I turn on a light?" He waited a heartbeat, then tapped the wall, feeling for a switch. The light cast a soft glow around the bedroom. I raised my head. Storms had dropped to a crouch. "Tell me now, Red. The truth."

"The children are missing. Carl, too." Tears trickled down my cheeks. "I'm so afraid something bad has happened to them."

"Did you call Ms. Beamish?"

Stunned that I had assumed the worst, I rose to my knees, grabbed my phone from my pocket, and dialed the number. The answering machine picked up, Carl Beamish's distinctive voice spooling out in typical fashion.

It's late. Call tomorrow. If this is Emma, the little bears are snug in bed, dreaming of more snow adventures. Rest easy. They'll be fine until tomorrow. I sank to the floor, buried my head in my hands.

"They're all right?" Tony said. I lifted my shoulders in silent acknowledgment. "Good. Now, talk."

I scrubbed my cheeks, sat back on my heels, and shook my head. "I don't want you to know."

"What don't you want me to know?" He inched closer, his crouching form filling the space, barring my escape, although I had no will left to run. I was making my stand here.

"About the man in the video. He's in Lorang's house, and he's coming to kill me."

"I'm pretty lost here, sweetheart. You're going to have to fill in the missing parts."

I rubbed the barrel of the gun, searching for words. "Josh told me to tell you, and he was right, but I wanted you to trust me and let me keep working with the vets."

Tony laced his fingers together, kept his eyes on me. "Josh knows what this is about?"

I bobbed my head, then stared at the ceiling. It would be easier if I didn't have to see his face when he learned how inadequate a wife I had been. "My husband is never coming to join us. He's dead. He was murdered, along with his other wife and a child he had with her. Imagine. A whole second family I knew nothing about." Bitterness colored my words.

"There's more." Tony settled onto the floor and scooted closer.

I set the gun down, worried the zipper on my coat, up and down, up and down. Wind rattled the window above the bed. I glanced toward the noise, heaved a sigh, and continued. "He was working some big undercover case with one of the agencies he consulted for, and the FBI believes the Kansas City mob killed him and his family there. But Gary must have done something else to piss them off because now, they're after me and the twins."

"Why do you think they're after you?"

I shook my head. "I don't know for certain that they are, but the Feds seemed very convinced. A killer, or killers, who would gun down an innocent baby... I can't take the chance that they might be after us. The

Feds offered to give us new identities, a new life, but I won't disappear into witness protection, erase who I am, who my children are."

"It would be safer."

"Would it?" I met his gaze and didn't look away this time. I had read his file. I knew he'd worked for the government. He understood how these things worked. Was he right? Had I done wrong by coming here? Tony edged closer until our knees touched. The contact should have felt intrusive. Instead, it steadied me.

"Okay, let me get this straight. Your husband cheated on you, then got himself killed, and you think the man staying at Denver Lorang's house is the killer?"

"Maybe. The same man showed up at my parents' condo in Florida and tried to find out information about Riley. Who she was. Where she lived."

Tony traced the scar along the side of his head. "I'm thinking I need a few more details. How about you go sit on the couch? I'll make some hot chocolate, and you can fill in the rest of the story."

I was too unsettled to argue. If Josh Waylon trusted Storms, I supposed I could, too. When he held out a hand, I grabbed it, didn't shake off his touch on the small of my back when he led me into the living room. He dragged the fleece blanket from the arm of the couch and tucked it around me.

"While the chocolate's brewing," he held up his phone and moved away, "I'm calling Josh."

I huddled beneath the blanket, the soft sounds of Tony's voice distant and unintelligible. How had that man found me in Wanakena? Something else was bothering me. Although David Yang had remained seated near Sinclair and Marner throughout the meeting, his eyes had followed me the entire time. The sergeant from Fort Drum, Klaman, did the same thing, clocked me every time I moved. The way he looked me over made my skin crawl. Was I just being paranoid? Could Yang be with the FBI? Or from the mob? And why would the army send a liaison officer now when, according to Tony, they had rebuffed previous requests? Who had tracked my escape to Wanakena? How had they done it? And how in the world could I keep my friends, all the kind people I had met here, safe from whatever violence seemed intent on finding me?

Storms returned carrying two mugs and a plate of cinnamon toast. He motioned me to move over, set the tray on my lap, took one of my sock-covered feet in hand, and rubbed it. My hands, heated by the mug of cocoa, thawed. I leaned back, closed my eyes, and fought the tears threatening to spill down my cheeks.

He rubbed my other foot, then tucked both feet back under the fleece, rescued his mug from the tray, and took a hefty swallow. His words, when he spoke, made me shiver. "Talk, Red. I'm listening."

I blinked. "I don't want to. It's horrible, and humiliating, and probably dangerous for you and for everyone I know."

"How about this?" He waited for me to meet his gaze, his dark eyes intent and serious. "We can trade horror stories and embarrassing moments, okay?"

I realized I still wore my wet hat. When I tugged it off, my hair tumbled forward, the mass of coppery curls a veil hiding my face. Tony brushed them back, his hand lingering on my neck as he waited for me to begin.

"Fine." I blew on the drink, gulped several mouthfuls, and, warmth pooling in my stomach from the chocolate and from Tony's intense gaze, I decided to speak. "I thought I had a good marriage and then I didn't. My hus—, Gary Pearson, betrayed me in the worst way a man can. He didn't just cheat on me. He had another wife, a second home, a separate, secret life in the city where he was doing undercover consultant work. I knew nothing about any of it until he was murdered, and the FBI showed up to question me."

Tony didn't interrupt my narrative. I took another drink and related the details as I knew them. The child born two and a half years after the twins. The house in a suburb of Kansas City. The horrific bloody murder scene. "Whoever murdered Gary also killed the woman, his wife, and their child." I doubled over as a gut-wrenching sob erupted. "What kind of monster kills an infant?"

Tony didn't say anything, but he didn't run away either. Instead, he refilled the mugs, checked that the doors were locked, and waited while I removed myself to the bathroom to cry in private. When I returned, I found him hunched over my laptop, a montage of newspaper articles about a Wilderness Strangler fresh from my printer scattered across the coffee table. He ran his fingers over the pages and motioned for me to sit.

"What is all this?"

"Quid pro quo, right, Red? My own sordid story...minus the initial incidents, how a lonely man, new in town, was played for a fool by a local woman, humiliated when she dumped him in a very public way, and almost made a play for Riley Finn even though he knew she wasn't for him. There's information about my accident," he touched the scar on his head, "and some about Gus Jernigan, who I thought was a friend. Turns out he wired a trailer full of drugs to explode and shot me as an added bonus. Hard to trust anyone after that."

I collected the printouts of the articles by a journalist named Mariah Kimby and read through them. I knew some of Tony's story from Riley's account of the summer of 2018, but I hadn't realized how close he'd come to dying. By the time I finished, the fire had burned low. Tony added a log and settled next to me. I laid the articles aside. "Did you love her?"

"Who?"

"Amanda Waylon, I guess, but maybe Riley, too." I didn't understand why I was so curious about his answer, an answer I was afraid to hear but unwilling not to.

"I don't think I know what love is, Red, or I never would have wanted Amanda. Riley was just," he rubbed the dimple in his chin, "she was cute and spunky, and, to be honest, I thought we could use her to flush out the Strangler. I was wrong, and I regret even considering using her as bait."

His sadness and regret were palpable. So were mine. I touched his arm, and he turned to face me. "I don't think we should ever be sad for wanting to connect with someone. You weren't at fault, and maybe neither was I. At least that's what my mother tells me every time I start down the self-pity highway. I didn't betray Gary. He did that to me. Amanda and Gus, they were the ones who used you, and they're to blame for all that happened."

Tony shook his head and covered my hand with his. "I wasn't smart. I trusted the wrong people. I won't make those mistakes again."

"So, what are you doing here then?"

He caught his lower lip between his teeth. "Damn it, Red, I don't want to like you. But you make it very hard not to."

"So, you're not going to fire me?"

He angled his body toward mine, slipped an arm around my shoulders. "No, sweetheart, I'm not going to fire you, at least not until Gordo comes back."

I started to ask when the man would be back. Tony placed a finger on my lips. "I'm trying not to like you," he repeated, "but I sure want to kiss you."

"Oh." I swallowed hard, peered into those dark, soulful eyes, the heat from his body thawing all the parts of me I'd placed in deep freeze. "We shouldn't."

"I know there's a but in there," he said, one hand cradling the back of my head.

"But I want to kiss you, too." I leaned into him, shivered at first contact, then surrendered to the comfort of his mouth and arms and body, relaxed into the kindness he had shown, the lack of judgment, his own guilt overriding any fault he might find in me. It had been so long since I'd been intimate that I thought it would be awkward, but I opened for him the moment his lips met mine. He tasted like chocolate and cinnamon and desire. I straddled him, wanting more contact, wanting what I knew I shouldn't, this man naked in my bed. A soft knock at the door startled us into breaking apart. Tony jumped up, snagging the blanket away when he stood. He replaced it around me, his hands lingering at my waist, then strode into the kitchen, my gun in his hand. When he undid the bolt and opened the door, Josh Waylon and Jesse Livetree swept in.

...complications...

The complication slumped lower in the wheelchair, mouth open, eyes closed. Swearing, Mouse tossed the wig he'd been wearing, cleared his throat, and considered his next move. He couldn't leave without an explanation. Too many people knew of his presence in Lorang's house. In retrospect, sharing space with a stranger had been an ill-advised plan, but he hadn't intended to be on camera during the meeting. Damn Lorang for dragging him onscreen. Double-damn him for exposing Mouse to the scrutiny of a roomful of nosy old men. He prided himself on blending in, on being an unremarkable man who didn't raise eyebrows or suspicions. Along the back of the house, a shutter rattled. The floorboard heating grate hissed as the furnace blew air around the room. Time to decide his next move.

Mouse did a quick walk through the house, his mind humming with scenarios. Best to make it look like an accident, but how to explain his inability to prevent Lorang from injuring himself? The whiskey bottles lined up on the counter drew his attention. He hurried to his room to retrieve a length of tubing, attached a spout to one end, and returned to the unconscious man. Prying the vet's mouth open, he inserted the tube, then poured the liquor into Lorang's stomach. The man stirred. Mouse paused the forced feeding to renew the chokehold, careful not to bruise the man's neck. When he was satisfied that the blood alcohol level would register high enough, he removed the tubing, bagged it, and stuffed it into the lining of his carry bag. Ignoring the ping of an incoming text, he wheeled Lorang to the front entrance and out onto the rickety ramp that led to the driveway.

The night sky was a dark disc along the horizon, the stars hidden by clouds. The temperature had dropped into the low teens, stinging his nostrils as he maneuvered the chair over the slick, rotting boards. The ramp groaned and shifted. Mouse jammed a hand into a glove, grabbed the railing, and twisted until it sagged more loosely over the edge of the ramp. When the fencing gave way, he steered the wheelchair into the gap, grasped the handles, and heaved. Lorang opened his eyes. Sluggish from the forced consumption of alcohol, the old man flung out his arms to stop the chair from rolling. His fingers grazed the damaged rail, the effort to catch himself ineffectual and doomed. Momentum tipped him forward, and he fell face down into a frozen drift of snow. Mouse remained on the ramp, waiting until the flailing ceased, and Denver Lorang, unable to lift his head and already suffering from hypothermia, slowly suffocated.

Back inside the house, Mouse sat down to drink himself into a stupor, thinking as he did so about the unstable David Yang and the soldier calling himself Eric Klaman. One of the two had to be the asset sent by the boss to assist Mouse. That situation he intended to deal with next. Charles Mouse worked alone, always. It was time for the boss to learn that the leash he held wasn't as tight as he thought. When the bottle was empty, Mouse staggered to the room Lorang had assigned him and collapsed onto the bed. Outside, the wind picked up. A mini flurry of snowflakes spiraled around the still form of Denver Lorang, coating him in an icy shroud.

...the best-laid plans...

I stood, clutching the blanket around me, and stared at the men. Livetree nodded as he folded his coat over the back of a chair.

"Emma," the older man intoned. "You good?"

"Yes." I looked at Josh. "Is Riley all right? Are the children?"

Josh gave me a one-armed hug. "They're fine, Em. I sent them to stay with my folks until we sort out whatever this is that's going on."

"Is that why you're here?"

Livetree guided me back to the couch and settled me there. Taking the spot by my side, he captured my hands between his. "Nobody comes to our town and threatens our people. Josh brought me up to speed on what's really going on here."

My cheeks warmed. "I didn't plan to involve all of you. I'm so sorry I brought this danger to your home."

"No need to feel bad, Emma. Not your fault what happened to your husband, nor is it your fault that someone is coming for you. Now," he picked up my mug, sniffed, and set it back down, "I, for one, could use stronger stuff than hot chocolate, no offense. What do you have to warm an old man's bones?"

Shrugging off the blanket, I shouldered past the men in the kitchen to reach the cabinet above the refrigerator. I dragged out the rum I'd stashed among the baking supplies I'd brought from Hopewell and set it on the counter. "I can make a *Cuba libre*," I said. "That's about as strong a drink as I can offer tonight. There are a few bottles of beer in the fridge."

"Deal. But I'll make the drinks." Livetree rescued the bottle from my shaking hand. He rummaged in the refrigerator for a Coke, tossed a beer at Josh, and made himself a drink. The Ranger straddled a kitchen chair, arms draped over the back. Storms leaned against the wall, face closed, thoughts his own. When we were all settled again, the mayor took charge. "Correct me if I mess up, Emma, but here's what we know. Gary Pearson and his Kansas City family were murdered as possible mob retaliation for his work as an undercover informant. The FBI considers you and your children possible additional targets for reasons currently unknown. You decided not to accept the offer of witness protection, resumed your maiden name, not all that difficult to trace, and came here to hide. Now, from what Josh and Tony tell me, your concerns have some validity. A man visited your parents at their Florida condo, asking about and finding information on our Riley and where she lives. Your parents shared a photo of the man with you, and you identified that man as the one who's staying with Denver Lorang and claiming to be a veteran himself. Storms," Livetree lifted his chin toward Tony, "interviewed the man, who calls himself Harlan Clouse, and another individual, who also claims to be a veteran, and who recently arrived in Wanakena. I won't lie to you, Em. We all have reason to be suspicious of these men. Almost no one moves here during the winter months unless they come to hunt in season, ice fish, or practice snowmobiling and other winter sports. Josh? Tony? Emma? Have I forgotten anything?"

I started to shake my head when Tony spoke up. "We had a third unexpected visitor at the Center tonight, Jesse, Sergeant Eric Klaman stationed at Drum. I've already left a message at the Fort asking to speak to someone about the man."

Josh rolled the beer bottle between his palms. "You think he's not who he says?"

Tony considered the question. "I've requested someone from Drum to work with us for the past year. It seems unlikely that the man would show up tonight. My gut tells me something's not right."

Jesse rolled his eyes. "Your gut? Come on, Anton, that's hardly a useful tool."

Tony faced Livetree. "I've ignored my intuition before, Tree. Look where it got me. It's time I paid attention to what the vibes are telling me, and everything about Clouse, Yang, and Klaman cries foul."

Josh took a long pull on his beer. "Fighting among ourselves won't help. Jesse, I'm with Tony on this. Three strange men in the space of two days? Not good. If the mob is interested in Emma, then she and the kids are in danger, and so is everyone else connected to her. That's why I sent Riley and my children away. Now, it's time to mobilize Wanakena. Start the phone chain. Remind everybody not to speak about Emma and the twins to anyone they don't know and to notify us if they see anything that seems out of place."

"Mobilizing the community's a good plan, Josh. Tomorrow there's a gathering at the History Museum. We can reiterate the warning and formulate a plan for informing the three of us if any strangers show up asking questions we prefer not to answer," Jesse said.

"I can just leave." I surprised myself with the offer. My voice didn't waver, but inside, I was shaking. I bunched my fists in the fleece. "If I'm not here, they won't bother any of you."

"No." Tony shrugged off Josh's arm to sit by me. "One way or the other, this ends here. Wanakena won't be bullied or scared into giving up its own."

I gave him a brief smile. "That's kind and generous, but I'm not one of you."

"Well," Jesse moved closer to us, "actually, you are, Red, like it or not. Carl proclaimed you one of us when she gave you the cabin."

"She didn't give me—" My protest died at the fierce pride in the mayor's words.

Josh and Tony shared a glance. Tony nodded, and the Ranger cleared his throat. "I have an idea, Emma. It's crazy, but I think it might work. I know of a hunting cabin near a fire tower on Long Tom Mountain. Tony and I will escort you there, get you out of harm's way while we flush out your pursuer. The twins can stay with Riley and the children."

"No." My denial rang out in the small cabin. "I won't be separated from my kids. I can't. They've suffered too much trauma. If I leave them alone, they might never recover."

"Em, the climb to the cabin is a trek in good weather. With all this snow, it will be treacherous. We'll have to snowshoe in."

"Carl taught them how to use the snowshoes. I mean, how hard can it be?" The men exchanged glances. Jesse cleared his throat. "What?"

"All due respect, Red, you don't know what you're talking about." Tony clenched his fists. "This will not be a walk in the park."

I surrendered. "You're right. I don't know anything about hiking up here. But I can't be separated from my children. Please don't make me do that. Besides, what's the point? I'll just be hiding again."

"Once we identify the people after you, we'll leave a trail of breadcrumbs, my dear." Livetree squeezed my hand. "Lead your pursuer into a trap. Our trap. You will be tucked away, safe and warm and unharmed."

I stared into the dying fire, trying to process their plan. When I looked up, they were all staring at me. "What will you do when you catch him?"

Jesse raised an eyebrow. Josh shrugged. Only Tony met my eyes. "Whatever needs to be done, Red, to make sure he never threatens you or Mollie or Evan again."

The silence spun out, leaving me to wonder if I was setting us all up for more betrayal. So much could go wrong. While Jesse added another log to the fire, Josh helped himself to a second beer. I reclaimed my hot chocolate, ran a finger around the mug's rim, then licked off the marshmallow residue. "I won't go without the kids. That's non-negotiable. And I want to know everything about your plan. And I'm taking my gun."

Instead of agreeing, Tony removed the .38 from his waistband and set it gently in my lap. "You won't be alone, Red."

"What?"

"You won't be up there alone. I'm going with you and staying until it's done."

Before I could protest, Josh and Jesse moved toward the kitchen. Josh stowed his bottles in the recycle bin, gave me another one-armed hug, and gestured toward Jesse. "It's late. You've been yawning for the last fifteen minutes, old man. We'll continue this discussion tomorrow, after we've all had a chance to sleep on it. You coming, Storms?'

"No. I'll stay a little longer, make sure nothing bothers Red tonight."

My mouth fell open. "I don't need a babysitter."

"No, but you do need a bodyguard. That's one thing I'm good at."

Jesse nodded. "I approve of that," he said. "Josh, you stopping with me tonight?"

"Sounds good. I'm kind of tired myself." His phone buzzed. He checked the message and smiled. "Baby Cara's pulling an all-nighter. Ri says hi."

My heart lurched at the look on Josh's face. I wanted someone to look like that about me. Then Tony's phone rang, the tone louder, the ring distinctly different from Riley's. He listened intently, his face clouding at whatever the caller was saying. Jesse and Josh sidled closer, the tension building. When he disconnected, he looked shell-shocked.

"That was Trooper Kellerman. Earlier tonight, she got a call from Denver Lorang asking her to stop by. She was on an accident call and only got around to checking on him thirty minutes ago, but Denver's a night owl, so she didn't think he'd mind."

Sensing the concern in Tony's voice, I moved closer. "What's wrong?"

Tony braced a hand on the wall. "Lorang's dead. His wheelchair broke through the railing of his access ramp, and he fell. Into a snowdrift. Suffocated or froze to death."

"But," I paused, not certain I understood, "doesn't he have that man there to help him?"

"Harlan Clouse." Tony spat the name. "Yeah, about that. Kellerman found him in bed, drunk and dead to the world."

...another iron in the fire...

The lights from the patrol car strobed red and blue, highlighting the frozen drifts and the crumpled remains of Denver Lorang and his wheelchair. The man calling himself Harlan Clouse swayed in the doorway, one arm gripped by Trooper Austin Camara. The EMT squad stood, silent and shivering, beside the corpse and waited for orders. Trooper Kellerman finished photographing the scene, swiveled to glare into the light behind the drunken Clouse, and fingered the radio clipped to the collar of her fur-lined jacket. "Camara?" When the trooper acknowledged the call, she gestured for him to take the drunken man back inside. "Get some coffee into him, Cam. I'll be in shortly."

One of the squad members crouched to shine a light over Lorang's still form. "Smells like alcohol. Didn't know Mr. Lorang was a drinker. What do you suppose he was doing out here at night?"

Kellerman joined him, slapping her gloved hands to keep the numbness from taking hold. "Good question, Fels. Tell me, what do you see?"

Lark Felsen looked over his shoulder at the broken railing, then glanced down at the body. "If my high school geometry teacher taught me well, the trajectory's off."

Kellerman nodded, patted his shoulder, and eased her tall frame to a stand. "When the coroner arrives, come get me. I'll be inside conversing with the man who was supposed to help our friend."

Wig once more firmly in place, Mouse started a pot of coffee. His bloodshot eyes drifted past the trooper, skittered around the cluttered kitchen and the unkempt living area, then refocused on Kellerman. The woman had an imposing manner and a stare that probably curdled most people's stomachs, guilty or not. Mouse wished his head would stop pounding. He must have imbibed more than he intended. He glanced at the empty bottle next to the computer, then plopped down by the table and rested his head in his hands. Kellerman did not sit.

"I understand you're a recent visitor to our locale. What brings you, Harlan Clouse, is it? to upstate New York in the dead of winter?" The coffee maker beeped. Clouse dragged himself up and shuffled past the trooper to pour himself a cup. He held it up in silent invitation. The Trooper shook her head. "Take your time, sir. Mr. Lorang's not going anywhere, and neither am I."

Mouse reseated himself and groaned. "Where is Denver?"

"You don't know?"

He raised tired eyes to hers. "We were toasting the fact that the vets are going to fix up his place. Got carried away, I guess. I'm not much of a drinker, and I don't remember anything after the third round except Denver urging me to go to bed."

"How is it you know Denver Lorang, Mr. Clouse? Are you old friends?"

Mouse tapped the mug with his fingernails. "I'm a professional photographer. Well, I was planning to be until a series of bad decisions left me broke and homeless. I was looking for a place to stay, hoping to acquire some photos for a winter calendar spread. Lorang offered me board in exchange for assistance with the house and his personal needs."

"And did you?"

"Did I what?" Mouse forced more coffee into his system. With each swallow, the fog on his brain lifted a bit more. He had to extricate himself from this mess as quickly as possible, get out of the house, and find out if Yang or Klaman was the assistant sent by the boss. He hadn't expected anyone to miss Lorang for days. How the troopers showed up so quickly was a mystery he had no time to solve. This was a big-time screwup.

"Help the man? Since he's currently lying face down and frozen in the snow, it's safe to say you failed in the one duty you had here, sir."

"Hold on." Mouse held up a hand. "Lorang's dead? But he was on the computer when I went into my bedroom."

"For the record, you're stating that you have no idea why your employer was outside in his wheelchair, alone, in the middle of the night on an icy, deteriorating ramp? That you heard nothing? No cries for help? No sound of the chair breaking through the railing?"

Mouse stood up too quickly. He reeled and fell against the table. Kellerman grabbed his arm and sat him down again, then crossed her arms and simply stared his way. Shit. He finished the coffee, burped, and gestured toward the pot. The trooper nodded her permission, and he poured a second cup, his mind skittering between close to the truth and an outrageous lie. Kellerman was, after all, only a local rube, hardly astute enough to see through his alibi. Maybe a little righteous anger would work. "You think I had something to do with Denver's passing?"

"His death, Mr. Clouse. Let's be clear about that. The man is dead. So, did you?"

"Look, officer or trooper or whatever the hell you are, I've only been here forty-eight hours. I hardly knew the guy, and I sure as hell have no idea why a man in a wheelchair goes out in the freezing cold in the middle of the god-damned night. My head feels like it's going to explode, and my gut wants to hurl every time I move." He held out his hands. "Want to arrest me? Go ahead. I'm the one should be pressing charges against you backwoods cops looking to jam up an outsider over what seems to me an unfortunate accident. Am I right?"

Kellerman narrowed her eyes and took out her phone. "Smile, Mr. Clouse, you're the prime photo on this backwoods trooper's suspect lineup, if not for contributing to a death, certainly for negligence and dereliction of duty. When Mr. Lorang's children arrive, they may wish to talk to you. In the meantime, this home is a potential crime scene. You'll need to vacate the house. But do stay in the area, sir. And leave Mr. Lorang's laptop right where it is. Trooper Camara will escort you to the Traveler's Inn in Governeur. It's two blocks from our backwoods police station in case we need to talk to you or you to us."

Clouse snatched his hand away from the keyboard, thwarted in his attempt to erase any history of searching over the past two days. He'd already stowed his passports in the lining of his travel bag. The tubing and funnel he'd smashed and fed into the septic system. When the phone in his pocket vibrated, he excused himself and stumbled to the bathroom. He locked the door, grabbed the phone, and held his breath when the message popped up.

Need to meet today Otto's Abode Noon

Clouse grinned. He might end up ahead of the game after all.

...hamburgers and history...

After the call about Lorang's death, Josh and Jesse hurried to their cars. Tony insisted on staying. I brought out blankets and towels, vacillated between asking him to sleep in my room, then settled for his presence on the couch as a sufficient deterrent. Despite our earlier close encounter of the romantic kind, the news about Denver had saddened us. I made sure Tony was comfortable, then crawled into bed, but I didn't sleep, at least not well. I missed the sounds of the children in the next room and felt humbled by the lengths Jesse, Josh, and Tony were willing to go to protect us, but the guilt weighed on me. Riley and her children had to leave their home because of me. My head ached with that knowledge while my body remained on high alert to the presence of Anton Storms in the living room. I couldn't stop thinking of our kiss, of the way my body responded to him. Sometime around five, exhaustion won, dragging me through dream landscapes that made perfect sense while in them and none when I opened my eyes.

Light had barely begun to seep over the wintry landscape when I dragged myself up to prepare for the day. I slipped out of bed and crossed the floor, only to smack into Tony coming out of the bathroom. His damp hair glistened. The scar from the gunshot stood out starkly, and his bare arms revealed the grafted tissue from the burns he'd suffered. Unable to resist, I ran a hand down one of his forearms, then looked up to find him frowning at me. He jerked away, covered the damaged skin with a towel, and swept back the hair that had fallen forward. "Sorry to make you cringe."

"You didn't." I snatched the towel away and curled my fingers over his arm again. "These aren't ugly, Tony. They're badges of courage. You didn't run away. You ran toward. I will never think they are anything except beautiful reminders of your strength."

"You're full of shit, Red." His breath was shaky, his eyes filled with pain.

"Shut your piehole, Storms. I'm not a liar, and I don't betray the trust of people I care about."

We stood still, locked in a moment of truth for a heartbeat, then two. Did we dare trust each other with our pain? I stepped closer, trailed my hand from his shoulder down his chest, my pulse thundering. He stood unmoving. "What are you doing, Red?"

"Honoring your courage, Tony."

"By touching me?" He raised a hand to push me away, hesitated, caressed my cheek instead.

"Do you want me to stop?" I held my breath. He shook his head and pulled me close. When his lips met mine, I moaned.

"Mommy!" The screen door banged open. Tiny fists pounded on the locked main door. "Mommy! Mommy, let us is. Auntie Carl has breskfusts for us."

Tony released me. I sighed. He hurried to pull on jeans and his shirt, then strode into the kitchen to unlock the deadbolt. I slipped into the bathroom, peed, and rinsed the lust off my face before the twins raced in. I gathered them close, raining kisses and endearments. Evan clung to me. Mollie wriggled free, ran to Tony, and jumped into his arms. "Stormy," she squealed, patting his cheeks. Carl set down a picnic basket emitting wondrous aromas and clapped her hands.

"Back to the kitchen, wee ones. Boots off and settle down, or no blueberry muffins." Under Carl's direction, the five of us tucked into the sausage and egg casserole, the fresh-baked muffins, the carafe of fresh-squeezed orange juice, and the thermos of coffee. The food filled our stomachs while the chatter from the twins about their overnight adventure restored a sense of balance to my soul. Twice I caught Tony staring at me. I did my best to ignore the butterflies his gaze evoked. Carl nudged my knee under the table and, mouth full of casserole, winked. "How'd you spend your night?"

I shook my head. "Not the way you think, Ms. Beamish. Jesse and Josh were here until quite late."

"That's particular. Does it have anything to do with the phone chain alert I received this morning?" She pulled out her phone to stare at the dark screen. "And the meeting at the Museum tonight?"

I wiped my mouth with a napkin to hide the trembling at the reminder of all we faced. Tony tapped my stockinged foot with his. "Ms. Beamish?" When Carl turned, he touched his lips and shook his head. "Little bears have big ears."

"We do not," Mollie said, waving her fork like a baton. "What's a mooseeum?"

Carl smirked. "Guess I'm rubbing off on them. Come, now, eat your breakfast. Mrs. Cleary will be waiting and wondering where you are. No, don't get up, Emma. I've got this. You and Anton take care of your business today. We'll talk about mooseeums later."

The stillness after they left felt heavy with thoughts unspoken. I cleared the dishes, put away the remainder of the casserole, and wondered why Tony hadn't stopped staring at me since Carl left with the twins. Unnerved by his gaze, I confronted him, hands on hips, hair framing my head like a cloud. Tony pushed away from the table and stalked toward me. "What?"

"Unfinished business." He wrapped his arms around me, pulled me against his chest, and pressed his lips to mine. I resisted only a second before relaxing into his warm embrace. His yearning for comfort and affirmation matched my own. I slid my arms around his neck and returned his kisses. When we paused for breath, he rested his forehead on mine. "Thank you, Red, for your kindness earlier."

"It wasn't just kindness, Tony. It was the truth."

"Will you come into work today? Everyone will be calling or stopping by now that Denver's gone."

"I can't imagine what they're all thinking. Do we need to bring in a counselor?"

"Let me make some calls. We're scheduled to take the Inlet guys to lunch."

"I remember. Will they still want to go?"

"Probably now more than ever, for the comfort."

I kissed him again and stepped away, fingers lingering on his shirt, then drifting to my side. "I need to shower and get the shoulder holster for this." I raised the gun from my pocket and held it up.

"You're sure you know how to use that?"

"I am. I took lessons. After they murdered Gary. I'm not going down without a fight."

"You're not going down at all, do you hear me?"

"I do, but it's not your fight."

"It wasn't, until they murdered Denver Lorang."

"You don't know they did that," I said, but I bit my lip and turned away, the possibility churning inside me.

"It's not your fault, Red, so don't guilt yourself for it."

"How do you know I am?"

"I see you, sweetheart. Much as I hate to say it, you and me? We're a lot alike."

Sadness welled up. "Maybe it really was an accident."

"No. I know my men, Red. No way Denver does something as stupid as falling through the railing. He knew it was dangerous. That's why he was so grateful for the fundraiser."

"If you're right, that means they're here. I should leave now."

He took my hands. "Promise me you won't do that, or I'm not leaving you out of my sight until we stop this guy."

"I have to take a shower." I tugged against his grip.

"I'm not averse to watching while you do." That dimple Riley had mentioned years ago made a sudden reappearance. I caught myself before I invited him to do precisely that.

"Okay, Stormy, I promise. Now, go. I'll be there soon."

One more enigmatic look, another kiss, and he was gone. I stayed by the back door, watching a man who had every reason to walk away demanding that I let him protect me. The tingling from our kiss and the warmth of his embrace pushed aside the fear.

...adapting to the new reality...

Mouse tossed his travel bag on the worn bedspread at the Traveler's Inn, then stood by the window waiting until Trooper Camara pulled away. Once he was sure the cop was gone, he removed the wig, changed clothes, and sent a reply to his contact that he'd meet him at noon. Next, he searched listings of local online sales for used trucks. A 2016 F-150 caught his attention. According to the seller, it needed new tires, but the photo showed a nondescript vehicle that would blend into the background in any parking lot. Replacing the tires could wait. He needed transportation now, and this one fit the bill. He offered a hundred dollars over the asking price if the seller could deliver the truck within the hour. Checking his documents one more time, he discarded the ones that were no longer useful. Once he'd found and disposed of the Pearson woman and her children, he intended to become someone else for good. He slipped the thumb drive he'd used to download Lorang's files and history into his laptop and set to work. The old man had done a thorough search for Harlan Clouse and even contacted one of those investigative services. The background Mouse's tech source had installed held up to routine scrutiny, but a deep dive would expose his real past. Good thing Lorang's skills were limited. He examined the driver's license photo and decided that, minus the wig and wearing different clothes, he could pass as Charles Mouse again.

Engrossed in plotting, he almost missed Lorang's email to Storms. *Tony, I changed my mind about this Clouse fellow. I'm going to tell him to leave tonight. So, I'll need a ride to Watertown next Tuesday. Tell Red I'm looking forward to talking football with her and hearing about her kids. Oh, and check out the attachment.* Mouse double-clicked the icon and a photo of the interior of his travel bag popped up, along with all the weapons spread out on the bed and the various passports. Damn! He'd badly misjudged Lorang. What else had he missed? He re-read the email, noting the mention of a woman and her children. Was Red the woman he'd come all this way to find? Had the universe delivered his prey at last?

A rapid-fire knocking brought him to his feet. Glock tucked in his waistband, he peeked out at a squat, muscular man in a red flannel and camo pants clutching the hand of a small boy in a snowsuit. Mouse undid the bolt and greeted the stranger. "Got my truck?"

"That car the one you're trading?" The man hooked his thumb at the compact Mouse had driven from Syracuse.

"It is, and it's yours plus the hundred extra. We good?"

The man barked a cough into his chapped hand and nodded. He reached into a pocket of the vest he wore over the flannel and extracted the title. "Already switched the plates, so, yeah, guess we are."

"Mind if I start her up before we finalize?"

"Be my guest." The seller followed Mouse to the truck, waited as the engine bucked twice before it turned over, then settled into a soft chug. Satisfied, Mouse hopped down, took the paperwork, and handed over the cash. "Keys?"

The seller held out a ring bearing a rabbit's foot and two keys. Mouse dropped his old set into the man's palm and waited until he and the boy left. Then he returned to the room, transferred all the photo equipment into the truck, left the room key on the bed, and headed toward Wanakena. After the meeting with his contact, he'd check out the woman at the Center. If she turned out to be Emma Pearson, he'd finish what he'd started and never look back.

...more clues to stir the pot...

The Center buzzed with the news of Denver Lorang's death. Clients gathered in the lounge, sharing Denver stories as they planned a celebration of the man's life. Despite the disabilities that had confined him to his house, Lorang had many friends. His quick wit and sense of justice appealed to the group. I took care of the drinks while Tony steered them toward a decision regarding the fundraiser that now had a different purpose. Once everyone had a coffee or soda, I settled at the desk to email Gordo. Whether he would return immediately or not, he deserved to know what happened. I kept checking the clock and the entryway, uneasy at the thought of strange faces on the monitor hooked into the brand-new ring camera at the outside door. Tony had installed it after he left the cabin, no explanation required. Patting the gun holstered beneath my fleece jacket, I decided to tidy up the old files on the computer. I caught myself falling into rabbit holes as I scanned the intake forms of older veterans before shifting them into folders labeled with branch of service and specific decades. Most of the men in the 1940s group were no longer alive. Maybe we should plan a special event for Memorial Day weekend, one where we read the names of all the local veterans from the greatest generation. I raised my finger to click into Tony's recent emails when he slipped up behind me.

J.E. Irvin

"Red?" His hand rested on my back, his thumb tracing a pattern against the fleece. A mix of responses flowed through me...surprise, sadness, arousal. I shook off the yearning for more bodily contact and pointed at the screen.

"Did you check your emails?" Before he could answer, I pressed a key, and the list of messages appeared. He reached over and closed the screen. "I'll deal with those later. You ready?"

"But there might be something important in there." I waved at the now non-existent list. He shook his head. "We'll be late if we don't leave now."

"Right. Let me visit the ladies' room. I'll meet you at the van." As I washed my hands, I stared into the mirror, wondering at the shine in my eyes. I tried to blink that away, reminding the image in the glass to trust no man, especially one whose touch awakened sensations I thought I'd lost. Not because I didn't want it, but because I wanted it too much.

An hour later, I slowed the van in front of the Diner. Tony helped the men clamber out, and I held the door as they shuffled inside. Once everyone was seated and had shouted out drink and lunch orders, the conversation drifted back to Denver, his wife Lucilla, deceased seven years ago, and the three kids who had all gone downstate seeking better-paying jobs. Only one had succeeded. The others scraped by with help from their father, which explained the shabby state of Denver's home and the planned fundraiser to help him restore the place. Theo Setter banged his glass of iced tea to get our attention. "No way Denver's death was an accident, and it definitely wasn't suicide. He may have lost his legs, but he never lost his sense of humor or his zest for life."

"I agree," Tom Sinclair said. "The man conducted surveillance ops for twenty years. He had a real instinct for sniffing out secrets. Maybe he found out something he shouldn't have."

"Now, Tom, Denver wasn't a conspiracy nut."

"Yeah, but he watched all those online programs about sleeper cells and infiltration targets. I'm just saying he could have chatted with the wrong people."

"Didn't he have some guy staying with him to help him out?" someone else asked. The men bobbed their heads. "Seems like he oughta be the one in Kellerman's crosshairs."

"Damn right," George Wattine chimed in. "The troopers ought to question that guy hard, find out what he was really doing last night." The conversation raged on even after the meals arrived. I nursed my tomato soup and cream soda and listened to them speculate, my attention flicking to and then away from Tony, seated at the opposite end of the table. He frowned at Tom's suggestion but held his tongue. Another member of the group spoke up.

"One of the EMTs said Lorang wreaked of alcohol."

Wattine cursed again. "No fucking way. Excuse the language, Red, but no f-ing way. After he was hospitalized for pancreatitis last July, Denver swore off booze."

"How do you know that, George?" Tony leaned in to hear more clearly above the clatter in the restaurant.

George scrubbed ketchup off his beard and tossed his napkin down. "Last time I stopped by his house, I commented on all the bottles on the counter. He insisted he was getting rid of them, offered me the vodka and rum."

"Did you take them?" Tony again, intent, focused. He homed in on Wattine's answer.

"I did. Still have them in my trailer. So, no way our friend drank himself to death." Wattine pushed to his feet and grabbed his cane. "Gotta visit the head."

Sadness settled over the table, smothering conversation. I slipped away to pay the bill with the card Tony had given me. These were good men, solid citizens. They were hurting, and I had brought this upon them. I snatched my coat and hurried outside. Leaning against the van, I took great gulps of air, waiting for the panic to subside. I should leave, take the children and go tonight before anyone else got caught in the aftermath of the Gary Pearson affair. *Hah! Good one, Emma.* I swiped at my eyes, the weight of the past heavier than ever. Tony's arm settled around my shoulders, causing me to jump. "Hey, Red," he pressed me against his chest, "breathe. It's not your fault. No one blames you."

"When they learn the whole truth, they will." I wanted to run. Instead, I did as he suggested, inhaling and exhaling until the weight on my chest eased. "If Jesse tells my story, everyone will see what I've done to all of you."

Before he could respond, the door to the diner creaked open, and the men filed out. Tony released me before they reached the van. I stood by to assist those who were ambulatory, then started the engine to warm up the interior while Tony worked the wheelchair ramp. Aside from an occasional comment on the weather, there was little chatter as we delivered the men to their respective homes. Once Tony and I were alone again, he leaned against his door and stared until I acknowledged him with a glance. "What, Storms? You know I'm right."

"No." He tugged on my seat belt, forcing me to lean his way. "You're not right. Didn't you listen to Josh and Jesse last night? You belong to Wanakena now, and we're not letting you go."

"You have no say in my staying or going."

"I don't?" He shifted closer to put a hand on the wheel. "Pull over, Red."

"You may be my boss, but you're not the boss of me."

"Hmm. That sounds like something Riley would say. Pull into that overlook." He exerted pressure on the wheel until I had no choice but to turn and park in the demilune of an observation point. The pond below the rest area was an icy wonderland, the pines surrounding it crusted with snow, the stark branches of deciduous trees rising above the frozen surface like alien monoliths. Tony unhooked his seat belt and scooted even closer. I had nowhere to go. "You act like a deer in the headlights, but I see the steel beneath the surface. You're going to stay here, and together we're going to catch the son of a bitch coming after you."

"Wait. You told me to leave. Multiple times. What changed your mind?" I glared at him, but the heat in his eyes stopped me.

"This." Tony pressed his mouth to mine, ran his tongue over the seam of my lips until, breathless and wanting, I opened for him. My body responded to his invitation, warmth and desire coiling between my legs. My mind teetered on the edge of submission. Yes. No. I rested a hand against his chest, intending to push him away. Instead, my fingers curled into the fabric of his jacket and drew him closer. When the kiss ended, we remained in place, eyes locked, breathing unsteady, until he cupped my head in his capable hands, pulled my hat tighter over the mass of curls threatening to spring free, and rested his forehead on mine. "We learned some important things today, facts I will share with Jesse, Josh, and Trooper Kellerman. You're not alone in this, sweetheart. Kiss me if you agree."

This Tony, somber then playful, sexy then practical, twisted my resolve. I thought back over the lunch discussion and kissed him. "All right. What are you planning to do about it?"

"Call everyone as soon as we get back to the Center. Tonight, after the meeting, the four of us will decide on the next step."

"I can't leave my kids, Tony." I hated how unnerved I sounded, but it was the truth. Tony covered the hand that still clutched his jacket.

"I know, Red. Whatever we decide, the twins are coming with us."

...no honor among the damned...

Mouse angled around the sandwich boards announcing all the offerings in Otto's Abode, then pushed his way into the store. The aroma of brewing coffee and fresh-baked bread assailed him. His stomach growled, reminding him he hadn't eaten since dinner last night with the now-deceased Denver Lorang. A man in the back turned to mark his approach, nodded, and reached into the cooler for a gallon of milk. Mouse recognized Jesse Livetree from his initial stop to ask for directions to Lorang's place. Bad luck that the man was here today. Behind the register, Otto Beamish raised his head. His eyes narrowed for a blink, then widened again. "Welcome back to Otto's Abode. You were with Denver Lorang when he died, right?"

Mouse blinked into the glare of the overhead light and sighed. "I'm sorry I couldn't do more for the man."

Otto pursed his lips. "You're right about that. Well, help yourself to a coffee, and let me know if you need anything. Jesse?"

The mayor strolled past the snacks and canned goods and thumped the milk carton onto the counter. He cocked his head toward Mouse. "Denver was well-respected in these parts. Now that he's gone, I wonder what's keeping you here."

"Man's got to be someplace, and that she-wolf of a state trooper told me to stick around. Man's also got to eat. I heard The Pine Cone serves a good meal."

Jesse crossed his arms. "You heard right, but you're out of luck. Pine Cone's closed until five. Of course, Otto has a selection of sandwiches that can be served hot or cold, so you won't starve."

Alert to their suspicions, Mouse started to back out when the front door banged, jingling the bell mounted above it. A man dressed in camo and heavy military boots stomped in, clumps of snow falling around his feet. His left hand clutched a camera strap, the other a tripod, which he shifted to join the camera. Hawk-nosed and a little over six feet, he cut an imposing figure. Livetree sidled forward. "Don't usually see many of you fellows from Fort Drum up this way in the winter."

The stranger removed his cap, revealing light-colored hair cropped close to his head. His eyes scanned the store, stared at Mouse a moment longer than necessary, and returned to Livetree. "Klaman, Eric. Sergeant. On assignment to the Veteran's Outreach Center. Maybe you heard I was at their meeting Monday?"

Livetree stroked his chin. "Can't say as I did. We've had a bit of a blow to our tight-knit community. One of our vets passed away last night."

Mouse watched the interplay, weighing his options. The sergeant bowed his head. "Sorry to hear that. I'll stop by the Center to offer my help with the funeral arrangements."

"That would be kind of you," Otto said. Klaman turned to Mouse.

"You look familiar. You're Harlan Clouse, aren't you? I read an article about you in *Amateur Photographer* last spring."

"Didn't think anyone read that piece." Mouse dropped his eyes, feigned embarrassment.

Klaman set the camera and tripod on the counter and replaced his cap. "Just came in to warm up. Thought I'd take a few shots of the bridge while the river's frozen. I understand the original structure got swept away in an ice flow some years ago."

Otto and Jesse exchanged glances. "You'd be right," Jesse said. "Quite a disaster, but we worked together to restore it. Coffee?" He held out a mug, which Klaman accepted, then ignored.

"Say, Clouse, would you mind showing me how you got those photos with the blurred backgrounds? I'm having some trouble finding the right settings."

"Guess I could do that." Mouse gulped his coffee, set the mug down, and slid two one-dollar bills toward Otto. Klaman retrieved his equipment, and the men left the store. As soon as they were out of earshot, Mouse confronted the soldier. "The boss send you to monitor me?"

Klaman lowered the camera and rested it in the crook of his arm. "You've got it all wrong, Mouse. I'm here to help you clean up this mess. The murder of the vet last night was sloppy, a complication we didn't need. Your control is slipping, and so is the boss's patience. Now, you and I have forty-eight hours to finish this."

"Or what?" Mouse pointed into the distance like he was giving instructions.

Klaman speared him with a predatory glare. "Do you need me to spell it out?"

Mouse gazed at the frozen river. He didn't know whether to believe the guy, but he was stuck with him. He decided to start with an apology. "I had no choice, believe me."

"There's always a choice. Did anyone see you at the dead guy's house?"

"Not the night before. But the cops did last night. No surprise there. They knew Lorang had hired someone to help him."

"Any way this can come back on you?"

"You're seriously questioning my skills?"

Klaman raised an eyebrow. "How sure are you?"

"One hundred percent."

"Good." Klaman raised the camera to pan the suspension bridge and the hill across the river. "Because I'm in charge now, and I'm one hundred percent certain that your life and the lives of your sister and her brats depend upon getting this job done and disappearing."

"I'm not the one who screwed up here."

"No?"

Mouse reached for the camera in case someone was watching and adjusted the focus. "The big boss is the one who trusted Gary Pearson, who gave him access to the accounts, which the man stole and copied. So, don't threaten me, asshole."

Klaman snatched the camera back, scowling. "Do your job, Mouse, or I'll do it for you and earn the rewards." Waving over his shoulder, he kicked a path toward the bridge and never looked back.

Mouse shoved his hands in his pockets and imagined several scenarios, all of which ended with Klaman, bloody and unbreathing, buried in the snow deep in the Adirondack wilderness. He retraced his steps to Otto's Abode, passing a young man in a deerslayer hat scuffing his way toward the frozen river. He recognized David Yang from the online meeting last evening. The troubled ex-soldier was frowning and mumbling to himself. Mouse changed direction to intercept the disturbed vet before he reached the dock, a new plan forming as he stalked Yang.

...a message from the spirit world...

Outside the door of the Center, a growing pile of flowers and tokens of friendship in Denver Lorang's name partially blocked the entrance, reminding me of the reality I faced. A man was dead because I'd come to the wilderness. Tony read the sorrow on my face and hugged me. "Let them express their grief right now," he said. "We'll clean this up tomorrow."

I followed him into the office, adjusted the temp to a more comfortable range, and tended to the blinking red light indicating voice mails. Most were condolences and offers of help. I noted each caller's name and number and promised myself to send personal notes later in the week. Then I pulled up the email screen. Tony still hadn't checked his account. I gnawed my thumbnail for a minute, debating the etiquette of invading personal message space, then hunching forward, whispered, "Fuck it," and entered his password. We could fight about it later.

The inbox was full of the same type of messages as the voicemail: friends and acquaintances wanting to share Denver stories, to rail against a society that would allow a man who had served his country to die of hypothermia, and to hint at conspiracy theories and secret vendettas. I added each to my list. We were going to need more stamps. On the third page, I noticed a shift in the time and the date, and then there it was, Denver's message to Tony.

Storms, I changed my mind about this Clouse fellow. I'm going to tell him to leave tonight. So, I'll need a ride to Watertown next Tuesday. Tell Red I'm looking forward to talking football with her and hearing about her kids. Oh, and check out the attachment. I clicked the icon. A photo of the interior of Clouse's travel bag popped up, along with a collection of weapons spread out on the bed beside a clutch of passports. Afraid I'd lose the email if I closed it, I gave the command to print. While the message spooled out, I sprinted through the lounge. Tony's door was open. He stood by the window, phone in hand, staring into the growing darkness. When he saw my face, he bolted over, grabbed my elbows, and ordered me to breathe. Again. I wriggled free, took his hand, and dragged him from the room.

"I told you to check your email."

He scowled. "And I'm going to."

"Too late. I already did." I shoved him into my chair and tapped the computer screen. "It's from Denver, Tony. He sent it before he died."

Tony read the note, opened the attachment, then scrolled through everything again. He scrubbed his face, ran a hand through his hair, and rose. "Did you make a copy?"

I snatched the printed materials and handed them over. "This Clouse, he has to be the one chasing me."

"I'm afraid I agree with you." He held up his phone and shared the pictures Jesse sent of Harlan Clouse and Eric Klaman outside Otto's that morning.

"Close everything down, Red. We're leaving now. Go home. I'll follow to make sure you get there safely, then talk to Jesse and Josh." He waved Denver's email and the pictures at me. "Tonight, when everyone's together, we'll set our plan in motion."

...a meeting of the minds and a shot in the dark...

Two tall pines stood by the road, guarding the approach to the restored dwelling now designated the Wanakena History Center. I stopped to admire the sign fronting the sidewalk and read the inscription to the twins. *The 1821 Rich Lumber Company home.* Once, it housed a family. Now it was officially a museum. The front porch ran the width of the building, a graceful entry point into the two-story structure now containing exhibits and artifacts from the hamlet's rich past. The twins tugged at my gloved hands, kicking at the snow piles along the sidewalk. Evan glanced over his shoulder repeatedly, checking to see if Stormy was still behind us. My cheeks warmed at the memory of his kiss in the van when the children weren't looking.

The interior of the Museum was crowded. Many locals who had contributed to the restoration had come out to inspect the displays gracing the walls. I found myself drawn to the timeline of the area but managed to read only three of the placards before Mollie insisted on pulling me toward a corner that had been set up, probably under Asa Cleary's competent direction, to entertain children who had accompanied their parents. The twins discarded their winter coats to plop down and work on crafting birdhouses using the materials spread out across a painter's drop cloth. Tony stepped up behind me.

"They'll be fine, Red. Jesse's waiting." He led the way upstairs to the front bedroom now serving as a meeting space for the evening. Amazed at the turnout, I edged my way around a couple who, turning, smiled like they knew me. The woman gathered me into a hug. "Amy Dugas," she whispered. "My husband's Ron. We own the Lodge, and we feel like we've known you almost as long as Riley. She told us all about her best friend."

I hugged her back, a reflex strengthened by the knowledge that this was the Amy Dugas, Carl's neighbor and Josh's cousin, who had stepped into the void left by my absence in Riley's life. She had been the one to provide support when Riley needed it the most. I swallowed a brief, bitter stab of jealousy. I was glad my friend had found this woman, and I told her so. Amy hugged me again, then let go, but not before she noticed Tony's hand on my back.

"Emma, you've already met Ron, and I understand that you now work for Wanakena's resident grump, the most overprotective male in the entire hamlet, maybe even the whole county." She winked. "You're in good hands."

I peeked at Tony, who scowled and looked away, unable to hide his grin at the compliment. In the middle of the scrum of residents, Jesse Livetree raised a hand and ordered us all to stop jawing and pay attention. Josh and two other men dressed in Ranger uniforms flanked the mayor.

"Good to see so many of you out and about this brisk winter night."

"Nothing better to do," a woman chirped.

"Well, hold your knickers, Gwen, because, by the time this meeting is through, you'll have a whole lot to do. Now, I want to introduce you to our newest resident and tell you why we need to protect this young woman and her children from some bad dudes from the outside world."

"Dudes?" The crowd howled. A young woman wearing oversized, black-rimmed glasses and carrying a steno pad shoved through the circle to confront the mayor. "I've never heard you use that word, Mayor Livetree. Care to comment for the record?"

Livetree took the young woman by the elbow and shook her gently. "Mariah, I thought you had a Chamber of Commerce meeting in Watertown tonight. What are you doing here?"

"I'm Wanakenan, same as you, Uncle Jesse, and I have every right to be here."

Jesse narrowed his eyes. "Don't be sassy, Mariah. Are you here as a journalist or as a concerned citizen?"

"Does it matter?" She looked at him over the rim of her glasses. Livetree pulled her closer. "It does, young lady, so you need to promise not to print anything until I okay it. Lives depend on it."

Mariah Kimby frowned. Carl scowled at the young woman. "Your granduncle's right, Mariah. Now, hush and let him speak."

Gesturing for me to stand by him, Jesse introduced me to a round of welcome greetings and nods. Then, without revealing all the details, the mayor summarized the story of my husband's murder, emphasizing the very likely possibility, based on evidence he couldn't get into, that the killer or killers had followed me to Wanakena. That provoked a ten-minute outcry, followed by colorful curses and an oath to teach the outsiders a lesson. Jesse waited for the outrage to subside.

"Do you have a plan?" Ron Dugas posed the question in the silence that followed.

"We do." Jesse motioned to Josh, his Ranger colleagues, and Tony. "The most important thing right now is to initiate our watch program. Josh?"

Waylon stepped to the front and held up a handful of flyers. "Thanks to Tony's recording of the last meeting at the Vet Center, Carl's photography skills, and my phone app, we have snapshots of at least three strangers who recently arrived in the vicinity. They may be asking questions. Under no circumstances should you confront them. If they inquire about a woman with two small children, do not tell them anything about Emma or the twins."

"In other words," Gwen piped up, "you want us to play dumb."

"As rocks," Carl said. The room crackled with laughter, then quickly sobered up again. Ron Dugas spoke next.

"How dangerous are these men?"

Josh rubbed his chin. "Enough for me to send Riley and my kids away. Probably not as dangerous for those of you who have no connection to Emma, but do not take any chances."

"I know you, Ranger Waylon. There's always more going on. What aren't you telling us?"

Josh grinned. "You're right, Mariah. There is more to the plan, and I'm not telling you or the rest of you any more than you need to know."

Kimby crossed her arms and pouted. "This is probably the biggest story of my career, and you want me to keep it a secret?"

Jesse placed a hand on her shoulder. "Mariah, a man, a woman, and a baby were slaughtered by unknown killers who may be here to do the same thing to Emma and her children. Do you want to be responsible for that happening?"

Mariah began to speak when a sharp crack echoed from the yard. Someone screamed. The men looked at each other, then ordered everyone down. As the crowd scrambled to the floor, Tony covered my body with his own. I twisted to look at him. "Was that a gunshot?"

"Kill the lights!" Josh called out as he and the two Rangers ran toward the stairs. I struggled to lift my head.

"Stay down, Red."

I pushed against him. "Please, Tony. I have to get the twins."

Leaning his weight on his hands, he continued to hover over me. When I stopped wiggling, he settled beside me and cradled a hand on my cheek. "They're all right. Mrs. Cleary would call out if anyone were hurt."

"What if Asa's injured? She might have been shot." I forced down the panic. "I need to check on them."

"They'll be all right." Tony's words were fierce, his voice a low growl. "They have to be."

"What if—?" I couldn't find the words to finish the statement. He shook his head.

"If anything happens to them, I'll burn down the forest to find who hurt them, and then I'll hurt them back."

Josh called out from his perch halfway down the stairs, "Mrs. Cleary, is everyone okay?"

Her voice wavered but carried to all of us lying on the floor. "We're all good, Ranger Waylon. Just a little scared."

"Stay together and stay down." Josh whistled softly. I heard his boots shuffle the rest of the way down and cross to the front of the house. A second set lumbered after him while the third Ranger moved toward the back. "Storms?"

"Here." Tony tugged me closer. I felt the vibration of his chest against my back as he spoke.

"You good to cover inside?" Josh whispered. He waited for Tony's affirmative, then added, "You armed?"

Tony relaxed his hold to tug free the gun holstered at his waist. "I am." When Josh heard that, he must have low-crawled from the front room to the double entry doors, the rasp of his clothing my only clue to his movements.

"Tony? With all the lights off and all the cloud cover, how will he see if anyone's out there?"

"Don't underestimate Waylon," Tony said, tugging me toward the window that overlooked the front of the property. We got to our knees and looked out. A faint wail from Route 3 announced the pending arrival of a trooper. "Josh won't wait for Kellerman. If someone's out there with a gun, he'll neutralize the threat."

"Neutralize?" I shivered. Josh's next word filtered up from the front of the house.

"Kent?"

The ranger accompanying him answered, "Ready."

"Tony?" Josh returned to the foot of the stairs. "We'll circle around, look for boot prints, snowshoe tracks, cartridge casings. You cover us. And, Storms, don't hesitate if it looks like the shooter is on the move."

"I hear you." Tony motioned for me to stay down. I shook my head, reached under my fleece, and unstrapped the holster.

"I can help." After a moment of hesitation, he pointed me toward the side window. I unsnapped the latch and shoved it upward. From that vantage point, I waited as Josh and Kent sprinted through the doors, kicking them shut as they exited. Vaulting the porch railing, they floundered through the drifts, heads panning the road in anticipation of an ambush. Josh turned down Second Street. He'd gone about five yards when a figure appeared out of the dark, slogging along the roadway. The Ranger whistled, alerting Kent to the intruder's location. Tony tapped my shoulder.

"Let's go, Red." We crawled around the prone bodies and slipped downstairs. The twins rushed to hug me. I returned their embrace, then set them firmly back in Asa's arms.

"Mommy has to help Josh and Tony catch a bad man," I said. "I'll be right back."

Gloveless and shaking, I followed Tony into the night. We were halfway to Josh when the shooter turned to look back. Tony ordered me down, then crouched and yelled, "Gun!"

I lifted my head enough to spot the outline of a long-barreled weapon rising above the man's shoulders.

"Stop!" Josh ordered. "Put the gun down and raise your hands."

The stranger lifted both hands, one still clutching his weapon. Tires crunched over the snowpack behind us. Blue and red lights strobed the darkness.

"There was a man on the roof." His voice, timid and trembling, carried in the frigid air. "I tried to scare him away before he hurt the children."

Ranger Kent approached the shooter from behind and remained in place, gun steady, finger not yet on the trigger. The stranger appeared distraught. What did he mean by a man on the roof? The Rangers and the shooter remained locked in place until Trooper Kellerman brought the patrol car to a halt and, service weapon drawn, got out of the vehicle. She sized up the situation, then directed her attention to the guy in camo gear still holding a hunting rifle above his head. "Sir, put the gun down and tell me who you are."

"They told me he would hurt the children." The stranger dropped the rifle at his feet and resumed standing with his hands in the air. Kellerman motioned for the Rangers to close in with her. While Kent cuffed him, Trooper Kellerman removed the man's ski hat and balaclava. Josh inspected the stranger's face. Before he could ask the man's name, Tony moved up behind him, placed a hand on the shooter's shoulder, and shook his head.

"Yang," he said, "what the hell are you doing here?"

...while the good guys debate...

Mouse flung open the door to The Pine Cone and looked around the small restaurant. Wooden booths arranged back-to-back filled the interior. A counter and stools ran along the rear wall below a window overlooking an expanse of yard that sloped down to Cranberry Lake. Strings of outdoor lights illuminated the wintry landscape. Several young students from the Ranger School up the road huddled over beers and textbooks. A man in a food-stained Henley and jeans, towel tucked at his waist, looked up from the bar and nodded. Before Mouse could ask if the man had seen his cousin, Klaman called a greeting. Mouse approached the booth closest to the back door and slid in across from his new associate. "I got your message."

"And I got yours. The distraction work?"

Mouse nodded, then turned to the bartender, who had sidled over unannounced. He ordered a local beer and waited for the man to leave before responding. "Kid's the perfect foil. They'll be tied up all night sorting out his story. You check out Lorang's place?"

Klaman rapped his knuckles on the table. "Crime scene tape everywhere. Laptop's gone. No prints where they shouldn't be. You did a thorough job. Still, they know you were there. You need to lie low, finish the job, and get long gone."

"I will, and when I do, we're done, too." Mouse splayed his palms over the table, ignoring the urge to reach across and rip out the man's throat.

"Did you locate the woman?"

The barkeep set a tall glass in front of Mouse and cocked his head. "We close in an hour. You need anything else, you let me know in the next thirty minutes, okay?"

Mouse laid a ten on the table and shook his head. "All we need is some privacy."

Micah raised his hands and backed away, but he held Mouse's gaze the entire time. Klaman was right. Time to get out before the locals turned feral and came at them in a pack. The owner retreated behind the bar and into his phone. Reaching into his jacket, Mouse pulled out a copy of a job application and laid it in front of Klaman. "Found this tonight at the Vet Center in a file labeled E. Evans. No photo, and the last name's different, but all the info lines up. Emma Pearson and her kids are here in Wanakena."

Klaman sipped his beer. "Where's she living?"

"Cabin down Reed Road. Sits behind a larger one."

"What's your plan?"

"Go in while everyone's tied up at the Museum. Locate the missing data files, then wait for her to come home. I'll make it look like a murder-suicide. After that, you can give me my discharge papers and go back to KC. I intend to melt like snowflakes into the night."

"You really want out?" Klaman waited for Mouse's confirmation, drummed the table, and scowled. "Any possible additional complications?"

Mouse rubbed his chin, then helped himself to a large swallow of beer. "That guy running the center, Anton Storms? He's ex-FBI, and I think he has a hard-on for the lady."

"I met him at the Center. Will he cause trouble?"

"If he does, I'll take him out, too."

"Best get to it, then." Klaman finished his drink, skimmed his mouth with a thumb, and shrugged into his coat.

"You sticking around?"

"Until I'm certain I'm not needed." Klaman cracked his knuckles, then reached out, quick as lightning, to grab Mouse by the wrist. "I'll be waiting at the hotel in Cranberry. Finish this tonight, you hear?"

Mouse growled a warning. Klaman relaxed his grip. He pointed his chin toward the exit. "Just making a point, Mouse."

"Point taken." Holding Klaman's gaze, Mouse zipped his jacket, settled a ski cap over his shaved head, and pulled on gloves. As he wound his way to the exit, he reviewed the list of all the items he'd need tonight, then added one more, an extra round for this guy, right through the man's fucking head. Aware of Klaman's eyes on his back, Mouse refused to turn around, instead checking out the shelves bearing homemade jams and syrups. The moment he stepped into the cold, a state trooper pulled in off Ranger School Road.

...are you the hunter or the hunted?...

David Yang, hands zip-tied and resting on his knees, huddled into himself, a deer frozen in place by the spotlight aimed at his head. The citizens of Wanakena filed by, scrutinizing the young man as they passed. The Rangers kept the crowd moving, escorting those who requested it to a vehicle or toward their homes, murmuring reassurances that there was no one else out there. I wasn't so sure. Yang appeared troubled, and he was obviously hiding something, but he didn't exude any true killer vibes. I shrugged off the derisive snort that accompanied that thought. How would I know what vibes a killer gave off? Carl offered to take the kids and bed them down for the night with their moosies and a happy story to erase the bad memories from the evening's scare. Although torn by the thought of being separated from them yet again, I decided I had no choice but to be present while Kellerman questioned the shooter. Once the Museum was empty of all but the Rangers, Livetree, Storms, Kellerman, and me, I listened in on their discussion of the best way to begin the interrogation. They had almost reached a decision when the trooper's phone pinged. Kellerman read the message, then pursed her lips.

"Seems your Wanakena pipeline is working as promised. Micah says the two strangers who showed up at Otto's are sitting in a booth at The Pine Cone, acting, he writes, like they have something to hide. I'd best check that out. Josh, are you, Jesse, and Storms good to watch Yang while I'm gone?"

Josh answered in the affirmative. So did Tony and Jesse. The other Rangers checked the yard for stragglers, conferred with Josh, and left. The slightly built, trembling Yang wasn't a physical threat to the bigger, stronger males. Once the Museum doors were secured, Tony sat in a chair across from the suspect and rested his elbows on his knees. "David, I realize this has been an upsetting evening for you, but we need you to be honest with us. Can you do that?"

Yang peeked at me, then burrowed into the collar of his coat. "I only did what he told me to do. I protected the children from the monster on the roof."

"Who is he?" Tony asked. "David? Is he someone you know?"

"He's a vet, too. He knows what it was like over there. How they hide in the shadows and shoot at us. He said they were after her." Yang lifted his chin in my direction. I sidled closer to Josh but kept my focus on the disturbed man.

"David," I said, "who's after me?"

"A monster wants to kill you and steal your children, Clouse said—" Yang's eyes widened. He pressed his tied hands to his lips. Tony flinched.

"Harlan Clouse? Is that the name of the man who told you to shoot at the Museum?"

"He made me promise not to tell." Yang twisted his ear between his manacled hands. "I think he lied to me. Because there wasn't a monster on the roof, was there?"

Tony and I shared a look. Josh caught it and cocked his head at me. "You know who he's talking about?"

I nodded. "One of the new vets who registered this week. I didn't meet him. Tony did his intake interview."

"So, you don't know him."

"I've seen his picture." I faced Yang. "Sounds like David's met him."

Josh stared at Tony. "Why the look, Storms?"

Tony kicked back the chair to pace the floor. "Harlan Clouse is the guy who offered to serve as Denver Lorang's caregiver. He claimed to be an Army veteran, had the paperwork to support his story. But Denver found a cache of weapons and fake IDs in his room and sent me photos the night he died. And Jesse saw Clouse at Otto's earlier today with the soldier from Fort Drum."

"Show me." Josh waited for Tony to pull up the email from Denver Lorang, then took the phone. While he read, the house museum settled into night, furnace chittering, fan whirring, old floorboards emitting the occasional crack as they slumbered. I studied Yang, how his posture slumped, but his eyes, clear and alert, flicked rapidly from Josh to Tony to me. Unnerved by his stare, I wandered into the kitchen area and dialed Carl. When she answered, I sighed with relief. "How are the twins?"

Ms. Beamish sniffed. "Finishing their hot chocolate and ready for bed. Do you want to speak with them?'

"Yes. Please. And Ms. Beamish—"

"Now you listen careful, Miss Emma," Carl said. "No harm will come to your cubs in my house. I'll defend them with my life. You do what you have to do to end this thing. Understand?"

I tried to speak, swallowed hard, and leaned against the wall. "I don't deserve you, Carl."

"Course you do. You're a fighter, Red, just like me. Here's Mollie bear."

I listened to my daughter, then my son recount their moosie adventures with Auntie Carl, assured them I'd see them soon, and reminded them to remember their manners. When the call ended, I rubbed my knuckles into my eyes, willing myself to stay strong for the children. The rasp of a boot over the floor caused me to look up. Tony stood in the doorway, frown in place but a hint of softness at the corners of his mouth. "Ms. Beamish will take good care of them," he said.

"That's my job." I squared my shoulders. "And I'm not doing it very well."

Tony moved closer, hands clenched. "Ready to go back to your place?"

"We can't do anything more here, can we?"

"I doubt it. Josh will take care of Yang until Kellerman returns." He eased me into his arms. "And I'll take care of you."

I tried to wriggle free, but he wouldn't release me. "I'm not a damsel in distress, Anton."

"No, you're our Red, and nobody messes with our girl."

"Who's our?" I fiddled with the collar of his shirt, comforted and aroused by the feel of his muscular body next to mine.

"The guys at the Center. The people of Wanakena." He tilted my chin to meet his gaze. "Me."

"You?" I weighed the look he was giving me against the things he'd said when I first arrived. "I don't—"

"You don't have to understand, Red, because I can't explain it either, but, damn, I can't stay away from you, and I can't resist the urge to kiss you."

I looked past him, aware of the men in the other room, but it didn't matter. Something was happening to my heart. The walls I'd built were crumbling under the need to feel desired. "You'd better do it, Storms, before someone comes in, or I lose my nerve."

The dimple in his chin appeared as he leaned closer. "What nerve is that, Emma?"

"The one that says I want to kiss you, too." I rose on my toes, our mouths meeting in a soft caress that morphed into a demand for more. I pushed away every warning and allowed myself to breathe him in. Tony kissed me with a hunger that matched my own, his tongue exploring, sucking and teasing, and sending messages to my breasts and between my thighs. I always loved sex, always found pleasure in the physical act coupled with what, for me, had been love. It was thrilling and terrifying to realize it was happening again. I didn't just need Tony Storms. I wanted him. The front door banged open. We sprang apart.

"Emma." He spoke my name like a caress against my cheek. "To be continued."

I staggered when he stepped away, caught the counter to steady myself. Tony wrapped an arm around my waist. Trooper Kellerman's greeting echoed from the front room. I started toward the footsteps scraping across floorboards, then paused. An unknown voice, one cold as the icicles lining the eaves of the Museum, rose above the roar of the furnace. "Why am I here, officer?"

"A formality, Sergeant Klaman. I want to see if any of these fine folks recognize you."

I peeked around the corner and drew back. Tony, at my shoulder, raised his brows. He put a finger to my lips, then peered into the room, pulling back as soon as he, too, recognized the soldier from the meeting at the Vet Center. What was Klaman doing here? The soldier's phone vibrated. He checked the screen and returned it to his pocket, a satisfied look gliding across his face. Yang continued his restless scan of the Museum but showed no sign of recognizing the stranger. Josh nodded at Kellerman's unspoken question. Easing past me, Tony joined the gathering. "Sergeant Klaman?" he said.

Trooper Kellerman hooked her thumbs in her belt. "So, Storms, you know this Sergeant Eric Klaman, out of Fort Drum."

"I do. He's been assigned as liaison to our Center."

Kellerman pursed her lips. "Funny. To my knowledge, there's no veterans group meeting tonight, right? And the soldiers from Drum rarely venture our way."

Klaman shrugged. "I had the day off and thought I'd scout the area. Met Mr. Livetree at the store this morning."

"That you did." Jesse folded his arms. "Said you were into photography. Asked that other man, Clouse, to help you with settings."

"You have a good memory, sir. I like the remoteness of this area. I'm thinking about settling here when my enlistment is up. Storms can vouch for me."

"All in good time, Sergeant Klaman," Kellerman interjected. "First, you and Mr. Yang are going to accompany me to Governeur. We're going to chat about relocating to Wanakena and Clifton in the middle of winter and other anomalies. Josh?"

"Tony and I will close up here," the Ranger said. "I'll bring Yang with me. Jesse, Tony, we'll talk tomorrow."

I remained hidden, observing the group as they headed for the door. Yang seemed resigned while Klaman inspected the room, his eyes lighting on my coat lying on top of Tony's parka. I had no reason except intuition to fear this man, yet I did. When he looked over his shoulder, I hunkered deeper into the shadows, afraid he could see me through the wall.

...one step too far...

The hamlet slumbered beneath its snowy blanket as Josh led Yang away. Tony and I followed until we reached his truck. I climbed in and stared out the window, the passage along River Street reminding me of fairy tale scenarios. I imagined myself a modern-day Red Riding Hood, lost and alone and pursued by shadow assassins hidden beneath the snow-covered limbs of the pines. Once predictable and tame, my life had devolved into a noir fable, where bogeymen stalked me in the night, and the secret my husband died to protect wove a noose around my neck. I kept my eyes on Tony and allowed myself to savor our kiss at the Museum and the one we'd shared in the van. Why did the man who warned me away now want to keep me close? How much could I trust him? He had his own demons to confront. How could he ever deal with mine? He turned down Reed and we cruised past the Lodge where the Dugas family lived. Their biggest concern? Filling the rooms of their establishment and containing the antics of their three children. I thought about Riley, nursing her newborn daughter while her boys slept and her husband spent his night escorting me from one disaster to another. I peered into the treelined dark, blinked hard, and grabbed Tony's arm. "Stop! Someone's been walking along the side of Carl's cabin. The drifts are all disturbed."

Tony cut the lights and the engine, then dialed Josh's number. When the Ranger answered, Storms barked one word, "Intruder."

"Is he coming back?" My whisper sounded loud in the enclosed cab. Tony shrugged. We sat in the dark, watching and waiting. Fifteen minutes passed. Suddenly, a snowmobile exploded from under the trees to the left of Tony's truck, scraped the side panel, and circled back. "Emma, down!" Tony wrenched his seat belt free and threw himself at me, smashing my head into the side door with one hand as he pressed us both below the dash. A bullet ripped through the driver's side mirror. A second shot slammed into the rear bumper and ricocheted into the snow. The Sno-Cat kept coming at us. A third shot glanced off the roof. Then the snowmobile tore off down the road, its runners banging over the steel bridge as it raced toward Route 3.

"Red?" Tony's hand brushed my cheek, slid under the ski cap to cradle my head. "You all right?"

"Yes. You?" I thought my voice would shake, but it came out calm and measured, the voice of a teacher trained to minimize her fear to ease that of others. A gloved hand banged on the passenger side window. Lights flared on in the Lodge and in Carl's cabin. Ron Dugas peered in at us, hunting rifle in hand. Carl stood on her stoop, down coat over flannel pajamas, her weapon aimed toward the truck.

"All good," Tony murmured. Ron blinked into headlights as Josh pulled up behind us.

The Ranger yanked open Tony's door and leaned in. "Anybody hurt?"

Tony assured him we were unharmed, and we all trudged back to the Beamish cabin. It took an hour to update everyone on recent developments. Josh contacted Kellerman, who had released Eric Klaman but sent Yang to Star Lake for observation by the psychiatrist in residence. Carl, with apparent reluctance, called Livetree. When Jesse arrived, he avoided eye contact with her and moved to stand by the fire. I was dying to ask why they were avoiding each other but now wasn't the time. Instead, I tiptoed in to check on the twins. I snugged the covers over their sleeping forms and positioned their stuffed animals between them before rejoining the group I had unofficially dubbed the Wild Gang. After dissecting the evening and the new information gleaned tonight, Josh rested his elbows on his knees and chewed his lip.

"Thoughts?" Jesse tapped the Ranger's shoulder.

"Time for Plan B, isn't it?" Josh looked at each of us. "You all have a say, but only Emma's counts."

...a predator in the night...

Mouse ignored the tingling in his fingers and the tips of his ears, shook off the ice crystals that blew into his face as the snowmobile roared out of Wanakena. He only had minutes to hide the Cat, and Klaman hadn't responded to his text. The runners glided over patches of hard-packed snow, shuddered against the exposed roadway, and blasted onto the thin strip of berm. Three miles...he had to go that far to reach his car, ditch the machine, and disappear into the night. He'd moved his gear from The Traveler's to the Hampton in Potsdam, not too close to Fine and uninterested in strangers with hotel membership cards checking in at odd hours. He didn't intend to stay there long. As soon as Klaman joined him, they'd resume the hunt. Too bad he'd failed tonight, but now he knew where she was. He patted the pocket where he'd stashed the only proof he needed, a photo of Gary Pearson's red-headed wife, the one the man had betrayed for the woman in Kansas City. Emma Pearson grinned into the camera, unaware of the chaos her husband's actions would bring down on her and their offspring. Mouse ignored the twinge of guilt beneath his ribcage. He couldn't afford sentimentality at this stage of his career. Besides, if he took care of the Pearson woman and Klaman, he saw a new path emerge, a way to take over the entire KC operation. It hadn't been on the drawing board earlier, but, damn, opportunity had come calling, and he was opening the door.

Off to his right, something wailed and went silent. Mouse checked behind him, buried the bottom half of his face in the collar of his coat, and swerved to avoid a chunk of ice that had dropped from someone's bumper. Another predator howled, closer than the first, followed by a rustling. From the corner of his eye, he spotted a plume of snow spraying upward. He skidded right, aiming the headlight toward the disturbance. A dark shadow emerged from the forest and paused, growling, the wolf's bright stare reflecting yellow in the beam of the snowmobile. Two more from the pack slunk out to join the first. Mouse swerved again and gunned the engine, searching from side to side for the rental car. He didn't look back to see if the wolves had followed him, although he imagined their powerful bodies bounding his way, their long strides covering the distance in swift, purposeful moves. Safety was a fantasy this night. The holstered Glock bumped against his hip. He spared a hand to loosen the strap. Wolves might be a protected species, but he didn't care. Survival dictated the rules, not the government.

No more growls behind him, but Mouse sensed their approach. He zigzagged down the road, grateful for the lack of traffic. At last, the light from the snowmobile reflected off the truck's fender. Mouse cut the engine of the Sno-Cat, steered toward the ditch along the highway, and jumped right before the snowmobile leaped forward to tumble down the side of the drainage ditch and bury itself in the snow. Just like Denver Lorang. He snorted at the thought and reached for his gun. Yanking at the driver's side handle, he slid onto the seat, slammed the door, and inserted the key. The truck coughed, stuttered, and died. He pounded the steering wheel, then tried again. This time the engine caught. He switched on the headlights to stare into the lowered jaws and intense stares of the pack that had pursued him. Releasing the brake, he jerked the car forward. The wolves scattered, howling as they ran. Mouse pulled out and headed toward Potsdam.

* * *

Fury rose like the tide as Eric Klaman exited the cruiser and slipped into his Jeep. Frost lay thick on the windows, forcing him to sit, stewing, while the defrosters went to work. He re-read the texts from Mouse, unhappy with the hitman's slow progress. He scrolled through the messages one more time, hoping to find something encouraging.

The Pearson woman and her two brats should have been an easy catch. Instead, she had eluded the FBI and the most experienced assassin the mob employed, forcing Klaman to come himself into this God-forsaken wilderness and pretend to be a Fort Drum soldier, only to freeze his balls off and be interrogated by a state trooper with a chip on her shoulder for outsiders. And, last but not the least of his indignities, he'd been forced to intimidate that son-of-a-bitch Charles Mouse into doing his God-damn job. It was only a matter of hours until the Ranger and that Trooper discovered that the real Sergeant Klaman had failed to report for duty three days ago. It would be months, if ever, before they found the man who now lay buried under five feet of snow somewhere outside of Watertown.

The wipers removed the last of the ice, and Klaman eased onto Ranger School Road. This woman had cost him. When he found her, there would be hell to pay.

... into the wilderness...

I held the future in my hands. My pulse beat in time to the challenge my friends had issued. Whatever they did next was up to me. But to take that next step, to set the plan in motion, I had to leave the children behind. My heart ached at the thought. If something happened to me, Mollie and Evan would have no one. The risk had grown greater than I could have imagined for the twins and me and all the people who had befriended me. Carl sat and rested an arm over my shoulders.

"Emma, you don't have to decide tonight, and you don't have to do this alone." Carl looked around the room, her eyes soft until they landed on Jesse. She glared at him, then resumed patting my shoulder. "Are you ready to check out your cabin? See if anything's missing? That may help you decide."

Josh slapped his hands together and rose. "Good idea, Ms. Beamish. I informed Trooper Kellerman about what happened, but she's still tied up with Yang and that Klaman fellow. Meanwhile, Ron and I will look around the property to see if our guy left anything behind that might help identify him. Tony, you and Emma go to the cabin. See if you can figure out what he was doing there."

The men recovered their coats and slipped into their boots. Ron hesitated. "I don't want to leave Amy and the kids alone. I'll go home and watch the road in case the intruder returns."

With a plan in place for the immediate future, I hugged Carl, then followed Tony down the path to the cabin, the sense of violation and outrage making me shake. The main door had been jimmied. Puddles of melted snow dotted the kitchen floor and led through the living room area and down the hall. Tony insisted on going in first, gun in hand. He inspected each room, keeping me behind him. When he was certain we were alone, he released the breath he'd been holding.

"Check out the rooms, Red. See if anything's missing." He ran a hand over the door frames before doing the same to the lamps in the living room.

"What are you doing?"

"Checking for bugs, the listening kind."

I started the search in the children's bedroom. Everything had been upended, the beds stripped, pillows tossed, but nothing appeared damaged or missing. I was glad the twins weren't here to see the mess left behind. My room was another story. The invader had removed every piece of clothing and examined each one before tossing it aside. Our suitcases lay open, the linings sliced and ripped free. The gun case had been pulled from under the bed. Dented by a heavy shoe or boot, it lay discarded on the floor. Our photo albums were strewn across the bed. I gasped when I realized which pictures were missing. Hearing my cry, Tony returned to the bedroom. "Tell me."

"Pictures of me with my husband, of us with the children. They're all gone. The bastard is trying to find us."

Tony scratched his chin. "Don't panic, Red. You already knew that was his intent. What's that?" He kicked at a small black rectangular object partially hidden beneath the bed.

I picked it up, juggled it from hand to hand. "It's an old recording device I used in my classroom to capture children reading from their favorite books to share with parents at conferences, to show how their kids were improving. I don't even remember the last time I used it, but Gary took it with him a few times, to record his speaking sessions, he said."

"Have you listened to it recently?"

When I shook my head, Tony took it from me. He loosened the Velcro fastener on the case and slid the tiny device onto his palm. He pushed play. The recorder hummed, followed by the sound of a child reciting a line from "Winnie the Pooh." We listened through five more readings until there was a pause, and then a man began to speak. My eyes widened at the shock of my husband's voice coming from the tiny amplifier.

"This is Gary Pearson..." The next words were muffled. I heard another name, followed by a baby crying and a woman pleading, her words faint but clear. "Don't do it, Gar." My husband kept talking. I didn't understand most of what he said until the last words. "The information about the bank accounts is on the thumb drives."

My memory skipped back to the talk I'd had with Riley, to the handful of drives I'd found and discounted. "Tony? Is that what I think it is?"

"Your husband's last attempt to do his job? Yes, and the reason the mob is after you."

I closed my hand over the recorder. "What should we do?"

"This won't excuse or erase what your husband did to you, Red, but if we can find those drives, it will put the guys he was investigating away so they can't harm anyone else. Josh and Kellerman can get this to people who will know what to do, how to locate the missing information, but it will take time. I might still have a few friends left in the FBI who can help, too. Meanwhile, we have to lead these mob guys away from Wanakena."

"I know where the drives are, Tony."

"What?" He grabbed my shoulders. "Emma, what are you saying?"

"I thought they were nothing but music collections. I gave them to Timmy Waylon."

"Are you saying the information Gary died for is with Josh's son?" I nodded. He rubbed his chin. "And no one knows about this?"

"Not even Riley. I left them by his gaming console. Is he in danger?" The thought of my carelessness putting Riley's family in peril chilled me.

"No, sweetheart, because no one but you and I know this, right?" I nodded again. "And we're going to keep it that way."

He paced the room. I could almost hear him thinking. "We're going, then? Into the mountains?"

"If you're willing, yes. Mollie and Evan can hide with Riley." He held my gaze, waited for me to think everything through, what I knew and what I suspected, the ruthlessness of the pursuers, all the good people now in harm's way. He waited while I paced, and then he rested his hands on my shoulders. "I don't want to put you in danger, but I think it's our only play."

"Will you go with me?"

"Every step, Red."

I thought about the past month of running and hiding, fearing every second that we'd be caught. I thought about the veterans at the Center and about Tony Storms, this man who cared about them. I weighed the courage it took to face an enemy and not back down, and I thought about the naked truth on Tony's face when he admitted how he wanted to be with me. All of it was worth fighting for. I placed his hand holding the recorder over my heart and nodded. "Guess we're going into the mountains."

...even a betrayed heart can learn to trust again...

Tony conducted a final check of the cabin while I packed up the twins' clothes and wheeled their suitcases into the hall. I glanced into my bedroom, shuddered, then took a purposeful step into the clutter left behind by the intruder.

"I can help." Tony settled a hand on the small of my back.

"How?" I moved deeper into the chaos and sank to my knees to gather the paperwork littering the carpet. "This room looks the way I feel, fragmented, shredded, a total mess."

Tony knelt beside me and took my hands. "That makes two of us, but you're not alone now."

I let my gaze linger on the scar along his temple, looked down at the evidence of the damage the explosion had done to his arms, then met his eyes, amazed at the determination in them. "How can you be so strong?"

He shook his head. "I'm not strong, Red. I'm bitter, and angry, and filled with guilt. I didn't see the truth about Amanda or Gus, and it almost cost me everything."

I offered a thin smile. "I did lose everything. How could I have been so blind to my husband's deceptions?"

"Did you love him?"

The question surprised me, reopened the wound of his betrayal. I probed it like a sore tooth and realized, with a shock, that it didn't hurt as much as before. "Once I did. We met at university, married after graduation. We were fresh out of college, with new jobs and big dreams. I think I mistook a girlish fantasy for love and bought into society's expectations. Get married, raise a family, live happily ever after. I suppose I liked the idea that we could have the good times without the trials. What about you? Did you love Amanda?"

"You asked me that before." I blushed. He leaned closer. "Why is it so important to you?"

"Because you don't like me, yet you're here," I whispered, "and you make me long for things I never thought I'd desire again."

Tony inched closer, his chest brushing mine. I inhaled sharply. He slipped his arms around me. "You want me."

I covered his heart with my hand, smoothed the flap over the pocket of his flannel shirt, traced the line of his jaw. "God help me, I do."

"That's good, Red, that's so good, because I want you, too, all the ways a man wants a woman. In my arms. In my bed. I can't promise easy, and I don't know how to do this long term. But you and your kids have cracked me open."

"Are you afraid?"

"Hell, yes. Aren't you?"

I outlined his lips with a finger, licked my own in anticipation. "A little, but I'm more excited. I want to taste you. I want you to taste me."

"Thank the gods, woman." He kissed me then, pulled me close. His arousal pressed against me, and my body, so long deprived, burned with desire. I refused him nothing, my tongue joining his in the age-old dance of pleasure. I worked the buttons of his shirt, eager to touch his skin. He broke our kiss to do the same to me, and when my breasts sprang free, he groaned and cupped them in his hands, bending to suck each hardened tip until I cried his name and whispered *please* and *yes* and *more*. He yanked the comforter from beneath the jumbled clothing and spread it out, then laid me down. I palmed his erection, worked the button and zipper of his jeans until he could kick them off and strip off his boxers while I shimmied out of my pants. He rose over me, eyes dark and yearning, and kissed me deeply before working his way down my body. He stripped off my panties in one long, slow motion that heightened my anticipation. When his mouth found my wetness, I cried out and cradled his head, urging him on with soft sighs and gentle pressure. And when I came, he held me tight, murmuring, "I've got you, sweetheart. I've got you."

"Tony." Tears ran down my cheeks, my neck. I sighed into another kiss and lifted his face to mine. "I need you. Now."

He stilled my hand against him, his next words filled with agony. "I don't have a condom."

I smiled. "I'm on the pill. I had months left on my prescription, so I just kept taking them."

"Another reason to thank the universe." He kissed me again, long and tenderly, as he settled between my legs. "Take me home, Red."

I guided him to my opening and lifted my hips, and when he thrust into my warmth, I echoed his cry. "Home."

...laying traps...

Otto listened to the boots tramping across the porch. He nodded to Jesse, who resumed his stance in front of the coolers at the back of the Abode. When the bell above the door tinkled, he liberated a six-pack of Canadian and moved toward the register. Eric Klaman removed his gloves, slapped them together, and looked over his shoulder at his companion. Mouse moved up beside him.

"Gentlemen." Jesse set the beer next to a pile of snack items and crossed his arms. "Can we help you with something today?"

Mouse stepped in front of his boss and wrestled out the photo of Emma and Gary Pearson. With his thumb over the man's face, he cocked his head and frowned. "Look, we haven't been exactly forthcoming with you."

"You haven't." Livetree's agreement reverberated around the store.

"No. I'm not just a retired vet with a penchant for photography. I do some private investigating on the side, and the Pearson woman's a client of the company I represent."

"Which company is that?"

"Erie Insurance Company. Ms. Pearson and her children suffered a terrible loss, and in her distraught state, she took the children and left her home. We think she came here to reconnect with her friend Riley Finn,

214

and since her cousin," Mouse pointed at Klaman, "is stationed here, we thought he might help us with our search."

Jesse pursed his lips. "Maybe the woman just wants to grieve in private."

Mouse sighed. "Thing is, I didn't lie about needing a place to stay, which is why I took Lorang up on his offer. My job's on the line if I don't find her. The company is anxious to finalize the payout on her husband's insurance. Now, we understand how stressful it has been for Ms. Pearson. The money might ease some of her burdens."

Otto stroked his beard. "How much money are you talking about?"

"The amount is confidential. But if you've seen her, it would certainly make my job easier." He held up the photo. Otto reached for it. Mouse held it just beyond his fingertips.

"This the same woman you were looking for the other day?"

"I don't believe I said anything about her the other day."

"Now that you mention it," Jesse said, "you didn't. Otto, go ahead and ring me up." Mouse drummed his knuckles on the counter while Otto tallied the mayor's purchases. Klaman paced, face tight, hands clenched. After Livetree placed his purchases in a sack, he turned to the strangers and grinned. "Maybe you should read the *Wanakena Gazette*. Might be something in there about a new move-in. That local reporter, Mariah Kimby, she has her finger on the pulse of our fair hamlet."

Klaman scowled and started toward Livetree. Mouse hauled him back. Otto offered a copy of the newest issue. "Fresh off the printer this morning," he said. "You gentlemen need anything else?"

Mouse grabbed the newsletter and turned to leave, pushing Klaman ahead of him. Outside, they stood by their car, watching Jesse Livetree head toward East Street, purchases in one hand, cell phone in the other. Otto noted their progress from inside, then read the alert crawling across his phone.

Crumbs in place Good job mariah Stay alert Wanakena The rats have taken the bait

...standing in the eye of the storm...

I burrowed deeper under the comforter, aware of Tony's warm, naked body twined around me. I ran a hand down his thigh, over his amazing ass, and sighed. Stirring, he buried his nose in my hair and tickled my ear with one calloused finger. "Is that a good sigh or a bad one?" he murmured.

"You know the answer to that, Stormy."

He laughed at my use of the twin's nickname for him. "You ready for today?"

"After last night, I'm ready for anything."

"It was good then?"

Facing him, I stroked the scar along his temple. "You were, you are, amazing, Anton. Don't ever doubt that."

"Back at you, Red. Among all the other good feels, you made me feel good about my manself again. I'll never be able to thank you enough for that."

I bit my lip. "Does that mean we're a one-and-done?"

He pulled me on top of him and lifted his hips so I could feel how ready he was to take me again. "For now, Em, only for now." He kissed me thoroughly, then eased away to rise and dress. I rescued clean underwear from the mess left by the home invasion, grinned into Tony's hungry eyes, and scampered into the bathroom. Closing my eyes against the glare of the overhead light, I relived our encounter, unashamed of my eagerness and my need. Gary Pearson had stolen enough of my life. I wasn't going to give him one minute more.

While I stuffed a backpack with items I might need, Tony helped fold and stow away the rest of the scattered clothing. The papers we simply piled in the closet, along with the framed photographs and other mementos of my life before the murder of my husband. With the room in better order, I turned off the lights, locked the cabin, and wheeled the children's suitcases down the path to Carl's.

Ms. Beamish had set the table and baked a fresh batch of scones. The kitchen was warm from the oven. Mutzi wound around Carl's legs in anticipation of a morning treat. The twins' voices carried from the great room as they invented moosie adventures for their new favorite toys. When they heard Tony and me, they rushed in to tug at my legs until I grabbed them and kissed them.

"Auntie Carl says we're going on another adventure today," Mollie intoned when I sat her down at the table.

"We are." Reaching for Tony, Evan wrapped his arms around Storms' neck. "She says Auntie Riley needs us to help with Michael and Cara. Are you coming, too, Stormy?"

Tony hugged Evan back, then settled a sippy cup of hot chocolate before him. I raised my eyebrows. "Carl? How do you have sippy cups already?"

Carl Beamish smirked as she took a seat. "I pay attention, especially when cups are likely to spill at least once every meal."

I blushed. "I should have mentioned that."

"No matter." Carl leaned over to pat my hand. "You and Tony go do what you have to do to make sure all our bears and moosies are safe. In the scheme of things, spilled milk is the least of our worrisomes."

Unable to respond without tearing up, I served the children, then filled my plate with scrambled eggs, a scone, and bacon. Tony did the same, and we ate while answering an endless stream of questions about the new adventure, and what moose ate in the winter, and why snowshoes were shaped like flat shovels. The food, the conversation, the smiles on their small faces made it seem like a normal family meal, something I'd missed for longer than I cared to admit. Maybe Wanakenans weren't blood relations, but they acted like they cared. I caught my breath at the thought that maybe our plan would work. Perhaps we would succeed in lifting the doom that hovered, cloudlike and threatening, over me and the children. I risked a glance at Tony, caught him looking at me. Heat gathered in my belly. I wanted him again. Carl looked between us, shook her head, and winked.

"Guess everyone slept well last night," she observed. "Good for you."

As soon as we cleared the table, I made my way to Carl's front stoop, coatless, shivering, and cursing my dead husband for all he'd done to bring this day upon us. Watching the twins ride away with Ms. Beamish tore at every heartstring. I was not an indecisive woman, but taking this step, putting myself in the path of a dangerous killer, seemed irresponsible. Still, what choice did I have? Keep running? Drag the children from one remote location to another and hope the pursuers tired of the chase? I turned to go back inside and bumped up against Tony. He pulled me in, closed the door, then grabbed my shoulders.

"Are you having second thoughts?"

"Of course." I shoved past him, my throat clogged with regret. "What kind of mother sends her children away so she can be the cheese in some elaborate mousetrap?"

Tony trailed behind, respectful of my space. His frown, when I faced him, deepened. "Do you want to call it off, Red?"

I clutched my waist, looked down at my fingernails. "I'm puzzled. If the killers found me, why hasn't the FBI?"

"I've wondered about that, too." He reached into a pocket and pulled out the recorder. "FYI, I made a copy of the recording and sent it to both of us. I also emailed it to a friend in the Bureau."

"Someone you trust?" When he nodded, I flopped into Carl's recliner and drummed my fingers along the leather arms. "Why do you think they haven't shown up here? The FBI?"

"Maybe they have, and we just don't know it. Wait, hear me out. You made it clear you didn't want witness protection, so they backed off, but my guys aren't stupid."

"Your guys?" I smiled.

"Well, they were before they put me on extended leave. They're still the best in the business of finding people. I think someone is here in Wanakena, shadowing you and waiting for the killers to make a move."

"Great. They stay hidden, and people like Denver Lorang get killed. I hate this uncertainty." I took a deep breath. "I guess we should get going.

The sooner we confront them, the sooner this will all be over. One way or another. I just don't want anyone else to get hurt. I couldn't bear it."

He knelt in front of me and put his hands on my knees. "Emma, you don't have to do this. Josh, Jesse, and I can make it look like you're with us."

I cupped his chin, searching those dark eyes for any hint of uncertainty, and kissed him. "Uh-uh. No. You all are not going without me."

"You're sure, sweetheart?" He ran his fingers up my arms, igniting all sorts of wicked thoughts. I kissed him again.

"With you beside me, how can I say no? Besides, this whole sorry drama reminds me of the chess match in Wonderland. I'm Alice, trying to keep my head, but who, I wonder, is the Red Queen?"

"The other Red Queen?" Tony slipped the recorder back into his pocket and tapped his watch. "You still call the shots, Red. You want to change the plan?"

"No. Josh's idea is a good one. We'll go to work, like any normal day. By the way," I chuckled as I slipped into my coat, "did you read Kimby's column in the *Gazette* this morning."

He laughed. "I did. She and Jesse are a pair, aren't they?"

I stopped him when we reached the car. "Tony, are you sure this is the right thing to do? I really don't want to endanger anyone else."

He placed a soft kiss on my cheek. "I promise you on my life, Red, the only ones getting hurt are the guys threatening you. Now, come on, my beautiful, sexy redhead, let's go checkmate a murderer."

Wanakena Gazette…January 28, 2022

Strange Tidings

By

Mariah Kimby

Record snowfall, bitter cold temperatures, and mysterious sightings have invaded our quiet hamlet this January. Our normally slumbering community has been the recipient of not one, not two, but three unusual events, the last one being the untimely and mysterious death of Mr. Denver Lorang. Rumor has it the poor deceased froze to death after his wheelchair took a header into a snowbank at his home. Lorang's dwelling was scheduled to be the beneficiary of a fund-raising event spearheaded by the Veterans Center under the direction of our own humble hometown hero, Anton Storms. Questions abound around the accident…or was it?

Couple Lorang's demise with the call for a town meeting at the new Wanakena History Museum last evening, where shots rang out, threatening the assembly, and this reporter must ask…has evil stretched its hand once again over our hamlet?

But, Mariah, you're thinking, that's only two strange incidents. What's the third? Well, my fellow citizens, consider the arrival of a mysterious, comely redhead with two adorable children in tow just as the new year began and who has taken up residence, if you can believe it, in a hunter's cabin on Long Tom Mountain. The lady has been spotted at numerous locations in and around Wanakena, but so far, not even Mayor Livetree or the irrepressible Carl Beamish has been able to ferret out her reasons for relocating to our neck of the Adirondacks.

If you have any information on any of these events, please send it to the email below. This inquiring reporter has a nose to know!

...a trek into the wilderness...

Tony and I arrived at the Vet Center with ten minutes to spare and still weren't the first ones there. The parking lot rumbled with engine sounds as everyone who could drive had come to discuss Denver's funeral, those plans replacing the ones for the fundraiser he had been so looking forward to. I was busy for the next two hours, fielding phone calls, refilling the coffee urn, and easing the minor tensions that erupted in a roomful of sad and worried survivors. Lorang's sons stopped by to request a military escort and a gun salute, which Tony assured them would not be a problem. More than fifteen Wanakenans called to report sightings or non-sightings of the strangers known as Harlan Clouse and Eric Klaman, who, as it turned out, was not a soldier from Fort Drum. In fact, no one seemed to know who he was or where he came from. Around eleven, Trooper Kellerman also came to check on me, then spent forty-five minutes sequestered in Tony's office. When she left, her face solemn and disapproving, I decided to slip in and pump Tony for information, but before I could do so, the office phone rang again. I ignored it until the voice on the recording device made me reconsider.

"Gordo?" I hugged the receiver to my neck and shuffled the papers on the desk until I located a pencil. "Are you on your way back?"

"Now, why would you think that, Red?" Phil Gordon sounded like he'd just come in from a run.

"You said you'd only be gone a short while."

"You having trouble with the job?" Gordo covered the receiver and spoke to someone. All I heard was mumbling, but it sounded like he was with a woman. Uh-oh, maybe he was in bed, but why call me then?

"The job's fine, but Denver Lorang passed away." I eyed the few stragglers from the morning still conversing by the coffee stand and lowered my voice. "Under mysterious circumstances, you should know."

Silence. I held the phone away from my ear, thinking we'd been disconnected, when he cleared his throat and spoke again. "Emma, listen to me. I can't leave yet, but if you, Tony, or the vets need assistance, I want you to call me here." He recited a string of numbers, pausing after each until I confirmed them. "Do you understand what I'm telling you?"

"I'm not sure." Gordo didn't know about my problem, so why did his voice sound so ominous? I tried a different tack. "You sound like you're in the middle of something important."

He didn't deny it. "Transfer me to Tony, Red, and then hang up the phone."

"Of course." A little miffed that he thought I'd eavesdrop, I punched the requisite button and announced Gordon on the line. I intended to hang up, then didn't. I covered the phone so they couldn't hear me breathing and listened as Tony filled Gordo in on my situation as well as what had happened to Lorang. The background noise on the call increased, and hearing everything they were saying became difficult. What I did catch made me shiver.

"Hard to believe they pulled you from here to follow up on her husband's murder in Kansas City," Tony said.

"Once the Ohio boys discovered Emma's connection to Riley, they suspected she might head there."

"So, why aren't you here, Gordo?"

"You'll have to trust me when I say it's all part of the job, Tony. Now, you do yours. Keep Red safe." The call ended with metallic rattling that made me think of SWAT teams and automatic weapons and raids. I set the phone down and buried my head in my arms. I felt like a swimmer caught in a riptide, one I hadn't anticipated, that was pushing me inexorably farther from the solid ground I thought I stood on. My hands shook. I needed an explanation, but to get one, I'd have to confront Tony and admit I had listened in on his conversation. When I applied for the volunteer position, Phil Gordon appeared to be nothing more than a retired soldier and Anton Storms a disabled vet in charge of helping other veterans, although if last night was any indication, Tony wasn't that compromised. My cheeks warmed at the thought of our lovemaking. Damn it. I had trusted him with my body. Had I been wrong again? I circled the office three times, counting each step, before Tony strolled into the reception area, folded his arms, and focused his attention on me.

"Red."

"Tony."

"You heard."

"I heard what?" I busied myself adding water to a packet of hot chocolate mix, trying to gather my thoughts, to frame an explanation that wouldn't sound lame.

Tony remained where he was. The room, empty except for us, emitted the usual sounds of a building flinching in the cold. Down the hall, voices echoed, then died away.

"Who is Phil Gordon?" Blowing on the drink to cool it, I took a sip, set it on the counter, and faced him. "Why did you tell him about me?"

"Gordo is who he says he is, but he's also more. He has a military intelligence background and frequently advises the Bureau on cases when they need his expertise. He likes the Adirondacks, so he lives here and works with us until they call on him for help." Tony slipped his hands into the back pockets of his jeans and moved my way. "He's also here to keep an eye on me."

The bitter edge to his words surprised me. "Why would he do that?"

"Because I want to return to the work I did before the explosion. He's deciding whether I'm rehabilitated enough." Tony was close enough to touch me now, but he kept his hands in his pockets. "Because there are still some concerns about my past associations with Gus and Torvald and the drugs Ben peddled."

The despair I saw on his face evoked my mother bear response. I grabbed his arms. "Why, after all you've been through, is there even a question?"

He shrugged, his eyes shadowed by loss and grief. "Because that bastard Torvald tried to get his sentence reduced by turning against his fellow dealers. He lied, said I knew what he was doing and looked the other way."

I didn't understand why someone would do that, but I recognized another betrayal when I saw it. "Did it work?"

"Not the way he intended. There was no evidence of complicity. None. Livetree stood up for me. So did Josh. But suspicion, once cast, is hard to erase."

"Tony." I traced his jaw, fingers rasping over the stubble he hadn't had time to shave away. "How do we make it go away?"

"We?" A hint of a smile. My heart stuttered.

"I see what a good man you are. Gordon does, too. How can I help?"

He wrapped his arms around me and tugged me close. "We'll worry about me after we handle your problem."

I pushed away enough to look at him. "Are you simply with me as my babysitter?"

He held my gaze. A muscle in his jaw ticked. "Emma, do you believe I'm that shallow?"

I searched for anger, found only sorrow at the position he found himself in, and took the biggest risk of my life. I chose to trust him. "No, I don't. Tell me what I can do to help."

"You want to help me, Red?" His lips met mine, his tongue coaxed me to open, and he spent a full minute exploring my mouth. A noise in the hall had us both blushing. He cupped my chin and smiled, really smiled at me. "You already have."

I studied him, looking for signs of deceit or hesitation, and found none. "All right. Let's go catch a killer."

At 9:45, we locked up, drove to Josh's, and hid our vehicles in the garage. Then we piled into the Ranger's work truck. The back overflowed with gear – heavy white down coats, crampons, snowshoes, hiking staffs, packs. Hemmed between the men, I determined not to second-guess my decision. When my cell vibrated, I had to squirm to extract it from my pocket. Josh chuckled. Tony whispered in my ear. I swallowed hard over the desire that swept through me and checked the screen. Riley.

"Hey, girlfriend," I choked out, "everything all right?"

"It is, and that's why I'm calling." One of the dogs barked in the background. I detected the yipping of puppies and the joyful sound of children laughing. "I thought you'd like to see what the kids made." Riley reversed the image to pan the crowded kitchen. The table was a mess of arts and crafts items. Popsicle sticks and graham crackers, chocolate chips and red licorice, and cups of white icing surrounded a precarious structure that vaguely resembled a medieval castle. "We've completed our STEM challenge for today and will now plop in front of our little screens for several hours of innocuous YouTube videos while Cara and I nap."

"Where's Julia?"

"Here, Em." Josh's mother stepped into view, apron stained with tomato sauce, wooden spoon raised in greeting. She looked tired and happy. "Thank you for allowing the twins to camp out with us for a few days. Brings back memories of when my children were little."

"Oh, Julia," I blinked back tears, "I'm sorry to invade your home like this."

Josh nudged me and spared a smile. "My mom's totally loving it, Red. Stop worrying."

I turned to watch the rambunctious puppies lick the remnants of frosting from the children's hands and faces. God, I wished I were there with them. Riley reversed the screen again and moved into the baby's room. "You can do this, Em. You've always been the brave one."

I scoffed at that. "I don't agree, but we can compare stories once everyone is safe and home."

"Tell my husband I love him," Riley said.

"You can tell him yourself." I handed the phone to the Ranger and leaned away to give him some privacy. Tony was staring at me, one finger on his upper lip, the frown he usually wore at the office now deepened into a tense line across his forehead. "What?" I mouthed.

He didn't speak, just wormed one arm around my waist and pulled me into his body, setting off the memory of him holding me the same way last night when we were both naked and trembling in the aftermath of orgasm. I closed my eyes, allowed a moment to wallow in his nearness, then forced myself to think about what we were about to do. Go into the mountains. Lure a killer to the site. Capture him...or make the kill and end the threat forever.

...picking up the trail...

WBRV out of Lowville paused their music streaming for a noon update on local events and the weather. Anxious to set the revised plan in motion, Mouse and Klaman tuned out most of the announcements until they heard a reference to the article in the *Wanakena Gazette*. Klaman turned up the volume and folded his arms, scowling as the story that had appeared in the paper that morning spooled. When the announcer moved on to a moose sighting, the boss pounded the table. "Time's running faster than a duck's ass around here," he muttered. "Did you identify any hunter's cabins on Long Tom?"

Mouse opened his laptop and clicked on a map of the mountain. "Most of the existing ones are not equipped for winter lodging," he said.

"Do you believe the woman described in here," Klaman held up a copy of the *Gazette*, "is Emma Pearson?"

"It's too much of a coincidence not to be her. Besides, after we left the store, I checked out the Waylon house. No one home there, at least not this morning. It looks closed up tighter than a tick."

"So, if she's in the mountains, we go after her there." The boss stabbed the map with his thumb.

Mouse finished his coffee, rinsed his mug in the bathroom sink, and stowed it in his duffel, his voice a tinny echo in the confined space. "You can stay here, Eric, warm and comfortable. If the cabin is as remote as the directions indicate, it won't be easy to reach."

Klaman released his weapon from the shoulder holster and laid it on the map. "You've dragged this out too long already, Mouse. Now, figure out what else we need to do to locate the Pearsons, gas up the truck, and get to it."

"We need another snowmobile, one that's not stolen."

"You have the funds. Use them. And just so you understand me, tomorrow I intend to be on a plane back to KC with the information that fucker Pearson stole."

"You think the Feds know the woman's in the area." Mouse made it a statement.

"I'm certain they do. My contact made it clear they were holding back until they believed the threat was imminent. Well, we're here, so you can bet your ass they are, too."

A knock at the door had both men drawing their weapons. They exchanged a glance, then flanked the entrance.

"Hello? Mr. Clouse? Housekeeping." The female voice, weak and quavery, paused. A shadow covered the window. "Mr. Clouse?"

Mouse stepped to the door, coughed loudly, and called out," Don't need anything right now, ma'am." He counted to ten, waiting until the footsteps crunched away down the sidewalk, accompanied by the rumble of cartwheels. Klaman peeked out and nodded. Mouse rechecked the items they'd need for a trek up the mountain, stuffed his kit into his duffel, and wiped the room clean of prints. His associate racked the slide on his weapon and, satisfied, returned it to the shoulder holster. "What are we hunting?" he asked.

Mouse patted his gun and smirked. "Red fox."

...into the mouth of winter...

The Ranger truck labored up the slope of Long Tom and into the gravel lot at the trailhead. Josh parked parallel to the sign detailing the length of the climb, expected duration, and altitude reached at the summit. The air was frigid, but a weakling sun made it bearable until the wind blew. We geared up, me following each step with care. I had dressed at the Center, pairing long underwear with flannel-lined jeans, a wool sweater, a fleece, and a ski jacket. Tony helped me add a Camelbak under my jacket and shirt, threading the tube under my bra strap to keep it in place. I wrestled my arms into an anorak that reached my knees. "What's the tube for?"

"Hydration." Josh wandered over, a length of rope in his gloved hands. "The water won't freeze if it's close to your body heat, and you'll need it. You've no experience with this kind of trek, Emma, so it's not too late to turn back."

"Yes, it is." I tried to lift my arms above my shoulders, but the weight and thickness of the clothing impeded my movement. "I feel like the Marshmallow Man."

Despite the seriousness of the moment, Josh smirked. Tony crossed his arms and shot me a look that warmed even my little toes. I punched at the thick down coat, then squatted to tighten my boots. Both guys helped me don the snowshoes, then circled my waist with the cord, clamping the ends to each of their belts.

"Why the rope?" I tugged at it. I peered through the goggles Josh insisted I wear and frowned as snowflakes drifted across my cheek. "It's snowing."

Tony yanked on the hook to be sure it was secure, then motioned me to follow Josh. Each of the men shouldered heavy packs. Skis tied across the back extended above their heads. Tony pulled a sled behind him, additional supplies lashed to the slatted bed. I followed the Ranger, ignoring the urge to drink until Tony poked me in the back, then gestured toward the water tube. "Hydrate, Red, and keep going, no matter what."

His words stoked my anxiety, but I pushed it down. The cabin lay four miles up the mountain, a challenging hike during the summer months, a grueling one under present conditions. In Hopewell, I had prided myself on staying fit, visiting the gym three times a week, lifting weights, running on the treadmill. But working out in a heated facility was no match for making my way through snow drifts in the middle of winter. I tightened the scarf covering my nose and mouth and focused on putting one foot in front of the other.

We paused frequently to assess the weather. Josh mentioned the potential for avalanches, then asked about our fingers and toes, concerned about frostbite and hypothermia. I considered asking for a restroom break, then discarded the notion. No way was I hanging my private parts out to freeze in front of these men, and I wasn't going to release myself from the rope to flounder into the woods for privacy. The guys didn't relax their vigilance. Josh scanned the snow for predator tracks while Tony checked behind for any sign of pursuit. Two and a half hours into the trek, we reached a rockslide blocking the trail. The wind had scoured the snow from the boulders, leaving behind a layer of ice. There was no way through. We would have to go around. Josh led us toward a grove of pines that offered protection from the falling snow and the wind, both now double what they had been at the beginning of the climb.

Using field glasses, Josh scouted the terrain ahead, then passed them to Tony, who repeated the action. I drank from the Camelbak, risked ungloving to tear open a trail bar and replenish my flagging strength. When both men had completed their inspection, the Ranger rubbed his chin through his face covering.

"Unexpected detour." He pointed toward the opposite side of the slide and then up the hill. "The southern route's a tougher climb, but we won't be as exposed to the elements as we would if we go up this side. Emma? You okay?"

I paused my chewing to nod. Tony rubbed a hand over my back when I shivered. I finished the snack, drank more water, and suppressed a burp. "I'm good to go. How much farther?"

Josh inspected the lashings on the sled, nodded, and moved away from the trees. "Come here." He waited for Tony and me to join him, then retrieved crampons from his pack. He removed my snowshoes to attach the spikes. When he finished with mine, he did the same to his and Tony's.

"Why are we changing footwear?" I lifted a boot to examine the added grips.

Josh raised an eyebrow, then turned my shoulders toward the top of the mountain. "Slope's steeper here. Crampons offer better traction. Look up. Can you see the top of a fire tower above that clump of trees at eleven o'clock?"

"Yes. Is that where we're going?"

Tony pressed closer, his presence reassuring, and pointed. "The hunting cabin is just to the right of the tower. You can't see it from here. With the detour around the rocks, it will take us two more hours to reach it."

"That long, huh?" I snorted and readjusted the scarf. "Better get going then."

"Good girl," Tony whispered.

"Not a girl, Storms," I hissed.

He pressed harder against my back. "You're right, Red, you're all woman. And you're mine."

He whispered the last word. I thought I misheard him, but the way he herded me after Josh belied that thought. How was it possible that, in a month, I had gone from swearing off men to being claimed by Anton Storms?

The snow that had danced around us on the first part of the climb now tumbled down in earnest. I had to wipe off my goggles every few minutes. Josh trudged on ahead, as did Tony behind me. Once we cleared the rockslide, we emerged onto a narrow trail nearly obliterated by the new snowfall. The upward climb was taking its toll. My breathing shortened, then turned into rasps as I labored over the drifts. I stumbled against a hidden rock and fell. Tony reached me first, hauling me up, then checking for injuries as much as possible through the thick clothing. Josh backtracked to join us. "We're almost there, Em."

"I'm all right. I'm all right!" I pushed them away and struggled forward, hands clutching the rope.

Tony removed his gloves to inspect my forehead. "You're bleeding, Red."

I batted his hand away, my tired mind recalling a line from an old Monty Python movie. "It's only a flesh wound." Josh frowned, but Tony roared.

"Damn, Red, you should have been a Marine."

"Shut up, Army. I'm cold, tired, and hungry enough to eat everything in your pack."

"On it, Evans," Josh said and, taking my hand, dragged me forward until we were all back in line. I gritted my teeth against the tingling in my fingers and toes, refused to think about frostbite, and concentrated on stepping wherever Josh did. My legs ached, and my face felt numb. Everyone was breathing hard as we labored up the last ridge, and the cabin finally appeared. Its weathered slump of a roof bowed under the weight of the snow. The windows were shuttered and dark. But a woodpile covered by a tarp secured with rocks signaled the promise of warmth. I almost cried as we approached but shook off the urge. Any moisture that leaked from my eyes would freeze to my cheeks.

Josh kicked his boots against a log beside the door, dug in his pocket for a key, and inserted it in the padlock. We hurried in, depositing our crampons and boots on a high-sided mat just inside. I stepped away to allow the men to work while I took stock of the one-room cabin. Cots were stacked along the wall to the right. Blankets and pillows nested in plastic bags next to a stone fireplace, a deer head mounted above. An opening at the back revealed an outhouse-type toilet seat with hand-written instructions on how to use a composting crapper nailed to the wall. I ran a finger down the list and shook my head. An in-house outhouse. This place probably got smelly at times. I suppressed a giggle and opened the cabinets to look for plates and eating utensils.

Josh found a Coleman lamp in one of the cupboards and coaxed it to life with an infusion of kerosene from a container in one of the lower cupboards. Tony peeled off his coat, and, matches in hand, set to work building a fire. Once the flames took hold, I hung my coat on one of the hooks lining the wall next to an array of fishing rods. Josh rummaged through the storage cabinets, pulling out a cast iron frying pan, a soup pan, and a handful of faded towels. He put his coat back on and went outside, returning with items from the sled. Tony helped him unpack while I opened two cans of chicken noodle soup. I found a grate attached to the fireplace that swung out over the fire and set the pan to warming. I spread a towel over the dusty table, then set out bowls, spoons, and bottles of water. The guys completed their transfer of provisions and eased onto the hard-backed chairs, their stockinged feet oriented toward the fire rapidly warming the interior. Once the soup was hot, I portioned it out. We sat silent, content to warm our insides and rest from the trek. Tony fished three chocolate bars from his pack, and we finished the meal staring into the flames. Finally, Josh spoke.

"To paraphrase an old Sherlock Holmes line, the game's in play. Once I get back—"

I interrupted him. "You're not making the trip back down today? It'll be dark before you reach the bottom."

The Ranger shrugged. "Can't leave the car there for our bad guys to see. Besides, more snow is predicted for later tonight."

"Josh," I sputtered, "you promised Riley you wouldn't take unnecessary risks. Going back now, that's a huge one."

He leaned forward, elbows on knees, eyes focused on his hands. "Emma, you have a part to play, as does Tony. This is mine."

"Tony, can't you talk him into staying until morning?"

Tony checked the time and shrugged. "Josh is right, Red. Besides, he knows his job. And, we have these." He held up a walkie-talkie. "Sophisticated technology designed for conditions like the ones we're facing now. It's also a tracker."

Josh looked at me. "I'll be fine, Emma. Will you?"

I crossed my arms and pouted. The idea of Josh going off alone scared me. If anything happened to him, Riley would be devastated, and it would add more guilt to the amount I already carried. "You'll be at the fire tower tomorrow?"

"That's the plan. Now, I'm going to sleep for a half hour and then start down. I should be able to ski most of the way."

"Oh, I forgot about the skis." I rose to clear the remnants of the meal, snatching an extra piece of chocolate from Tony's bar. I grabbed the soup pan, carried it outside to rinse, and hurried back into the warmth. My toes ached from the cold. By the time I had everything stowed away, Josh was asleep and Tony splayed out in his chair, brooding. I spread a blanket on the floor close to the fire and sat down. I took out my phone to check for a signal. Not one bar. I rooted in my pack, retrieved Gary's gun, and began to clean the weapon.

...an unexpected clue...

The search for Emma Pearson and her children led Mouse and Klaman on a fifty-mile wild goose chase. Everyone they spoke to seemed certain of the location of the mysterious redhead and the hunting cabin she supposedly now called home, but when they reached the various sites, the places were locked and empty of humans. Cold, exhausted, and in a rage, the hitmen returned to the Cranberry Inn to find a note taped to the door of their room. *Check with reception when you get in.* "You go," Klaman ordered Mouse, "and bring back some food. I'm pissed, starving, and convinced everyone in this punk-ass wilderness is lying."

Surprised to find he agreed with Klaman's assessment, Mouse trudged to the main building, startled once again when the woman behind the desk, whose nametag read Mariah, handed over a manila envelope with Harlan Clouse printed on the outside. "When did you get this?" He shook the contents, wary of what might be inside.

Mariah straightened the oversize tortoise-shell glasses she wore and shrugged. "Found it on the desk when I arrived for my shift."

"And when was that?" Mouse slammed his palms on the counter. Mariah jumped.

"Ni-nine o'clock this morning. Don't shoot the messenger, sir." She waited until he moved toward the restaurant before taking out her phone to type a message. Mouse tapped his foot while the grill cook filled the order, then hurried back to the room, eager to open the envelope and see what was inside.

Klaman was too hungry to care. The men ate in haste, talking little. When only two wings and a thigh remained, Mouse sat back, belched, and picked up the envelope. Greasy papers from the carryout lay discarded on the floor, the odor of fried food lingering in the closed space. "I'm opening this now."

Snatching the missive from Mouse, Klaman extracted a single sheet from inside and stretched the lined yellow paper over his knees. He read and re-read instructions printed on the page. Stuffing a French fry in his mouth, he chewed, swallowed, and barked out orders. "Someone's trying to do us a solid," he said. "Google hunting retreats near Round Lake."

Mouse rolled his eyes. "Could be a trap."

Klaman grunted and handed over the laptop. While Mouse worked, he unfolded a map of New York State, located Wanakena, and searched for the coordinates printed in red ink in the mysterious message. The two worked steadily until Mouse handed over the list he'd made. The other man began to make calls, systematically inquiring, when anyone answered, whether his cousin had rented their cabin for the winter. It took an hour and a half, but they finally narrowed Pearson's location to an old hunting lodge near a fire tower on Long Tom Mountain.

"This bitch is making me work too hard," Klaman mumbled. "I'm going to enjoy making her talk."

Mouse cleaned up their food cartons. "How certain are you we're not being misled again?"

"Even if we are, these wilderness fucks are no match for professionals like us." Klaman eyed him. "You second-guessing me? You want out?"

"I don't renege on my deals, Eric." He drawled the fake name, smirking when the man's ears pinked. "You and the real 'boss' better stick to the one you made me."

"As long as I get whatever Pearson stole, the arrangement holds."

Charles Mouse crossed his arms. "You don't even know exactly what we're looking for either, do you?"

Klaman shoved him aside to grab his travel bag. "I know it's enough to tank everything and send us all to prison for a very long time, so you better hope the woman knows what and where it is."

"And if she doesn't?"

"Either way, she's not getting out alive, and neither are her kids. That fucking husband of hers stole more than information. He played me, played my sister. But she didn't have to die. That's on you."

"Your sister was married to Pearson?"

"He got her to marry him. Put her in danger to steal our financial data." Klaman pounded his chest. "No one does that to me. An eye for an eye, you know?"

Disturbed by the personal rant, Mouse skirted the man's flailing arm to collect his coat. "You plan to head up to this cabin now?"

"I do. The sooner we find her, the sooner we can get out of this fucking armpit of the country."

Mouse refrained from commenting that many, including him, said the same about Kansas City.

...more grist for the mill...

The shadow of the mountain shifted with the light, spreading an impenetrable darkness over the cabin. I finished cleaning the gun, stowed it in my pack, and stretched, groaning as the muscles in my back protested. Josh snored softly. Tony had joined me in front of the fire, head cradled in his arms. I allowed myself a moment to peruse his sleeping form, recalling those muscular limbs wrapped around my body. He hadn't minded the soft belly that motherhood had left behind, had caressed the stretch marks now a permanent fixture on my once-toned stomach. Alone with my thoughts, I blushed, the warmth climbing my neck and across my cheeks. My thighs warmed, too, reacting to the memory of soft kisses and fingers that touched in all the right spots. I scolded myself for acting like a creeper and added more logs to the fire, then slipped around Tony's sleeping form to shuffle through the food packets. The trek up the mountain had left me ravenous. The men must be hungry, too. I had unwrapped three dried packets of lasagna when Josh stirred. He noticed the food in my hands and grinned.

"Fix that for me now, Em. I'll be heading back as soon as I eat."

I wanted to rail against his leaving, but when I looked at him, I realized it was futile. Ranger Waylon had made up his mind. Instead of arguing, I lifted the kettle simmering over the fire and, adding water to the pasta, handed it over. Josh practically inhaled the serving, returned the empty food pack, and kicked Tony's booted feet. "Hey, Storms, rise and shine. We've got criminals to catch."

Tony rubbed a hand through his hair and rose to his knees. "What do you want me to do?"

Josh gestured toward the bear traps hanging on the back wall and grinned. "Had a little off-season trapping in mind. Space those out around the cabin and bury them about five inches into the snow."

"Sounds like a plan." Tony visited the indoor outhouse before pulling on his hat, coat, and gloves. Josh was already dressed and releasing the skis strapped to his pack. He pointed at the handle of the gun poking out of my backpack.

"Listen to me, Red. If anyone other than me, Tony, or the Rangers you met at the Museum approaches the cabin, do not hesitate."

He didn't need to spell it out. I had already decided what I would do. The men stepped outside, closing the door tightly behind them. I listened to their goodbyes, then moved to the single window to watch Josh start his run down the mountain. Soft thumping sounds clued me in to Tony working his way around the cabin as he buried the traps. I checked my watch, squatted to retrieve my phone, and was opening the solitaire app when I noticed an object peeking from beneath one of the bags the men had used to carry supplies. I reached for it, fear crawling up my spine. I thumbed the call button and spoke into the receiver. "Josh?"

Tony's voice crackled back. "Red? What's wrong?"

"Josh is heading down the mountain, and he left his walkie-talkie behind."

"Okay, don't panic. I'll go after him." His line went dead. I told myself not to worry, but I felt the nausea take hold. I thumbed on my device and called Tony again.

"Red?" He sounded winded already.

"Come back, Tony. You can't follow him and take both talkies, and you can't leave one behind because—" I choked on the next words.

"Because then I'll have no way to reach you or you me."

"Oh, God, Tony. What if Josh runs into the killer on his way down the mountain?"

"Don't go there, Red. I'm almost done. We'll talk this through when I'm back inside."

I thumbed the off button, my gut churning. If anything happened to Josh, Riley would blame me, which she had every right to do. I had brought this horror down on all of them. I brushed away the tears, but they kept coming as I cursed Gary Pearson and the choices he'd made that had put all the people I loved in jeopardy.

...more than wolves prowl the mountain...

The brakes growled, tires slipping, when Mouse pulled into the trailhead. He turned into the skid and eased next to the Ranger's truck. His companion drummed his fingers on the dash, then tugged on a ski cap and exited the vehicle. Klaman laid a hand on the hood of Josh's truck, snorted, and put his glove back on. "Been here a while."

"You couldn't tell that from the snow covering the windshield?" Mouse turned away from the other man, whose constant complaining had made the drive more unpleasant than expected. He circled the Ranger's vehicle, inspecting the ground for additional proof that Waylon himself had been there. "Only the one truck, but there's evidence of more than one pair of boots. See the indentations in the snowpack? If he and another Ranger are around, it could be nothing more than a routine patrol."

"Or maybe they're checking on the Pearson bitch. Hand me that note again." Klaman snatched the paper as soon as Mouse wrestled it free, read the directions, and, grinning, stuffed it in his pocket. "Seems this is the right place. All we have to do is climb the mountain."

Mouse retied his boots, tucked snowshoes under his arm, and lifted the bag of firearms from the back seat. "When's the last time you did any cold weather training?"

Klaman got in Mouse's face, spittle flying from his mouth. "You think I'm not up for this?"

Mouse didn't back down. "Do what you want, Eric. You're the boss. But I was hired for a reason. I know what I'm doing. And I'm pissed that you keep questioning my abilities."

"Fine. Forget I said anything." Klaman held up his hands and stepped away. He motioned toward the snowmobile they had trailered in. "That was a waste of money."

Mouse scrubbed his chin. He looked off into the four-foot-wide fire cut that wove through the pine trees and disappeared. "Actually, no. We can ride for a while, see how it goes. I'm more concerned about the light. Four-plus miles up this sloping terrain is a slog in good weather, especially through this snowpack. Any additional accumulation and we could end up stuck someplace we don't want to be."

"Enough." Klaman secured a long rifle across his back, slung a pack over one shoulder, and lowered the gate on the trailer. Mouse helped him muscle the machine down the ramp. They climbed on, tugged balaclavas over their faces, and roared off, unconcerned about the noise they made. Mouse maneuvered the machine up the first rise and dipped out of sight. As soon as they disappeared, two Rangers sprinted from the forest. One jimmied the lock on the driver's side of the car and popped the hood while his companion stood guard. Once the engine was disabled, they returned to their snow blind, radios in hand, and tried to contact Ranger Waylon again.

...even the best-laid plans must change...

The snow continued to fall, leaving a powdery covering over the tracks Josh, Tony, and Emma had made on their trudge up the mountain. Josh paused to adjust the clamp on his right ski and resumed his run down the hill. He made good time, reaching the rockslide in just over an hour, when he heard the rumble of a snowmobile. He crouched behind one boulder and peeked around the jumbled pile. The south side remained canted and unstable, the stones jutting out at odd angles, their icy covering buried under the fresh snow. Despite his desire to get off the mountain before full dark, he had no choice but to divert to uncharted territory now. He couldn't allow the men on the snowmobile to catch him out in the open. He tightened the skis and headed forward, increasing his speed on the downhill grade. He had almost cleared the rockslide when a strong gust of wind pushed him to the right. The tip of one ski nicked a rock concealed beneath the snow. Josh leaned left to compensate, but gravity had other ideas. The ski bent forward, snapped back, and he went airborne, twisting to land on his shoulder. He rolled twice, then slid down an embankment and into a depression, missing the trees that lined the ridge.

When he tried to stand, pain brought him to his knees. He slowed his breathing, grimaced, and tried again. The fall had wrenched his arm from the socket. Dislocated shoulder or not, remaining where he was not an option. Tony expected him to check in. So did the Rangers waiting at the base of Long Tom. Sliding the pack from his good shoulder, he eased it away from the injured limb and, breathing through the pain, rooted in the mesh pocket for the walkie-talkie. He came up empty. He unzipped and checked each section until, arm throbbing, Josh Waylon faced the fact that somewhere along the trail, he'd lost his only way to communicate with the team.

* * *

Tony stomped into the cabin, brushing snow from his boots, then deposited all the wet gear by the door. I looked up from my perch by the fire. "All done?"

He joined me, hands reddened from the cold. "If you go outside, do not wander near the corners of the cabin. Either hug the walls or follow the path we made with the sled when we arrived."

"Otherwise?"

He nudged me with his shoulder. "Otherwise, Red, you'll be caught in a bear trap, which is not an experience you want. The initial release will break your leg. The continued pressure could lead to amputation."

"Well, that's an unpleasant thought. Maybe the asshole following me will find your hidden treasure. How did you hide the traps and cover your tracks? Are you a fisherman and a magician?"

"Stop deflecting." Tony wrestled me onto his lap and nuzzled my neck until I cried uncle. He kissed my nose. "You said asshole."

"Why, Mr. Storms, did I shock you?"

He grew still, his dark eyes hooded. "You are a constant shock to my system, sweetheart, one I was totally unprepared for."

Oh, truth time. I swallowed hard, but I didn't push him away. "I didn't mean to shatter your image of me, but this man, whoever he is, is an asshole. He has endangered everyone I love, and I hate him for it."

A log snapped, sending sparks across the slate hearth. Tony slipped a hand around my waist, then lower to cup my behind. The other cradled my head, fingers moving among the fiery strands. He swallowed hard, gnawed his lower lip, and sighed. "I didn't expect to want you, Emma. I tried not to. I'm terrified of letting you into my heart, but I can't stop my desire for you."

The naked need in him tugged at my resolve. Straddling him, I cupped his face, searched for the lie, and found nothing but anguish. "I want you, too, Anton. My body aches to have you inside me again, and my heart, damn it, my heart feels torn between running to you and running away. I swore I'd never let another man close to me. How did this happen?"

He kissed me softly, deliberately, his lips saying what his words could not. I returned the kiss, unable to stop the moan that escaped. "Too many clothes," I murmured, tugging up his shirt to run my fingers over his skin. He pressed me harder against his arousal, broke the kiss to groan against my neck.

"When this is over." He shoved away the neck of my sweater to suck the hollow of my neck, cupping a breast through the thick wool. I kissed him again, grinding against his erection, the ache to have him inside me roaring through my veins. I pulled back and rested my forehead against his.

"When this is over." I pushed off, straightened my clothes, and motioned toward the table. Josh's radio lay beside the plates, a reminder that, for now, we were out of touch and vulnerable. I handed him a meal packet, and we ate, our fingers occasionally brushing together, desire strung between us like a thread, while awareness of the danger coming up the mountain droned beneath the wanting. He helped me tidy up. We took turns in the in-house outhouse, unwilling to spoil the new-found intimacy with baser needs and powerless to avoid it. Darkness shrouded the cabin, obscuring the view through the only window. Tony stoked the fire, brought in more firewood, then crouched next to me to rest a hand on my knee. I saw the confusion in his eyes.

"You're not leaving me here alone, are you?"

"I don't want to, but with Josh out of contact, we can't afford to be blind. I'm going up the tower." He reached for the weapons in the duffel, lifted out the sniper rifle. "This has a night vision scope. With it and these goggles, I'll be able to spot the pursuit in time to warn you."

I shook my head. "No, Tony. Please. I can't lose one more person. Do you understand?"

He trailed a hand up my leg, sending coils of arousal into my core. I released the breath I was holding. He looked me in the eye. "Where's your gun?"

I reached into my pack and pulled out Gary's weapon. "I told you I know how to use it, Tony. I took a course after Gary... after what happened."

"If anyone, I mean anyone, you don't know comes through that door, do not hesitate." He took both my hands, held them to his heart, kissed the tips. "I've set the talkies to the same frequency. Keep yours on. If the battery runs low, replace it. There are more in the food bag."

"It's freezing out there. How will you stay warm?"

"You worried about me losing fingers or toes?" A corner of his mouth twitched.

"Now who's deflecting." I inched closer. "Maybe I'm concerned about a more important body part."

Tony groaned, buried his head in my lap, then stood and pulled me up against him. "Unfair, Red, and thank you."

"For what?"

"Some lightness to make this night easier."

"It's an impossible situation, has been from the start." I handed him his coat, hugged him quickly, and retrieved the shoulder holster. I strapped it on and settled the gun. "Do I look like a badass?"

Grabbing my arms, he pressed me back against the door, lining up all the parts that had fit together so perfectly the night before. "We'll talk about your ass later, okay? For now, stay alert, check in every ten minutes, and, Red, don't forget what I said. Don't hesitate. Shoot to kill."

I shivered in the doorway, watching him head across the trampled snow. He turned to wave and headed up the mountain toward the fire tower, its silhouette rising above the trees like a monolith. When I could no longer make out his form, I closed the door, trimmed the lantern wick, and settled into the mound of blankets in front of the fire. Walkie-talkie clutched in my hand, I listened to Tony breathe as he moved farther away from me.

... decisions with deadly consequences, part one...

The roar of a snowmobile carried up the mountain. Josh bent over, hands gripping the poles, skis crusted with ice, and waited for the sound to diminish. When it didn't, he estimated the distance from his current path to the tree line and made slow, painful progress toward shelter. He felt lightheaded and sweaty, his body's attempt to compensate for the injury interfering with his ability to keep moving. He'd have to spend the night on the mountain, but first, he had to get out of sight. Cursing the carelessness that left him unable to communicate his position or warn Tony and Emma, he resolved to concentrate on staying alive. He reached the pines seconds before the snowmobile skidded up the path, heading straight for the rockfall. Maybe the idiots would crash there. One could only hope. Or maybe they'd abandon their vehicle, and he could steal it. But that would mean hiking back to the main trail. With his injury, he'd never make it, not with night closing in and the temps dropping to zero.

He slumped beneath the lower branches of a hemlock, grateful for the needles that protected him from the wind, and listened to the men mutter over the engine noise. Two, then, and no way to contact his friends. He waited for the voices to fade and thought about Riley, how her dark hair slid over his chest as she rode him, how she whispered his name when she came. He thought of Timmy and Michael and little Cara, his newborn daughter, already a glowing light in his life. He had been lucky to find and fall in love with Ri, to build a family with her. He wouldn't let go of that, no matter what.

246

... decisions with deadly consequences, part two...

Mouse's hands shook on the handlebars as he fought to keep the snowmobile from sliding off the trail and into the trees. Klaman gripped his waist, his curses indistinguishable above the engine's whine. The slope increased, making it harder to keep the snowmobile upright. When a dark mound loomed ahead, Mouse fishtailed the vehicle to a halt and slumped forward, exhausted. Klaman slid off and circled the snowmobile, then kicked at one of the exposed rocks at the bottom of the slide. He raised a fist at the hovering sky. "What now? We're losing the light."

"We walk from here." Mouse shouldered his pack, adjusted the rifle on his back, and pointed at the depressions in the drifts that skirted the rockfall. "We'll follow their tracks."

Klaman huffed his way to Mouse and, slapping him on the back, gestured toward the narrow path between the tumble of boulders and the forest. "How much farther?"

"Couple hours. If the map is accurate, we won't reach the cabin until after nightfall."

"Maybe we can use that to our advantage. They won't see us coming."

Yeah, Mouse thought as he picked his way up the slope. *We'll all be shooting in the dark.* He shifted the pack higher, checked the compass, and followed Klaman up the mountain.

J.E. Irvin

Snow fell, steady and silent, laying new cover over any previous tracks and muffling all but the sound of their breathing beneath the balaclavas they wore. They pressed deeper into the wilderness. One, driven by the promise of freedom from the life he'd led, considered the approaching victory with mixed feelings. The other, fueled by revenge and desperation, savored the thought of enacting a final indignity on the man who had wronged him and his associates. They spoke little, stopped briefly to piss or re-orient themselves. When Mouse spotted a light up ahead, he halted, scanned the terrain, and handed the night vision binoculars to Klaman.

"No sign of movement, but someone's inside the cabin." Klaman motioned toward the smoke curling up against the faint streak of starlight. "I'm going closer. Cover me."

"We should wait." Down on one knee, Mouse dug a gloved finger into the snow. "Make sure there are no surprises."

"Get real, Mouse. The woman has no clue we followed her and her brats here."

"Maybe. But that Ranger is around somewhere, and that old man at the store suspects something. He might have alerted her."

His companion snorted. "If he fucked us, he's a dead man. If you see the Ranger, take him out."

A distant howl raised the hair on Mouse's neck. "Fine. I'll wait here until you signal the all-clear."

Setting his pack in the snow, Klaman checked his gun and edged toward the left side of the cabin. Mouse tracked the boss's approach, aware of the trail they were leaving, then shrugged. By the time help reached this spot, the woman would be dead and the secrets her husband left behind destroyed. And so would his associate. Somewhere along the climb up the mountain, Charles Mouse had decided to erase all witnesses. He used the binoculars to track Klaman's progress. The man crept closer to the dwelling, his hunched figure a darker shadow in the night. He had almost reached the front wall when a shot rang out. Klaman's body jerked and slumped forward, collapsing into a snow pile at the corner of the cabin. He floundered, then screamed, one arm flailing. The muffled thump of a hinge snapping shut accompanied his cry. Mouse flattened himself against the snowpack, rifle balanced in his arms as he traced the report of the gunshot to the fire tower rising on the hillside above.

248

Silence squeezed Mouse like a vise. His heart pounded, but his vision was clear. He listened for the sound of someone approaching. Had the shooter spotted him? Where were the woman and children? Probability said they were cowering inside while someone, maybe the Forest Ranger, protected their flank. He had to get inside for the answers, but first, he had to eliminate the man in the tower. It was too much to believe that the Emma Pearson he'd followed from Hopewell had the training to make a shot like the one that took down Klaman. Then he heard it, a mewling from the lump of darkness that was his boss.

"Mouse! Help." The plea ended in a whimper, then rose again. "That piece of shit shot me, and I'm caught in some kind of trap. Fuck, it hurts."

The last word ended in a wet sob. Mouse considered his next step. One trap probably meant more, but whoever laid them would have left a safe way in and out. If he remained hidden, the sniper might not know he was there. He simply had to wait him out. Already the cold was seeping in through the layers he wore, but Charles Mouse was a patient man. Sooner or later, someone would make a move, and then he'd have them.

...decisions with deadly consequences, part three...

When I heard the shot, I scooted into the corner near the window, dragging the blankets with me. I strapped the walkie-talkie to my wrist with a bungee cord, afraid that if I panicked, I'd drop it or forget it the way Josh had. The mic crackled. Tony's voice skittered out.

"Red?"

"I'm all right. You?"

"Good. I shot someone."

"Is he alone?"

"Unknown. Stay down. No noise." I heard rustling, the snick of a bolt slamming home. "I'm coming down."

I heard the injured man call out, groaning in pain. My training and temperament as a caregiver dueled with the knowledge that this man had probably killed Gary and the family he had hidden from the world. Instinct warned me not to show myself. From all the reports Jesse and Otto had shared, he wasn't working alone. Tony could walk into a different kind of trap. It was up to me to end this now. I thumbed the on button. "Don't you move, Storms. If there are others out there, they'll see you. I can't," I paused, unwilling to show hesitation or weakness, "allow them to hurt you."

"Red, don't you do it."

"We'll talk about it on the other side." I low crawled to the door, clawed my coat and hat from the hook, and wrestled them on. I moved to the table and shuttered the kerosene lamp. Now the only light came from the fire, which had mellowed to a bed of deep red embers. I unlatched the door, allowed it to creak open, and inched forward, staying low. "Who's out there?" I let a quaver escape, just like my high school drama coach taught me. "Are you hurt?"

"Help me, you bitch," the man moaned, "or I'll have Mouse skin you like a rabbit."

"Sounds like the only rabbit around here is the one caught in a bear trap," I cooed. The man tried to growl but only managed a slurping sound. "Mouse? Funny name for a killer. You out there, Mouse? Your friend needs help."

Before either man could respond, I rolled back inside, kicked the door closed, and counted to twenty. The panic careening through me receded, replaced by an ice-cold resolve. I returned to my spot by the window. It was a waiting game now.

...echoes in the night...

The distant crack of a rifle reminded Josh how far away he was, not only from the danger Emma's pursuers presented but also from help. First things first. He groped for an energy bar and the water bottle and finished both before strapping his injured shoulder to his chest with duct tape. One-handed and in pain, he used his teeth to unzip the pack. He set the flashlight at an angle and pulled out everything he'd brought: rope, knife, matches, one-person inflatable tent, extra thermal socks and gloves, water, energy bars. He hadn't included a sleeping pad or bag, but he did have a wool Army blanket. With only one working arm, setting up the tent took longer than it should have. Once he had it anchored, he crawled inside, zipped it closed, and fell asleep, waking only an hour later when he rolled onto his dislocated shoulder. With a groan, he sat up to wrestle off his boots, grateful for their waterproof exterior. He changed his socks, replaced the Timberlands, and his wet gloves, then drank more water before curling up beneath the blanket. His thoughts bounced between Riley and the children and Emma and Tony, alone on the mountain with two professional killers.

* * *

Tony edged down the slick tower steps, alternately cursing Emma and feeling proud of her courage. He ignored the ache in his chest at the thought of losing her. He didn't know where these feelings were leading him, and now was not the time to figure it out. He had gone down two sections of steps when a muffled curse floated up from the bottom of the tower. Crouching, he set the rifle aside and raised the night vision goggles. There, twenty yards downhill, a figure moved through the drifted snow. Tony thumbed the radio, praying Emma had remained inside the cabin. No answer. If she had made it out undetected and was coming to him, he didn't dare shoot. But if the approaching figure was the second killer, he had no choice but to take him out. He cradled the rifle and resumed his scan of the hill. No movement, only that humped shadow, closer now to the bottom of the tower. Tony slithered down another five steps, raised the weapon, and sighted on the figure creeping toward him. Shoot or don't shoot? He fingered the trigger. The walkie-talkie buzzed against his chest. "Emma?" Even a whisper carried in the frigid night air.

"I'm in the cabin. Where is he?"

"Coming my way. The injured guy?"

"He's either passed out," she choked on the words, "or dead."

"Stay where you are, Red." He settled the rifle against his shoulder and waited for the shadow to inch closer. When the man reached the tower's base, Tony pulled the trigger.

...one more game of cat and Mouse...

The bullet tore through Mouse's jacket and the muscle of his left arm, the burn replaced by a fiery throb as it exited the back and buried itself in the snow. He raised his gun and peppered the tower in the direction of the shot. An object clattered and bounced against the wooden structure, struck a side rail, and disappeared under the snowpack. Static sputtered from the dropped radio. He started forward to retrieve it, paused, hung back. He wasn't certain the man he'd shot was dead. Besides, the woman was the priority now. With his associate out of play, Mouse didn't have to leave the job for good. Klaman knew too much to be only a hitman. Was it possible he was the big boss and had come to the Adirondacks to oversee the retrieval of the lost data? If so, the man, injured, perhaps dying, had no more power. Mouse could eliminate the woman and her kids, retrieve the missing data, and return to take over the entire operation. Without the boss, the KC mob was his for the taking. *God bless America.* His breath puffed out. Something wet trickled down his arm. Damn. He leaned against the tower and reached up his sleeve to inspect the damage. Blood oozed into his palm. Yanking the scarf from his neck, he used his teeth and good hand to tighten it around his upper arm. He was in no shape to climb the tower, but the shooter didn't know that. If he kept out of the line of sight, he could return to the cabin. Grimacing, he stumbled into deeper drifts, hugging the tree line, and avoided the open stretches. The Pearson woman was going to fix him up. Then he'd beat the shit out of her and her kids until she gave up the missing info. Too bad he didn't know exactly what it was stored on. One more oversight to blame on Klaman.

When Mouse spotted the cabin, he halted to consider what path to take to avoid more traps. He used the barrel of his gun to probe each mound of snow before he moved, circling the rear of the structure before stumbling down the ruts the sled had left behind. At the door, he stopped to catch his breath. He felt nauseous and light-headed, but interrogating Emma Pearson would make him feel better. He shifted the rifle from his shoulder to his good hand, checked that the scarf was still secure, and opened the door.

...revenge is a dish best served cold...

The fire was dying, and the warmth of the cabin with it. I piled another blanket over my legs. I'd heard the gunshots and the walkie-talkie banging as it fell. Tony must have dropped it, because I couldn't, wouldn't believe he was gone, that I alone remained to confront the monster. Boots crunched over the crusted snow. I removed my gloves. Gary's service weapon lay in my lap, hidden under the blankets and pointed toward the door. I mouthed the mantra I'd been reciting since Tony left to climb the tower. *No one threatens my children. No one threatens my children.* The recorder in my pocket whirred. I didn't know how long the batteries would last. *Please, just long enough*, I prayed. An ember popped and I jumped. The door creaked open and the man from my parents' video, the one who had chased me across the country, staggered in.

"There you are." He kicked the door closed and braced himself against it. Dark stains dotted the sleeve of his parka. Blood. Was it Tony's? No time for that now. I could grieve later.

"Been waiting for you, asshole." I kept still, kept my hands beneath the covers.

"Quite the mouth on you, Pearson. But, like they say, sticks and stones may break my bones. Your words, however, are harmless."

"Your partner's dying. Maybe he's already dead."

Mouse raised his chin, winced at the pain coursing through him. "You might think I care. I don't. He was useless before. Doesn't matter now. All he had will be mine, including the information your husband stole from him. I'd appreciate your cooperation, but one way or another, I'll have it by sunrise. Get those kids of yours out here. Now."

"Sorry to disappoint. My children are nowhere near here." He lurched forward, scowling, bumped against the table, then backtracked to lean against the door again. I smiled. "I'm not sure you'll make it till the sun comes up. You look a little shaky."

"Shut the fuck up." He shuffled to the table and sat down. The gun wavered in his hand. "I'm going to count to three, and then I'm going to shoot you in the foot, then the legs, then the arms. By the time I reach the gut, you'll be begging me to stop, and I will. As soon as you hand over what I came for."

"I don't know what you're talking about. Whatever my husband did in Kansas City, you must know by now he didn't share any of it with me." My bitterness escaped, along with the anger Gary's betrayal had left. I blinked. How foolish it was to cling to that hurt. Yes, Gary Pearson had wounded me deeply, but I didn't have to allow his betrayal to leave a permanent scar on my soul. The intruder reached for the water I'd left on the table, gulped it down, and licked his lips.

"You must know something. Other than you and the two kids he didn't want, what else did Pearson leave behind when he departed this world? I mean, I'm not sure he wanted the other woman either, but that wife, Sherrie, was the sister of the soon-to-be-deceased guy out there. Falling for your undercover cop husband was not a wise move. Two lost, stupid people going up against a syndicate."

"And you killed them." I shifted my legs, repositioned the gun. He wiped a hand across his forehead.

"I didn't intend to kill that baby, but I didn't lose any sleep over it. Neither did the boss." He racked a bullet into the chamber and lifted the gun. "One. Two."

I raised the blanket, aimed, and pulled the trigger. The shot roared in the confined space. Blood and brains exploded across the cabin floor. I screamed, prepared to shoot again, when he fell onto the table and tumbled to the floor. My ears rang. I shook my head and waited for him to move, but the man who had haunted my nightmares for five months was dead. I dropped the gun, buried my head in my arms, and wept. When the door to the cabin banged open, I scrabbled to find the weapon. Panting, a thin trickle of blood smearing his left cheek, Tony Storms swept in. He kicked the dead man, slammed and bolted the door, and gathered me into his trembling arms.

...every lost sheep comes home...

After the adrenaline rush faded and the tears stopped, I turned to face Tony. I expected him to take me to task for my decision to fight, but all he did was brush my hair back, kiss me tenderly, and turn to stoke the fire. Then he squatted next to the hitman's body. He nudged the man's gun away but didn't touch it. "You good, Red?"

"No, but I will be. What about the one outside?"

"He's not going anywhere. I'll take photos of him while you do the same in here if you're up to it. Forensics will need them later." He raised his head, those dark eyes probing mine for weakness or indecision.

"Go." I lifted my chin toward the door. "When you come back in, I'll bandage your head. Then what?"

Tony stood and folded me into his arms once more. "Two choices, sweetheart. Stay here until dawn or start down the mountain in the dark."

"Leave him, them, here? What about," I twisted to face the window, "wolves?"

"We could load the bodies on the sled, take them down, but that destroys the crime scene."

I slumped into him, his strength a buffer against the guilt, regret, and sadness threatening to take over. His body responded, sending the messages he couldn't voice aloud yet. I sighed. "One step at a time, Storms. Document, then decide."

"A sound plan, Emma Evans. I'll cover the body outside with a tarp and weigh it down with wood. Maybe that will keep the predators away until morning. Josh would approve."

"Josh." I teared up, thinking about the Ranger alone on the mountain. "What if..."

Tony placed a finger on my lips, stopping the speculation. "Waylon knows this mountain better than anyone, and he wouldn't be caught unaware. Concentrate on now, Red, okay?"

I bit my lip, eased free of his embrace, and reached for my phone. Tony put on his coat, grabbed the flashlight, and slipped into the night. Alone with the cooling body of the man called Mouse, I steeled myself against the sight of brains and blood spattered across the floor and went to work, preparing to email each shot as soon as I had enough bars on my phone. After I finished, I covered the corpse and took stock of the remaining supplies not spattered with gore. The radio still worked. I thumbed it on, hoping to hear Tony's voice, but all I got was crackling. The door banged open, and Tony stomped in. He glanced at the radio in my hand and rubbed his forehead. "That's no good, Red. I lost mine in the snow during the gunfight at the tower."

"Sit." I set the talkie down and opened the first aid kit while Tony removed his hat. Wincing, I cleaned the path the bullet had carved through the scar on his head. "What is it about you and bullets?"

"Maybe the better question is how many chances do I get before one of them does me in?"

I paused, bandage and tape forgotten as I stared at him. How many chances did any of us get to do things right? Between us, we had eliminated the threat to the twins. Tony had sent Gary's recorded message on to the FBI. Once I handed over the thumb drives, maybe they could find what he'd hidden among the music collections. If so, I would have completed my husband's mission, whatever it had been. Did I have a path forward from there? Was the yearning to be with Tony nothing more than the any-port-in-a-storm reflex, or was there something more between us? I knew there was desire, yes. And lust. Recalling how he called my name when he came had warmth curling in my belly. But now we owned the deaths of two human beings. As twisted and evil as those men were, they were still people. That was not a shared experience destined to further intimacy, was

260

it? Tony caught my hand, pressed a kiss onto my palm. "That's enough deep thinking, Red. Finish up, and we'll leave."

"You think we should head down?"

"I don't want to stay here, do you?" I shook my head, and he nodded toward the window. "It's stopped snowing. The clouds are breaking up, and there's enough of a moon to guide us part of the way. We have a compass, a sled, a tent, if we need one, food, and water. The Rangers will be starting up at first light. And I really don't want you here with that dead man any longer than necessary."

I bandaged the wound and wrapped his head with gauze to keep the dressing in place. "Do you feel strong enough, Tony? Because if anything happened to you..." I lowered my gaze. He didn't have to know how I felt about him now, especially if he didn't feel the same.

He touched the head wrap, tugged his cap back on, and pulled me onto his lap. "In the middle of this clusterfuck of a cabin, I have a reason to be strong. You. So, kiss me like you mean it, and let's go."

I cradled his face, the strain of the night's events reflected in his eyes, and molded my mouth to his, savoring the way his tongue met mine. His hands pushed beneath my sweater, skin to skin, his touches a caress and a comfort. When we broke apart, I sensed a new bond between us. Rising, I layered on coat and snow pants, handed a pack to Tony, and shouldered mine. We left the warmth behind, lashing the packs to the sled and the snowshoes to our boots. The radio continued to crackle. I left it on. Before the batteries ran out, maybe one of the other Rangers would discover our frequency. Tony led the way. Neither of us looked back.

...finding a way down...

The snow had stopped, leaving behind a thin sprawl of fresh powder and a sky threaded with wispy clouds. The moon peeped out, scattered blessings on the land, and flirted with stars. Josh woke chilled but rested. He packed up, the pain forcing him to take frequent breaks. He paused to look up the trail, hoping Tony and Emma were the ones who emerged triumphant from the gun battle that echoed in his fitful sleep. Riley would never forgive him if he let her best friend die. Too late for regrets. If he had stayed, it might not have changed anything. By now, his men would be wondering where he was and, concerned, already planning to mount a search. With luck, he'd make it down before they started. He labored back to the trail, maneuvered around the rockslide, and inched his way down, aware that another fall might render him incapable of getting up again. One step at a time, he told himself. He planted the ski pole, angled his body down the slope, rested, and repeated the sequence. Despite his insulated boots and change of socks, his feet were cold and getting colder. He checked his watch, squinting to make out the time. Two a.m. He had at least three or four more hours to reach the bottom. He kept a steady pace, one foot forward, then the other, recalling the first time he saw Riley, her petite form balanced out the door of her car, dark hair blowing as she shouted into the air. Despite the constant throbbing in his shoulder, he smiled at the memory of her brandishing the hair dryer like a weapon. As different as she and Emma Pearson were, they did share one thing, courage. Neither woman backed down from a challenge. He wondered if Tony Storms was Emma's puzzle to solve. He hoped so. She had the strength to bring his friend back from the edge of the abyss that Josh's ex-wife Amanda had pushed him into. One step forward, then the next. Deep in the shuffle of memory, Josh didn't react the first time he heard his name. Someone called again, louder, the shout echoing faintly down the trail between the leafless trees. *Josh!* The voice sounded close. No, two voices, male and female. Was he hallucinating? He considered stopping, he might not find the strength to start again if he did.

"Josh?" The call sounded only a short distance behind. Then a hand on his shoulder. He yelped. A figure shuffled around to face him. "Hey, man, are you hurt?"

Josh planted his good hand atop the ski pole and stared at Tony Storms. "Dislocated shoulder. Are you real?"

Emma tromped up next to him and rested her hand over his. "Thank God you're okay, Josh." She hugged him gently while Tony probed the Ranger's arm and shoulder.

"Son of a bitch, Waylon. How are you still standing? Red, help Josh with his coat, then clear the supplies off the sled. I'm going to reset that shoulder, and it will hurt. But then it'll feel much better. Josh?"

The Ranger was already unbuttoning his coat and shirt. Emma dumped the packs into the snow and helped Josh settle onto his back on the sled. He winced when the cold slats met his exposed flesh. "Steady now." Tony probed the shoulder joint once more. Then, whispering a prayer, he braced Josh's arm and pulled. Josh swore as the bones aligned and then popped into the socket, but the relief was instantaneous. With Tony's hand at his back, he sat up and allowed Emma to tape the injured arm to his chest.

"Red, can you pack snow into one of the small bags in my pack? And get out some pain reliever. I think there's a bottle in the side pocket of my pack." Emma soon had the cold pack strapped to Josh's shoulder. She helped him dress, tugged his cap tighter, and, with Tony's help, got him standing. "I'm good, Emma. Let's go home."

The three trudged on, grateful for the company but quiet, each locked in their own private thoughts. Dawn strutted over the mountain, fists of light flexing along the eastern horizon. When they reached the final stretch toward the trailhead, Josh stopped to take in the crowd gathered at the base of Long Tom. "You didn't tell me what happened at the cabin. Do I need to know?"

His companions exchanged a glance. "The threat has been eliminated," Tony said. "All the rest is detail."

"Good enough. What about forensics?"

"They'll figure it out." Tony reached for Emma's gloved hand.

Josh tapped Tony's bandaged head and raised an eyebrow.

"A reminder," Tony said, "to dodge faster when in a gunfight, but that's the last one for me. Let's go home." They started down the trail when the walkie-talkie in Emma's pack rasped out a call.

"Red? Tony? Josh? Will one of you answer the god-damned radio?"

Tony looked at Emma and grinned. "Gordo," they all crowed.

...an explanation for almost everything...

The EMTs sprang to Josh's side, taking vitals and asking about his injury. He spoke to his men, then directed them to Tony for additional information before climbing into the idling ambulance. Satisfied that his friend was being cared for, Tony corralled the Rangers, Officer Kellerman, and her deputy. "You're going to need a forensics team and two body bags. A chopper to bring them down the mountain would help. Your choice. I covered the corpse in the snow, but I don't know if the tarp will keep the predators away." They listened, then began preparations to ascend to the hunting cabin. Tony advanced on Gordon, dragging me with him.

"What are you doing here, Gordon?"

"My job, Red. Glad to see you're all right. Storms, can we talk?" Phil Gordon gripped Tony's elbow to escort him away from the crowded staging area. I followed on their heels in time to hear Gordo say, "We got the stuff you sent, Storms. An investigation is underway in Kansas City."

"Hold on." I crossed my arms, grateful for the heavy blanket one of the first responders had placed around my shoulders. "How do you know about all that?"

Instead of answering, Gordo waved at an SUV parked at the far end of the turnoff. Two men got out. I recognized the agents who had shadowed me and the twins back in Hopewell. "You knew," I said, my voice rising with each word. "All this time, you knew who I was and why I was here, and you never said anything."

"Gordon, you son-of-a-bitch. You put Emma in danger," Tony grabbed Gordo's jacket.

Gordo stood his ground. "Calm down, Tony. I told you on the phone we had her covered. The Bureau's known about Red's connection to Wanakena through Riley even before Pearson's murder, and, Emma, when you turned down protective custody, we knew you'd run. I can't say as I blame you, but we couldn't allow you to remain here unprotected. Sooner or later Mouse, would find you."

"Charles Mouse?" I spit out the name. "That's the man I shot? You knew about him, too?"

Gordo nodded. "He was one of ours, and then he wasn't. We didn't know his whereabouts until he showed up at your parents' home in Florida. We figured he'd head here next."

"But you work at the Vet Center. How are you connected to this?"

"I do the same thing your husband did, Emma. I work undercover."

"Wait, you knew Gary." I wore a clear patch in the snow with my pacing. "Were you there, in KC, when it all went down? And you kept that from me. Damn it, Gordo, I trusted you!"

"I know, and I'm sorry, Red, but there are big fish to catch, and we still haven't located the thumb drives Pearson mentioned on the tape. Here's the truth. I consult for the Bureau and go where they need me, and, yes, I knew your husband. I knew everything."

I inhaled sharply, blew out a breath, and tried not to scream. Tony and I knew where the drives were. Should I reveal that fact or hold it to use as leverage later? I exchanged a glance with Storms, who shook his head. I kept pacing. Gordo's deception was one more betrayal on the growing list of reasons not to trust men. I wanted to slap him, to rage against the world my husband inhabited. I opened my mouth, but Tony beat me to it.

"She was vulnerable." He threw off Gordon's grip. "You used me and the vets. And Denver? He got caught in the middle of your power games. If you'd told me, I might have warned him."

"I'm very sorry about Lorang, Tony. Charles Mouse had a very complicated MO. None of us expected him to do what he did. But that's not why I'm here now."

"You're not here to gloat over another successful mission? My husband's killer is dead. That man admitted he murdered Gary and the woman and the baby. I have his confession on tape." I gathered my thoughts as the truth of the hitman's actions washed over me. "He threatened to shoot me, and I killed him. The other man got caught in a bear trap and died in the snow. And I'm not sorry about that either."

"Klaman's dead?"

"He is." Tony gathered me in. "I laid the traps like Josh asked me to. When I shot him, he fell into one. End of story."

Gordon leaned closer. "It's not. Mouse was a trained assassin. Klaman may have acted like the boss of this operation, but he was just a go-between. There's one more player in this game."

I looked at Tony. "We have to go. If there's someone else out there, my children are still not safe."

"No, you've done enough. Your children are fine, Red. We have men stationed at the Waylon property and at his parents' house. Riley and all the children are safe."

"Then why don't you arrest the last player and put an end to this?"

Tony tightened his arm around me. "Because they don't know who it is, right, Gordon? And they don't have all the data Pearson took."

The man had the grace to look uncomfortable as he shook his head. "We know they are here. We don't believe they have the information Pearson gathered and that they will try again to retrieve it."

"No!" Tony's shouted. All the personnel at the base of the mountain turned our way. He grabbed Gordon's jacket and hauled the man close. "No. You will not use her again."

I touched Tony's arm. "It's time to end this. And don't argue. I'm tired and sore and angry and scared, but I will not live like this anymore, afraid of every shadow. I have four bullets left in Gary's gun. It's enough." I climbed into Josh's truck and rested my head on the dash, the thermal blanket wrapped around my quivering legs. What I wouldn't give to be back in a classroom or snuggled by a fire with the twins beside me. *Not my fate*, I whispered. No ghostly whisper contradicted me. There was no way back.

...one more mission...

After a long shower, a grilling by Julia Waylon about our overnight adventure, and a quiet goodbye from Tony, I lingered by the back window of the senior Waylon's residence, staring into the forest and pondering my next move. Josh huddled with Riley and his children, baby Cara in his arms, then left to set up a meeting of the Wanakena brain trust at Otto's Abode. I cuddled with Mollie and Evan until they fell into naptime, shared tea and hugs with Riley, and took off to join the group. But first, I stopped at Riley's house, found the key hidden under the mat, and let myself in. The thumb drives were right where I left them. I shoved them into my pocket, replaced the key, and waved to the federal agents in the SUV at the end of the drive.

Josh and I were the first to arrive. While the others filed in, accompanied by intermittent blasts of cold air and snow, Otto served coffee, tea, and brandy. Still ignoring each other, Carl and Jesse staked out territory at opposite ends of the counter. Gordon and the petite Mariah Kimby settled onto the bar stools. Tony edged up behind me, snaked an arm around my waist, and drew me close. The atmosphere reeked of tension. When Jesse rapped his knuckles on the countertop, I flinched. He patted my hand and cleared his throat. "Phil and I have discussed all the options and have arrived at what we believe is the best course. Once again, Emma, are you certain you want to go forward with this?"

I folded my hands around the mug of chocolate, encouraged by the warmth bleeding into my palms. "Tell me what I have to do."

Gordo glanced around the group. "The Vet Center has a special memorial service set up for Denver this coming Thursday. Emma, you'll get there early and stay late to close up afterward. You and Tony will argue. After he storms out, you'll be alone in the building."

Mariah raised her hand. When Gordon acknowledged her, she straightened her oversized glasses and took out her notepad. "What do you need me to do?"

While Jesse dictated the information for the Gazette article, Carl sidled up to me. "Want to come back to my place when we finish here?"

"Thanks, Carl, but I'm going to pick up a few things from the house and go back to the kids."

"Are you sure no one's watching you?"

"Oh, I'm certain they are. Gordo assures me I have no privacy left to protect unless I'm in my bedroom. It sucks."

"Well, that's consternatious indeed. But we're on the last lap, right, Jesse?" Carl's eyes blazed at the mayor. "You're taking care with this one, aren't you?"

"Carl, please. Can you stop being angry with me until this crisis is resolved?"

She huffed and turned her back. "Man owes me big time, Red. Sometimes you have to make them work for it. Now, that one," she cocked her head in Storms' direction, "he's up to the task. Tony!"

He stepped away from the men when she called his name. "Carl, what's up?"

"Our girl needs a few things from the cabin. I'm staying here to help Mariah write her article. Gordon says his men are in place, but I'd rather Emma not go alone. Can you see she gets what she needs?"

I blushed at the blatant innuendo in Carl's words but accepted Tony's offer to drive me home and then follow me on the drive back to the Waylon homestead. We didn't speak in the truck, although he rested a hand on my thigh, which sent a thrill of anticipation rushing through me. I waited while he scouted the exterior and inspected the cabin before returning to escort me in. The rooms, empty of the laughter of children, echoed sadness. I hurried to pack clean clothes for the twins. The task force claimed we had at least three more days of surveillance before we could return and feel comfortable in the space. Anxious to get moving, I swept out of the kids' room and collided with Tony. His arms immediately folded around me, igniting the longing I'd tamped down. Dropping the bags, I hugged him back, then looked down the hall. "Gordo said they planted cameras in the kitchen and living room."

"Did they?" He walked me backward toward my bedroom.

"Tony?"

He stopped, molding his body to mine, and traced his thumb over my bottom lip. "Sweetheart, I will never force you to do anything you don't want to do, but I want you so bad. Let me love you, sweetheart."

"Tony." His name slipped out, a prayer, a plea. He kissed me, his mouth firm and commanding. I didn't feel fearful or guilty, only safe, desirable, and willing. "I don't want to hurt you."

"Are you planning to?"

I ran my fingers down his stubbled cheeks and over his lips. "No, but look where we are, what we have ahead of us."

"Don't do that, baby." He held me steady. "No yesterday, no tomorrow. Only us here, today, remember? Are you okay with that?"

I smiled against his mouth and rose to kiss him while my hands tugged his shirt from his jeans. "I'm okay with that."

He guided me into the bedroom and closed the door with his foot. We worked to shed our clothes without breaking contact. His gaze turned steamy as it swept over my pebbled breasts and the lace-trimmed panties I wore. He was down to his briefs when I tugged him closer and wrapped my hand around his erection. "Yes," he breathed, lifting me onto the bed. He settled between my legs and pinned my wrists to the mattress. "We have time today, Red, for me to do this right, and I'm going to make you so glad you said yes."

"Make me come, Tony, with your mouth and your hands and your cock. Please." I lifted my hips and ground against him, moaning as the sensations powered through me. This, with him, was more than sex. It was ecstasy. Apprehension crept over me, retreating under the onslaught of kisses, and when he licked a nipple, I let go of my reservations. We were here together, and I wanted him. He took his time, whispering endearments and dirty promises that had me quivering with need, and when his tongue flicked over the tender spot between my thighs, I wept, shuddering, coming apart beneath him and feeling powerful at his look of awe as he watched me climax. When my breathing slowed, he began again, only whispering one word against my skin. "More?"

I reached between us to touch and stroke and tease until he pulsed with need, and then I spoke. "More, Tony. All of you."

"Baby, you got it." He lined up and pushed in, withdrew, thrust deeper in strong, steady strokes, making me gasp with pleasure. He stared into my eyes as our bodies moved together and our heartbeats joined. When the climax swept over me, Tony quickened the pace, my name on his lips, then his mouth wedded to mine, the only thing between us the fever of desire.

...an end to pursuit...

The vets hung their coats on racks in the hall and crowded into the meeting space. I greeted each one with a hug, handed out programs, and checked their names off the list. The chatter died down as the last of the group trickled in. I was surprised to see the young man who had shot at the supposed intruder on the roof of the Museum. He slipped through the door, hat in hand, avoiding eye contact, but crowded next to me, our elbows touching. "Is it too late to come in?"

His breath smelled of fish and beer, but his hands didn't shake, and his eyes, when I met them, sparked with excitement. "I'm sure there's room, Mr. Yang." Annoyed by his proximity, I stepped back. His lips twitched at my movement.

"I'm sorry about the other night," he said, his voice lower, more intimate. "Forgive me?"

What else could I do but nod, then steer him toward an empty chair. Tony watched from across the room, frowning. At the back of the gathering, Gordo also noted the exchange and signaled to Storms, who stepped to the podium to start the service.

The program began with a thoughtful tribute to Denver Lorang, a man who had served his country with distinction and his hometown with gruff kindness and a sense of humor. Those members who knew him best offered testimonials and anecdotes. The minister from Denver's home church offered a closing blessing. After the formal service, I kept the drinks flowing and the appetizer and cookie trays full while the crowd mingled and shared condolences. Twice, when our paths crossed, Tony rested a hand on my back, his touch reassuring and, when it drifted lower, inviting, but I couldn't see a way for us to be together again. Josh and Riley had returned home, taking all the children with them. I planned to spend the night there, then, once we'd caught the last of my pursuers, return to the cabin, to my life, whatever that would look like, when all this drama ended.

The evening ended with a shared rendition of Denver's favorite song, "Amazing Grace." The men and women filed out, shaking hands, clapping backs, wiping their eyes surreptitiously. When only a few remained, Tony grabbed my elbow and waved a sheaf of papers in my face.

"I told you," he rasped, "not to leave these lying around."

I struggled against his grip, but he yanked me closer. "You just can't resist screwing up my life, can you?"

Two of the veterans turned back, but I waved them off. "It's fine, guys. Nothing to worry about."

"Nothing to worry about?"

"Stop, Tony. Now is not the time. We can talk about this later."

"You're damn right we can, tomorrow when we discuss your termination. C'mon, everyone. Leave this shitshow for Evans. She's good at making messes. She can damn well clean up this one."

Gordo had disappeared early in the exodus. Tony herded the last vets out and followed them, slamming the door as he left. Even though I'd expected it, the vitriol in his words stung. Maybe he wasn't acting. Did he really believe I created chaos? I sighed and started stacking the chairs. Night closed in before I finished stowing away the supplies. I wiped down the counter, wet-mopped the floor, and set out coffee cups for tomorrow's visitors. I longed to put in earbuds and tune out my anxious thoughts, but I feared missing any noise that might alert me to the arrival of the last of my pursuers. The idea that Tony might have meant what he said refused to go away. I checked the clock — ten after eleven, and still no sign of a stalker. Perhaps the ruse hadn't worked. Maybe Gordo's men had given up, too, and I was truly alone.

I tugged down the oversize sweater covering the bulge of the gun on my hip and, keys in hand, headed for the door. A thump near Tony's office made me pause. Had someone come out of his room? The lights were off, even the night light in the wall outlet, which had been on earlier in the evening. I held my phone to my ear, called Tony's number, and hissed a warning. "In the lounge." The soft shuffling of a boot had me backing toward the hall. A shadow moved past the sofa and around the high counter. I clutched my keys and scuttled under the desk, angling the desk chair to block the figure rushing at me. The shadow resolved into a man who roared as he grabbed the chair and yanked. I hauled it back, shouting as the man wrenched it from my grasp and hurled it across the room. Fumbling for the gun, I kicked out. The intruder lunged toward me, his face looming close in the dim glow of the computer screen, which popped on when the desk jiggled. David Yang. The soldier who feigned crazy had fooled us all. I cradled my phone and shouted into the receiver, "It's Yang."

Praying that someone was listening, I kicked out again, catching Yang in the groin and eliciting another roar. One hand grabbed his crotch. The other aimed a Glock at the middle of my forehead. He stumbled back but didn't lose his footing.

"Out, bitch. Now." I huddled deeper beneath the desk. My hand closed over Gary's gun. I didn't want to shoot anyone else, but I couldn't let him live to threaten Mollie and Evan again. I raised the weapon, my finger sliding toward the trigger, when a body slammed into Yang, driving him to his knees. An arm wrapped around the hitman's neck while the other wrestled the hand holding the gun. Tony. He growled a warning to Yang to put it down. Then Gordo arrived. He chopped down on the gunman's arm, and the weapon skittered across the floor. More agents swarmed in to subdue Yang, who twisted and howled until, exhausted, he lay cuffed and panting on the floor. Tony crawled toward me, held out his hand, and drew me from the hiding place. He and Gordo exchanged a look. Then Tony was helping me into my coat and carrying me to his truck. He didn't let go of my hand until we reached the Waylon home. My breathing had returned to normal, but my heart was a shuddering mess. As soon as we pulled in, the door opened. Riley and Josh, accompanied by Mollie and Evan, waited for me to come inside. I turned to Tony, a question forming. He waved it away.

"I need to help Gordo tie up loose ends."

"Then you'll need these." I grabbed his hand and laid the thumb drives I had retrieved earlier in his palm.

Tony stared at the drives, tucked them in his pocket, and took my hands. "Thank you, Red, for the gift of yourself. I'll treasure it forever."

"I'll see you tomorrow, right?"

"I'll be back as soon as I can."

What choice did I have but to agree? I climbed from the truck, cast one more look at the man who had saved me, then ran toward the light.

...when spring and hope return...

Carl placed the last suitcase in the trunk of my car and folded her arms, the grim set of her mouth an indication of everything she wanted to say and couldn't. The twins had attached themselves to her legs, leechlike. I pried them loose and coaxed them into their car seats.

"It's time I closed out this chapter of my life, Carl. Please say you understand. My parents are flying home to help with final arrangements for the sale of the house."

"Oh, I get it, Red, but you promised them puppies." Carl swiped her eyes with her knuckles. "It's not right for mommas to break their promises."

I pulled the older woman into a hug. "I need to bring this all to an end. And I can get puppies wherever we live."

"Not Ike and Ivy's pups. Besides, Riley was just getting used to having her best friend back in her life. And there's more, Ms. Evans. Wanakena made a place for you. You really going to throw all that away?"

"I haven't decided yet, but there are depositions to give and a grand jury to testify before." I hugged her tighter, then let go.

"What about Anton?"

I bit my lip and hugged my sweater closer. "He has his own demons to sort, and he hasn't come to see me since the night we captured Yang."

"Holy moose balls, Red, you've been working at the Vet Center together. Don't tell me you haven't, you know," Carl looked away, uncharacteristically tactful, "talked about things."

"Tony's been more reserved than usual, Carl. I don't know what that means, but I can't figure it out until I get the rest of my life in order."

"Suit yourself, youngling." Carl huffed up the stoop. "Heard the school offered you a teaching job for next fall. Oughta take it, is all I'm saying."

I accepted the advice with a nod and joined the twins in the car. It was two days and seven hundred miles back to Hopewell, plenty of time to think about what I wanted to do with the rest of my life.

*   *   *

Spring comes late to the mountains, blushing its way up the slopes, hiding the evidence along the banks of streams and beneath the needled forest ground. I left the window down, eager to smell the perfume of the land awakening once more. The three months the twins and I had been gone felt like forever. I looked forward to surprising Otto and the mayor and the veterans I had come to know and care about. The contract to teach in Clifton-Fine was tucked in my purse, as was Carl's note, reminding me that the cabin was still mine if I wanted it. The woman had also promised to keep our return a secret, something I doubted. But I was due for a break, so I chose to remain optimistic. I glanced in the mirror at Mollie and Evan, the miracles I was most familiar with. I had finally explained their father's passing simply and honestly. We cried together and visited the cemetery as a family. The sadness that had clung to them all winter was slowly lifting. They were excited to return to Wanakena, to see the friends they had made, especially Timmy and Michael and baby Cara, who according to Riley, was already rolling over. I felt my own awakening, a return of joy as well as trepidation. Tony had texted during my time away, but he hadn't called. I didn't know what that meant, but I wasn't shying away from whatever truth lay between us. As soon as the twins were settled in at Mrs. Cleary's, I would confront him.

The Vet Center parking spaces were empty, just as they'd been the first time I'd shown up there. I gathered my purse and my courage and made my way into the office. Gordo was back at his place behind the desk, opting to make the takedown of the Kansas City mob his final mission before full retirement. He had purchased a condo on Isle of Palms in South Carolina and planned to spend the rest of his days scouring the sand for hidden treasure. When the door closed behind me, the sergeant looked up. He wasted no time drawing me into an embrace. "I knew you'd come back to us, Red. He needs you, you know."

I hugged him, then shook my head. "I'm not so sure, Gordo, but that's why I'm here. To find out."

He nudged me toward the lounge. "He's in the office, brooding as usual. Go give him hell. I'll just slip out for a while, put the closed sign on the door."

My cheeks heated, but I smiled back. "I doubt that's necessary."

"Shows how much you have to learn."

"Has he been sleeping here again?"

Gordo rubbed his head. "Every night since you left. Go."

I dropped my coat and purse on the desk, crossed my fingers for luck, and tiptoed to his door. It squeaked open. Startled, Tony looked up. He gaped at me as I approached the desk.

"You came back."

"Did you doubt it, Anton Storms?" I refused to take the final step toward him. It was time for Tony to claim what he wanted. If it was me, I was ready. If not, I would shove the ache in my heart into a box, swallow my pride at being rejected again, and make a life for me and the children in this place that had fought with me and for me. He hesitated only a moment before circling the desk to enfold me in his arms. His lips claimed mine, traveling down my neck to suck the tender skin where my neck met my shoulder.

"I hoped, sweetheart. I prayed. But I didn't know."

I pushed him far enough away to put some distance between us, unable to say what needed to be said when our bodies were touching. "That's not the question, though, is it?"

He drew me close again and met my gaze with clear and keen desire. "No, that's not the question."

"When I first came to Wanakena, you told me to go back where I came from."

"I did."

"Do you still want me to leave? Because that's no longer an option, Tony. For better or worse, I've come home."

"Home." His gaze heated as we both remembered the first time we'd made love, how he seated himself inside me, and I welcomed him home. I shivered, longing and fear at war inside me. I should go. He wasn't ready. I wriggled free. He tugged me back. "No, you don't get to run away again. Now that you're here, you need to listen very carefully. I've had months to think this through. I've gone to therapy. The Bureau has offered me my job back if I want it. Yeah, they did, but I'm not deciding until you hear me out. Are you ready?"

I took the hand he offered and held on, bracing myself. "I'm ready."

"When you first got here, I pushed you away because I was afraid of what might happen." He ran his knuckles over his chin. "The moment I saw you, I knew you were going to change my life, and I didn't know how to handle that. But I do now. I want you, Emma Evans. I want your kids and those puppies Josh has been keeping for you and all the messy business that having a family means. No, don't interrupt me, woman, not yet. I planned to wait one more month before making the trip to Hopewell. To get you."

"Did you plan to kidnap me, Mr. Storms?" I smiled. He frowned.

"No. I planned to wear down your arguments, to court you the old-fashioned way. To tease you with promises until you came to my bed willingly and as much in love with me as I am with you. So, tell me, Red, did you come back to be with me or to tell me there's no chance for us?"

This time I didn't back away. Instead, I burrowed into his arms, working my hands beneath his shirt to touch and caress, to remind myself what I had missed in those months away. "Tony, I love you."

"I know, Red. I love you, too, and it scares the hell out of me, but I want it, and I want you." He lifted me onto the desk, scattering the papers to the floor, and helped me wriggle off my slacks. I wrapped my legs around him as I worked the zipper of his jeans, moaning when I lifted him free. He took my hand and wrapped it around his cock. "I can't wait, baby."

"Me neither. I've missed you so damn much." I shifted my hips to allow better access. He pulled my panties aside, lined himself up, and slid into me. We both groaned at the rightness of our joining. He withdrew, thrust deeper, and slipped a hand between us to tease me closer to climax. I tightened my legs around him, met his kisses with demands of my own, and when he came, whispered the words we both wanted to hear, "Welcome home."

...will you be my stranger?...

The Wanakena Wild Gang gathered around Carl's moose-themed dining table to rehash the latest news regarding the capture, indictment, and upcoming trial of David Yang, boss of the Kansas City mob. The complicated embedding of the financial data onto the thumb drives through something called steganography had everyone but Tony scratching their heads. When we had recounted every last bit of rumor and fact, the mayor turned to Tony.

"Anton," Jesse glanced at Carl, whose frosty demeanor toward him had thawed, for confirmation. "Don't you have something to show Emma?"

Tony touched the scar along his temple, glanced at the tattoos on his arms, and shrugged. "It can wait."

Carl rounded the table to bop him on the head with a moose potholder. "No, it can't. Go on with you. We'll all be here when you get back."

I took in their smirking faces and blushed. They couldn't possibly know about our encounter at the Vet Center or his sneaking into my bedroom last night after the kids fell asleep. I rose to clear the table, hiding the hickey in the collar of my turtleneck. A chorus of admonitions shamed Tony into conceding. He grabbed my hand and towed me to his truck. We cruised down Reed, crossed the bridge, and passed Otto's before heading toward Ranger School Road. Past the Pine Cone and the school, he turned into a lane that ended in front of a two-story clapboard house with a covered portico on the right and a sunroom or library to the left. The backyard sloped toward Cranberry Lake. A boat dock nestled against the bank. A SOLD sign covered the realtor's sign in the front yard.

"Tony?"

He placed a finger on my lips and shook his head. "No questions yet." Withdrawing a key from the lockbox, he ushered me inside. Although empty of furniture, the house exuded warmth and charm. Wainscotting, freshly painted, lined the living and dining rooms on the left. Ahead, down the hall, lay the kitchen with a door that opened onto a wood deck and a garden beyond. I wandered around, ran my hand over the fireplace mantel, and admired the views from the windows before he cornered me by the stairway to the second floor. "Do you like it, Red?"

I opened my arms and spun around. "It's gorgeous. But it's sold. Why did you bring me here?"

"Because it's mine, Em, and I want to share it with you."

"Wait, what?" I clapped a hand over my mouth. Tony knelt in front of me, fumbled a box from the pocket of his jeans, and swallowed audibly. "Emma Evans, I want to share this house and my heart with you. Will you marry me?"

"Oh." I blinked away tears. They came back. I looked into his eyes, full of hope and trepidation, examined my own path to this moment, and smiled. "Oh, Tony, yes. Yes!"

He slipped the ring on my finger, then stood to fold me in his arms. "Thank God. I was about to have a heart attack."

"Don't you dare," I said, slipping my fingers into the waistband of his jeans. "Not before I let you know how much I mean yes."

"In that case," he kissed me, "welcome home again, Mrs. Storms."

The End

A Note from the Author

I'm so very proud and excited to present this sequel to BROKEN *Love and Murder in the Adirondacks*. BETRAYED is Emma's story, and it's also the continuing saga of the people who choose to live in the wild, wonderful, challenging wilderness of the Adirondacks. In a larger sense, it's a celebration of the inhabitants of small towns across our nation and the world, where neighbors care for and support each other when times get tough. There is a third book on the horizon, BLINDED, which will tell the story of Carl and Jesse's relationship and the cold case they pursue that will uncover more than one skeleton in Wanakena's fictional past.

As always, I must thank my editor, Donna Laugle Griffith, who never fails to make my work better. My sincere thanks, too, to Mark Friden, resident historian for the Clifton-Fine-Wanakena area. He advises me on the geographic, cultural, and historic parts of my tales. While medical issues curtailed his assistance on this novel, I remain grateful for all the things he did make clearer. Any omissions or commissions in the story are mine alone. And those details that diverge from the actual landscape? Necessary to the fiction, readers!

For their constant support and encouragement, my thanks to my friend Jeannie Smith, my writing colleague C. L. Pauwels, and the fabulous writers at Central Ohio Fiction Writers and Contemporary Romance Writers. Bonus points and much love to my husband Gregg, who waits for me to finish the day's work and fixes dinner when my mind is off wandering trails and exploring plot lines.

Dear Reader, if you like a book, please consider recommending it to your friends and posting a review on any social platform. Interested in future Byrd & Crowe mysteries or more novels by this author? Sign up for J.E. Irvin's newsletter at www.janetirvin.com for exclusive information, details on forthcoming books, and giveaways!

===

NewAtlantianLibrary.com or
AbsolutelyAmazingEbooks.com
or AA-eBooks.com

For sales, editorial information, subsidiary rights information
or a catalog, please write or phone or e-mail

AbsolutelyAmazingEbooks
Manhanset House
Shelter Island Hts., New York 11965, US
Tel: 212-427-7139
www.AbsolutelyAmazingEbooks.com
bricktower@aol.com
www.IngramContent.com

For sales in the UK and Europe please contact our distributor,
Gazelle Book Services
White Cross Mills
Lancaster, LA1 4XS, UK
Tel: (01524) 68765 Fax: (01524) 63232
email: jacky@gazellebooks.co.uk

www.ingramcontent.com/pod-product-compliance
Lightning Source LLC
Chambersburg PA
CBHW070443030726
47503CB00004B/877